A FARRELL &

A young girl is snatched in
school and later found hang

When recently retired Sa
Farrell, sees this on the news, he realises his worst nightmare
has just come true. The same brutal killer a government
agency stopped him from putting away twenty years before is
once more on the loose.

As the killer wreaks a trail of blood and destruction across
North America, Bob Farrell teams up with rookie cop Kevin
Kearns and sets out to track down their lethal prey. But Farrell
& Kearns are not playing by the rules any more than the killer
is, and soon the FBI have all of them in their sights...

Author Sean Lynch is a former Lieutenant and Commander
of a San Francisco Bay Area Detective Division. A visceral and
heart-wrenching cross between *No Country For Old Men* and
The Silence of the Lambs, this is an exhilarating and thrillingly
authentic debut.

SEAN LYNCH

WOUNDED PREY

EXHIBIT A
An Angry Robot imprint
and a member of Osprey Group

Lace Market House,
54-56 High Pavement,
Nottingham NG1 1HW
UK

www.exhibitabooks.com
A is for Authentic!

An Exhibit A paperback original 2013
1

A catalogue record for this book is available
from the British Library.

UK ISBN 978 1 90922 306 6
Ebook ISBN 978 1 90922 308 0

Set in Meridien and Franklin Gothic by EpubServices

This book is respectfully dedicated to that rare breed of police detective who track sex offenders.

These cops truly hunt in the dark places.

CHAPTER 1

Nevada, Iowa. November, 1987

Vernon Slocum sat waiting in the driver's seat of a stolen Ford station wagon. When he saw the children his eyes narrowed.

They were right on time.

The wagon was parked on University Drive, less than a block from Franklin Roosevelt Elementary School. The engine was running. Both of Slocum's hands were thrust into the pockets of his faded green army jacket. His left hand was a clenched fist. His right hand gripped a government-model .45 caliber pistol.

Slocum was a large man at six feet two inches. What gave him the appearance of even greater stature was the girth of his chest and shoulders; a product of his Germanic ancestry and a lifetime of physical labor. His breathing was uneven and his nostrils flared.

He sat up straighter in the driver's seat when the group of second graders came into view. They were accompanied by two adults. An elderly matron was in the lead, and a student aide of no more than twenty-one brought up the rear. The procession was returning from a field trip. The youngsters were bundled in mittens and scarves and clutching leaves and other local flora in their tiny hands.

The children neared where Slocum had strategically parked his car.

He checked the ignition to ensure the screwdriver was still in place. The first teacher, leading the procession, saw the battered station wagon and began scrutinizing its lone occupant suspiciously. She saw a large, disheveled man with a tight crew-cut, unshaven face, and dark eyes.

Slocum felt the teacher's challenging gaze and knew it was time to act. With agility and speed unusual for a man his size, he burst from the stolen Ford. He moved towards the children, leaving the driver's door open.

The elder teacher saw him approach and stopped, the first signs of alarm wrinkling her face. The children continued on, oblivious to anything but their playful thoughts.

Slocum gained the sidewalk in a few powerful strides, ignoring the frightened eyes of the teacher.

He grabbed for the hair of seven-year-old Tiffany Meade. In her red mittens was a sheaf of autumn leaves which were to be the mainstay of her science project. She'd selected them on the basis of their still-green appearance, despite the lateness of the season.

He caught the girl's shoulder-length hair and pulled her to him. The force of his seizure wrenched the breath from her lungs. The old teacher screamed and released her hold on the two children she held at either side. Slocum encircled the girl's neck with his left arm and drew the .45, thumbing off the safety.

The teacher ran at Slocum with arms extended, her face contorted.

"No!"

Her shriek, part command and part plea, shattered the serenity of the crisp November morning. Slocum waited until she was at arm's length to fire. The heavy slug struck her above the right eye, and her head snapped back violently. He didn't remain to watch her fall. He made off with his struggling cargo, his pistol trailing smoke. He strode towards the car while stuffing the handgun into his coat pocket.

Slocum didn't notice the terrified wails of an entire second grade class; the sound couldn't penetrate the roar in his head. And he didn't see the still-green autumn leaves fall gently to the ground from Tiffany's thrashing hands.

CHAPTER 2

Kearns ran along the river, the steady pounding of his neoprene-soled shoes creating a pleasant rhythm. He'd been running for just over ten minutes and was beginning to even his pace and regulate his breathing. From here on, for the next twenty minutes or so, it would be smooth sailing. The first ten minutes were the hardest.

Once he despised running. A hitch in the army as an infantryman did little to alter that sentiment.

It took the Iowa Law Enforcement Academy and a charismatic physical training instructor to instill an affinity for running. It had been several months since he'd graduated the police academy, and he was now a rookie deputy sheriff in rural Story County. Unlike his academy classmates he still ran regularly, even though there was no longer an army drill sergeant or police academy PT instructor to mandate it.

Kearns jogged along the Skunk River and turned onto University Drive. The Franklin Roosevelt Elementary School lay ahead.

He took the air in slow, through his nose, and watched his breath leave in a visible plume. It was late November, and winter was still a few weeks away. Though the TV weatherman raved about the mild weather central Iowa was experiencing, he could feel the coming season in the sting of his lungs. Folks were saying it was going to be a hard one.

He chuckled to himself. He couldn't remember when an Iowa winter wasn't a hard one. Looking far ahead, Kearns yielded the sidewalk to a group of schoolchildren who were hogging it; a wandering mob herded by two harried adults.

He gave them a glance, and went back to focusing on that point on the ground avid runners seem unable to look away from. He jerked his head up with a start when he heard the scream.

It was a short scream. The word, "No!" was all he heard. But in its tone was a stark, bone-chilling quality that made Kearns unconsciously break stride. He held his breath to listen better. It was what he saw, however, that brought him to a complete stop.

Approximately seventy yards ahead a large man was holding a child. Kearns could see the child's legs kicking spastically, well off the ground. The man wore a green army jacket, and all Kearns could see was his back. The man retreated towards a clunky-looking station wagon parked nearby. An elderly woman, perhaps the one who'd screamed, ran towards the man with her arms outstretched. In her every move, even from his distance, Kearns sensed desperate terror.

Deputy Kevin Kearns instinctively started running again, this time in a sprint. His heart raced as the drama unfolded before him. Suddenly everything seemed to be occurring in slow-motion. He ran with all his strength, but felt he would never reach the children.

He formed no plan of action for his arrival. All his concentration was focused on simply getting there. His legs pumped furiously and he stretched his arms to lengthen his stride. The elderly woman's outstretched fingers almost reached the jumbo-sized man holding the child.

To his horror, the man drew a pistol from his coat pocket and leveled it point-blank at the approaching woman.

With twenty yards to go, Kearns saw the flash of the pistol's muzzle. The sound of the gunshot reached him a split-second later. The woman's head jerked and she stopped in mid-stride, crumbling to the ground. The big man turned away and began walking towards the car. He seemed oblivious to the weight of the child struggling in his grasp.

Kearns hoped the killer didn't hear the sound of his fast-approaching footsteps. The big man looked up just as the deputy reached him.

CHAPTER 3

Slocum caught motion from out of the corner of his eye and whirled, causing the girl's short legs to swirl in an arc. He saw a man running at him full speed. The man was medium-sized, with a muscular frame under a set of gray sweats. He was young, in his early twenties, with short, military cut hair. Slocum's eyes locked with those of the approaching man's. They were innocent eyes, eyes unlike his own, eyes that belonged to a man who had never drawn fresh blood.

Slocum braced for the impact.

Kearns lowered his head and hit the bulky figure in a running low tackle with every bit of momentum his hundred-yard/thousand mile sprint had summoned. Kearns, the big man, and the little girl hit the ground in a pile of flailing arms and legs.

Kearns was dimly aware of children screaming and scampering around him. He rolled in an effort to regain his feet. He realized the man must outweigh his own one hundred and eighty pounds by at least fifty.

Kearns got up and watched his opponent do the same. He marveled at how the big man shrugged off the collision. Kearns squared-off, and saw the man reach into his pocket for his pistol; the same pistol which moments before had cut down a defenseless woman. There was no time to think. As a drill sergeant once taught him, it was kill or be killed.

He closed, clasping the man's right arm with his left. At the same time he brought up a knee into the larger man's groin. He was rewarded with a grunt and felt hot breath on his face. He also felt the hard steel of the pistol in the man's pocket and clenched with all his might over the hand holding it.

Dazed by the groin shot, the man swung a quick left to the deputy's head. Kearns saw it coming and ducked, taking most of the momentum away from the punch. It still hit him hard, and stars danced in his head. He sent out a right hook of his own, and followed up with a headbutt to the man's nose. Though he knew they were powerful shots, they seemingly had no effect.

Kearns realized he couldn't match his adversary's strength. With rising panic he felt his grip on the gun-hand slip. If he didn't stop the man from drawing his pistol, he would join the courageous teacher in death on the sidewalk.

The little girl was crawling on her hands and knees away from the two men locked in mortal combat a few feet from her. She tried desperately to scream. There were tears of anguish in her eyes, but she'd yet to recover her breath.

Kearns hammered away at his foe's head with his right fist, punches that bloodied the distorted face. In his adversary's eyes he saw hypnotic darkness. It momentarily distracted him.

The giant seemed able to withstand a tremendous amount of punishment. With a Herculean shove he pushed the deputy, catching him off balance. Both went down, the larger of the two men on top.

Kearns knew it was over. He fell backwards and lost his grip on the gun-hand. He groped desperately with both of his hands to regain his restraining grip on the pistol. He felt a vice-like hand clamp his throat.

His eyes widened as he saw the pistol emerge from the coat pocket. He recognized it as a US government .45, the same model he'd been issued in the army. With all the strength he could muster he strained against the weight of the large man straddling his chest. Kearns could almost feel the bullet enter his skull and winced; death was a trigger-squeeze away.

The man's face was a bloody pulp. He cleared the pistol from his pocket and brought the gun-butt down on Kearns' head. The blow landed over his left ear, on the temple, and rendered him instantly unconscious. Switching the pistol slightly in his hand to get his finger in the trigger guard, he pressed the muzzle against Kearns' forehead.

An instant before he pulled the trigger, the man again sensed motion out of the corner of his eye. Looking away from Kearns' inert body he saw Tiffany Meade get to her feet.

Forgetting the deputy, the man rose to his own feet. In several quick strides he had the youngster once again in his grasp. She shrieked and struggled. He was more dazed by his encounter with the deputy than Kearns would ever know, and he silenced the girl with a savage punch to the head. The second grader went limp in his arms.

The man looked around. People were running out of the school. He ran to the idling station wagon and hurled his unconscious bundle into the car. He got in and slammed the door with a jolt.

••••

Kearns fought himself groggily to consciousness; splashes
of color and unidentifiable sounds overlaid the agony in
his head. He couldn't get up, and for a moment fought
the overwhelming urge to vomit. Blood ran freely down
the left side of his face, obscuring his vision in that eye.
What images he could see through his right eye were out
of focus.

He tried to push himself up but his arms wouldn't
work. He heard a car door slam, very near him, and
rolled over on his back to bring his right eye towards the
origin of the sound.

He saw the mass of the station wagon bearing down
on him. Kearns rolled again, hard, with the last vestiges
of his dwindling strength. He felt the crunch of tires as
the car grazed past, missing him by inches. He looked
up in time to see the station wagon screeching away. He
dimly noticed the car had no license plates.

Pain seared through his head, and he felt consciousness
slip away again. His cheek hit the ground, remarkably to
him, with no sensation from the impact.

The last image Kearns saw through his fading vision
was a leaf, oddly green for so late in autumn.

CHAPTER 4

Slocum drove away from the school and the carnage he'd wrecked there. The seemingly lifeless form of a seven year-old girl bounced on the passenger seat as he gained speed.

He wiped snot and blood from his nose. He knew it was broken by the shooting pain he experienced when his forearm brushed the tip. There were seeping cuts over both eyebrows and his eyes were beginning to swell. Slocum was no stranger to pain, and willed the rising tide of hurt from the front of his mind into one of its many dark recesses.

Slocum took a direct route to the viaduct which spanned the Des Moines River. He eased the station wagon off the street and onto an unpaved road near the railroad tracks, out of public view.

Slocum pressed a finger none too gently against the neck of the girl. Her breathing was shallow and her pulse weak, but she was alive. Slocum breathed a sigh of relief.

It was too early for death.

He drove the station wagon directly under one of the huge concrete pylons that formed the bridge's legs. Parked near the wall was a beat-up Dodge pick-up truck. It was an inconspicuous vehicle in a part of the country where people made their living from one facet of agriculture or another.

Slocum got out of the Ford pulling the girl towards him across the seat by her legs. A faint groan emerged from the child's lips. He took her roughly in his arms and carried her to the truck, opening the door with his elbow. He placed the semi-conscious child on the passenger seat as he'd done in the station wagon. Reaching past her and onto the truck's floor, he grabbed a canvas tarpaulin and completely covered the inert girl. The key was already in the Dodge's ignition, and a moment later he was pulling out of the gravel lot and back onto the street.

He shifted through the Dodge's gears and picked up speed. He struggled out of the faded green army jacket and set it aside. Under it he wore a sweat-stained shirt, its ragged sleeves rolled up past thick, muscular forearms. A squatting bulldog wearing a campaign hat and a snarl sat above the letters USMC, tattooed on his right forearm. Slocum shrugged into a plaid work-shirt, pulling the collar up. He added a John Deere baseball cap in green and yellow, and wiped the blood from his face with a grease-stained rag. He finished by tucking his pistol into his waistband.

He was almost out of town. He passed the minimart and the First Presbyterian Church with its pointed roof. He reached over and removed the tarp from the girl. An ugly bruise was forming along the child's jawline where he'd silenced her frantic struggling.

Slocum's breathing got irregular for the second time that morning. His vision started to narrow, and within the confines of the warm cab of the Dodge he could smell the acrid scent where the little girl had urinated on herself.

The scent of urine.

He involuntarily rocked back and forth. Whining sounds emanated from his mouth. His eyes closed, and he remembered how his own urine smelled when his father struck him with the hickory switch. The smell of urine also brought back the sound and thunder of mortar rounds slamming into the earth, and the screams of the dying. He breathed deeply the familiar musk and became lost in a maelstrom of stark, hell-wrought images.

The crunch of gravel and the angry blare of a horn snapped him back to reality. The smell of urine vanished as he opened his eyes and straightened the steering wheel.

He'd faded again. The truck edged over the center divider, narrowly missing another oncoming pick-up truck. Slocum steadied his hands on the wheel. He shook his head to clear the cobwebs from his mind.

He squeezed a Pall Mall from a wrinkled pack on the dash and lit it with a worn Zippo lighter extracted from a hip pocket. On one side of the Zippo was engraved an eagle, globe and anchor.

He took a deep drag from his cigarette and nudged the truck south towards the interstate.

CHAPTER 5

Kearns woke to the sound of an amplified voice asking for Doctor Somebody to please report somewhere, and to a blinding white light. His mouth felt thick and his head felt like it weighed a ton. He tried to sit up and found restraining hands pushing him gently back onto whatever it was he was lying on.

Gradually his vision cleared, and through his right eye he could see a rubber-gloved hand over his face at close proximity. He couldn't see at all through his left eye. He realized he was in a hospital. The person wearing the rubber gloves dragged stitches through his scalp.

"Where am I?"

A deep voice answered from out of view. "You're in the hospital, Kevin. You've taken quite a thump on the head."

He recognized the voice of his boss, Sergeant Dick Evers, a former trooper who'd retired from the state police and joined the sheriff's department a couple of years ago. Kearns could feel the tingle of anesthetic on his head as the rubber-gloved hands tugged stitches through his skin. He realized the blinding light he'd awakened to was the spotlight framing the physician's face. It prevented him from knowing the identity, or even the sex, of the attending doctor.

"How long have I been out?"

"About an hour," said Evers' bodiless voice.

"What happened?"

"You were there; you tell me. But you'd better talk fast. The sheriff's on his way, and there's gonna be State Division of Criminal Investigation boys coming shortly. There's also more reporters than you could shake a stick at. It's a regular parade. Buck'll be in heaven."

Evers was referring to Sheriff Robert "Buck" Coates, their Commander-in-Chief. Buck wasn't liked by his men, and his swaggering style did little to endear him to anyone else. Sheriff Buck spent most of his off-duty time at the Elk's Lodge in varying stages of intoxication, nurturing voter support along with his Kessler's. Anywhere the press could be found, Buck Coates could be found too.

The doctor finished the final stitch and stood up, nodding to Evers and leaving the room. Evers followed him to the door and closed it. He went back to where Kearns lay flat on the gurney and helped the bandaged deputy sit up. He handed Kearns a cup of water.

Kearns gulped the water and looked up, meeting his tall, lanky boss's gaze. Finishing the drink, he threw the cup on the floor.

"The old lady's dead?" he asked, wincing.

The sergeant nodded. "She took one right between the eyes. You think it was gonna be a flesh wound?"

"I had to ask."

"Didn't mean to snap at you; I'm a little edgy, that's all. We rolled up and found thirty hysterical kids in every stage of blind panic. One teacher was stone-dead, and the other teacher, a young thing, was in catatonic shock. I got a daughter no older than her."

Kearns said nothing.

"And to top it off, I find you in a puddle in the street like goddamned roadkill, blood leaking out every which way. I thought you'd taken a bullet in the head yourself."

"By all rights I should have," said Kearns, remembering the .45's muzzle pointing at his face.

"It took some time before we could find anybody coherent to tell us what happened. The school janitor, a Korean War vet, heard the shot and the screams and called it in, but he didn't see anything. All the kids could tell me was that a man 'grabbed Tiffany,' and you tried to stop him."

Kearns winced, memories of the schoolyard tightening his stomach. The waves of pain cascading through his head suddenly magnified. He remembered the little girl. Her name is Tiffany, he thought.

"Sarge, we've got to get a broadcast out. He's probably still got her. We've got to–"

"Take it easy," interrupted Evers. "We're on it. I got enough of a description from some of the kids and the surviving teacher when she finally snapped out of shock. We've already put out a statewide BOLO for the guy, and the car, as well as a photo and description of the little girl."

"How'd you get the little girl's picture so quick?"

Evers paused before replying, suddenly very interested in the scuffed toes of his wellington boots. "I sent a deputy out to the girl's house. I got the address from the school."

"So the kid's parents know?"

"They had to find out sometime. Besides, I needed a picture of the kid pronto."

There was a long silence. Evers broke it.

"Kevin, do you know how big this is?"

Kearns' puzzled look was his answer. Evers grimaced, shaking his head.

"It's big. And messy. And it's going to get bigger and messier."

"I don't care how big or messy it is. We've got to find that kid."

Evers grunted. "You don't say? Now there's an original idea. Hadn't thought of that. Good thing you're here, deputy. You've been a cop what, six, eight months? Catching the bad guy and getting that kid home safe to her folks should be easy for an experienced law enforcement officer like yourself. Probably have her home by supper."

Kearns felt his face redden. "That's not what I meant."

"I know. You didn't deserve that. I'm just cranky. This is as foul a crime as I've ever seen, and I've been a cop over three decades. I don't mean to take it out on you."

"Forget it. I know I'm a rookie, and don't know shit. I just want to get the son-of-a-bitch, that's all."

"You ain't alone. But be careful what you say. Folks are listening."

"Huh?"

"Look around you. You wonder why you're not in the ER?"

For the first time Kearns noticed he wasn't in the emergency room. He was in a private room. He looked quizzically up at Evers for an answer.

"There are thirty, grade-school aged, psych-trauma cases in the ER right now. There's also a lobby full of panicked parents, a pair of grief-stricken parents, and a DOA under a sheet who was once a sixty-one year-old schoolteacher and grandmother. There's ten or twenty city and county cops, a posse of reporters, and plenty more cops and reporters burning pavement to get here. There's also FBI guys from Des Moines en route, as well as forensics people. It's only been an hour, for Christ's sake, and it's already a three-ring circus."

Kearns felt a sinking feeling overtake him.

Evers went on. "We both know that kid is gonna be dead and buried before sundown. That ain't something I like, but I've been a cop too long to think otherwise. Everybody wearing a badge is going to want to bag this guy, and it's going to get political. I've seen this kind of thing before. Especially when the federal boys arrive; they can't take a piss without calling a press conference."

"Sarge," said Kearns, standing up on shaky feet. "I don't give a shit if they call the ghost of Elvis Presley in from Graceland. I want that kid back and I want the fucker who snatched her."

Evers' brow furrowed, not unkindly. "What you want doesn't matter, Kevin. You're out of it, now. You'd better heed my advice and mind your tongue. You're under a microscope."

"What's that supposed to mean?"

"It means, when shit like this happens, it spells trouble. Political trouble. People looking to make careers over it. Blame gets laid. People get hurt. You'd best keep your yap shut and your head down. You're a little fish. Little fish that ain't careful get chopped up for bait."

"I don't know what you're driving at, but I think I can guess. I really don't care who catches the bastard, and gets the credit, as long as he's caught. And as far as taking the blame, I did all I could do. The bastard damn near killed me. I tried to—"

"Take it easy, kid. You don't have to convince me. I'm the guy that scraped you off the sidewalk, remember? But others might not see it that way. You're too new to police work to know this yet, but I'll clue you in on a universal truth of law enforcement: cops always get the blame. Always."

"That's ridiculous."

"Maybe so, but it's true just the same. That's what cops are; a place for the buck to stop."

Kearns wasn't convinced. "I'd like to see my critics take that guy on. He was like the goddamned Terminator. Anyone who witnessed the fight would know I did all I could do. All anyone could do."

"Who are you trying to convince? Me, or yourself?"

"That's a cheap shot."

"Agreed. But you'd better get used to it. It ain't gonna be the last shot fired at you. You'd best be ready."

"I did all I could to save that kid," Kearns insisted again. "The best I could."

"Yeah?" said Evers. "That little girl's mom is outside in the ER getting sedated as we speak. Tell it to her. It ought to be a real comfort."

CHAPTER 6

Trooper Dale MacKenzie pressed his foot further on the accelerator, nudging the Chrysler past the eighty mile-per-hour mark. He rolled up the window, the siren too loud for the police radio with the window down. It was past noon and traffic on Interstate 80, though not heavy by metropolitan standards, was heavy enough to warrant extra caution.

The feminine voice of the dispatcher asked for any unit in the vicinity to respond to the report of an injured child along the westbound section of the interstate east of De Soto, near the rest stop. The dispatcher said the report was phoned in by an anonymous caller from a phone booth there.

MacKenzie heard the "Be on the Lookout" advisory, or BOLO, two hours before over the radio. The broadcast announced missing/presumed kidnapped Tiffany Meade, a white female, aged seven, last seen wearing a brown corduroy skirt and plaid scarf. The suspect was described as a white male, approximately forty years old, over six-foot, large build, last seen wearing a green army jacket. The suspect vehicle was described as an older, full-sized, American-manufactured station wagon, white or cream in color.

The dispatcher's voice cautioned that the suspect was considered armed and dangerous, and presumably still in possession of a handgun used in the commission of the offenses of murder and kidnapping. There was no known direction of flight.

Trooper MacKenzie had over fifteen years of service, and was experienced enough to know the seriousness of the bulletin. He was also the father of two little girls. He spent the past two hours searching the highway for the suspect vehicle.

So when the report of the injured child came in, MacKenzie dropped the Styrofoam cup of coffee he'd purchased at the minimart and headed for his car at a trot. The two incidents were too rare to be unconnected, and even if they weren't, MacKenzie wasn't going to take the chance.

He cut a quick U-turn in the truck-stop parking lot and headed for the onramp, switching on the lights and siren. MacKenzie's 1986 Ford LTD Crown Victoria purred, and he was on the interstate in less than a minute.

MacKenzie was less than ten minutes from the reported locale of the injured child, making him the closest unit by far. He blurted his call sign into the radio's mike, signifying he was en route. He barely heard the dispatcher's acknowledgment over the roar of his engine and the shriek of the siren.

MacKenzie's heart raced as he passed first one motorist, then another. He grabbed the mike again and asked the location of his nearest cover unit. Through the static came the voice of another trooper, giving his position as north of Winterset on Highway 169, with an ETA of twenty minutes. MacKenzie clicked the mike button in response, not surprised. Unlike city cops, highway patrolmen and rural deputies were accustomed to having their back-up a long way off, often in another part of the county entirely.

MacKenzie saw the outline of the rest area in the distance and began pumping his brake in quick bursts to control his deceleration. He saw a lone eighteen-wheeler parked in the rest area's lot, its engine running. He grabbed the mike from its dashboard mount a final time, telling dispatch he was on-scene. The cruiser skidded to a halt.

He scanned the vicinity of the semi-truck for its driver. MacKenzie ran over to the truck's cab and jumped up on the step, peering into the cab. There was no one inside.

The trooper went around the far side of the rig and headed towards the small brick building which housed the public restrooms. The rest area consisted of the restroom building and a series of picnic tables in a grass courtyard nearby. At the edge of the grass he found the truck's driver.

He approached a tall, heavy-set man in a blue nylon windbreaker and cowboy boots. The driver was bent over, his hands on his knees. He appeared to be out of breath, taking in thick gulps of air, which he let out in wheezing rasps. MacKenzie approached him, crinkling his nose at the smell of fresh vomit.

"What happened? Where's the injured kid?" He could see a puddle of puke at the driver's feet, some of which had splashed onto his trousers and cowboy boots. The truck-driver didn't respond to the trooper's questions.

"Talk to me; I need some answers." MacKenzie put his hand on the driver's shoulder. The driver looked up, his eyes wide.

MacKenzie asked again, "What happened? Are you alright?"

The driver finally nodded, spittle dripping from his chin. He wiped his mouth and stood up.

"Did you call in a report of an injured child?" The truck-driver nodded again, and MacKenzie realized the man was experiencing dry heaves and couldn't speak.

"OK, take it easy," he said soothingly. "You're going to be alright. Where's the kid? I need to know where the kid is."

Tears began to form in the big trucker's eyes, and a sob escaped his lips between dry heaves.

MacKenzie was losing patience. "Damn it, you called in an injured kid. Where's the kid?"

In answer, the truck-driver turned and pointed to a clump of elm trees framing the picnic area. MacKenzie followed the man's fingers.

Hanging from one of the tree's branches was a little girl. She was upside down and her throat had been cut, a thick pool of blood staining the brown grass and autumn leaves below her. She was hung by her ankles, and what looked like a fishing gaff was threaded through each Achilles tendon, the connecting chain draped over one of the elm's thick branches. Her lifeless eyes were open and staring directly at Iowa State Trooper Dale MacKenzie.

Trooper MacKenzie felt his own stomach lurch, and he grabbed at the portable transceiver on his belt. He began to speak, working to suppress the tremor in his voice and the shaking of his hands as he keyed the mike. He almost gagged, but caught himself. He tried, several times, to look away from the staring eyes of the dead child. Even when he closed his eyelids he could feel her eyes burning into him.

Until the end of his life, Iowa Highway Patrolman Dale MacKenzie would still find himself occasionally waking to the sound of his own screams and the nightmare image of Tiffany Meade's sightless eyes.

CHAPTER 7

It was late in the afternoon when Sergeant Evers and Deputy Kevin Kearns discreetly left the hospital through a side door to avoid the throng of reporters. Kearns was still in his blood-spattered work-out clothes and was chilled to the bone. Evers drove them to Kearns' apartment for a change of clothes. Kearns asked to stay home and clean up, but Evers only shook his head. "We've got to get your statement," was all he'd say.

Once at the sheriff's station, Kearns was allowed the comfort of a shower. He let the steaming water wash over him. The ER doctor told him not to get the stitches over his left eye wet, but he ignored the warning. The water not only cleaned him up, but cleared away the remaining fog from his recent concussion. Feeling better, he dressed in jeans and boots and topped them with a fresh T-shirt and a sweater. He wished he'd remembered to bring a coat; the thermometer was falling rapidly.

He'd finished dressing and was combing his short, bristly hair when Evers walked into the locker room. The physician had shaved a portion of Kearns' hairline on the left side to sew the stitches, and it gave him a somewhat ghoulish appearance.

"C'mon," the sergeant said. Kearns followed his boss up the stairs from the locker room, grabbing his revolver and badge as he closed his locker.

Once upstairs, Evers led him to the Inspectors' Division. All investigative functions of the sheriff's department were handled from that section of the substation. As a rookie deputy assigned to patrol duty, Kearns had only been up there a handful of times.

He was greeted by the stares of several men in the area. Some of them he recognized: district attorney's inspectors and sheriff's investigators. Others he didn't know.

Evers nodded to a seat at one of the tables and Kearns sat down, feeling the eyes on him. Evers accepted a cup of coffee from one of the DA's men standing nearby. Nobody offered any to Kearns.

One of the men moved forward. He was of medium height and wearing an expensive-looking three-piece suit on a bony frame. He had a receding hairline he tried to conceal with a perm and dye job. His tie tack was a Phi Beta Kappa key.

"Deputy Kearns, I'm Steve Scanlon, Special Agent in Charge of the Des Moines Bureau. This is Special Agent Tatters, and Special Agent Lefferty." Scanlon nodded his head at two nondescript men lounging on the far wall. "We'll be overseeing the investigation into today's happenings."

Kearns looked to his sergeant for any sign of how to respond. Evers silently mouthed the words, "Watch out," and turned his attention back to his coffee.

Scanlon continued. "As you know, a young child was kidnapped and murdered today. Also murdered was the teacher in charge of that child."

"Wait a minute; I didn't see the child get murdered. I only saw–"

"Apparently you haven't heard. The child's body was found hanging from a tree on the interstate earlier this afternoon."

Kearns felt the room begin to spin. He put his face in his hands. Through his fingers he asked, "Why wasn't I told?"

Evers cut in. "I had instructions not to inform him, direct from the sheriff."

Scanlon put his hands on his hips, an exasperated look on his face.

"Tell me," blurted Kearns, looking up. "I want to know."

"You might as well know, Deputy," Scanlon said, no attempt to disguise his disdain at being interrupted. "Tiffany Meade was found with her throat cut out on I-80 twenty miles west of Des Moines. We suspect she was sexually assaulted as well. She was hanging from a tree like a slab of meat. A passing trucker spotted her."

"Jesus Christ," Kearns said under his breath.

"We're going to need a full statement from you," said Scanlon.

"I already gave one, at the hospital," replied Kearns, with no inflection. He was thinking of how a seven year-old girl spent her last moments on Earth. He was replaying images of his fight with the girl's abductor, and remembering the screams of the other children. He closed his eyes, and a vision flashed of an elderly woman falling to the ground with a .45 slug in her brain. He began to tremble.

"You'll give another statement, Deputy. And another after that, if I think it's necessary. Until I find out how your negligence resulted in two deaths."

Kearns stood up and hit Federal Bureau of Investigation Special Agent Steve Scanlon a stunning left hook to the center of his face. He followed it with a right, the knuckles already skinned from the fight in the schoolyard. He crossed his wrist expertly and leaned into it, driving from his hips. The agent's head rocked back. He slumped to the floor unconscious, blood spurting from his shattered nose.

The two remaining agents lunged at Kearns, who stood his ground. Several of the sheriff's detectives and DA's inspectors intervened and grabbed them, and Evers swiftly moved to a position between Kearns and the fuming feds.

"You motherfucker!" Agent Tatters howled, fighting the restraining hands. "I'll kick your ass!"

Evers faced the agents. "That's enough. Calm your butts down."

The two feds shrugged off the men restraining them and instantly began straightening their ties. Evers hid a grin. The detectives and DA's men looked away, grinning also. Sergeant Evers bent over the unconscious Scanlon and held his chin.

"He's out cold. His nose is busted, too." Evers motioned to the red-faced feds. "Get him to a doctor, and when you get back you can resume your little taskforce. I think we can manage without the illustrious FBI for an hour or so."

The two agents stooped to pick up their limp boss. "Rest assured, there's going to be documentation on this," said Tatters.

"Kiss my ass," Evers said. "Scanlon was way the hell out of line. Where does he get off talking to my deputy like that?" Evers bent his thumb at the unconscious FBI man. "Get him the fuck out of here."

Once the agents left, Evers gave Kearns a hard look.

"What the hell is your problem?" he asked the deputy.

"What did you want me to do?"

"I guess when I was your age I was about as stupid. How's the hand?"

"Not bad," said Kearns bitterly, "considering it's only good for knocking out bureaucrats. It's child-killers I wish I had better luck with."

Evers poured himself another cup of coffee. "I already told you at the hospital it was going to get rough. When shit like what went down today happens, it might be nobody's fault, but people look for someone to blame. It's gonna be you if you don't put a lid on your temper."

Kearns nodded, not really listening.

"Office pogues and reporters launch their careers on high profile crimes like this one. Scanlon's no different. Hell, you know what he did?"

Kearns stared at his sergeant for an answer.

"Scanlon already had the mother identify her kid's body. Can you fucking believe it? Walked right up to her and showed her a Polaroid. He said, 'Is this your daughter?' Mom went ballistic. She tried to do to Scanlon what you just did, with less success. She had to be sedated."

"What an asshole."

"You ain't kidding." Evers sipped coffee. "But it doesn't change things."

"Everyone is acting like I did something wrong. Like this was my fault."

Evers wrinkled his nose and poured the remaining coffee in the sink. "Listen kid, I know you did all you could, and you know it. But the rest of the world doesn't know, and they don't forget. This ain't LA or New York. This is a rural county, in a rural state, where things like child-killings aren't supposed to happen. And when they do, it grabs headlines. People around these parts have long memories."

"Look, Sarge," said Kearns, calmer. "I realize you're looking out for my best interests. I can handle it. I'll weather the storm."

Evers reached into a pocket and pulled out a stack of Polaroid photographs. He tossed them on the table in front of Kearns. "Got these from Scanlon," he said.

Kearns looked at the photographs, not really wanting to. The first picture was a close-up of what was once a seven year-old girl. She was hanging upside down from a tree. He didn't want to look, but couldn't take his eyes away. He shuffled through the stack of photos, each grislier than the first; a deck of cards from hell. After the third one he put the pictures down, his hands shaking.

"She was killed not long before she was found," Evers said, "by her body temperature and the coroner's estimation of the coagulation of her blood in relationship to the temperature outside."

Kearns was ashen. Evers continued.

"There were reporters everywhere; even more than at the hospital. It's all over the news. Still think you can weather the storm?"

Kearns said nothing.

"Go home. Get some sleep. Stay by the phone. I'll call you and tell you when to report."

Kearns stood up and walked to the door. "Sergeant," he began, "I want you to know–"

"You don't need to say it. Go home."

CHAPTER 8

By the time Kearns got to his apartment the sky was overcast and the temperature had dropped twenty degrees. Flakes of snow were starting to descend, and his hands shook when he inserted his key into the apartment door. He didn't know whether the shaking of his hands was from the falling temperature or the day's events. After several tries he got the door open and switched on the light.

Kearns' apartment was sparsely furnished. He'd had little time and money to obtain furniture since his police academy graduation. The apartment did have a sound heater, however, and he turned it up to take the chill from his bones.

His head hurt, and he was exhausted, but he knew he couldn't sleep. Over and over again he replayed the day's stark scenes in his mind. He couldn't erase the images and sounds of the murderous attack. The crunch of his shoes on the pavement as he jogged; the frantic voice of the now-dead teacher; the chorus of terrified children; the deafening report of the pistol; the big man's emotionless eyes. It was a nightmare he couldn't wake up from.

Kearns went to the kitchen and started a kettle to boil. He felt cold and weak, and knew the adrenaline deficit was responsible. He removed his revolver from his belt and placed it on the kitchen table.

The weapon, a Smith & Wesson Model 19 .357 magnum with a 2 ½ in barrel, was purchased when he'd graduated the police academy as an off-duty gun. His departmentally-issued duty revolver was still at the station in his locker.

Kearns stared at the blue steel of the compact revolver and wished he'd had the weapon when jogging this morning. The kettle's whistle broke his reverie. He gripped the kettle with both trembling hands to keep from spilling the boiling water. A pounding on his apartment door startled him, and he nearly scalded himself.

He heard several loud voices outside his apartment door. Someone was knocking on the door and ringing the bell simultaneously. Cursing, he put down the kettle and answered the door.

He was immediately blinded by a flash. A din of voices bellowed, and he blinked his eyes to clear them. He was aware of people crowding his doorway. Gradually his vision returned.

The group was carrying an array of cameras, videocams, and sound-recording gear, like peasants bearing pitchforks and torches as they stormed a castle during a revolt. Kearns was puzzled and angry all at once. How did the reporters find out where he lived?

"Deputy Kearns," a woman's voice erupted from the crowd, "did you know the child was murdered today?" Without waiting for an answer, the same voice asked, "Did you know after the kidnapper got away from you, that the child would in all likelihood be killed?"

Another voice, a man's, came fast and harsh. "Deputy, do you know the kidnapper? Have you ever seen him before? Was he–"

Still another voice interrupted, "Deputy, have you spoken with the child's parents? Did you know they were at the hospital at the same time you were?"

Kearns reeled, as more questions were hurled. Camera bulbs flashed sporadically, and he was aware of microphones in various shapes and sizes being thrust at him like weapons. The crowd of reporters pushed towards him, as those in the rear moved forward to get their microphones and cameras in. He tried to close his apartment door and found feet blocking it.

The deputy pushed his way into the crowd and moved the bustle of reporters away from his door. As soon as he cleared a path, he backpedaled into his apartment and closed the door and locked it. Instantly the doorbell began to ring again and the pounding resumed.

Kearns' hands fumbled the phone from its cradle. After several tries he dialed the number of the sheriff's department.

"Sheriff's office, is this an emergency?"

"This is Kevin Kearns. Get me Evers."

After a moment, "Dick Evers here."

"Sarge, it's Kevin."

"You're gonna have to speak up," Evers said. "I can barely hear you."

"That's what I'm calling about. There's a mob of reporters at my apartment. They won't leave."

"How the hell did they find out where you live?"

"I don't know. Maybe somebody followed me."

"Sit tight. Don't talk to any of them. I'll be there in a few minutes."

"Thanks."

He hung up the phone and sat down on a worn sofa he'd bought at a garage sale. His tea grew cold, and he didn't have the energy to make more. His head pounded in concert with the incessant pounding on his door. He felt like screaming.

Instead, Kevin Kearns put his face into his shaking hands and cried.

By the time Evers arrived Kearns had wiped away his tears and calmed his breathing. He wasn't proud of his crying jag, but once over it he found his hands had steadied. He poured the remainder of his tea down the sink and ran cold water over his face. He noticed the pounding on his door had stopped. This silence was followed a moment later by Evers' familiar drawl.

"Open up, Kevin, it's me." Kearns opened the door, hoping any evidence that he'd been crying had washed away under the water.

Evers came in, his breath visible. Behind him came Detective Rod Parish, who Kearns had only met once before. Kearns could see two uniformed deputies outside, roughly dispersing the crowd of reporters.

Evers made introductions, and Parish and Kearns shook hands.

"I didn't know what to do," Kearns said.

"This was bound to happen," said Evers. "Besides, we need to move you anyway."

"Move me?"

It was Parish who answered. "Kevin, things went to shit after you left the station. The sheriff held a press conference and opened his big goddamned mouth. There're at least a hundred people at the department, and more coming every minute. Reporters from every network, school administration people, church groups, plus the usual troublemakers and rubberneckers. It's a zoo." Parish looked around for a place to spit tobacco. Kearns found a plastic cup emblazoned with the Iowa State Cyclone and handed it to the detective.

After Parish spit, he continued. "The citizens don't know what happened, and they're all worked into a lather. Folks are confused; they're grieving, and angry, and some of em are asking how come the girl's dead and you ain't. The press ain't helping things any, either. I've never seen anything like it."

"It's a mob alright," Evers added. "It's ugly as hell, and getting uglier."

Kearns felt a stab of pain in his stomach.

"Like I told you at the hospital, people get crazy at times like this; they don't think. Some are jumping to foolish conclusions. Folk are looking to make sense out of something nobody can make sense of. They want someone to blame." Evers took off his hat and wiped his brow. "They're blaming you."

"He's right, kid. Things are really hot," Parish said, around his plug. "There have been threats."

"Threats? Against me?"

"Take it easy. Like I said, people get crazy."

Kearns ran his hands through his hair, flinching when he inadvertently rubbed the fresh stitches. "What the hell did I do? Why would somebody want to threaten me?"

"It's what they think you didn't do, Kevin. Folks are worked up and looking to lash out," Parish said. "You're the most convenient target."

"I'm not responsible for what happened to that little girl! Is somebody implying that I caused the girl's death? That I'm responsible?"

"Sheriff Coates didn't exactly say you weren't," said Evers.

"That fucking blowhard can't keep his mouth shut," said Parish. Evers nodded in agreement, cursing under his breath.

"What did the sheriff say?"

"He didn't say you were the cause of anything," Evers said, kneading his hat in his large, calloused hands.

"But he damn sure didn't say you weren't," finished Parish. "Buck's no JFK when it comes to public speaking on a good day, but with the crowd the way it was, he should have kept his mouth shut. I think he was trying to showboat and score a few votes, but all he did was rile everybody up. Damn near caused a riot right out in front of the station."

"How did reporters find out where I live? My address and phone number are unlisted."

"I wouldn't be surprised if somebody at the station leaked it," Parish said. "Besides, it's a small town. They'd have found you eventually."

"Buck goes up for re-election in less than a year," Evers explained. "He's already campaigning, and he's afraid of voter backlash. He wants to distance himself. The sheriff's got no loyalty to you; you're a rookie. Hell, you're still on probation. And now you're a source of controversy. He ain't saying you did anything to cause today's crime spree, but he damn sure ain't sticking up for you, either."

"And that ain't all," said Parish. He spit a wad of brown juice into the plastic cup for emphasis. "That FBI fucker you crowned, Scanlon? He's madder than hell. He was at the hospital getting his face repaired when all the reporters showed up. He's been running off at the mouth about what a reckless asshole you are. Said even though the investigation is still in preliminary stages, he can't eliminate you as somehow connected to the kid's disappearance, that sort of shit."

"Swell," said Kearns. "What am I supposed to do?"

"First off, we get you out of here," said Evers.

"Yeah," agreed Parish. "We've got to move you. You're a hot potato. At this point, I wouldn't put anything past anybody."

"You're not taking the threats seriously, are you?"

All Kearns got for an answer was a hard look from both veteran cops.

"Pack a bag," said Evers. "Take plenty of clothes. I don't know how long you're going to have to lay low."

Kearns began stuffing clothes and toiletry items into a green army duffel bag. The last thing he packed was the snub-nosed Smith & Wesson magnum from the table and a box of cartridges. He followed Detective Parish and Sergeant Evers from his apartment.

Parish led them to an unmarked sheriff's sedan parked nearby. Evers dismissed the two deputies who stood guard, and they left in their patrol car. There was half an inch of snow on the ground, and more was coming down. Parish fired up the cruiser and the trio drove off. Kearns sat in the back with Evers riding shotgun next to Parish.

No one spoke as they drove past the city limits and onto Interstate 35. The snow was getting thick on both the road and the windshield, and the wipers worked hard. After ten minutes on the highway Parish pulled into a roadside motel.

All three men exited the car, and Parish produced a key to a room on the ground floor. Kearns lugged his bag in, followed by the two deputies. He didn't ask why Parish didn't check in.

"OK, Kevin, you're on your own," said Parish. "Don't go out of the room. There are a lot of out-of-town folks, especially reporters, who are going to be flooding these roadside motels. Don't give them a chance to spot you. We'll check in tomorrow."

"I'm supposed to hide out? Like a criminal?"

"Don't think of it that way," said Parish, spitting in the snow. "More like a witness."

"Easy for you to say. You're not being stashed in a shitbox motel with orders to keep out of sight."

"It's only for a while," said Evers. "Until things cool off a bit. Try to relax."

"Could you?"

Evers and Parish exchanged a look. "We'll be in touch. Lock the door behind us." They left.

Kearns looked around the dingy room. The bed had a device which vibrated if you inserted coins. There was a rotary phone, a bible, two white towels in a bathroom which smelled too strongly of Lysol to be truly clean, and a battered color TV with cigarette scars on its simulated wood grain plastic top.

He placed his bag and took off his coat, removing his revolver from the pocket. He opened the wheelgun and made sure there were six cartridges nestled in the cylinder. He replaced the handgun into his coat and slung it over a battered chair.

Kearns checked his watch. It was past 10 o'clock. He switched on the TV and found a news station. The picture wasn't great, but the sound was adequate. He settled on the bed, watching and listening intently. The television was tuned to a nationally-broadcast news network.

"In political news today, the Tower Commission released a damning appraisal of the Reagan administration's direct involvement in the Iran-Contra affair. What President Reagan personally knew of his administration's decision to sell arms to Iran through Israel in exchange for the release of hostages held by Hezbollah is still under investigation."

Kearns switched to local news.

"Tragedy struck in rural Iowa today. An unidentified gunman apparently kidnapped a seven year-old elementary schoolgirl after gunning down her teacher during a brazen daylight attack. We have received unconfirmed reports that after making his getaway, the lone gunman sexually assaulted the child and killed her by unknown means."

Kearns held his breath and wrapped his arms tightly around his chest.

"What made this particular act of violence especially brutal," droned the monotone voice of the anchorman, "is the fact that the suspect, according to law enforcement sources speaking on condition of anonymity, apparently left the victim's body at a well-traveled highway rest stop. Steve Buchanan, on location, has more on the story."

The TV picture switched to a shot of the Franklin Roosevelt Elementary School crime scene, with cops, ambulances, and a large crowd milling about. The location reporter, Buchanan, was babbling away in the same monotone as the anchorman who'd introduced him. Kearns barely heard him. In the background, medics were loading a sheet-covered stretcher into the back of an ambulance.

From there the image changed to a still-photo of a matronly woman in horn-rimmed glasses, standing proudly by a group of small children. The reporter described the woman as a dedicated teacher, churchgoer, and grandmother who died courageously trying to save a child in her care.

Kearns felt queasy. He wanted to turn off the TV but couldn't take his eyes from the screen.

The TV shifted to a picture of Tiffany Meade. The shot showed a small girl with a kitten in her arms sitting in front of a Christmas tree. She was wearing pajamas and an ear-to-ear smile. Kearns flinched, tears forming in the corners of both eyes.

The camera changed once again. It switched back to the reporter, Buchanan, this time standing in a field.

Snow was falling and his breath was visible. In the background, ringed by yellow crime-scene tape, were state troopers and sheriff's deputies. There was also a crowd of onlookers. The reporter motioned to a grove of trees, and indicated those very trees were the location where young Tiffany Meade's body was discovered.

Kearns closed his eyes hard in an effort to stop the flow of tears. He opened them an instant later to see footage of the hospital, taken earlier that afternoon. Hospital staff scurried about tending to the hysterical children and adults in shock. He knew while those pictures were filmed he'd been inside the hospital getting his head sewn up. He listened to Buchanan's estimation of how hard the solid, blue-collar community was rocked by the tragic event.

"We are receiving mixed reports that an off-duty sheriff's deputy may have been somehow entangled in the day's events. Unconfirmed rumors have surfaced that the deputy has refused to cooperate with the FBI task force. There's been no comment from the deputy, who's been tentatively identified as Deputy Kevin Kearns, a rookie with less than a year's tenure on the department."

Kearns' jaw dropped. He watched his police academy graduation photo displayed on television. He was shaking his head in disbelief when the familiar face of Sheriff Buck Coates lit up the screen.

"...assure you that my department will do everything possible to apprehend the individual responsible for today's crime. You all can count on that. You have Buck Coates' word on it."

Kearns couldn't believe his ears. Coates was using the incident as a campaign platform. He began to understand Detective Parish's assertion that a scapegoat was in the making.

The news story continued with a sketch artist's rendering of the suspect. The description was given to detectives earlier by Kearns at the hospital. The story ended with an admonition that the suspect was considered armed and dangerous.

The news broadcast returned to the stern but friendly face of the anchorman, who said the current Tri-State manhunt for the suspect was the most extensive in the region's history. Kearns switched the TV off.

He wiped the tears from his eyes angrily and drew the curtains apart. He hadn't turned on the lights inside the motel room. Outside, gentle but heavy snowflakes descended on a blanket of fresh snow and reflected off the neon lights of the motel sign, casting an eerie glow. Kearns watched the falling snow. It reminded him of the picture of Tiffany Meade on the TV a moment ago. She was cuddling a kitten near a Christmas tree. But Tiffany Meade would never see another Christmas.

Eventually Kearns lay down fully dressed on the bed. He spent the remainder of a sleepless night reliving each anguished moment of the past day. Each time he dozed off he would awaken moments later in a cold sweat amidst visions of children hanging dead from snow-covered trees.

CHAPTER 9

Robert Farrell rolled over in bed and squinted at the digital alarm clock on his nightstand. Its radiant blue face read 7.43am. He rubbed his eyes and sat up, his bare feet searching the floor under the bed for his worn slippers. He stood, grabbed a tattered robe from the bed knob, slipped it over his rounded shoulders, and headed for the bathroom. There was a pack of Camels in the robe pocket, and he lit one with a wooden match while he relieved himself. Inhaling, he suppressed a cough and looked into the mirror.

San Francisco Police Inspector Robert Farrell, retired less than a month after over thirty years of service, stared at his sagging jowls and grunted. His thinning hair, which he'd grown long on the left side of his balding head and slicked over to the right, had flopped the wrong way during his sleep and stood straight up like an erection.

Exhaling smoke through his nostrils, he patted down his errant hair and said to his reflection, "At least one part of my anatomy will still stand up."

Farrell left the bathroom and headed towards the kitchenette. He stopped at his apartment door long enough to pick up his morning newspaper and tossed it on the small kitchen table. He took a moment to open the windows. The atmosphere in his apartment was a haze from last night's cigarettes. The moist San Francisco air filled the room, and he drew his bathrobe tighter about his chest.

His Lombard Street apartment resonated with the sounds of traffic as the morning commuters made their way through the city below. After putting on coffee, Farrell closed his windows. Most of the smoke had dissipated, leaving the apartment noticeably colder. After taking a final drag on his cigarette, he tamped it out and tossed it into the sink.

For over thirty years, Bob Farrell had been getting up and reporting to one of San Francisco's police stations. Now retired, he found old habits hard to break. He always told himself he would sleep late in retirement, and on weekends actually did sleep in an extra hour or so. But on weekdays, like today, he was wide awake in time to report to a job he no longer held.

Pouring a cup of coffee, Farrell sat down at his tiny table and glanced at the *San Francisco Chronicle*'s headlines. The phone rang behind him. He picked up the receiver without getting up.

"Hello," he barked, sticking another unfiltered Camel in his mouth.

"Bob, it's me. I called to..."

He rolled his eyes and took the receiver away from his ear. He instantly recognized the voice of his second ex-wife, Ann. Though separated for nearly four years, their divorce had been finalized only a few months before Farrell's retirement. It had been a long and bitter dispute. By the time Bob and Ann Farrell finally completed their divorce even the lawyers wanted it to end.

Putting the phone back to his ear, he said, "Look Ann, I don't want to talk to you. Do you know what time it is? If this keeps up I'm going to change my number again. Or get a restraining order."

As soon as he said it, he knew it would have no effect. Ann would simply obtain his new phone number from Jenny, their daughter, whom Farrell would naturally give the number to. It was a no-win situation with Ann. He sometimes wondered if she merely enjoyed bothering him for the sake of bothering him.

"Now look here, Bob, if you think..."

Farrell took the receiver from his ear again and set it on the table. He heard Ann's voice prattling away like the drone of a beehive from the earpiece. He lit his second cigarette, sipped his coffee, and turned his attention back to the *Chronicle*.

He skimmed the headlines, and was turning to page two, when his eyes widened and the cigarette dropped still burning from his mouth. Suddenly the room was much colder than the damp San Francisco air could have made it. The tiny mechanical voice of his ex-wife on the phone faded from his ears.

At the top of page two was the caption,

MASSIVE MANHUNT FOR MIDWEST CHILD-SLAYER CONTINUES.

Beneath the headline was a picture of a group of police officers and state troopers standing around a tree. In the tree, vaguely discernible in the photograph, was a body, hanging upside down.

Farrell picked up the phone and interrupted his babbling ex-wife. "I've got to go," he blurted, and hung up. Then he stamped out his cigarette.

He located the article beneath the photograph. He read the grim tale of a seven year-old girl who was kidnapped, slain, and found hanging from a tree in a rural Iowa. The article announced that the largest manhunt in Iowa's history was underway. Local law enforcement authorities had no leads on the identity of the suspect.

He let out a breath slowly and looked away from the paper, his mind in a trance. He shook another cigarette from the pack in his robe with trembling hands. It took four matches to light it. After inhaling deeply, he looked again at the blurry picture of a snow-covered Midwestern plain and the silhouette of a small body dangling from a leafless tree.

He sat motionless for many minutes, his eyes unfocused. The cigarette burned to his knuckles and jarred him back to reality.

"He's back," Farrell said aloud. "He's come back."

CHAPTER 10

Saigon, Republic of Vietnam. April, 1967.

Staff Sergeant Bob Farrell nodded to the sentry as he walked briskly past the interior security perimeter and into the compound.

Farrell was sweating profusely. He'd never acclimated to the humid climate. Even though he was far enough from the jungle, Farrell considered Saigon more of a jungle than a city, and the barefoot throngs of people who occupied its crowded streets did little to dispel this belief.

He took off his cap after entering the building and checked his .45 with the desk officer, going past him to the CO's office.

"Howdy, Bob," said Colonel Edgewater as Farrell entered. "Thanks for coming. Coffee?"

The thought of coffee in the intense heat nauseated Farrell instantly. Shaking his head, he shook a pack of Camels from the breast pocket of his fatigue shirt, offering one to his boss in the same motion. After both men lit up, Edgewater broke the silence.

"So how is he?"

"Eerie," replied Farrell. "Eerie as hell."

The colonel was referring to a young Marine who was at that moment locked securely in a cell at the Armed Forces Provost Occupational Headquarters, Saigon, one building over. Farrell, the Criminal Investigation Division's Non-Commissioned Officer assigned to the case, had spent the better part of a day-and-a-half trying to elicit information about the Marine, without much success. He was irritated at being pulled from the investigation for an impromptu conference with Edgewater. To Farrell the colonel was little more than an overblown prison-keeper and of scant help in investigative matters. Farrell was too new in-country, however, to object.

Farrell had been a San Francisco police officer for almost ten years when his army reserve unit, the 390th Military Police in Oakland, was activated and sent to Vietnam. His MP unit's mission was to supplement the staff at the Joint Services Provost Headquarters, in Saigon. Though Farrell disliked leaving his wife with her mother in San Leandro, he welcomed the unique challenges a year in wartime Vietnam would present. He packed his bags, and was off to the Criminal Investigation Division under Edgewater.

Though in-country less than three months, Farrell had earned a reputation as a tenacious investigator and a good cop. His superiors relied on his street experience obtained in the States, and he got along well with the MPs and soldiers he worked alongside. His present case was quite unique, and giving him more than the usual amount of grief.

A young Marine, hailing from somewhere in the Midwest, had been arrested the night before by MPs under Farrell's command. The Marine had violently resisted his arrest. This resulted in the injury of two military policemen, one seriously. But it was the crime the young Marine committed which created the real problem.

Farrell had become accustomed to a strained relationship between the residents of Saigon and the American occupational forces. The problems associated with the recreational behavior of thousands of American servicemen in a foreign country were a constant source of irritation to both the Vietnamese and American war efforts.

There was also intense political and racial strife between the Vietnamese and the American GIs. The United States military and its political overlords in Washington wanted to dilute this conflict at all costs. The war was escalating, and the Pentagon was becoming sensitive to the wavering public support for the war effort stateside. This created a delicate situation for the military police.

While trying to diminish the stigma of being an occupational army, the MPs had the tough job of not only keeping a leash on the off-duty servicemen, but had to do it in a manner that wouldn't bring international attention to the increasing levels of American-involved crime.

The case of the young Marine was a compelling and grisly one. Two nights before, a young Vietnamese prostitute reported her four year-old son missing from the upper floor of the tenement brothel where they lived. She would never have reported it to the American military police at all, except that she'd been servicing US troops on R&R when the incident occurred.

The young woman told the MPs that several of her fellow hookers saw a tall, husky American with a crew-cut and a distinct limp carry the screaming child from the brothel. When several of the girls tried to stop the American, he beat them savagely and made off with the boy. The child's mother was careful to explain that these women, all prostitutes like herself, did not wish to come forward and become embroiled in an investigation.

The report of the missing child was taken by the desk officer, and broadcast to roving foot and mobile patrol units. Farrell, a CID investigator, would never have been involved at all had the incident ended there. It did not.

Within six hours of the report, the son of the Vietnamese prostitute was found hanging upside down from a lamppost in one of the more secluded districts of the slum-ridden city.

The child was dead, his throat cut, and both ankles were wrapped in green parachute cord which was used to drape the body over the streetlight's arch. The boy had been sodomized, and had apparently been hanging only a short while when discovered by an intoxicated sailor who'd detoured into the alley to relieve himself.

Farrell was assigned to investigate, but within minutes of the body's discovery the crime scene had to be abandoned. When the local Vietnamese discovered the body, anti-American sentiment in the neighborhood became understandably ugly. A full-blown riot ensued, with every available MP in the city dispatched to assist.

Farrell suffered a cut over his ear from a thrown bottle, and before the night was over, many other MPs received similar treatment at the hands of the enraged Viets. Only through the use of teargas and riot batons were the embattled MPs able to retrieve the body of the child. Farrell had the body taken to HQ, where the child's hysterical mother made the identification.

Though no stranger to violent crime, Farrell was nonetheless deeply disturbed by the murder. Back in the States he was only a beat cop, and the investigation into such a brutal crime would have been handled by a team in the Inspectors' Division. But in Saigon, Staff Sergeant Robert Farrell was delving into the investigation of a heinous child-murder virtually singlehanded.

That a fellow American was responsible for the killing was not lost on the young cop. Farrell, like most soldiers of his generation, had been largely supportive of the war effort and indifferent to the growing tide of anti-war sentiment. But three months as a cop in Saigon had done much to plant the seeds of doubt in his mind. The constant contact with American soldiers whose behavior ranged from drunk and disorderly, to assault, to rape was taking its toll. As a stateside cop, he'd dealt mostly with a separate and distinct criminal element, easily distinguishable from the average citizen.

As a Saigon MP, Farrell found more and more of the servicemen he was arresting appeared to be ordinary guys. Often they were young men with no prior history of criminal offending. They had come to Vietnam to fight a war as innocent boys next door, and somewhere in-country had become drug addicts, sexual predators, and hardened criminals. It became harder for Farrell to see the difference between the good guys and the bad guys. What was once black and white became gray.

The war made things fuzzy.

He committed himself to capturing the child-murderer. His office became the command post, and he stayed around the clock. Photographs of the child hanging from the lamppost were piled on his desk, and the more he looked at them, the more disturbed and determined he got.

Farrell believed the suspect was a frequent patron of the many Saigon prostitutes, but the task of checking all the brothels in the bustling city was a momentous one. The suspect met a very general physical description, and there were thousands of American servicemen in Saigon on R&R.

It was an idea he got from one of his MPs that eventually led Farrell to the child-killer.

As a group of MPs came straggling in from another night of riot-breaking in the wake of the murder, they more closely resembled crash victims than a military police detachment. Splinted fingers and hands, bandaged heads, and torn uniforms seemed the order of the day.

As Farrell watched the troops stumble in, it occurred to him that the suspect was described by several of the prostitutes as walking with a limp. Maybe the killer wasn't on R&R? Perhaps the killer was a patient at the naval hospital, or the army medical center, where countless servicemen wounded in the field were transferred for treatment? Many of these wounded personnel, though not fit for return to full duty, were allowed leave within Saigon during their recovery. Maybe the limp was a battlefield wound?

Farrell had his invaluable translators re-query the prostitutes who'd witnessed the child snatching. They all concurred; the suspect limped on his right leg.

He dispatched MP units to each of the medical facilities within the Saigon Command. It didn't take long to hit pay dirt.

At 1630 hours, Farrell received a call to respond to the naval hospital regarding the apprehension of a suspect in the child-murder. He drove to the hospital code three.

When he arrived he was greeted at the entrance by a shore patrolman and a hospital staff officer. They led him to the emergency room, where one of his MPs was seated on a table.

Corporal Vincente Gomez looked like he'd gone ten rounds with the Brown Bomber. One of his eyes was swollen shut, and his normally dark-brown complexion was a sickly yellow pallor. His right hand was being wrapped in a cast by a navy doctor.

"Vinnie, what happened?" asked Farrell.

"We were checking with the orderly, Sarge, just like you told us, and giving him a description of our man."

Gomez took a moment to swallow, his voice shaky. He looked as if he were about to throw up. "Go on," Farrell said anxiously.

The corporal nodded. "The orderly told us to check the convalescent barracks where the outpatients and walking wounded are billeted. Orderly said there are too many dudes around here for him to keep tabs on. So me and Rick head over there."

Farrell knew Gomez was referring to his partner, Rick Bryson, and wondered where the young MP was. "OK," Farrell said, the nervous edge to his voice showing through, "get to the point."

"So we go into the convalescent barracks, and the first guy we run into is this huge jarhead with a bunch of tattoos. He spots us coming into the room, and makes a bee-line for the rear exit. Only problem is, he's got a limp, so we catch him in about three seconds."

The young corporal grimaced as the doctor wrapped his hand. "So Rick says, 'We want to ask you some questions, you'll have to come with us,' and the guy shrugs and sort of comes along, you know, real mellow-like."

Farrell was looking intently at the MP. "Then what happened?"

"Hell, Sarge, I don't know. Next thing I know this guy hits Rick in the throat. Rick goes down. I grab the guy, but he wiggles out and knees me in the groin."

Farrell now knew the origin of Gomez's sickly pallor. "OK, then what?"

"So I pull out my .45, but before I can plug the fucker he grabs my hand, and whammo, the next thing I know my hand is fucked up, and my gun is on the floor. I bent down to pick it up, and he kneed me in the face."

"So where is the suspect now? You reported you had him in custody," Farrell said impatiently.

"I guess Rick wasn't completely out, because the next thing I hear is a shot. There's Rick, puking blood, and his gun is smoking. And there's our man on the ground."

"Where's Bryson now?"

Before Gomez could answer, the doctor interjected.

"Sergeant, your man is in the adjacent treatment room. I think you'd better see to him."

Farrell went next door, where he found Private First Class Rick Bryson lying face down on a bed with his shirt off and clear plastic bags of ice on both sides of his neck. Under his mouth, on the floor, was a drip-pan full of bright, frothy blood.

It was obvious Bryson couldn't speak. Farrell asked the doctor leaning over Bryson, "How is he, Doc?"

"Not good, but much better than it could have been. His larynx is badly bruised. We think we've bled out most of the fluid, and the swelling is down. His lungs aren't in jeopardy. We'll know soon if he'll need a trach."

"In English, please?"

"Your man has had a lot of damage done to his throat. I won't know for a while if we'll have to cut his throat open and do a tracheotomy. I believe we'll be able to avoid that, and he'll eventually have a full recovery, but I can't say for sure. It's too soon to tell."

Bryson was in obvious pain. Tears formed in the corners of the young soldier's eyes as he listened to his injuries discussed so casually.

"Just patch him up, will you?"

"I hope to have him good as new."

Farrell silently prayed that Bryson wouldn't suffer permanent disability. He patted the young MP gently on the shoulder.

"You take it easy, Rick, and soak up all this flatbed time. I'm going to work your ass off when you get back. I'm also going to put you in for so many medals you're going to have to lug them around in a shopping cart."

Bryson forced a smile. Farrell nodded a goodbye, and headed out to the main lobby. The same shore patrolman who'd greeted him at the entrance was still there.

"OK," said Farrell curtly. "Where is the son of a bitch?"

The SP led Farrell to a surgical room, and had him don an apron and facemask. He entered the operating room.

He found a surgeon, as well as a group of nurses, huddled around a man laying face down on a surgical table. No one looked up as he entered.

The man on the table was huge, with a thickly muscled torso. The man's face was obscured, and he wore the deep tan of the field soldier. There were jagged scars running up and down the man's back, and Farrell could see several of the circular sphincter-scars that only gunshot wounds produced. The man had a crew-cut, and a Marine Corps eagle, globe, and anchor tattooed on one of his massive forearms.

Farrell imagined getting slugged in the throat by one of those beefy arms, and cringed as he remembered the nineteen year-old MP spitting blood in a room down the hall.

"I'm going to have your ass on a platter, motherfucker," Farrell said between clenched teeth. "You're never going to see the outside of a prison as long as you live."

At Farrell's outburst, the physician and nurses looked up.

"What are you doing in here?" the surgeon asked.

"That man you're operating on is in my custody," replied Farrell evenly. "How badly is he hurt?"

"He's very lucky. He was shot in the buttocks, and the bullet deflected off his hip and exited. Would you care to see?"

"I'll take your word for it."

By the time Farrell left surgery and got out of his gown, three of the MPs from his detachment were in the lobby. He issued orders requiring twenty-four hour babysitting of the suspect. Once the suspect was awake, he was to be put in irons, the doctors be damned. And once medically cleared for release, the suspect was to be transported forthwith to the detention facility at the Provost HQ. Farrell assigned two of the MPs this task.

The third MP was to see that MPs Bryson and Gomez were taken care of. He was also ordered to obtain the medical records of the suspect and dispatch them to Farrell's office immediately. He left strict orders that no one was to talk to the suspect. He then left to catch some much needed rest.

Farrell was not to sleep, however. By the time he returned to his billet, a message was waiting for him to report back to his office to take receipt of the suspect's 201 file, or military service record. He took a hurried shower, stuffed a fresh pack of Camels into his pocket, and drove back to Provost HQ.

One of the GIs in the office brought Farrell some sandwiches. He unbelted his .45 and sat down at his desk. The clerk came in a moment later and he signed a receipt for the Marine's personnel file. It was as thick as a phone book.

Lance Corporal Vernon Emil Slocum, United States Marine Corps, was only twenty years old. He'd enlisted in the Marine Corps at age seventeen after being signed in by his father, a farmer from Ogden, Iowa.

There wasn't much background on Slocum. He'd never graduated high school, and was one of four children. His military record was considerably more detailed.

After boot camp at Parris Island, Slocum was attached to the 1st Battalion, 6th Marine Regiment, already in Vietnam. He was assigned as an M-60 machine-gunner, probably due to his large stature and physical strength. His unit was a Battalion Landing Team in the Da Nang area.

Farrell lit another in an endless stream of cigarettes and labored over the file. Slocum's service record read like Audie Murphy's.

In late '65, and early '66, Slocum was in the Cam Ranh Bay doing platoon recon. His unit was ambushed by a significantly larger NVA force. Though wounded in the chest and back by rocket fragments, he so effectively suppressed enemy fire that his platoon was able to escape. He did this after both his assistant gunner and team leader had already been killed.

After a brief stay in a field hospital, Slocum was back with his unit, this time with a Purple Heart and Bronze Star.

Then Farrell found an unexplained gap in the records, and Slocum was reassigned to another platoon. Again he distinguished himself in combat, earning the Silver Star for singlehandedly halting a Viet Cong ambush in the Chu Lai Peninsula that would have resulted in a complete rout of the Marine defensive perimeter had it succeeded. More battles, and even more medals, were chronicled in the file.

Farrell was completely engrossed in the documents and lost track of the time. He was jarred back to reality by the desk sergeant's voice.

"Hey Bob, your baby-killer's CO is here. He wants to talk to you. He's in the colonel's office."

So Farrell found himself in Edgewater's office, irritated at the interruption, and curious what Lance Corporal Vernon E Slocum's company commander would have to say about what his Marine had done.

"What do you mean, 'eerie'?" asked Edgewater.

"Well sir, I haven't had a chance to talk to the suspect, but I've been going over his 201 file. I'd like to get back to it before I interrogate him."

Edgewater said nothing in response, looking at the floor and exhaling smoke through his nostrils. It made Farrell nervous. Finally he spoke.

"Bob, you've done a good job on this, and I'm proud of you. But I think you should talk to this Marine's commanding officer. He's outside in the waiting room. I've already had a chance to chat with him."

"Why didn't you tell me he was here? You could have saved me a couple of hours of reading."

"I have my reasons, Sergeant." He ground out his cigarette and pressed the intercom button on his desk. "Send in the captain, will you?"

The door opened, and a tall Marine came in. He was wearing filthy, sweat-stained fatigues, and looked as if he hadn't slept in at least as long as Farrell. It was clear he'd come in from the field. Edgewater made the introductions.

Farrell stood and shook a hand thick with the dirt of the jungle. Both sat down.

"I've already briefed the captain on the status of the investigation and the charges against his Marine," Edgewater said. Turning to Bradshaw, Edgewater added, "The industrious sergeant here has been going through Slocum's 201 file."

Farrell didn't like the tone of Edgewater's voice. There was a hint of something veiled, something that spelled trouble to the young cop.

Bradshaw sighed deeply, and pulled a battered pack of Marlboros from inside his tunic. After he had lit one with an equally battered Zippo, he looked at Farrell through the smoke and said, "Sergeant Farrell, Corporal Slocum is certainly one helluva Marine."

"There are a lot of gaps in his file, Captain. I was hoping you could fill some of them in."

The captain sighed heavily again, and Farrell realized the Marine officer was several years younger than him. Bradshaw displayed a weariness not borne solely from lack of sleep.

"Sergeant, Corporal Slocum is without a doubt the most efficient fighting man I've ever known. You've seen his file; you've probably guessed that already."

Farrell took umbrage. "Sir, he may be a super-trooper, but do you know what he did? Are you aware of what he's being charged with?"

Bradshaw said nothing for a long minute, staring solemnly at Farrell.

"Sergeant, have you ever been in combat?"

"No, sir, I have not."

"Then it's going to be hard for you to get perspective on Corporal Slocum. I'm not sure you would understand."

Farrell found himself growing angry. "Sir, with all due respect, I'm not sure I care to understand. To you, Slocum is a squared-away Marine. To me, he's a child-killer. Your troop buttfucked and murdered a four year-old boy and left him hanging like a piñata. When he was questioned about it, he attacked two of my men, severely injuring one, and tried to escape. I don't give a goddamn about his war heroics, or the Corps, or how rough it was out there in the jungle. He's a monster. And I'm going to see he gets the death penalty, or spends the rest of his miserable life in Fort Leavenworth."

Farrell half-expected the Marine captain to lash back. He knew he was out of line, but didn't care. Edgewater glared at him hotly; he was pushing the limits of insubordination. Instead, the Marine officer shook his head slightly, smoking in silence. After a final drag, Captain Bradshaw put out his butt and looked at Farrell in contempt.

"OK," the captain said finally, his voice a whisper. "You want to know about Lance Corporal Vernon Slocum? Listen and learn."

CHAPTER 11

Captain Bradshaw reached in his pocket for another Marlboro. He looked at Farrell coolly, appraising him. After he lit his cigarette he began to speak.

"Slocum came to my Company in November of '66, as part of a replacement group from Da Nang. We'd been hit hard, and were due some light defensive posturing in the Chu Lai Peninsula as a result. I should have known by how fast we got our replacements we'd be heading straight back to the bush."

Bradshaw rubbed his unshaven chin. "Slocum was not a popular Marine. He's a big motherfucker and twice as strong as he looks. He kept to himself, and didn't get along too well with the guys in his squad. A lot of rumors followed him; real nasty ones."

"What kind of rumors, Captain?" asked Farrell.

Captain Bradshaw's face broke into a skeletal grin. "What kind of rumors, Sergeant? Rumors you can't confirm, or deny, or even dare ask about."

"Captain, I'm conducting an investigation. I need to know."

The Marine exhaled smoke. Farrell was grateful the infantry officer was smoking; the odor of unwashed body emanating from him was strong.

"I asked you if you'd been in combat for a reason. When you've been out in the bush for a long time, away from the world, things change."

"Could you be a little more specific?"

"You sure you want to hear this?"

"I asked, didn't I?" Farrell said.

Bradshaw ground out his cigarette. "OK, cop; you want specifics, I'll give you specifics." The tension between the grunt officer and the CID sergeant was palpable. "Shit happens. Is that specific enough for you?"

The Marine's eyes flashed, and Farrell heard the escalating tone in his voice. He knew he was angering the captain but refused to back off. He needed answers, and as Slocum's commanding officer Bradshaw was uniquely qualified to provide them. He didn't want to piss him off too much, however; Bradshaw looked like a man capable of anything.

Bradshaw stood up and walked over to the window. He resumed speaking, his back to Sergeant Farrell and Colonel Edgewater. He appeared to have calmed somewhat, but since Farrell could no longer see his face he couldn't be sure.

"Sergeant, let me offer you a hypothetical. Let's pretend you're a grunt in an infantry company, here in Vietnam. Pretend you've been out in the bush for a couple of months. You're so fucking far away from the civilized world that you don't remember what it's like to shit in porcelain or eat from a plate. And for the sake of my hypothetical, we'll pretend that Vietnamese children approach you with grenades stuffed in their armpits. We'll pretend snipers shoot at you all day. And we'll pretend that every once in awhile, as you walk through the bush, one of your buddies steps on a tripwire and gets splattered all over you without warning."

The captain lit another smoke, his face still turned away.

"All you want to do is go home," Bradshaw went on, "with both arms, both legs, and both balls. There ain't no rules; just get home in one piece. Now pretend that some of the guys in your unit, guys you sure as hell wouldn't choose to have as friends back in the States, are crazy fuckers. You still with me?"

"I'm listening, sir," Farrell said quietly.

"Outstanding. You realize we're only talking hypothetically, don't you?"

"I understand."

"Good," Bradshaw said. "I want to make that clear. Pretend some of the troops in your unit are truly psychotic. One hundred percent, dyed in the wool, certifiable, batshit crazy. Whether they were like that before the war, or got that way after being in it a while, is inconsequential isn't it? Every war has them, right? Guys that like it; dudes that enjoy killing. And not surprisingly, these whack-jobs are often the best soldiers in your unit."

Bradshaw turned around suddenly to face Farrell, his eyes burning. Farrell sat motionless, afraid to speak.

"Well Sergeant, these troops I'm talking about, hypothetically, of course, aren't boy scouts. They cut off ears, and slice off dicks, and hang bodies up in the trees as a warning to the enemy. They go into villages like Gia Binh, or Gia Lang, or other godforsaken shithole places, and kill civilians, fuck children, burn hooches, and generally have a merry old time."

Bradshaw's voice was gradually rising to a fever pitch, and his eyes were glowing coals of contempt. Farrell was conscious that he'd checked his .45 with the desk sergeant when he came into the compound, and missed its reassuring weight on his hip.

The Marine backed away from Farrell and began to pace around Edgewater's office, his hands folded behind his back. The colonel sat impassively, taking in the scene as if it were on TV.

"What was I saying, Sergeant?"

"You were telling me about the villages, sir."

"Ah yes; the villages. Well, Sergeant, in the villages, things happen. Unpleasant things." Bradshaw's voice was again the epitome of control. Farrell found the captain's calm demeanor more disconcerting than his angry one.

"Let's pretend, still for the sake of our hypothetical scenario, that you're in a squad with one of these mad motherfuckers. Because they're crazy, they aren't afraid of anything. And they genuinely like their jobs. Maybe one of these weirdoes has even saved your life a few times; maybe a lot of times. Maybe the only reason you're alive and able to even fucking breathe is because one of these bloodthirsty nutjobs has pulled your ass out of the grease."

Bradshaw paused to take a drag from his cigarette.

"So there you are, waking up every morning praying to survive another lovely day in the Nam. And when you get to a village and meet some of the friendly citizens of the bountiful country you're trying to liberate, some of these weirdoes in your squad start having their special brand of fun. Just what are you gonna do?"

"It would present a challenge," Farrell said.

"Outstanding, Sergeant. You move to the head of the class. Maybe you don't like what this madman is doing, but you're too busy trying to stay alive to notice."

Bradshaw's voice was starting to rise again. Farrell wasn't sure the Marine captain wasn't one of the crazies he was talking about.

"Or maybe," Bradshaw spat, his voice again at a fever pitch, "there's an even more compelling reason to look away. Maybe this guy is so crazy he makes the other gung-ho types look like Sunday school teachers. Crazy enough to singlehandedly stand off an ambush and save you and your whole platoon. Crazy enough to carry your wounded ass to safety through two hundred yards of mine-ridden rice paddy under heavy fire. Or crazy enough to cut your throat in your sleep if he gets a hint that you don't approve of his extracurricular activities." Bradshaw smiled without mirth. "Hypothetically, of course." He threw his third cigarette to the floor and ground it out with his heel, staring at Farrell.

When the Marine spoke again, his voice was again quiet.

"You asked me about the rumors that followed Lance Corporal Slocum? You tell me he sexually assaulted and murdered a gook kid in your city? What do you want me to say? That I'm shocked? That I've never seen anything like that before? Wake up and smell the napalm, cop. You ain't in Kansas anymore."

"Sir," Farrell asked hesitantly, "are you telling me Slocum has committed this kind of crime before?"

Captain Bradshaw looked at Farrell as if the CID investigator was from another planet.

"I'm not telling you anything at all, Sergeant. I was only speaking hypothetically, remember?"

Farrell stood up. "I'm sorry sir, but I don't buy it. War is hell, and all that shit, but it doesn't bring back a dead child. A kid whose dying moments were sheer horror. I don't give a damn if your Corporal Slocum planted Old Glory on Iwo Jima all by himself. He might be Audie Murphy to you, but to me he's a fucking monster. And he ain't in the bush anymore; now he's mine."

To Farrell's surprise, Bradshaw began laughing.

"You're a kick in the ass, you know that Sergeant?"

"What the hell is that supposed to mean?"

"It means you haven't heard a thing I've said, have you? Do you think you're the only one full of righteous indignation? Do you think that just because I understand something, I condone it? Grow up."

The Marine officer again moved his face to within inches of Farrell's.

"Like I said when we were talking hypothetically, you're a grunt in the bush, and you want to stay alive, you ignore things. It doesn't have to be murder, you know. A guy like Slocum, an experienced ground-pounder, he doesn't have to pull the trigger himself. He just doesn't speak up when he sees your foot stepping toward a tripwire. Or during a firefight, you walk into a bullet. It's nothing overt, but you're just as dead, and nobody's the wiser."

Bradshaw headed for the door. He stopped before reaching it.

"For what it's worth, thirteen months ago I would have felt outraged, too. But it's been a long time since I felt a whole lot of anything."

Captain Bradshaw put his cap on. He looked briefly at the colonel, and then back at Farrell. "I didn't come here to give you a hard time. I respect what you're doing. I've already been briefed by Colonel Edgewater. I was only trying to soften the blow."

Farrell listened, puzzled.

"One more thing, Sergeant; watch Corporal Slocum very carefully. Don't turn your back on him for a second. He's the most dangerous man I've ever known. Good luck."

"Sir," blurted Farrell as Bradshaw walked out the door, "don't you want to know what's going to happen to your Marine?"

Shaking his head slightly, Bradshaw said, "No, Sergeant, I don't. Do you?" The door closed behind him, and he was gone.

Farrell turned to Edgewater, who hadn't spoken during the exchange between the young cop and the hardened Marine.

"Sir, what did he mean when he said he'd already been briefed?"

"Sit down, Bob, and let me have another smoke. We've got to talk."

Farrell didn't like the tone of Edgewater's voice, or the fact that his commanding officer didn't look him in the eye when he spoke. He shook two cigarettes from his pack.

"Bob, you're a good soldier, and a good cop. I like having you work for me, and like I said, you've done a helluva job on this baby-killing thing."

There was an overly long pause as Edgewater exhaled smoke, still not meeting Farrell's eyes.

"Try to understand; there are things going on here that are out of my control."

"I get the feeling that you're about to give me bad news."

"I'll get to the point. The investigation is over as far as we're concerned. I had Captain Bradshaw brought here to advise him that Corporal Slocum was no longer his responsibility. Some men will be arriving shortly to take custody of him. I want all files and paperwork on the investigation turned over to me immediately. Your work will be noted in your enlisted evaluation report."

Farrell was dumbfounded. He couldn't believe what he was hearing.

"It's over? Just like that? I'm off the investigation?"

"Bob, I'm trying to be reasonable. You've got to try to be reasonable too. You're not being taken off the investigation. The investigation is over."

"What do you mean, over? And who's taking custody of Slocum? The JAG's Office? The Naval Investigative Service?"

The colonel finally looked directly at Farrell; it wasn't a friendly expression. Neither was the tone of his voice.

"Sergeant, you don't need to know who's coming to get Slocum. It's out of our hands. There are influential people who are aware of this situation, and have taken the necessary steps to remedy it. I haven't been given a clue about what's going to happen to him, and I'm a full-bird colonel. You, as a staff sergeant, ought to know better than to even ask. Like you, I follow orders."

Farrell worked to control his mounting rage.

"This is going to be buried, isn't it?"

Edgewater ground out his cigarette angrily. "What did you expect? This is political dynamite. You can read the writing on the wall, can't you? If Slocum gets prosecuted for his crimes through regular UCMJ channels, there'll be no way to keep a lid on it. How do you think this would look if the press got hold of it? Jesus Christ, you just came from the States, didn't you? This Slocum murder is exactly the kind of thing the hippies are chanting about during their campus protests. That the US military is in Vietnam killing babies. Isn't that what they call us back home? Baby-killers?"

"Sir, I understand the political ramifications. But you can't expect me to sit quietly and let Slocum walk? That Marine is a fucking time-bomb. He needs to be put somewhere where he can't do this kind of thing again. Sir, we aren't talking about friendly-fire casualties occurring in the heat of combat. We're talking about an American serviceman committing a premeditated murder in cold blood."

"That's enough, Sergeant," Edgewater said. "You are under my command, and you will do exactly as you are ordered. I told you, it's out of my hands. This has already attracted the attention of some very high-ranking brass. I will not let you, or anyone else, fuck up my command, and create an embarrassing international incident over an isolated criminal act. Hell, Bob, we're at war. What's one dead gook, more or less?"

Farrell held his tongue, and ground out his cigarette in the ashtray on Edgewater's desk. He went for the door.

"I want all the paperwork on my desk in fifteen minutes. All of it."

"Roger that," Farrell said over his shoulder as he slammed the door.

He left the headquarters building after picking up his .45. He walked briskly to his own office in the adjacent building and went directly to his desk, where he'd left Slocum's 201 file. He walked out to the administrative office and made a mimeographed copy of the arrest sheet. Tucking the copy into his breast pocket, he took the file over to the desk sergeant.

"Have the CQ runner get this over to the colonel's office immediately. Edgewater wants it yesterday."

The desk sergeant took the file. Farrell stopped him before he left.

"Is the suspect still in the holding cells?"

"Where else would he be?"

"Thanks. Put a rush on that file, will you?"

Farrell walked out of the administrative offices and across the courtyard, this time in the opposite direction of Edgewater's office, towards the detention center. Once there, he checked his pistol with the sentry and signed in on a log. From there he proceeded to the desk sergeant's post.

"Where's my boy?"

"Cell B-4. End of the hall. You want some company?"

"He still shackled?"

"Damn straight," said the desk sergeant. "You see the size of that guy?"

"I'll be OK. Lemme have the key."

"Here you go," the sergeant said, handing Farrell a large brass key. "You need anything, holler."

Farrell walked past the jailer's station and was buzzed through a large metal door. Once inside, he went to section B, and found cell number four.

Looking through the bars, he saw Slocum lying on a bunk. The lance corporal had a thick leather belt on, and both of his hands were securely fastened to it by steel cuffs.

Slocum was wearing an olive-drab T-shirt and green boxer shorts. To his buttocks was taped a large patch of gauze and cotton, brown with congealed blood. It looked painful as hell to Farrell, and was undoubtedly the aftermath of the surgery to treat the gunshot wound he'd received during his arrest. Farrell inserted the brass key and noisily turned the lock. Slocum looked up as he entered.

Farrell saw a cherub-like face set under a tight crew-cut. Slocum's neck was a thick trunk of muscle, and his arms were corded powerhouses. If he was in pain or discomfort from his wounds he didn't show it.

It was Slocum's eyes however, that made Farrell the most uncomfortable. They were deep and black, and seemed devoid of emotion. He'd seen pictures of predatory animals with such eyes.

"Who the fuck are you?"

The deep voice snapped Farrell from his silent appraisal. In the voice was the hint of a Midwestern accent.

"I'm Staff Sergeant Farrell, CID. It was my men that caught you."

A grunt was all he got for a reply.

Slocum returned his stare for several long seconds, finally saying, "So what the fuck do you want?"

Farrell shook his head. "I wanted to see what talking shit looks like."

The big Marine unexpectedly sat upright, with a speed that startled Farrell. It made him forget for an instant the suspect was shackled. He stepped back reflexively, and Slocum laughed.

"This shit sure scared you, mister big-shot CID-man."

Then the laughter was gone from Slocum's features. Replacing it was an expression Farrell would never forget, an animal visage on a human face.

"I could kill you the way you turn off a light," Slocum said.

Farrell was more shaken by the Marine than he cared to show. He'd seen a lot of criminals, but never before one with such depraved viciousness seeping from every pore. He hoped Slocum couldn't detect how unnerved he was.

"What's the matter, Sergeant? Cat got your tongue?"

"I came to tell you I'll enjoy knowing you'll be locked up for the rest of your life. It makes me happy."

Slocum produced a feral grin.

"If I told you what makes me happy, you'd have nightmares."

Farrell suddenly didn't know why he'd come to see the child-killer, and wished he hadn't. With a confidence he didn't feel, he said, "Enjoy your life in prison, Corporal."

Farrell left the cell, locking the door. As he walked down the corridor he heard Slocum's chilling voice behind him.

"Maybe I'll see you around someday, Sergeant."

Minutes later, three men wearing civilian clothes but sporting military haircuts and Ray-Ban Aviator sunglasses pulled up in a jeep. Ten minutes later they drove away with Lance Corporal Vernon E Slocum, still shackled. Farrell watched them drive off from the window of his office, a cigarette smoldering between his lips. He sincerely hoped he would never see Corporal Vernon Emil Slocum again.

It would be twenty years before he did.

CHAPTER 12

San Francisco, November, 1987

Farrell sat at his kitchen table and stared at the blurry newspaper picture. His thoughts drifted back to the here and now from Southeast Asia of 1967.

Eventually he put the newspaper down. Rubbing his eyes, he took in a deep breath and exhaled slowly. He got up and poured his lukewarm coffee into the sink. He reached into a cabinet and took out a bottle of Jim Beam. He poured bourbon until the ceramic mug was full to the brim. He took a gulp, grimaced, and put another Camel between his lips and lit it.

Farrell closed his eyes and let his thoughts wander to the past again. He thought of the young Marine corporal in shackles, his face a mask of evil. He remembered the riots in the Saigon ghetto, and the sound of batons hitting bodies as MPs held outraged Viets at bay. He could almost hear the tormented wailing of the Vietnamese prostitute as she identified the gutted body of what was once her child. And he remembered the impotence he felt as he watched Slocum being whisked away by Agency men in mirrored sunglasses. These images dredged up a maelstrom of half-buried feelings and long-suppressed fears, and brought a twinge to his stomach.

He opened his eyes and wiped his forehead, not surprised to find it damp with sweat. His stomach was queasy, the painful reminder of a recently-diagnosed ulcer. Farrell took another drink of bourbon.

He picked up the phone. After dialing long distance information, he was connected to the editor's desk at the *Des Moines Register*.

"City desk, can I help you?"

"Hello," said Farrell. "This is Dave Riley calling long distance from San Francisco, at the *Chronicle*. I wanted to see if you had any more insight into that kid found hanging out on I-80? What's her name, Meade? How about a motive or a suspect?"

"Well, Dave," came the voice of the Midwestern newspaperman, "to tell you the truth, nobody knows a thing. There was a press conference at the FBI office here in Des Moines about an hour ago. They gave out the usual, 'We're following a number of promising leads at this very moment' bullshit, but nobody thinks they're doing anything but blowing smoke up our asses. They ain't got shit."

"Thanks a lot. You saved me some legwork," Farrell lied.

He hung up the phone, his brow furrowed. He took another drag from his smoke and slurped down the last of his Jim Beam. He picked up the receiver again and dialed a number from memory. It was picked up on the second ring.

"Carruthers and Lyons," said a falsetto woman's voice.

"Yeah," Farrell spoke around his cigarette, "lemme talk to Vinnie Carruthers."

"One moment," was the curt reply.

The secretary didn't ask who Farrell was because he'd called his lawyer by the name Vinnie. Vinnie Carruthers' real name was Leonard, and nobody but his close friends called him Vinnie.

"This is Leonard Carruthers, can I help you?"

"You can cut the formalities Vinnie; it's Bob Farrell. I need to ask a question about my will."

"Don't tell me you're back in the sack with that broad. After what I went through getting you two divorced, I'll kill you. Do you understand me? I'll fucking kill you."

"Take it easy, will you?" Farrell interrupted the torrent. "I didn't mend any bridges. You'll be happy to know she's still my ex, and she still hates my guts."

"That's a relief. You scared me for a second."

"Believe me, if I was hooking back up with that crazy bitch I'd want you to kill me. But speaking of getting killed, I have a question about my will. If I croak, Jenny's going to get my pension, right? It's not going to go to either of my ex-wives, is it?"

"No. That was all finalized with the divorce. I thought you knew that. I gave you a copy of the settlement. Didn't you look it over?"

"Nice talking to you." He hung up.

Farrell didn't have a lot. He owned the few pieces of furniture in his apartment, and a shiny new 1987 Oldsmobile he'd bought as a retirement present to himself. What he did have, however, was a respectable pension that would have transferable benefits, ideal for his college-age daughter to finish school, or take out a loan against after graduation.

He looked again at the grainy photo in the newspaper. A monster was loose, a predator in the heartland. He read the article below the picture again. The identity of the killer was unknown.

Farrell put out his cigarette and left the kitchenette. From his closet, high on a cluttered shelf, he withdrew a rusty metal box. He sat on the bed and opened it.

Inside the box were several faded black-and-white photographs from his time in Vietnam. There were assorted papers, a couple of medals, and a lock of his daughter's baby hair. He sifted through the contents until he found what he was searching for.

Folded into squares and yellowed with time was Slocum's mimeographed arrest sheet. He read the name on the paper and felt a shiver traverse his skin.

Within minutes he was in the shower and scraping a disposable razor across his face. He toweled off and dressed, hastily knotting a tie over a white dress shirt. He put on one of his inexpensive detective suits and finished with a pair of highly shined black oxfords.

He peered into the mirror. He saw a gaunt, pale man with a scant hairline and double chin. Grunting at his reflection, he stuffed his pockets with keys, wallet, penknife, handkerchief, notebook, pen, and finally his badge case and .38. It was a five-shot Smith & Wesson Bodyguard with most of the bluing worn off. Though retired, he'd been wearing a gun for over thirty years and would no more leave his apartment without it than leave without trousers. He also took Slocum's arrest sheet.

Farrell left his apartment, lighting another cigarette. He walked down the stairs to the parking garage. It felt good to have purpose again.

Inspector Robert Farrell, like many retired cops, found that retirement wasn't all it was cracked up to be. The first few weeks were relaxing, and he'd done a lot of things he always told himself he would do when he finally got the time. He went on more fishing trips in a month than in the previous thirty years. He made a road trip south on Highway 101, to San Luis Obispo, where he and Ann spent their honeymoon twenty-five years ago. It was better without Ann. He contemplated driving out to Nebraska where his daughter was in her senior year at the university there, but decided to postpone the trip until her graduation in the spring.

Farrell had nothing but time. He found himself fidgeting a lot, and smoking and drinking too much. His doctor warned him to ease up on the sauce when he'd been diagnosed with an ulcer. He noticed he spent a lot of days since his retirement watching daytime TV and pondering the past. Reminiscing about his police career and stewing over his failed marriages.

By the time he reached the carport he was moderately out of breath. He walked to his car, marveling at its beauty.

To him, the Oldsmobile was American craftsmanship at its finest. No Asian-manufactured, high-tech junk for Robert Farrell; no siree. The Olds was two tons of steel, polished chrome, velour upholstery, stereophonic sound, and smooth 442 cubic inch V-8 ride. He treasured it, and its deep burgundy paint was the color of fresh blood.

He went to the car's trunk. Inside, along with the spare tire, were the contents of his desk when he'd been a burglary inspector. He'd yet to unpack the heavy boxes and lug them up the three flights of stairs to his apartment.

He rummaged through the boxes. He smiled when he found a silver flask full of bourbon. With the flask were several cylinders of breath mints and a pocket-sized bottle of Listerine. After tossing away his cigarette, he helped himself to a snort of the flask's contents to ensure they hadn't evaporated.

"Beats the hell out of Geritol," he said aloud, wiping his lips on his sleeve.

He put the flask and breath mints into the pockets of his coat and continued rummaging.

In a moment he found what he was after. It was on the bottom of a stack of heavy boxes, and it took him a bit of grunting to wrench it free. With a final tug he came up with a battered shoebox.

Inside the shoebox was one of his most invaluable investigative tools: business cards. Hundreds of them. He'd made a habit over the years of collecting business cards from every person he made contact with: crook, victim, witness, or John Doe. He'd even taken them from the desks of his fellow cops.

He grabbed a handful of cards and put them into his pocket. Tossing the shoebox into the trunk, he closed the lid and got into the car.

Within minutes he was out of the city and on the Bay Bridge, looking over Treasure Island. The morning mist hadn't lifted yet and the fog left him with only a few car-lengths visibility.

He had the radio tuned to KDFC-FM, a classical music station broadcasting from San Francisco, and before he knew it, was eastbound on Highway 580 in the Oakland hills. Exiting the freeway in San Leandro, he drove into the parking lot of the Oak Knoll Naval Hospital.

Leaving the comfort of the Oldsmobile, he entered the hospital lobby. Once inside he straightened his tie and popped a breath mint into his mouth. He approached the receptionist at the main desk.

"Can I help you, sir?"

"Yes," said Farrell coughing, "I'm Lieutenant Donovan, OPD, and I'd like to examine some of your records."

When Farrell said this he snapped open his badge case and briefly flashed his seven-point San Francisco star. The only difference between it and the Oakland Police Department's badge were the small letters denoting the name of the city engraved over the number. He handed the receptionist a business card that read, Lieutenant Paul Donovan – Criminal Investigation Division. The card was handsomely engraved with the OPD crest and Chief Hart's name.

The receptionist took the card and went into an office. In a moment she returned with a tall African-American man wearing eagle's wings on his white uniform. The captain was holding the business card Farrell had given the receptionist.

"I'm Captain Pracon. How can I help you?"

"I'm not sure. I need some information."

"What kind of information?"

"Well," Farrell said, "I'm trying to track the whereabouts of a Marine who left the service from Vietnam about twenty years ago. He was wounded, and would possibly have come to this facility for medical treatment."

Pracon seemed puzzled. "Have you tried the Veterans' Information Center in San Francisco? I believe they would be better suited to provide information regarding Vietnam-era vets."

"I already tried that facility," Farrell lied smoothly. "They referred me here."

He didn't tell the captain the reason he hadn't contacted the Veterans' Administration was because that organization was accustomed to fraudulent attempts to access veterans' personal information. Subsequently, the VA had safeguards preventing inquiries from anyone but sanctioned US Government personnel.

The navy captain rubbed his chin. "Let's see what we can dig up. Follow me."

Farrell knew the naval hospital was a long shot, and wasn't convinced he was on anything but a wild-goose hunt. Slocum could have been routed through Japan, and then stateside, after medical treatment, or could have returned to any of a number of hospitals from Vietnam. But then again, many Marines came through Oak Knoll for treatment, especially after tours in Vietnam. And even if Slocum hadn't been routed through Oak Knoll, he was betting on the navy having a system by which they could track his records, regardless of where he'd been treated.

He followed Pracon to an elevator and the two rode down to the basement. When the door opened Farrell found

himself in a damp, cold, and musty storage facility. In one
corner a clerk sat at a cluttered desk, the glow of a computer
terminal illuminating his face.

"AJ, this is Lieutenant Donovan, OPD."

The two men shook hands. Captain Pracon said, "Do
what you can for him, and let me know what you find."
Pracon said. "Goodbye," and disappeared into the elevator.

"OK, Lieutenant, what can I do for you?"

Farrell wasted no time. "Last name Slocum, S-L-O–"

"I can spell real good," interrupted the clerk. "Give me
the rest."

"Anything you say. First name: Vernon, middle name:
Emil. He was in the Marines, and would have gotten out in
'67 or '68." He read Slocum's birth date and serial number
from the yellowed arrest sheet.

The clerk turned to Farrell with a smirk on his face. "Do
you have any idea how many Marines came through this
facility since the war? And you want me to track one who
might have been here over twenty years ago?"

Farrell took out his pack of Camels and lit one. The clerk
said, "There's no smoking in this wing, sir."

He offered the pack and the clerk took one. He lit the clerk's
smoke with a match. Farrell then took out two twenty-
dollar bills and tossed them on the desk. The clerk grinned
broadly, saying nothing. He tossed another twenty on the
desk, then returned the clerk's look of bored disinterest.

The stalemate lasted until the clerk was convinced Farrell
would put no more money down. Finally he stood up,
scooping the three bills into his hand.

"C'mon," he said, motioning for Farrell to follow. "Records
that old are put on microfiche. If we're going to find your
boy, it'll be there."

Farrell followed the clerk, an acne-faced kid in his late
twenties. He was led to a dusty microfiche terminal across

the room. The clerk took a stack of microfiche folders from a shelf and began shuffling through them. Over his shoulder he said, "Get comfortable, this could take a while."

Farrell took his flask from his pocket and had a gulp, timing it carefully so the act was beyond the range of the clerk's vision. He had a lot of practice, and if the clerk noticed he didn't show it. Farrell pulled up a chair and sat down.

More than an hour, and half a pack of Camels later, Farrell was nearly asleep. He squinted through barely open eyes, his chin resting on his chest.

"Got him," blurted the clerk, jolting Farrell from his near-nap. "Here's your man. Slocum was the name, right Lieutenant Donovan?"

Farrell had forgotten the name on the business card, and it took him a moment to realize he was Lieutenant Donovan. "You found him?"

"Right here; Slocum, Vernon Emil, Lance Corporal, 1st Battalion, 6th Marine Regiment. Admitted here in July of 1968. Transferred to the veterans' hospital in Des Moines, Iowa, a month later. Doesn't say what he was here for. Got his admittance and release dates, and some personal shit. You want to take a look?"

Farrell moved his chair to a position enabling him to see the dim microfiche screen. Taking Slocum's arrest sheet from his breast pocket, he compared the social security number and birth date to the data on the microfiche terminal. They matched.

When Farrell had gotten all he could from the machine, he reached into his pocket and handed the clerk another twenty-dollar bill.

"Thanks, kid. I'll see myself out. You didn't find anything, if your captain asks."

The clerk accepted the bill and smiled. "Find what?"

Farrell drove back to his apartment in silence, the melancholy sounds of classical music wafting from his car stereo. His stomach was bothering him, and he knew he had to eat something soon or his breakfast of cigarettes and bourbon would have his ulcer bleeding in no time.

He was beginning to remember things he'd forgotten long ago. Things he'd hoped were put to rest. He thought he'd exorcised Slocum from his nightmares, but seeing the name again reminded him he was wrong.

Sometimes he'd see Slocum's eyes watching him in his dreams. He felt those eyes on him today when wide awake. When he read the newspaper.

Farrell tried to convince himself his trip to the Oak Knoll Naval Hospital was sparked by little more than morbid curiosity and fueled by boredom. But somewhere in the corner of his mind, a corner dark for two decades, a voice was calling. A voice he tried to convince himself he couldn't hear.

The voice howled in frustration over a career toiling in a justice system that couldn't stop criminals like Vernon Slocum. The voice shrieked in concert with the cries of tortured, dying children. The voice moaned in shame for failing to deal with a monster when it had the chance. The voice wailed in self-pity over a life spent watching loved-ones drift away. It was a voice Farrell tried to drown in a sea of bourbon, yet could still be heard.

It was a voice Bob Farrell could ignore no longer.

When he got home he poured himself a stiff shot of bourbon. He again stared at the picture in the morning's paper. He was grateful the picture didn't show the girl's eyes.

Eventually he put down the newspaper and started to pack.

CHAPTER 13

Buddy Cuszack burrowed deeper into the dirty quilt covering his bed and tried to ignore the barking of his two hounds, tied to a post outside. It had snowed another six inches during the night, and the snow had come with sub-zero temperatures and high winds. It wasn't even December yet. His dogs usually didn't bark unless someone was approaching. Who could be coming up the driveway at this hour of the morning?

Buddy was what Inspector Robert Farrell, had he known him, would have called a "lowlife." He lived in a trailer on a remote piece of acreage on the outskirts of the bustling metropolis of Audubon, Iowa; population 8559. He stood under six feet tall, and weighed under one hundred and forty pounds soaking wet. He had a full beard and a penchant for bathing when it suited him. It didn't suit him often.

Buddy worked only occasionally, doing farm labor and odd mechanic jobs here and there. He spent most of his time consuming tequila, smoking the local marijuana, known as "Iowajuana," and snorting methamphetamine when he could get it.

Cuszack was known to associate with a local motorcycle club known as the Sons of Silence, and dreamed of promotion to full membership. His only known companions beyond the renegade biker's club was a three-hundred pound throwback named Sunshine, who visited him for sex on occasion, and two large, unhealthy hound-dogs affectionately named "Douche" and "Bag." These two dogs were responsible for rousing him from his alcoholic slumber.

The dogs continued to howl, barking with a ferocity usually reserved for the bi-annual visit from the sheriff's department. Buddy put a worn pillow over his head, but the high-pitched barking penetrated easily. His headache was a grim reminder of how much tequila he'd consumed last night.

Buddy heard a car door slam, followed by the sound of heavy footsteps crunching in the fresh snow. He sat up in bed, wondering if all those traffic tickets he'd yet to pay had turned into warrants, and if the footsteps came from a deputy with a writ for his arrest.

Someone pounded on the trailer door.

"Shit, fuck, piss!" Buddy hauled his bony body out of the squalor of his bed. Wrapping a worn blanket around his waist, he waddled to the trailer door, which was still vibrating with the pounding of a fist.

"Jesus fucking Christ, I'm coming! Ease up, will ya?"

Cuszack opened the door and squinted into the blowing snow.

Standing on the doorstep, like an apparition, was a huge and vaguely familiar silhouette. Buddy peered through his alcohol-blurred eyes to make out the face.

"Who the fuck are you?"

"It's me," said a voice surprisingly soft for the size of its owner. "Vern." It took a moment for Cuszack's booze-impeded brain to recognize the man standing before him.

"Vern! Vernon fucking Slocum! C'mon in, man. It's freezing, you know? Damn!"

Cuszack stepped aside and let the tall man into the trailer, closing the door after him. "Sit down, man. I'll get some clothes on."

Slocum brushed aside a stack of magazines from a battered sofa. Most depicted naked girls or motorcycles on their covers. He swept snow from his worn fatigue-jacket and sat down.

Buddy returned a moment later wearing a sweater and buttoning the suspenders of his bib-overalls. It was cold enough in the trailer to see breath. Buddy switched on a portable heater and sat down opposite Slocum on another battered sofa.

"Well, hey, Vern, it's good to see you. I mean, it's been what, twelve, thirteen years? What you been doing with yourself? How you been?"

"Buddy," he said, "I need your help."

Buddy's eyes finally adjusted to being awake and semi-sober, and for the first time since his visitor arrived he got a good look at him. It made his eyes widen.

Slocum wore his hair in a crewcut, the unshaven stubble on his chin almost as long. His nose was puffed and bruised, and both eyes were swollen and ringed in black. Dried, crusted blood seeped from both nostrils, and there was matted blood on his chin. Beneath the swollen eyelids, in the depth of his eyes, a fire burned fiercely.

"Uh, OK Vern," stammered Cuszack, biting his lip, "whatever I can do, I'll do. I mean, you need a place to stay, or whatever, you can count on your old pal Buddy. What are friends for, right?"

Slocum said nothing, simply stared at Cuszack with his burning eyes. He reached into his jacket and came out with a pack of Pall Malls. He stuck one into a corner of his tight lips and lit it, the momentary flash of the lighter in his face casting a demonic glow on his already frightening countenance.

Tossing the cigarettes to Cuszack, Slocum said, "I need some weapons and some crank. I've got money. You can put me in touch with people who can outfit me. I need to lay low for a few days."

Buddy Cuszack gulped and blinked. He didn't know what Slocum wanted weapons for, and by his appearance it didn't look like target practice. The dope was no problem, if Slocum really did have money. He lit one of Slocum's cigarettes nervously.

"Vern, I can get you the dope. No problem. You got the cash I got the stash, right? But I don't know nothing about no weapons. I stay clear of that kind of bad news, you know?"

"You owe me, Buddy," Slocum said, "and you'll get me what I want."

Buddy almost choked on his cigarette. Slocum's words were not a request. And Cuszack knew he must deliver.

Buddy Cuszack met Vernon Emil Slocum in the autumn of 1968, at the Veterans' Hospital in Des Moines. Buddy had been captured by the Viet Cong in February of '66, when his helicopter was shot down. He'd spent nineteen months as a prisoner of the Viet Cong before being rescued when the POW camp was liberated by Australian troops. In those nineteen months, Buddy Cuszack experienced every form of degrading humiliation that could be devised by his brutal captors.

By the time Buddy was physically healed, his mind still had a long way to go. He was shipped to the psychiatric observation ward of the veterans' hospital in the capital of his home state, Iowa, and spent several long years fending off his demons before being released.

During those years, the years from 1968 to 1974, Buddy Cuszack made the acquaintance of a lumbering Marine named Vernon Slocum, who was housed in the psych ward as well. Slocum was there when Buddy arrived, and remained when he left. Slocum seldom spoke, but didn't seem to mind Buddy's incessant babbling.

The reason Buddy Cuszack developed an affinity for the stoic Marine was out of necessity. Like many of the veterans' hospital's residents, he'd developed a severe drug dependency. The lithium, Valium, Thorazine, and countless other pills that were dispensed like candy at the facility soon became his reason for living.

It was like being back in the VC prison camp. Cuszack found himself groveling at first, and then performing sex acts with hospital staff members and less-dependent residents for the drugs he craved. It was another nightmare to add to his burgeoning collection.

It was Slocum who broke the cycle and freed him from his servitude. One day the big Marine started giving his medications to Cuszack for no apparent reason. He would feign swallowing his own prescribed pills, and hide them under his tongue. He'd later give them to Cuszack without demanding the sex others who offered the same service demanded.

Then, for some inexplicable reason, Slocum put a stop to others using Cuszack. He began shaking down patients for their medications and giving them to Buddy. Slocum took no payment for this; he simply handed the meds over to the depraved addict without a word. Slocum's reward was the pleasure of extorting the other residents.

Some of the incidents were notable. A huge African-American former Marine at the psych ward was one of the more serious offenders in the game of brutalizing Cuszack. Not only would the Marine, named Jackson, force blowjobs from the sniveling Cuszack, but he would take the pills Cuszack already had in his possession.

Slocum faced off Jackson in the residents' lounge, where both shared clean-up duty. Jackson's response to Slocum's demand to leave Cuszack alone was to break a mop handle to a sharp point and lunge at him.

When the other patients and staff heard the screams, they went running into the lounge. They found Jackson on the floor, shrieking hysterically and bleeding profusely from an empty socket that was once his left eye. Slocum was conveniently gone, and they never found the missing eye.

Another time, one of the residents who'd been abusing Cuszack loudly remarked that Slocum was keeping all of Cuszack's ass for himself. The next day that same resident leaned over to drink from one of the water fountains and a powerful hand materialized and slammed his head down savagely onto the spout of the fountain. Nothing was heard from that resident for some time because his shattered jaw was wired shut for several months.

When Cuszack was discharged from the hospital in September of 1974, the last thing he saw was the expressionless face of Vernon Slocum staring silently after him.

That same expressionless face was now staring back at Cuszack more than thirteen years later.

"You got anything to drink around here?" asked Slocum in a monotone.

"I got some tequila and bourbon; whichever you want, old buddy."

"Both."

Cuszack disappeared into the kitchenette and reappeared a moment later with a bottle of Jack Daniel's and a bottle of Cuervo. It hadn't occurred to him to bring a glass. Slocum took the bottles.

"I'm going to rest here for a while," Slocum said, after taking a long swig from each bottle. "When I wake up

I want you to have somebody lined up for me to deal with. You know some people who can help me, don't you Buddy?"

"Yeah, sure Vern," sputtered Cuszack. "How much you willing to spend? I mean, if I knew the price range it would help."

"Don't worry about money. Just set it up." Slocum stared into Cuszack's frightened eyes. "You ain't gonna let me down, are you Buddy?"

Cuszack swallowed hard. His hands trembled and the cigarette between his lips twitched. "Course not, Vern. You can count on me. Don't worry. You just go to sleep, and I'll get right on it."

"OK." Slocum took another long pull from the bourbon bottle, and tossed Cuszack the keys to his truck. "It's got a full tank of gas, and it's a four-wheel drive. It'll get you around in this storm. When you get back, wake me up."

"Sure, anything you say." Cuszack put on his parka.

"One more thing, Buddy," Slocum said. "Don't tell nobody I'm here. Nobody. You got that?"

Cuszack nodded. Slocum appeared out of the past like a phantom, with blood on his face and his eyes burning. He wanted weapons and meth, and barked requests like orders. Things didn't look good to Buddy Cuszack, but he knew better than to disobey. He tried to conceal his fear of the imposing figure sitting on his couch, drinking his liquor.

"What are you waiting for?"

"Nuthin', Vern. I'm leaving." Cuszack left the demon from his past sleeping in his trailer and went out into the snow.

CHAPTER 14

Deputy Kevin Kearns was going stir-crazy. He'd been sitting in the dingy roadside motel for the better part of two days with nothing but the daily game shows, soap operas, and MTV for company. If he never saw another Terence Trent D'Arby or Cyndi Lauper video, or heard U2's "With or Without You" again, it would be too soon. Meals he ordered from the truck stop across the highway. If he never had another piece of chicken-fried steak again, it would also be too soon.

Sergeant Evers phoned last night but had nothing to report. He told Kevin in his relaxed drawl to sit tight. He promised to call sometime today.

Kearns was doing push-ups alternating with sit-ups. He'd done hundreds of these each day, partly out of boredom, partly out of necessity. The exercise briefly took his mind off his troubles. He didn't know when he was going to get a chance to visit a gym or run again.

He got up from the worn carpet and wiped the sweat from his brow with a motel towel. He went to the window and parted the curtains.

The world outside was pristine white, the sky a haze of snow-filled gray. Occasionally trucks and automobiles braved the road, but Kearns could tell by their greatly reduced speed that it was slick outside.

An illuminated clock/thermometer/billboard at the truck stop showed the temperature as five degrees Fahrenheit.

Kearns left the window and sat on the bed. He hadn't slept much during the two nights he'd been at the motel. Visions of the incident at the schoolyard played again and again in his head, and would jar him to wakefulness each time he drifted to sleep.

What happened at the station also nagged at him. He knew he shouldn't have hit the FBI man, but saw red when the agent implied he was responsible for the loss of Tiffany Meade. How could he have been responsible for what happened? He did all he could. He'd been lucky to escape with his life.

He knew the public's perception of the horrific incident was clouded with anger, grief, and a need to lay blame. A child was dead, and doing his best to prevent it hadn't been enough. A brave schoolteacher was also dead. Like him, she'd done her best to prevent the tragedy and it cost her life.

What Sergeant Evers told him at the hospital was true. People would try to make sense of what happened, though maybe there was none to be made. And part of that process for many people would be finding someone to blame. Folks were struggling to understand why he survived and Tiffany Meade did not. He'd be easy to point the finger at; he was a cop. When the sheep get attacked by a wolf, they blame the sheepdog. Even Kearns, with less than a year on the job, knew that.

Kevin Kearns had been raised by his mother as an only child. It wasn't until he was thirteen he learned she'd never married his father, and didn't even know his whereabouts. He took the news indifferently. It was hard to miss what he'd never known.

Kevin's mother died of lung cancer when he was in the army. He took it hard, grieved, and returned to finish his tour in the infantry. He was thankful she wasn't alive now to experience the events currently occurring in his life.

Sheriff Coates could be counted on to disassociate himself from Kearns, and according to Detective Parish had already begun doing just that. And the FBI could now be counted as an enemy, though hardly friendly before.

He didn't know what to do next. The TV newscasts reported the "dragnet," as it was being called, had netted no suspects and few leads. The child-killing, almost three days cold, continued to dominate the news. There was a lot of speculation, and many different theories, about the identity and motive of the killer. Kearns' name was mentioned occasionally, followed by hints of police cover-up. It was unsettling, and he would have switched off the television, except that it was his only contact with the outside world.

He got off the bed and headed for a shower. He was undressing when the phone rang. He leaped over the bed and picked up the phone by the end of the first ring.

"Hello."

"Kevin, it's Dick Evers. How you doing?"

"I'm getting a little edgy, Sarge. Otherwise I'm OK."

There was a long pause on the other end of the phone.

"We've got to take you to the station. I've delayed it as long as I could. The investigation's going nowhere and you've got to be re-interviewed." After a too-long pause, Evers went on, "There's something else. They're going to charge you with assault and battery on that special agent you clouted."

"I figured as much," Kearns said. "That way they can roast me in the press. The FBI's got to have a reason to explain why they haven't made any progress on this thing yet. I'm going to be the reason."

"You knew it was coming," Evers said. "The Full Blown Idiots are under a lot of pressure, and they're experienced witch-hunters. By attacking you they divert attention away from the fact they've got zilch on the killer."

"Am I going to be suspended or fired?"

"I don't know, Kevin. Maybe both. You've got to prepare yourself for the worst. I'll be with you as long as I can, and so will Detective Parish. But don't kid yourself; it's going to get rough. I want you to get a handle on your temper this time around; do you read me?"

"Loud and clear. I promise not to deck any more federal bureaucrats."

"That's exactly what they want you to do. They'll bait you; don't let them. Your freedom could be riding on this."

"Don't worry," said Kearns, dejectedly. "I'll keep it together."

"Rod will be out to get you in an hour. It'll take that long to reach you, the way the roads are. He'll drop you by your place to change into something nice; a suit if you've got one. Use the time to rehearse what you're going to say; go over different scenarios in your head. It'll help prepare you."

"Do you really think it'll be that bad?"

"I'll see you in an hour." Evers hung up.

CHAPTER 15

Retired San Francisco Police Inspector Robert Farrell parked the rented Oldsmobile in a visitors stall at the Story County Sheriff's Department and got out of the car reluctantly. The Iowa wind was like nothing he'd ever experienced; it tore through him like a blade. The thin lining of his California raincoat did little to impede the frigid air's passage through his equally thin body. With his feet crunching and slipping in the snow he skidded to the rear of the Olds and opened the trunk with numb fingers.

"Jesus, Joseph and Mary!" he cursed in the flailing wind. "How does anybody live in this icebox?" His thinning hair flew over his exposed head, and he ducked under the trunk lid for the windbreak it provided. Rummaging through the trunk he located his shoebox filled with business cards. After sorting through the box with numb fingers he found the card he was searching for. He also brought out a worn but expensive leather briefcase.

In the Sheriff's Department lobby was a large sign which read, RE-ELECT COATES FOR COUNTY SHERIFF. A VOTE FOR BUCK WILL BRING YOU LUCK!

He took a moment to comb his hair and straighten out his storm-disheveled appearance. Looking around to ensure there were no onlookers, he withdrew his flask from a side pocket and took a long gulp. It warmed him instantly and took away the involuntary shivers that had racked his body since he got off the plane in Des Moines. He popped a breath mint into his mouth and approached a sergeant sitting at a desk at the end of the hall.

"Can I help you?"

"I'd like to speak with Deputy Kevin Kearns, please."

"I'm afraid that's impossible. There's no visitors allowed. You press?"

"No," Farrell said in an indignant voice, "I am certainly not the press. I'm his attorney. If he is in conference without me present there will be grave consequences. Please notify whoever is in charge immediately."

The sergeant gave Farrell a look which denoted the feelings all cops have for attorneys and picked up a phone.

"Someone will be down in a minute to get you."

"Thank you, Sergeant. You've been most helpful."

"No sweat," said the sergeant sarcastically. "Anything for a member of the Bar." The sergeant turned back to what he was doing before Farrell came in.

Farrell stifled a grin, reassured by the sergeant's demeanor. Cops are cops, he thought, no matter where they are.

A moment later two men entered the lobby from an interior door. Farrell recognized one as a Bureau man instantly. The FBI had a dress code as distinct as the Queen's Royal Guard, and could be spotted a mile away by anyone with any previous exposure to the agency.

This one looked in his early thirties, with a salon-trimmed hairstyle and a three-piece suit that did a poor job of concealing the revolver on his hip. The man accompanying him was surely a cop. He wore a look of bored disinterest and was clad in a wrinkled, off-the-rack

suit. His hair had the look of the six-dollar barber, and
he was sporting a large wad of chewing tobacco in his
distended jaw. They approached Farrell.

"Hello," spoke power-suit first, "I'm Special Agent
Lefferty. What can I do for you?" The fact that the FBI
man didn't introduce his associate was not lost on Farrell.
Farrell stuck his hand out to the cop and said, "I'm Bob
Lyons, from Legal Defense. Who are you?"

"Rod Parish, Sheriff's Department."

"Good to meet you," said Farrell. "Where's my client?
I'd like to talk to him."

"You're representing Kearns?" interjected Lefferty.
"We weren't advised of any attorney. I'm going to have
to get this approved with my supervisor."

"You'll do nothing except take me to my client,"
Farrell cut in. "You have been advised of my identity
and purpose. To deny my client legal representation is
in violation of his Peace Officers' Bill of Rights, state
law, and the Constitution. I'm surprised as a Bureau
man you don't know that. You will take me to my client
immediately, or believe me, Special Agent Lefferty, there
will be consequences. I thought all you FBI chaps had
law degrees these days. You should know better."

The sheriff's detective was smiling, obviously deriving
pleasure at the discomfort of the special agent. "C'mon,"
he said to Farrell. "I'll take you to see Deputy Kearns
right away."

"Thank you, Detective," Farrell said courteously. As he
followed Parish into an elevator, Lefferty remained in the
lobby. The FBI agent picked up the desk sergeant's phone
and feverishly began dialing numbers. The elevator doors
closed. Farrell grinned at the sheriff's deputy. The deputy
spat a glob of brown juice on the elevator floor. "God I
hate those pompous fucks."

Farrell laughed. "Where I come from we call the FBI, 'Fan Belt Installers.'"

Parish chuckled. "I'll remember that one. But it's only fair to warn you: I don't like attorneys much better."

"Who could blame you?" Farrell answered truthfully.

The elevator doors opened and he followed the deputy to a room filled with lounging men. Most wore the look of the working cop so familiar to Farrell, but there were a few who looked federal. Their attention was focused on a glass window through which was visible a young man seated at a table. A tape recorder was on the table and two men were inside the room, obviously interrogating the seated man, who appeared relaxed. The appearance was deceiving, however; Farrell noticed patches of sweat soaking the man's underarms, chest, and back. Deputy Kearns, no doubt.

Farrell felt a hand on his shoulder. It was Lefferty, the snotty special agent. He must have come up the stairs.

"Mister Lyons, my supervisor would like a word with you. If you'll come with me, please?"

Detective Parish edged close to Farrell and whispered, "Watch your back, Lyons. If you think Lefferty is a dick, wait till you meet his boss."

"Thanks for the warning."

Farrell followed the special agent into an office. Behind a large desk sat a fat man with the reddened face of a regular, heavy drinker. Farrell knew the look well. On the desk was a gold-embossed placard reading,

BUCK COATES, SHERIFF.

Standing next to the desk was a short, thin man in a pin-striped suit of expensive cut. The man had a plaster cast taped over his nose, and both eyes were rimmed in black. He vaguely resembled one of those weirdly masked professional wrestlers on Spanish TV. Farrell suppressed a chuckle.

"Bob Lyons, from Legal Defense," Farrell extended his hand. In it was a business card reading Carruthers & Lyons, Attorneys at Law. Below the title was an elegantly engraved Union Square address in San Francisco. Sheriff Coates took the card, and after glancing at it briefly, handed it to the other man.

"I'm Steve Scanlon, Special Agent in Charge." Scanlon didn't offer his hand to Farrell. "This is Sheriff Coates, whose department has territorial jurisdiction." Scanlon was still glancing at the business card Farrell handed him, and did not look up.

"What's an attorney all the way from San Francisco doing here, Mister Lyons?" His voice was altered because of his broken nose, and made him sound as if he had a terrific head cold. "Mister Lyons" came out as "Bister Lyods."

"My firm contracts to Legal Defense for peace officers, and I go where I'm sent," Farrell lied smoothly. He spoke as if this was a question he answered regularly with a prescribed response. "As you probably know," he lied on, "this case has already garnered a high degree of notoriety and has national implications. Therefore it is being monitored by watchdog organizations who wish to ensure the propriety of the investigation."

"What kind of double-talk bullshit is that?" asked Scanlon. "What watchdog organizations? I've never heard of any such organizations, and I've overseen a few investigations in my day. I don't like you, Lyons, and I don't like what you stand for. Maybe you'd better leave."

Farrell noticed a look of chagrin on Sheriff Coates' face. It confirmed his suspicions of how little power the sheriff wielded in this incident. Coates obviously didn't want to pick up any bad press going into re-election season next year and had subsequently given the feds free rein. It was the smart thing for a rural county sheriff to do. If the child-killing investigation was successful he could share the spotlight and the glory. If it flopped, he could distance himself and let the Bureau take the fall. Either way, somebody else did all the heavy lifting and took all the heat.

It accounted for why the young deputy he saw in the interrogation room was getting the third degree by the feds with no intervention from Coates. They were going to sacrifice the deputy. Offer up a scapegoat to divert the negative public sentiment towards the sheriff's department and Bureau in the wake of the child-killing. Farrell had seen it before in high-profile investigations.

It was time for Farrell to take the offensive. He set his briefcase confidently on Coates' desk and smiled. Coates still looked nervous and Scanlon was watching him warily.

"So, you don't know who I represent? And because you haven't heard of an organization, it must therefore be bogus?" Farrell paused, shaking his head for dramatic effect. "Your ignorance is profound. Just who do you think you're dealing with?"

Scanlon's face reddened. He wasn't accustomed to being spoken to in this manner. It contrasted sharply with the white plaster on his nose. He didn't answer Farrell's question.

"I'll tell you who you're dealing with. Who heard of child kidnappings five years ago? It was an isolated crime, dealt with on the local law enforcement level. Not any more. Now we have prime-time TV shows devoted to the issue. Watched *Donahue* lately? We have missing and exploited children on the sides of every milk carton from here to Hong Kong. We have delivery trucks, union delivery trucks I might add, using their valuable advertising space to broadcast pictures of missing kids."

Farrell looked up from his briefcase to see if his words were having effect. They were. Sensing advantage, he pressed on.

"Do you think my coming here is paid for out of charity, Special Agent Scanlon? Are you that naïve?"

Scanlon still said nothing in reply.

"I would expect the sheriff in a rural Midwestern county to be somewhat uninformed, but I'm surprised at your apparent lack of awareness. Evidently the Bureau relegates its more adroit agents to the larger jurisdictions. The missing/exploited-child phenomenon is now overseen by political action groups so powerful they can easily afford to send attorneys from San Francisco to Iowa on a whim."

In the face of Lyons not appearing intimidated in the least, Scanlon now clearly sensed he may have bitten off more than he could chew, and switched to a more diplomatic posture.

"Perhaps I was somewhat hasty in my initial assessment of your purpose, Mister Lyons," he said nervously. "You must realize, as Sheriff Coates can attest, we are under a tremendous amount of pressure in our efforts to apprehend the suspect in this tragic case. Please forgive me if I seemed abrupt."

Farrell smiled, accepting the conciliatory gesture. "I understand. These are troubling cases. We're all on the same team."

"By all means. How can our office be of help?"

"First off," said Farrell, "are there charges being filed against the deputy?"

"Well, it's like this..." began Sheriff Coates.

"At this time," interrupted Scanlon, "we are pursuing the possibility of leveling charges at Deputy Kearns for battery, against me as you can probably see. We are also considering further charges for disruption of an investigation and refusal to cooperate with same."

Just as I surmised, Farrell thought. They're going to crucify the kid. "I see," he said. "Pursuant to charges, has Deputy Kearns been given legal counsel at this level, or admonished of his Peace Officers' Bill of Rights?"

"We felt no need at this point," said Scanlon, in his head-cold accent. "We're still in the preliminary phase of his interrogation. Also, we're only considering charges, as I said, and should they be leveled we would certainly comply with all safeguards established to protect the deputy's civil liberties."

I'll bet you would, thought Farrell. "I'm not trying to raise anybody's hackles," he said. "I only want to get some background."

"Of course," said the federal agent accommodatingly. Behind him, Coates sat at his desk and nodded in agreement.

Farrell bit his lip, appearing deep in thought. Looking at his watch, he spoke. "Special Agent Scanlon," he said in his most sincere voice, "I don't want to be any further trouble, and I know you're busy enough with supervising this investigation. May I offer a suggestion?"

"What are you proposing?"

"Well," he went on, again looking at his watch, "it's after 11. I'll take my client to lunch and return around 1 o'clock. I'm sure I can be finished in an hour or so. That way I could be on a flight back to California by this afternoon, and you could continue your investigation without me in the way."

By the flash of Scanlon's eyes Farrell knew the federal agent took the bait. Offering to be rid of the nuisance lawyer from California was too tempting.

"I think we could arrange that," Scanlon said, a little too quickly. "What do you think, Sheriff? He's your deputy."

"Fine by me," babbled the sheriff. Farrell could smell the familiar odor of Listerine on the sheriff's breath and smirked. He realized why the sheriff had been so quiet, sitting impassively behind his desk; his breath was worse than Farrell's.

"If that will be all, Mister Lyons, I'll have one of my agents bring Deputy Kearns to you. I'm sure you're anxious to get back to California."

"Considering the weather here," said Farrell honestly, "I'd like nothing better." He picked up his briefcase and headed for the office door.

"Oh, there's one more thing," Farrell said, turning back towards Scanlon. "May I have one of your business cards?"

"Of course," replied Scanlon, anxious to be rid of the bothersome attorney. He reached into the breast pocket of his tailored suit.

"Thank you," said Farrell pleasantly as he tucked the FBI man's card into his pocket.

"I hope I've been of some help to you," said Scanlon, as Farrell opened the office door.

"You'll never know."

CHAPTER 16

Buddy Cuszack squinted through the windshield wipers and tried to see the road ahead. The snow was coming down heavily, and visibility was less than fifty feet. He was forced to rely on the snowbanks on either side as his guide to keep the truck in the middle of the road.

Weather reports were predicting the blizzard would last through the night. Local schools had closed early so the rural children could get safely home, and school was canceled tomorrow. Today was the first of December, and winter wasn't officially to start for nearly three weeks.

Slocum lay napping in the passenger seat. His large body seemed impervious to the cold, and Cuszack wondered how anyone could sleep in the fierce chill of the frigid night. The temperature had dropped another ten degrees, and Cuszack's teeth chattered louder with every falling notch on the thermometer.

He wondered what caused Slocum to appear in his life after so many years. One day there he was, as if he'd never left. Buddy didn't ask about the blood on Slocum's face or the pistol he'd seen protruding from his pocket. He didn't want to know. All he wanted was for Slocum to get what he wanted and leave.

He claimed to be seeking refuge, drugs, and weapons. Cuszack knew he owed the big former Marine drugs, maybe even his life. But the appearance of the man from the past was a bad omen. He sensed Slocum wanted more than merely shelter, dope, and guns, and thought that whatever it was, it spelled trouble.

At Slocum's demand, Cuszack had spent the day at Zeke's place in Coon Rapids, twenty miles northeast of Audubon. Coon Rapids was off Highway 141, and boasted less than five hundred people. The town was little more than a whistle-stop on the Burlington Northern Railroad line. It had taken the better part of two hours to drive to Zeke's. There he'd bargained for Slocum's needs.

Returning from his meeting, Cuszack had gone back to his trailer. Slocum had awakened and insisted they return to Zeke's immediately to get the merchandise. And at a time when the Highway Patrol broadcast an advisory on the radio to stay off the roads.

Exhausted from the tedium of the two-way drive, Buddy had dug into his emergency stash of crank to wake up enough to drive back.

Zeke Fornier operated a clandestine methamphetamine laboratory at his Coon Rapids farm and used addicts like Buddy Cuszack as mules to distribute his product.

Zeke Fornier was also a Vietnam veteran, and spent his post-war years in the penitentiary at Fort Dodge for trafficking narcotics. Fornier put the three years of college-level chemistry he'd obtained prior to Vietnam to good use. His lab supplied much of the crank used from Des Moines to Omaha.

Zeke lived north of Coon Rapids on a farm chosen for its seclusion and large machinery shed. The shed housed the major components of his rural laboratory. It was also a constant party at Zeke's place, and if you wanted crank, or guns, or stolen car or motorcycle parts, or hot VCRs, or the latest music cassettes, or jewelry, or tools, or anything else an addict or burglar would trade for methamphetamine, you could probably find it at Zeke's. One of the rooms in the farmstead was even a home-movie studio. Zeke had branched into pornographic filmmaking, and hoped to begin marketing VHS cassettes of the people who came to him with nothing more than their bodies to barter.

It hadn't been easy for Cuszack to negotiate with Zeke. Cuszack wasn't able to tell Zeke much about Slocum, because he didn't know much. He only had Slocum's word that he had money, which didn't assuage the skeptical Fornier. One of the reasons Zeke had been successful as a drug dealer was his predisposition to distrust strangers. He had a well-paid informant in the Carroll County Sheriff's Department who would tip him off if the County Narcotics Enforcement Task Force began snooping, but he took no chances. And he wasn't particularly fond of Cuszack.

Unbeknownst to Cuszack, Zeke viewed him as a docile junkie. Cuszack had value to the drug dealer only because he craved drugs to the point of servitude. And well did he serve. He would do anything, anytime, to score dope. To a man in Zeke's business that was an asset if exploited properly.

Cuszack was actually one of Zeke's more consistent mules because he was always available. The only way to avoid surveillance or entrapment was to be as random as possible in delivery, and Cuszack was always only a phone call away.

Today was different. Cuszack asked for a meeting between Zeke and an old friend who wanted to make a big purchase. He was short on details and long on pleas. Zeke had agreed to meet Cuszack's friend because he was bored.

Now past nightfall, Cuszack fought the sliding truck over the snow-covered treachery that was Highway 141. Slocum was still asleep beside him, oblivious to the difficulty of guiding the truck to its destination. Eventually the truck's headlights cast their illumination on the entrance to Zeke's place. Slocum sat up.

"Back the truck up in the driveway," he said gruffly, "and leave the keys in the ignition."

Cuszack complied and got out of the truck. Slocum stood in the drifting snow, and Buddy watched him rack the slide of the .45 and chamber a round. He then put the pistol back into his pocket. Cuszack shuddered.

Yelling to be heard over the howling wind, he said, "Vern, what's the piece for? This guy is my friend. You don't need no gun."

Slocum turned to face the addict, his eyes harder and colder than any Iowa winter could ever be. "This guy ain't your friend. You ain't never had a friend in your life. Get me in the door, and don't worry about nothing else."

Buddy Cuszack was scared, just like in the Viet Cong camp and the VA hospital. Once more he felt powerless, his life spiraling into a place he didn't want to go. He began to whimper; a pathetic figure standing in a snowdrift in an Iowa field.

"Vern," Cuszack begged, "don't do this. It's fucking crazy. Don't do it. Let's just get the fuck out of here. C'mon Vern, please?"

Slocum's hand sliced viciously across his face, knocking him to the snow. As soon as he fell the same strong hand scooped him up by his collar and pulled him shakily to his feet.

"If you fuck this up, everything that ever happened to you is going to seem like a holiday weekend. You owe me. It's time to pay up."

Cuszack looked into Slocum's feral eyes. He wanted to cry out, but the sheer evil in those eyes frightened him into silence.

"You owe me Buddy," said Slocum's hoarse monotone again. "If you ain't gonna pay up, tell me now so I don't waste any more life on you."

The words were crystal clear. Standing in two feet of snow at an Iowa farm, in the middle of a blizzard, nothing ever seemed clearer. All Cuszack's feeble brain could register was that to fail this monster, this phantom from his nightmare past, was certain death. "OK, Vern," Cuszack heard himself sputter. "I'll get you inside. Relax, OK?"

He felt the steel grip of the hand around his collar relax, and he discovered he could stand by himself. He started towards the farmhouse on wobbly legs. Slocum followed several paces behind.

When they reached the porch Cuszack wasted no time. Any longer outside and he would be deep frozen. He pounded on the door with a bony fist.

The door opened and Zeke Fornier stood in the hallway.

"Well, well, well, what have we here? Looks like my good friend Buddy Cuszack. Come on in, before you freeze your ass off."

The speaker was a man of medium height and more than medium weight. He was slovenly-looking, with the sallow complexion and rotting teeth of the regular methamphetamine user. He wore boots, jeans, and the obligatory Harley-Davidson T-shirt. His thinning hair was greasy and grew past his collar, and his scraggly beard had the same oily quality. Over his T-shirt he wore a bathrobe. In one hand was a cigarette, in the other a glass of Jack Daniels.

Fornier stepped aside and allowed Cuszack and Slocum to enter. A fire roared in the hearth. The house was cluttered with an assortment of turntables, audio speakers, televisions, power tools, and various other items of stolen property. The television was on, and *Married with Children* was playing.

Sitting on one of several sofas were two females, one a woman and one a teenager. The woman was perhaps thirty years old but appeared much older. She was wearing skin-tight jeans under a halter-top which exposed most of her large, sagging breasts. The insides of both elbows were bruised and scarred from the ravages of too many needles, and most of her teeth were gone. Like Fornier, she was holding a drink and a cigarette.

Seated next to her was another female, perhaps fifteen years old. She might someday be beautiful if she shed her present company. As it was, she could expect to resemble her companion in the not too distant future.

The teenager was clad only in a too-small bathrobe which exposed her ample body. She had long blonde hair and a pouty mouth, which was undoubtedly the reason for her presence in Zeke's home. Both women had the jaundiced pallor, glazed eyes, and diseased teeth that went with chronic methamphetamine addiction.

"Don't be rude, Buddy," Fornier said. "Introduce me to your friend."

"Oh, yeah," stammered Cuszack. "This here is Vernon Slocum. We was in the hospital together after the war."

Fornier took this in. "Pleased to make your acquaintance, Mister Slocum," he said expansively. "Any friend of Buddy's is a friend of mine."

The girls giggled at this. Cuszack nervously forced a smile. Fornier began making introductions of his own. "Gentlemen, meet Rhonda and Missy."

Slocum nodded at the girls. An immense figure emerged from another room, tightening suspenders over his shoulders.

"Godfuckingdamn, Zeke," bellowed a thundering voice. "I just took a shit a Kodiak bear would be proud of. A real cornback rattler. Why don't you girls come to the shitter and take a look? I didn't flush it yet."

At this Zeke smiled, and the girls burst into uproarious laughter. Zeke said, "Buddy, you remember Wolf, don't you? Mister Slocum, meet Wolf. Wolf handles my security."

He turned to face the emerging figure. The man stood easily three inches taller than Slocum, and weighed well over three hundred pounds. Wolf had a blonde beard which grew to his chest, and he was clad in overalls.

"Now that we've made acquaintances, let's get down to business. Rhonda, turn that shit off." The older woman switched off Al Bundy mid-punchline. Zeke sat down on one of the sofas and motioned for Slocum and Cuszack to do the same. Wolf took a seat next to Rhonda and put his large hand inside her shirt. Fondling Rhonda's breast, he leered at Slocum.

"I'm being a poor host," Zeke said melodramatically. "Please, help yourself."

He motioned to the coffee table which was littered with drugs and drug paraphernalia. Lying among the rolling papers, straws, razors, needles, bongs, and pipes was an ounce of meth. It looked like oily sugar, and several lines were already neatly and expertly chopped. There was also weed, and an open bottle of Jack Daniels.

Cuszack bit his lip. Never before had Zeke offered him anything for free, especially crank. It was a bad sign.

Slocum reached down and scooped up some meth, placing it onto the web of his hand. Putting his hand to his nose he inhaled deeply. His face flushed, the veins in his thick neck distended, and his nose began to run. He wiped his nose on his sleeve.

"Do you like my product, Mister Slocum?"

Slocum didn't answer. Instead, he looked around the room. He saw Cuszack's nervous eyes darting to and fro. He saw Zeke's too confident expression. He saw Wolf seated on the sofa; one hand conspicuously on Rhonda's breast, the other inconspicuously out of view. The fifteen year-old returned his stare, secure in the power of her sexuality.

"I want a half a pound," Slocum said at last.

"Only half a pound?" asked Zeke in mock surprise. "That's a pretty large order from a guy I just met." His eyes narrowed. "But then again, you're a friend of Buddy's. I trust Buddy like a brother. Any friend of his is a friend of mine. Right Buddy?"

"Uh... yeah," babbled Cuszack. "Partners, brothers, and friends."

It was Wolf who spoke next. "I heard you're interested in weapons, tough guy. What exactly are you looking to score?"

"What you got?"

"Wolf can get you anything you want," Zeke interjected. "That is, if you're not full of shit." When he spoke he cast a sidelong glance at Wolf. Cuszack noticed.

"So tell me, Mister Slocum, are you full of shit?"

All but Cuszack and Slocum began to laugh. Zeke's double chin bobbed up and down. "If you're a friend of Buddy's you've got to be full of shit, right?"

"Hey, Zeke, you don't gotta talk to me like that. I thought we was friends. I done a lot of work for you. Why you making me look bad in front of my friend?"

"Shut the fuck up!" Zeke roared. He stood up and walked towards Cuszack, who began to cringe. He grabbed Cuszack by his collar and slapped him across the face. Slocum watched impassively.

Zeke Fornier drew back his hand to strike Cuszack again when Slocum rose from the sofa and threw a lightning fast punch to his jaw. It dazed the drug dealer, and when he fell back Slocum slammed a fist into his solar plexus, doubling him over. Wolf started to get up, the hand not full of Rhonda's breast emerging with a revolver. He tried to bring the muzzle to bear on Slocum. He was too slow. Slocum had already drawn his pistol.

Slocum shot Wolf in the face. The heavy slug took the giant above the mouth and snapped his head back. Wolf fell dead, the pungent smell of his relaxed bowels filling the room. His revolver clattered from his lifeless hand.

Both women began to scream; primal, terrified howls. Cuszack curled himself into a fetal position on the floor and lay trembling, saliva dripping from his quivering lips. He was too terrified to scream. Slocum stepped over Wolf's body and grabbed Rhonda's hair. He chopped down on her head once with the butt of the .45 and she quieted instantly, collapsing into unconsciousness. Missy frantically scrambled over the sofa in a futile attempt to escape.

Slocum caught her by the hair, and with another savage chop of his pistol put her down. He strolled casually over to where Zeke was on his hands and knees vomiting convulsively from the punch to his gut. He grabbed Zeke by the hair, replacing the semi-automatic into his coat, and hurled the puking meth-cooker onto the sofa the two females had vacated. He stood over Fornier, his face impassive.

"Where?" he asked calmly.

Zeke Fornier's head rolled back and forth, and vomit-spittle ran down his chin onto his Harley-Davidson T-shirt. He looked up at Slocum. "You'd better say your prayers, asshole, because you are one dead motherfucker. Do you know who you're fucking with? My friends will be down on you like stink on shit. You'd better get the fuck out of here while the getting is good."

Slocum ignored the tirade. "Where?" he repeated.

"Where's what, motherfucker?" shouted Zeke. "You want something from me, you can fucking kiss my ass. You ain't getting shit."

"I want your stash, and I want your guns. I won't ask again."

"Fuck yourself!"

Slocum stepped from Fornier and returned to the inert body of Rhonda. He picked her up by the shoulders and held her at arm's length with no apparent strain. He put her neck in the crook of his left elbow and placed his right forearm under her chin, gripping his left wrist in his right fist. Then he twisted; a quick and powerful jerk of his shoulders and waist. Rhonda's neck snapped like a dry bundle of twigs.

The instant Rhonda's neck broke, Fornier twitched involuntarily and emitted a shriek. Cuszack rocked back and forth on the floor, whimpering, and repeated, "Oh dear God, oh my God, oh Jesus, oh God, oh my God…"

Slocum strolled casually back to where Zeke sat on the sofa. Zeke had urinated in his jeans and was sobbing. Slocum grabbed his unkempt hair and lifted his face to within an inch of his own.

"Where's the shit?"

Fornier's eyes had a disconnected look and his lids blinked spastically. "All I got on hand," he stuttered, trying to get the words out too fast, "is a couple of pounds. I swear. It's all I got. You're welcome to it. It's in a coffee can under the water heater in the basement."

"Buddy," barked Slocum. "Come here."

Still babbling incoherent prayer, Cuszack complied.

"Go down to the basement and find it."

"Anything you say, Vern." Cuszack staggered towards the basement.

"If you're lying to me Zeke, I'll make you eat the shit out of Wolf's dead ass. Do you understand me?"

"I promise, man," Fornier whined, "I'm telling you the truth."

"What about guns? Where are they?"

"I don't know about guns. Wolf takes care of that shit. If he's got anything, it'd be in his room. I swear, man, I don't know nothing about it." Fornier refused to look into the smoldering coals of Slocum's eyes.

"Here it is, Vern." Cuszack returned from the basement. He seemed to be in a trance. He was carrying a large coffee can.

Inside the coffee can, which was lined with plastic, was approximately five pounds of the same brown-paste methamphetamine on the table. In that quantity it gave off a strong odor, similar to human sweat.

Slocum replaced the lid on the coffee can after inhaling another pinch of crank. He turned his attention back to Zeke.

"You're a good cook."

Slocum drew the .45 smoothly from his pocket and shot Fornier in the forehead, execution style. Fornier's body slid to the floor with a thud, his eyes open.

Cuszack sunk to his knees and resumed sobbing. Slocum ignored him, and walked over to where Missy lay unconscious. She was face down, her legs askew, and her scanty bathrobe no longer covered her. A trickle of blood ran across her cheek from behind her ear where she'd been pistol-whipped. He effortlessly picked up the limp girl and disappeared with her into one of the bedrooms.

Cuszack wrapped his arms tightly around himself and rocked back and forth on his knees, mumbling under his breath.

It wasn't long before he heard Missy's screams.

CHAPTER 17

The Oldsmobile fishtailed along the icy road, skating from one lane to the other.

"Done a lot of driving in the snow, have you?"

"Hell, kid, I haven't done any." Farrell pulled the big sedan over to the side of the highway. He opened the door and got out.

"Take the wheel, Deputy," he said over the howling wind, "unless you want to end up in the ditch."

Kearns complied. Farrell replaced him in the passenger's seat and closed the door. He turned up the car's heater a notch.

"You Iowans ought to do something about these winters." He lit a cigarette and inhaled deeply.

"It's still fall. Where to? You said something about lunch."

"I'm not hungry."

"Neither am I. I haven't had much of an appetite for the past couple of days."

"Nix on lunch, then. OK, the next stop is the veterans' hospital in Des Moines. The lady at the airport who rented me the car said it wasn't far from here."

"It isn't," said Kearns, easing the car into gear and back onto the road. "It's just down the Interstate about thirty miles."

116

"Then let's get going. We've got a lot to do today."

Kearns headed for the freeway onramp.

"Sergeant Evers said to be back by 1 o'clock. If we drive to Des Moines there's no way we'll be back in time, especially with this much snow on the roads."

Farrell grinned, showing nicotine-stained teeth. "Just get us to the veterans' hospital Deputy Kearns. Let me do the worrying."

"My name is Kevin, as long as we're going to be chummy," he said, loosening his tie. "It's going to be hard to let you do the worrying if I don't trust you." He glanced at Farrell. "No disrespect intended, but I didn't even know who you were twenty minutes ago. I'm in enough trouble already; I don't need any more. Not showing up at the sheriff's department on time is more trouble."

"You're in a lot of trouble, alright. I've worked with the FBI before. And your sheriff ain't your friend, either. Between the two of them, they're going to hang you out to dry. You don't have a prayer."

Kearns skidded the Oldsmobile to a stop. He turned in the seat to face the older man.

"What the hell does that mean? And who're you to tell me what's going to happen, Mister California hotshit lawyer? I didn't ask for your help, and I'm not sure I need it. I think we'd better go back to the station."

Farrell listened to the outburst indifferently. Fury radiated from the young cop, and he thought for an instant Kearns might hit him. He smoked in silence and waited for the deputy to cool down. After a moment Kearns calmed, and he turned to the windshield, making a pretense of looking at the falling snow. There were tears forming at the corners of his eyes.

"I'm not trying to make things harder on you. I've got an idea of what you're going through–"

"No, you don't." The flash of rage had passed. His voice was calm.

"You might be surprised. But blaming yourself isn't going to help."

"Tell that to Tiffany Meade's parents. Or to that FBI asshole, Scanlon. Or to the redneck citizens of that hick-town." He rubbed his eyes, wiping away the tears. "I thought you were supposed to be some kind of legal expert. That you were going to help me. That's what Detective Parish and Sergeant Evers said. They said you were my lawyer and I should trust you."

"Don't you?"

"I don't know who to trust. I only graduated the police academy six months ago. This is all new to me. And now it's all down the toilet."

He rubbed his temples. Farrell could see where his hairline had been shaved back to sew the gash on his head.

"Listen," Farrell said. "Things might not be as bad as they seem. Come with me this afternoon. Give me a few hours of your time; it's all I'm asking. What have you got to lose?"

Kearns smiled, but it didn't reach his eyes. "Apparently not much."

"Then why not trust me?"

"What have I got to lose, right?" Kearns shrugged and put the Olds back on the road. Fortunately the storm left traffic on the interstate at a minimum. He concentrated on his driving. Farrell stared out the window and smoked. Neither spoke.

After a while Kearns broke the silence.

"I'm sorry about the outburst back there. I'm not a high-strung kid."

"You've been through a helluva lot in the past few days, if what the newspapers print is even close to true.

Besides, if I had to work for that shitbird sheriff of yours I'd have snapped long ago. Forget it."

The car plowed over the snowy highway. Kearns asked, "You've been a lawyer long?"

"You might say I've been practicing law most of my life. How about you? What did you do before you became a deputy?"

"I was a soldier."

"How's your family taking your involvement in this mess?"

"I wouldn't know. I don't have any."

Farrell didn't know how to answer that, so he didn't.

Kearns merged the Oldsmobile onto westbound Interstate 80. Once on 80, the roads improved.

"We'll be at the veterans' hospital in about fifteen minutes," he said, "and it's nearly 1 o'clock now. Scanlon is going to be pissed. He hates my guts."

"I'm not surprised. I got a look at his face. Why did you crown him?"

"I lost my cool. He said the little girl got murdered because of my negligence."

"I'd have punched him, too." Farrell appraised the younger cop. He could tell the FBI agent's accusation struck a nerve. One look at the deputy's tortured eyes and it was as plain as the plaster cast on Scanlon's face.

"Kevin, you're damned lucky to be alive. You nearly got yourself killed trying to stop that madman. Believe me, I know. You did all you could."

"A lot of folks don't see it that way. As far as they're concerned I stood there with my thumb up my ass and let that guy waltz away with the kid. They don't understand why the kid's dead and I'm still alive."

They exited the freeway onto Merle Hay road. With the exception of a Des Moines PD cruiser and the occasional snowplow, the streets were deserted. Soon the Olds was eastbound on Douglas and pulling into the parking lot at the veterans' hospital.

Kearns turned off the ignition. He was surprised to see the California attorney withdraw a flask from the pocket of his trench coat and tip it to his mouth.

"Takes the sting out of this arctic weather."

The smoky odor of bourbon filled the car. Farrell offered the flask to Kearns, who declined with a wave of his hand and an incredulous look on his face.

Replacing the flask into his pocket, Farrell said, "Deputy, we're going to go in there and talk to some people. No matter what I say or do, I want you to play along. Follow my lead and keep your mouth shut. Do you understand?"

"Are we going to rob the place?"

"I'm your lawyer and I know what's best. You'll have your answers soon. In the meantime, you've got to trust me. When we come out of the hospital you can ask me anything you want. But while we're inside, keep your lip zipped. Got it?"

Kearns started to speak, but thought better of it. He didn't know why, but something in the Californian's demeanor gave him confidence. And for the first time since the incident in the schoolyard somebody was showing confidence in him. "Alright. But I want some answers when we come out."

"Agreed. Straighten your tie."

CHAPTER 18

Buddy Cuszack sat groggily up, his body racked in shivers. He could tell it was well past morning, and when his eyes finally focused enough to read the hands of his wristwatch he noticed it was indeed after noon. The room was frighteningly cold, and he stood up to find a blanket.

The first thing he saw was Zeke Fornier on the floor, his legs contorted in a position no living person could tolerate. There was a hole in his forehead, with no trace of blood coming from it. Under the back of his bearded head however, was a congealed mass of blood and tissue. The .45 slug had taken most of Fornier's brain with it when it exited.

Cuszack stepped gingerly over Zeke's body and switched on a portable space heater in the corner of the room. He reached for the bottle of Jack Daniels on the table and took a large swallow of the amber fluid.

Across the room was the mound of flesh that was once Wolf. Wolf was semi-seated on the couch, his eyes and mouth gaping. He too had a hole in his head, but this one wasn't neat. Cuszack was spared the view of the back of his head. Near Wolf's right hand was a revolver.

Cuszack took another hit from the bottle. On the floor adjacent to Wolf was Rhonda. Like Zeke, she was contorted into a posture no one alive could comfortably assume. Her skin had turned a mottled blue, and she had small pools of scabbed-over blood in each ear. The angle of her head relative to her shoulders was extreme.

Cuszack hazily remembered the night before. Slocum was a death-dealing juggernaut, like that RoboCop character he'd seen at the movies last summer. Buddy's head was foggy and his hands trembled. He remembered falling asleep on the floor of Fornier's living room in an exhausted panic.

Taking another gulp of bourbon he went to the window. He didn't know where Slocum was. Had he left during the night? He hoped so. He parted the curtains and looked out.

Though not snowing as fiercely as the night before, it was still snowing. At least two feet of the white powder covered the ground. Cuszack could see Slocum outside, shoveling snow from under the truck. He must have known the snowfall would be heavy. If they'd parked the truck nearer the house, it would be buried in drifts.

The room was beginning to warm up. Cuszack went over to the coffee table and found a cigarette. He also found more of Zeke's product in a paper bindle. Despite the trembling, he was able to get some of it to his nostril. He inhaled sharply, wiped his nose, and let the rush take him.

He was lighting the cigarette when he heard the back door open and slam shut. Slocum entered.

"You're awake."

"Yeah, I finally got up," said Cuszack, uneasily. "I miss anything?"

Slocum said nothing in reply. He sat on the couch next to Wolf's huge body and lit a Pall Mall. He smoked in silence.

Cuszack felt strange. He knew he should be terrified of the big man, who only last night threatened to kill him if he didn't assist in gaining entrance to Zeke's home. Yet he felt oddly calm. He handed the bottle of Jack Daniel's to Slocum.

Slocum accepted the bottle and took a long drink. Wiping his unshaven jaw with a snowy forearm, he looked down at Zeke's body.

"He was lying," he said.

"Huh?"

"He was lying. He wasn't ever going to make you one of his gang. And he had a lot more than a couple of pounds in that coffee can." He kicked at Zeke's lifeless body. "I found his guns, too," he said matter-of-factly.

"Well what do you know about that?" answered Cuszack, as if discussing the weather. He had to suppress an urge to giggle. He didn't know why, but he felt strangely giddy. Maybe it was shock. Maybe it was the crank, or the alcohol. Maybe it was all three. Somewhere in the back of his mind he knew he should be running madly away from this daytime nightmare. But he wasn't. In fact, at the moment, the whole thing seemed pretty amusing. He took another swig from the bottle and grinned.

"Be leaving soon," Slocum said, "before the snow gets any worse. Give me a hand loading the truck."

"Anything you say. But lemme take my morning piss first."

Still wrapped in his blanket, Cuszack ambled down the hall towards the bathroom. His half-smoked cigarette drooped from his lips, and he carried the bottle of Jack Daniel's. One of the bedroom doors was half-opened, and when he passed by he glanced inside. He wished he hadn't.

Hanging upside down by her ankles was Missy, Zeke's fifteen year-old consort. Her ankles had been lashed with telephone cord to a ceiling fan in the center of the room. She was naked, and her eyes were open and staring. She swung in a slow circle. Her throat had been cut from ear to ear, and her face was obscured in the flow of dried blood from the wound. It was obvious the girl's throat had been cut after she'd been strung up. A large puddle of congealed blood lay below her on the floor.

The room was in disarray. On the bed were bloodstained sheets. Cuszack knew it was there Slocum raped and tortured the girl before her death.

Cuszack stared in horror. The cigarette dropped from his gaping mouth, and the bourbon bottle fell to the floor at his feet. He felt warm urine streaming down his thighs, and wasn't aware the whimpering, animal-like sounds he heard were coming from him.

He shuffled back to the kitchen, where he could hear Slocum rummaging. He suddenly remembered falling asleep to the sounds of Missy's screams.

Slocum didn't appear to see Cuszack walk up behind him. He was busy loading canned goods from Fornier's pantry into a large suitcase. Lying next to the suitcase on the kitchen table was a sawed-off shotgun and an AR-15 rifle. Several handguns were on the table, and boxes of ammunition. There was the five-pound coffee can of methamphetamine, and several stacks of currency wrapped in rubber bands. He couldn't discern the denominations, but noted there were a lot of them. The whining sounds he emitted caused Slocum to whirl and face him.

Cuszack fell to his knees sobbing, his face in his hands. Slocum grunted in disgust and turned back to stuff everything but the AR-15 into the suitcase. Slinging the rifle over his shoulder he hefted the heavy suitcase and left through the rear door, leaving it open. Blasts of icy air slammed into Cuszack, who couldn't control his sobs enough to stand up. He vomited.

Slocum walked to the truck and tossed the rifle and suitcase inside. He then went to the machine shed, where Fornier's methamphetamine lab was. He'd spent the morning foraging, and found Zeke's lab almost immediately. Inside the shed he found an industrial stove, several tanks of ether and propane, Freon canisters, acetone, red phosphorus, industrial-sized boxes of coffee filters, and a five-gallon can of gasoline.

He splashed half of the can's contents throughout the lab. Using his Zippo, he ignited the gasoline and headed for the door.

Moments later the shed exploded. Slocum walked from the engulfed shed back to the house with the remainder of the five-gallon gas can.

Cuszack had regained his feet. "Oh Jesus," he babbled, drool spraying from his lips. He tripped over the splayed legs of Zeke Fornier, falling headlong to the floor. He got up and ran through the front door. He fell down the porch steps, but was up in an instant and scrambling from the Fornier farm in a loping trot.

Slocum re-entered the house through the back door and poured the last of the gasoline randomly throughout the house. Another explosion roared outside in the shed, as more of the volatile chemicals in the clandestine laboratory fell prey to the flames. Standing on the porch, Slocum put a Pall Mall to his lips. He watched Buddy Cuszack thrashing through snowdrifts trying to reach the road.

He lit his cigarette and put the flame of his lighter to the gasoline-soaked carpet. In seconds the interior of the living room was engulfed.

He closed his eyes, feeling the heat from the burning farmhouse. His mind wandered.

Gia Binh.

There, he was a Marine; the baddest in the jungle; walking death. He remembered the oppressive heat and the stench of rotting bodies. There, he was a million miles from the hell of his Iowa home, and from the backbreaking labor and torment he endured each day. Away from his father, and sister, and brothers. In Vietnam he was supposed to kill; it was why they sent him. It's what they trained him for. What he lived for.

He'd left his mark. Children dangled from village trees for all to see. So they'd know Lance Corporal Vernon E Slocum, 1st Battalion, 6th Marine Regiment, had paid a visit.

Slocum snapped out of his trance. He didn't know how long he'd been standing on the porch, but it was time to leave. The entire farmhouse was in flames, portions of the roof folding in on the walls. The heat was tremendous. He spat out his cigarette and waded through the deep snow to the truck.

While the engine warmed up he snorted a pinch of crank. The brownish powder warmed him, but started his broken nose bleeding again. He eased the Dodge from the snow bank and onto the road.

Less than a quarter of a mile down the road he found Buddy huddled in a fetal position in the snow. Slocum stopped the truck and got out. Cuszack looked up at him in stark terror. The only sounds he made were whimpers.

Slocum opened the passenger door of the truck. Cuszack's eyes widened even more.

"Get in, Buddy. Let's go."

CHAPTER 19

Farrell took a moment to pop a couple of breath mints into his mouth before approaching the main desk of the veterans' hospital. He smiled a greeting at the receptionist.

"I'd like to see someone from your records department, please."

Farrell flashed open his wallet showing his badge. At the same time he handed the receptionist a business card. By the time the receptionist read the card, Farrell had the wallet and badge back in his pocket.

"One moment, Agent Scanlon. I'll have to notify my supervisor."

"We'll wait right here."

The receptionist left. Kearns was livid, his eyebrows jumping.

"What the hell do you think you're doing? You gave her that FBI guy's card! You're impersonating a federal agent! That's a crime!"

"Keep your voice down, will you? I told you outside to play along, didn't I?"

"Yes, and I agreed," said Kearns in a loud whisper. "But that was before I knew you were going to impersonate an FBI agent!"

"There's a lot you don't know, deputy. But if you know what's good for you, you'll quiet down before you give us away."

"Us? Who the hell is us?"

"I said I'd explain when we got outside. Now shut your piehole."

Before Kearns could protest any further the receptionist reappeared.

"Doctor Kennedy will see you; third floor, room 305."

"Thank you, ma'am."

Farrell strolled to the elevator with Kearns on his tail. There was no one else aboard.

"I don't like this."

Farrell was busy watching the ceiling. "You agreed to trust me, outside in the car. We've already started this, so we've got to play it out. Who knows, maybe it'll pay off?"

"What will pay off? What are you talking about?"

"Shhhhh," Farrell said. The elevator doors opened. He walked out to room 305. Kearns hustled behind him, cursing under his breath.

A secretary looked up from her typing and said, "You must be the gentlemen from the FBI. Come in; I'll tell the doctor you're here."

The secretary disappeared through a door and returned a moment later. "You may go in."

Farrell and Kearns stepped inside the office to find a portly man of about sixty years sitting behind a mahogany desk. He was nearly bald, and wore an expensively-tailored suit. Farrell couldn't help thinking the man was truly obese if he looked portly in such well-crafted attire.

"I'm Doctor Kennedy, senior administrator here."

When the doctor spoke he stepped from behind the desk and offered a soft hand to Farrell. Taking it, Farrell said, "Steve Scanlon, Des Moines Bureau. This is my partner, Kevin Smith." The doctor shook Kearns' hand. Kearns merely nodded.

"To what do I owe the pleasure of a visit from the FBI?"

"We're here as part of an ongoing investigation into possible medical fraud."

"My goodness," exclaimed Kennedy, the first signs of worry showing on his face. "How does that investigation involve this hospital?"

"We aren't certain yet," Farrell said melodramatically. "We're hoping the allegations will be groundless. As part of investigative protocol we're going to have to examine some of your records."

"An audit? You're talking about an audit, aren't you?" Small beads of sweat began to form on the administrator's brow. "We've always been given several weeks' written notice prior to an audit. This is most unusual. I'm afraid before I allow any inquiries into the administrative workings of the hospital I'm going to have to call my legal staff." He picked up the phone.

Kearns felt sweat trickle under his arms. One phone call and the doctor would discover the two men in his office were attempting to fraudulently gain access to hospital medical records by impersonating agents of the Federal Bureau of Investigation. How did he let himself get bamboozled into such an insane act?

How he'd gotten himself into the charade no longer mattered. Kearns only knew it was time to get out. He cleared his throat, and was about to speak up and tell Kennedy the truth about his and Farrell's identity, when Farrell acted.

Farrell yanked the phone violently from the physician's hand from across the desk. "Who do you think you're dealing with?"

Kennedy's eyes widened as Farrell walked around the desk and closed in. Kearns' stomach lurched. The Californian was now going to add assault and battery to the list of crimes they'd committed since entering the facility.

"Do you think we're here to play games?" said Farrell indignantly. "Do you think you can cover up your improprieties with a phone call to your lawyer?"

"Cover what up? What improprieties?" Kennedy babbled, his eyes wide.

"Don't mince words with me!" Farrell accused, a bony, nicotine-yellowed finger pointed at the doctor like a gun. "I don't know who you're used to dealing with, Bucko, but you're talking to the Federal Bureau of Investigation now."

"Agent Scanlon, if you think..."

"Did you think we were going to be put off by such tactics? Do you think we're amateurs?"

"No, of course not. I would never–"

"That's right, of course not." Farrell put his hands on his hips and glared at Kennedy, shaking his head. Over his shoulder, he said, "Isn't this a tragic way to administrate a federally-funded hospital, Agent Smith?"

"Uh... yeah. I mean..." Kearns stammered.

Kennedy mopped his glistening brow with a handkerchief. "I was only going to verify–"

"Verify what? We're federal agents, remember? Do you think we need your approval to inspect a federal hospital? Our authority comes from the United States Constitution," Farrell lied. "Are you challenging our patriotism, Doctor Kennedy?"

"Goodness, no! I would never impugn–"

"I didn't think so. But I'm skeptical. A hospital administrator guilty of no improprieties has no need to call his legal staff. Frankly, it's suspicious. Perhaps we need to take a much closer look at this facility. We were originally only going to conduct a cursory examination of some of your EPA records to see if this hospital is in compliance with federal asbestos-contamination standards. But now we may have to widen the scope of our inquiry. What do you think, Agent Smith?"

Kearns loosened his tie and glanced nervously around the room. If he could only slip quietly out and get back to the station...

"There's no need for that!" Kennedy pleaded. "You can keep the scope of your inquiry as narrow as you want!"

Sensing the upper hand, Farrell switched tactics. His demeanor again became that of the courteous civil servant.

"Certainly my colleague and I don't want to believe you're guilty of any impropriety."

Kennedy sat heavily down in his chair, drained. Farrell continued.

"Initial reluctance to cooperate fully with a federal investigation is often tantamount to having something to hide. You don't have anything to hide, do you?"

Kennedy only shook his head.

"Then I can report to my superiors that you cooperated fully?"

"Anything you need. Help yourself."

"Your cooperation is indicative of your patriotism, and it's always a pleasure to work with a fellow patriot. Agent Smith, make a note of Doctor Kennedy's patriotism."

"Uh... duly noted."

"Very good," said Farrell cheerfully. "If that's settled, we can get down to business. We'll need to see all patients' records from 1967 to the present, in alphabetical order."

Kennedy wasn't even listening. He pressed a button on his desk. The secretary appeared. "Eva, take these gentlemen down to records storage and have the staff there show them full cooperation."

"Your country thanks you," said Farrell to the deflated administrator.

Doctor Kennedy halted them. "Forgive me, Agent Scanlon, but is there a number where I can reach you? In case my superiors want to follow up?"

"Here," said Farrell. "Take one of my cards." Kearns gagged.

Farrell and a relieved Kearns left the administrator's office and followed Kennedy's secretary to the elevator.

"I'll leave you here, gentlemen," she said at the elevator. "Go to the basement and proceed left until you get to the east wing. The staff there will be expecting you."

"You've been most helpful," said Farrell with a Cheshire cat grin. Eva left them.

Kearns exploded. "What in the hell kind of a stunt were you trying to pull up there? Do you want to get us thrown in jail?"

Farrell ignored the angry deputy and uncorked his flask. After a quick swig he stashed it and popped a breath mint into his mouth. The elevator stopped and the doors opened.

Farrell headed for the records section. Kearns trailed behind him muttering obscenities under his breath.

The records department implied an office complex; it was not. It was a dank, dusty, dungeon of a room of vast proportions. Hundreds of crates of records lined the water-stained walls. It was cold enough to see your breath. The "staff" there was an old man in janitor's coveralls. He stood leaning on a mop and stared at Farrell and Kearns.

"Sir, I'm Special Agent Scanlon of the FBI, and this is my partner, Agent–"

"I know who you are and what you're here for," snorted the old man. "Just don't mess the place up." With that he left.

Farrell shook his head, chuckled, and lit a cigarette. "How ironic. All those theatrics to get access to medical records, and all we needed was a pair of coveralls and a mop."

"I don't even know what we're looking for."

"All in good time, my impetuous young deputy." Farrell began examining boxes. Each box had a series of dates scribbled on it, as well as alphabetized letters to denote the names contained within. He spent a long time looking at the writing on several of the boxes using his lighter for illumination. Eventually he found the one he was looking for.

Kearns watched as Farrell pulled a box from a lower shelf. The box was bulging, and on one side was written in black marker, SH-SP. After scrolling through the box for another minute or so, he extracted a thick folder. Setting it aside, he carefully replaced the box into its original position on the shelf. He tucked the folder inside the waistband of his pants and buttoned his coat over it.

"OK," he said with finality. "Let's go."

Kearns breathed a sigh of relief and checked his watch. It was a little after 2 o'clock. Scanlon and the Sheriff were probably wondering why he wasn't back.

"I've got to get back to the station. It's late as hell."

"I said we were done, didn't I?" He ground out his cigarette.

They walked through the musty basement to a stairwell. Light filtered in from above. Farrell mounted the steps and opened the door with some difficulty because it was blocked by drifting snow. Both men squinted in the outside light. When they reached the parking lot Farrell tossed Kearns the keys.

"I fulfilled my part of the bargain. It's your turn. You said you'd explain when we came out. We're out. What gives?"

"Deputy Kearns," said Farrell, "I promised you answers, and I'll deliver them. But could we at least drive away? I don't want to be stopped and questioned by a real FBI agent when Doctor Kennedy finds out he's been flimflammed."

Kearns hesitated, biting his lip. How much further was this going to go? The Californian's suggestion to leave was prudent however. He got in and switched on the ignition.

"OK, we'll go. But if I don't get answers soon one of us is going to be walking. I've taken about all I'm going to take today."

"Fair enough," said Farrell jubilantly. "I think you'll find your answers worth the trouble."

The snow was falling more heavily than when they'd entered the hospital and the roads were even slicker. Kearns noticed more traffic on the streets. The evening commuters were leaving early in anticipation of the poor road conditions.

Kearns turned north on Merle Hay Road and headed for the shopping mall there. He pulled into the parking lot. Christmas ornaments were draped over the lampposts, and the faint melody of an Andy Williams holiday tune was audible in the distance. He could hear the cling-clang of a Salvation Army volunteer ringing a bell. He parked the Oldsmobile in a remote corner and left the engine idling to run the heater.

"Mister Lyons, it's time to come clean. What the hell's going on? What was that scene at the VA hospital all about?"

"Easy, kid. I said you'd get answers, and you will." Farrell paused to light a cigarette. "But before you get them, I want to be sure you really want them."

"I'd better start getting some answers. Or you're going to end up looking like Special Agent Scanlon."

Farrell ground out his unfinished cigarette. "I'm sorry, Deputy. The last thing I want to do is play games with you. I know you don't believe me, but I know what you're going through."

"How could you possibly know what I've been through?"

Farrell reached into his coat and pulled out the file he'd taken from the veterans' hospital. He opened it and shuffled through the stack of documents until he produced a photograph. He handed the photo to Kearns.

"How do I know what you're going through? Because I let the same man slip through my fingers twenty years ago."

Kearns listened, not believing what he was hearing. He accepted the photograph from the older man and stared at it.

He looked at the faded black-and-white picture. Staring back at him was the face of the child-killer.

The picture was of a man in a dress-blue USMC uniform. It was undoubtedly the same man Kearns had confronted in the schoolyard a few days ago, only much younger. The eyes were the same, though. Unchanged by time. Evil eyes. They glared back at Kearns.

"That's him," he said almost inaudibly. "That's the man from the schoolyard."

"I know," said Farrell soothingly. He put a hand on Kearns' shoulder. "His name is Vernon Slocum."

Kearns set the photo on the dashboard and looked at Farrell skeptically. "You know who he is; you've known all along. I don't understand. Why haven't you told the authorities?"

"I have my reasons."

"We're heading back to the station right now. We're going to get this Slocum guy's identity broadcast so we can get him locked up."

Kearns started to put the sedan into gear when he felt something very hard jab into his ribs. He looked over to find Farrell leaning towards him, a snub-nosed .38 in his fist. The muzzle poked into his side.

"Not so fast, Deputy. Turn off the ignition and take out the keys."

Kearns silently cursed himself. How could he have been so foolish? Hadn't the Californian's actions been warning enough he was capable of anything? First he'd been duped into impersonating a federal agent. Now he found himself at the business end of a gun. And he knew no more about the man holding the gun than when they'd met.

He complied with Farrell's request, but instead of handing over the keys he tossed them at the older man's face. He expected Farrell to flinch, and hoped for an opening to make a grab for the gun. Farrell didn't flinch.

"Put your hands on the wheel. If you try any more stupid tricks I'll blow your lungs out."

Kearns did as he was told.

"Sit quiet. You wanted answers, didn't you?"

Farrell leaned back in the seat, away from Kearns, and took the gun from against his ribs. He lit a cigarette, covering the younger cop with the revolver.

"You were howling for an explanation a few minutes ago. If you don't like what you hear we'll drive back to the station. You have my word. Is it a deal?"

"If the alternative is having my lungs blown out, I'll take the deal."

CHAPTER 20

Special Agent Steve Scanlon was not a happy man. He sat in Sheriff Coates' office blinking his eyes as hard and as regularly as possible. Through this facial contortion he was able to move his nose slightly inside its plaster cast and alleviate the itch that was driving him crazy.

It was after 1600 hours, and there was still no word from Deputy Kearns or his smart-ass lawyer. Sergeant Evers had been on the phone for over an hour trying to locate the young deputy. It was likely the blizzard had delayed their return, but even that possibility was becoming remote.

Evers checked with the State Patrol, and though many of the highways were closed due to the storm, there were no reports of accidents which would account for the deputy's absence. He was supposed to be back at 1300 hours; that was the arrangement with his attorney. Even if he'd been delayed, surely he could have made a phone call. Sheriff Coates could offer no explanation for the loss of his employee and Scanlon was beginning to suspect a conspiracy by Evers or that wise-guy detective, Parish. Scanlon hated the redneck cops and their scarcely concealed contempt for the federal agents, and wished he didn't have to work with such backwoods clods on so sensitive and important an investigation.

Two of the agents assigned to him had already been diverted, accompanying the State Fire Marshal to a remote area of western Iowa known as Coon Rapids. Apparently there'd been an explosion and fire there, and sheriff's deputies on the scene reported the origin of the fire as a possible clandestine narcotics laboratory.

Washington was calling daily, contributing to Scanlon's problems. The Assistant Director wanted constant updates on the status of the investigation, and promised to send agents specializing in Crimes Against Children as soon as the weather permitted it. He was relieved the storm delayed the additional personnel, as he wasn't ready to relinquish control of the investigation until a solid lead was produced. Scanlon didn't mind extra help, but too much of the FBI's resources were devoted to promoting the Bureau's public image and the political aspirations of the Washington division chiefs, and not enough to the agents in the field.

So far, the investigation had turned up little in the way of actionable leads. The autopsy on the teacher revealed she was shot at point blank range with a .45 caliber handgun. Ballistics details would take several more days, even with the priority assigned to this case. The shell casing found at the scene, a standard brass .45 ACP Federal, was worthless without the gun that fired it. The shell casing would be invaluable in identifying the gun once located, but of little help in locating the firer. The indentation on the primer, and the extractor and ejector markings, were as distinct as fingerprints; but like fingerprints, worthless without fingers to match.

The victim, Tiffany Meade, was found west of Des Moines on Interstate 80 hanging from a tree. Preliminary autopsy information indicated the child suffered a fractured jaw and cranium prior to death. Scanlon took comfort knowing Tiffany Meade likely never regained consciousness from her original concussion. She'd been raped and sodomized, with semen residue discovered in both vaginal and rectal orifices. The bodily fluid evidence was also useless without a suspect to match for comparison. The hair and fiber evidence left by the suspect was limited for the same reasons.

There wasn't much else to go on. The station wagon used in the kidnapping was found under a bridge in Ames, Iowa, and Detective Parish himself personally supervised the latent fingerprint search of the vehicle. The only such prints found in the car were those of the retired farmer who reported the vehicle stolen two days prior to the kidnapping. The farmer's alibi and character were credible and airtight.

An accurate suspect description was also proving difficult to obtain. Besides Deputy Kearns, the only other witnesses were a terrified young teacher and a group of preschool children. Kearns gave an Identi-Kit description to Detective Parish which was remarkable in its detail. But how good could a drawing be? And how accurate could Deputy Kearns' observations of the suspect be if he suffered a concussion just after making them. So, as Scanlon saw it, the only reliable description of an at-large child-murderer was based on the memory of a rookie cop who'd been knocked unconscious immediately after viewing the killer.

The thirty miles distance between the kidnapping-murder and the discovery of the child's body indicated the suspect obviously had access to another vehicle; it too was probably stolen. All stolen-auto reports were being checked and re-checked.

Scanlon's men, as well as deputies, were also checking the known sex offenders' files. The records check was tedious and time-consuming, and so far yielded no results. Deputies, detectives, state police, and special agents rounded up known sex offenders and conducted interviews around the clock.

There'd been a tremendous media blitz; beneficial in some respects, and a hindrance in others. Scanlon had to badger the sheriff to issue orders forbidding deputies from conversing with the press. The kidnap-murder was commanding most of the TV and news coverage, both on the local and state level. The only good thing produced by this media frenzy was the Identi-Kit drawing of the suspect was being broadcast on every television from Chicago to Omaha. Maybe somebody would see the suspect and call it in. It sometimes happened, but was extremely rare, and Scanlon didn't believe in luck.

Editorials in the local papers called for stepped-up police and sheriff's patrols, and it was a blessing the blizzard kept children from school. Much was being written in the press about the bogeyman, as one *Des Moines Register* columnist dubbed the suspect. Though far from panic, popular sentiment surrounding the child-killing was closer to hysteria than Scanlon would have liked.

Not that he didn't expect it. From the moment the child was found hanging from a tree in broad daylight he knew it would be a career case. Scanlon knew all too well that FBI careers were made or broken during investigations like this one. He intended to ensure it was the former and not the latter.

As much as he hated to agree with the lawyer from California who'd crashed into his office this morning, Lyons was right. The issue of exploited and abused children was receiving ever-increasing focus, and America was paying attention.

Thinking of the Californian started Scanlon's nose itching again, and he resisted the urge to scratch it with the eraser on his pencil. The doctor who set it warned him any unnecessary movement could result in complications. He reached into his pocket and withdrew the business card he'd been given by the Californian attorney.

Dialing long distance, he punched in the number at the bottom of the card. After only one ring a feminine voice answered.

"Carruthers and Lyons. May I help you?"

"Yes," said Scanlon in his newly acquired nasal twang. "This is Special Agent Scanlon of the Des Moines Bureau of the FBI. I'd like to speak to someone in charge, please."

There was a brief pause. "Sir, if you could tell me what this is about, perhaps I could help you."

"I'm calling long distance from Iowa in regards to Mister Lyons. I'm having a bit of trouble locating him since he left my office this morning. Could you tell me which hotel in the greater Des Moines area he is staying at? You see, we're in the midst of a blizzard and–"

"Sir," interrupted the voice, "I'm afraid I don't know what you're talking about. Mister Lyons just left the office for a golf date twenty minutes ago. Are you sure you have the right number?"

Scanlon felt his throat sink into his stomach. He looked at the elegantly engraved business card in his hand and quelled the impulse to crumble it in his fist.

"Sir? Are you there?"

He hung up. Taking a deep breath, he picked up the phone again. "Get me Sheriff Coates, please."

"I'm sorry, Agent Scanlon," said the voice of the dispatcher. "The sheriff is out for the day. I can leave a message if you like?"

"Yeah," barked Scanlon angrily into the phone, "leave him this message. Tell him to get his drunk ass back to his office, pronto. Got that?"

"Yes sir. I'll relay the message."

"Thank you." He slammed the phone down on its cradle. He went to the office door and opened it. The Investigations Division was filled with agents and deputies busily at their duties.

"Tatters," Scanlon called to one of his agents. "Round up Evers and Parish. Then you and Lefferty bring them to me in the sheriff's office as soon as you can."

"OK, boss."

Within minutes the two special agents arrived with Evers and Parish in tow. After the group entered the office Scanlon told them to close the door. Evers and Parish both looked as though they hadn't slept in several days. Parish munched on his trademark wad of tobacco.

"Gentlemen," Scanlon began dramatically. "You're probably wondering why I called you here."

"Wow," said Parish. "You gonna read us your will?"

Evers laughed, and the two agents looked scornfully at the two deputies.

"This is no laughing matter. I believe we've been duped."

"Duped?" asked Evers. "What the fuck does that mean? Duped?"

"Don't try to figure it out," snickered Parish. "That's secret agent talk. It's above our heads. They learn that shit in Quantico, along with how to be snotty and use a decoder ring."

"That will be enough. We have a problem; one which will prove as embarrassing to my agency as yours."

"What are you babbling about, Scanlon?"

"Our young deputy has disappeared."

"Disappeared? What do you mean, disappeared? Just because he's a little late returning to your inquisition doesn't mean he should be put on the Ten Most Wanted list. He's out with his lawyer. You're the one who let him go, remember?"

"I have only now discovered the attorney's credentials were false. The organization which he alleged to represent claims no knowledge of him. I just got off the phone with them."

Evers glanced at Parish. Parish shrugged.

"So," Scanlon went on, "since nobody seems to know the current whereabouts of our young deputy, and since he's several hours past due, I think we can safely assume he's flown the coop."

"For Christ's sakes," Parish said. "What possible motive could Kevin have for splitting? He hasn't done anything wrong. Why would he take off?"

"I don't know, but the fact remains he's gone. And he happens to be the most significant piece of the investigation we have right now. Why wouldn't he call, if he was merely late? And why would the man he left with falsify his identity in order to get him away from us?"

"He's right, Rod," Evers said, shaking his head. "It's pretty goddamned fishy. I don't like it at all."

"Come on, Dick," Parish said. "You don't think Kevin would do anything crazy, do you?"

"No, I don't. But I can't be sure."

"Well, what do you gentlemen suggest we do?" asked Scanlon.

"I'll send a deputy to his apartment," said Evers. "And phone around to some of the local eateries favored by cops. He's got no living relatives. I can't think of anywhere else to try."

"How about a girlfriend?" asked Parish.

The tall sergeant shook his head. "He never mentioned one. And he's only been in the area a few months, since he got out of the academy. He was just remarking the other day about hardly knowing anybody in town."

"What if these efforts are fruitless?" Scanlon asked. "What then?"

"What do you want to do?" Parish said. "Put out a 'pick up and hold' on him?"

"I was thinking of exactly that," said Scanlon.

"I was joking," Parish said. "Are you out of your fucking mind? He's a cop, not a criminal."

"I'm not so sure," Scanlon said.

"Fuck you."

"Take it easy, Rod," Evers said. "Much as I hate to admit it, Scanlon's right. Something's going on here. Kevin is our only solid material witness. What if we get a line on this creep? Who's going to identify him?"

Parish spit a large glop of brown juice on the carpet. "I don't believe it! You want to put out a BOLO for one of our own deputies?"

"Detective Parish," Scanlon said, "calm yourself. It's not my intent to cause trouble for the deputy. But we've got to find him. What if something happened to him? This impostor waltzed in here and took him right out from under our noses. I thought he was an attorney with appropriate legal access to Kearns, and so did you. What if that's also what Kearns thought?"

"You think Kevin was kidnapped?"

"It's a possibility I haven't eliminated, Sergeant. What if the killer had an accomplice? There are a number of possible explanations, but none of them add up. What I don't know is who that man was who came in here and took Deputy Kearns or what his motives were. Do you?"

"No, but I agree with you. We need to find out."

"Dick, don't tell me you're siding with this pencil-necked asshole?"

"Rod, I ain't siding with anybody. Scanlon is right; we've got to find Kevin. Something is definitely wrong."

"OK, let's find him. But do we have to put a BOLO in the system for Kevin? Can't we list him as a missing person?"

Evers looked to Scanlon. Scanlon shrugged. "Why not? If we list him in BOLO, it'll appear as if Kearns is a suspect. Better to list him as a missing person. Either way, the press is going to have a field day."

"Yeah," said Parish. "I can see the headlines now. 'Deputy vanishes. Only witness to child kidnapping whisked away by mysterious stranger.' We're going to look like a bunch of butter-fingered idiots."

"I suggest we don't dwell on that too much," Scanlon said. "Let's get to work."

Evers and Parish took their cue and headed for the office door. Halfway out, Detective Parish turned back to Scanlon.

"I'm sorry I called you an asshole and a pencil-neck, Agent Scanlon. I was pissed off and flapping my gums. I didn't mean it."

"It's forgotten," Scanlon said loftily.

Parish nodded and closed the office door. When they were well away from the office, Evers halted Parish with a hand on the shoulder.

"You really sorry?"

"Nah," said the sheriff's detective. "I had my fingers crossed when I apologized. He's still a fucking pencil-neck asshole."

"I figured."

CHAPTER 21

Kearns stared through the windshield at the blowing snow. With the engine of the Oldsmobile turned off the car was getting noticeably colder, and would soon be intolerable. Next to him, in the passenger seat, sat a man from California aiming a gun at his belly.

Kearns glared at Farrell, who exhaled smoke and stamped out his cigarette. He tucked the revolver into its holster under his coat.

"If you'll be civil, Kevin, I won't need the gun."

"Only my friends call me by my first name. I ought to punch your lights out."

"Could we turn the heater back on?" He handed the keys to Kearns. "I'm freezing. Besides, if you punch my lights out you won't get answers, will you?"

Kearns angrily switched on the ignition. A minute later the interior of the Olds was comfortably warm. Farrell extracted another cigarette from inside his pocket. He offered the pack to Kearns, who declined with a shake of his head.

"Do all attorneys in California carry guns?"

"Only in Los Angeles." Farrell opened his wallet, displaying his San Francisco star and ID. "I'm not a lawyer. I'm a cop from San Francisco. My name's not Lyons; it's Bob Farrell."

Kearns examined the wallet. "The ID card says you're honorably retired. I guess you're not even a cop anymore."

"I guess not," said Farrell lighting his smoke. "Aren't you wondering why a retired cop from San Francisco is in the middle of Iowa freezing his ass off?"

"What I'm curious about is why you haven't told anybody about this Slocum guy. It's obvious you knew who he was all along. Your games have done nothing but delay his capture and get me in deeper trouble."

"A little more trouble won't matter one way or the other."

"What's that supposed to mean?"

"The newspapers said you were a rookie," Farrell said, "but I didn't realize until I met you how green you were. You're expendable, Deputy Kearns, and don't even know it."

"Bullshit."

"I wasn't just fucking around back at the VA hospital," Farrell said. "I thought Slocum was the perp, but I couldn't be sure. I needed you to see a picture of him to confirm it. I had to be certain."

"So why not get the file and show me the picture at the station?"

"You still don't get it, do you?"

"No, I don't get it," Kearns said in exasperation. "Why don't you assume I'm as dumb as you think, and spell it out for me?"

"If you'd calm down, I will."

Kearns answered with silence.

"Twenty years ago I was in the same place you are. With one exception: I caught him."

"Apparently he didn't stay caught."

"Hell, kid, I don't think he ever went to prison. It was in Vietnam. I was a military cop in Saigon."

"I'm listening."

Farrell ground out his cigarette in the rapidly-filling ashtray. "This guy Slocum is the real deal; an undiluted badass without a shred of remorse. He's also a textbook sociopath, if you're familiar with that term. One tough hombre, too."

"You don't have to tell me the guy was tough," Kearns said, pointing to the stitches on his head. "I danced with him, remember?"

"You must be a bit of a badass yourself to have survived the encounter. But your peers at the sheriff's department don't believe that, do they? They think there was something more you could have done. They think you should have stopped him. Prevented the kidnapping and murder. They're confused about why you survived and the kid didn't."

Kearns kneaded the steering wheel, his face flushing.

"You and I know something those fools will never know," Farrell said. "We know who and what Vernon Slocum is. He left his mark on us both."

"How did you meet him?"

"He kidnapped and murdered a Vietnamese kid in Saigon. Left him hanging from a lamppost just like Tiffany Meade. Couple of my men caught him; he damn-near killed them both. During the investigation I discovered he'd been doing a lot of that kind of thing out in the bush. The other Marines in his unit looked the other way; they were afraid to take him on."

"I can see why. But you said you caught him. Why wasn't he locked up?"

"I'm not sure how familiar you are with the history of the Vietnam era, but if you view it in the context of the times, it's not hard to figure out. This was in '67, before the Tet Offensive and My Lai Four. A boy-next-door Marine, buttfucking little children and hanging them in the trees with their throats cut? Wouldn't sound too good coming from Walter Cronkite on the evening news."

"Same modus operandi as the schoolyard," Kearns said.

"You got it. Slocum would go into a village with his unit, usually on a long-range patrol, and they would burn the village to the ground. Before they left he would leave one of his little playthings hanging from the trees."

"His superior officers knew about this? They condoned this behavior?"

"I wouldn't say 'condoned' is the right word. His officers were out in the field with him for very long periods of time. Not only were they dependent on his considerable skills to survive, they were entirely at his mercy should they piss him off."

"I get it. Nobody in his unit would rat on him for fear he'd frag them. How did your men catch him?"

Farrell pulled his flask from his side pocket. "He was wounded, and was sent to Saigon for treatment. Nothing serious; otherwise he'd have been shipped to Japan. But he forgot he wasn't in the bush; he killed a kid in downtown Saigon."

"That must have been political dynamite."

"You ain't kidding. It started a race riot. The two of my men who confronted him ended up a lot worse off than you. They had to shoot him."

"So what happened?"

Farrell took a quick sip from his flask. "The government couldn't very well bring charges against him. That would mean a court martial, and a court martial couldn't be contained. It would expose the many other crimes Slocum committed in the field. War crimes. Crimes other

Marines witnessed, along with Marine officers. That would have been extremely embarrassing to the war effort. It would have been impossible to keep out of the press."

"So they buried it?"

"What else could they do? It was 1967, remember? The war was just starting to lose popularity at home. Most people still viewed the US forces as the good guys fighting for democracy and the American way. Nobody was paying attention yet to the hippies chanting that Uncle Sam was turning America's hometown boys into baby-killers. If what Vernon Slocum did leaked out, America would pay attention."

"Let's not embarrass ourselves over a few dead kids?"

"That's about the size of it."

"And they just let this Slocum guy walk?"

"I don't think they let him walk," Farrell said. "I think they put him on ice."

"On ice?"

"He didn't go to Leavenworth, because I checked. And as far as I could tell, he never served time in any civilian prison. I had access to that information at work."

Farrell glanced out the window at the falling snow.

"I guessed they locked him up in one of the VA hospitals somewhere; it would be the perfect place to stash him. Turns out I was right."

"Why a VA hospital?" asked Kearns.

"Veterans' hospitals have psych wards. A lot of guys come back from combat with their brains scrambled worse than their bodies. I figured the navy had Slocum locked up in a VA hospital psych-ward under the guise of being a mentally disturbed combat casualty. That way they could dope him up and keep him docile. Make him a zombie, and nobody would be the wiser."

"Now I know why we went to the veterans' hospital. But how'd you know his records would be in the Des Moines facility?"

"Slocum was from Iowa," Farrell said with a shrug. "And after I read in the paper about the kidnapping of the Meade girl, I put two and two together."

"So you learned about the kidnapping from the San Francisco newspaper and figured it had to be the same guy?" Kearns couldn't hide the disbelief in his face.

"Look, kid," Farrell said with a hard grin. "You're a cop long enough, you stop believing in coincidence. There couldn't be two guys who snatch their victims in a military raid and hang them up in the trees after sexually assaulting them. If there are, we're in a world of trouble."

"You're right. It's too distinct. What you said just now, about the military raid? What did you mean?"

"From what the newspapers said the suspect drove up to the schoolyard, got out of his car, and snatched a kid in broad daylight. Then shot a teacher who tried to intervene. That about how it went down?"

Kearns' stomach tightened. "That's how it went down."

"Don't you see? That's Slocum's signature. He didn't take the kid quietly, on the sly, like he was afraid of getting caught. Most sex offenders would have waited till their victim was alone and nobody was looking; they wouldn't want to get arrested. Slocum took his victim as if he was on a military raid, like in Vietnam. During the war, he was a member of a long-range reconnaissance unit whose mission was to penetrate deep into the jungle and disrupt the enemy at his home. Guerrilla tactics; gun and run. Most of that sort of thing was credited to Special Forces, Ranger units, and Navy SEALs, but a lot of it was done by the Corps in the delta regions with fair success. Slocum is merely following a pattern like he's still in Vietnam. He commits his crimes like he's in combat; not like a criminal trying to avoid apprehension and prosecution. Slocum isn't a criminal. In his twisted mind, he's still at war."

"That sounds pretty far-fetched."

"Maybe so. But when you've been a cop as long as I have, very little seems far-fetched anymore. Especially when it comes to sex crimes."

"Is that what you did for SFPD?" asked Kearns. "Sex crimes investigation?"

"No. I was Property Crimes Inspector."

Both men were momentarily silent.

Finally Kearns spoke, looking over at Farrell with narrowed eyes.

"OK, Mister Farrell; you've explained a lot. But it still doesn't answer all my questions. Why involve me? You didn't need me to prove it was Slocum, you knew it already. By dragging me along you put me in deep shit."

"You can afford it, Deputy. You're bought and paid for. You were marked as a scapegoat long before I came into the picture."

"How can they make me the bad guy?"

"I told you: because the public is outraged and looking for someone to blame. Every time a ghastly crime occurs John Q Citizen screams, 'Why didn't you cops prevent it?' Your boss, the good sheriff, has his job only with the support of the voting public. The investigation, from what I can tell, has gone stale. It's in the damage-control phase now. It's switched from a criminal hunt to a witch-hunt. And you're riding the broom."

"I did all I could."

"I believe you. But do you honestly believe the people in these parts are ever going to forgive and forget?"

Kearns hung his head.

Farrell rubbed his chin. "I can even tell you how they're going to do you in. You signed your own death warrant when you punched out that FBI agent."

"That rotten bastard said it was my fault that the kid got killed."

"I didn't say he didn't deserve it. I'm saying you'll be portrayed as an irresponsible hothead. It'll be implied your lack of judgment, or your inexperience, or your temper, had something to do with your inability to prevent the kidnapping. Nothing will be stated outright, but the implication alone will be enough for people to draw conclusions. I've seen it done before, and nobody does character assassination better than the FBI. The press will be more than willing to help. It sells papers."

The men's eyes met, and Kearns knew the older cop was right.

"They've got to cover their asses," Farrell said. "That's just the way it is. If you believe the sheriff, and Scanlon, and the rest of those fucks aren't going to sell you down the river, you're even greener than I thought. Let me ask you something; has anybody yet made a statement to the press, or to anyone for that matter, in your support? Has anyone come out and said, 'Deputy Kearns is a good cop who put his life on the line and did all he could to save a little girl'?"

"No one's risen to my defense. They all keep looking at me with those accusing eyes. They don't have to say a word. I know what they're thinking."

"What's that?"

"They're thinking, 'How did you let him get away with that child, Deputy Kearns? Why didn't you stop him, Deputy Kearns? Why are you still alive, Deputy Kearns?'"

He put his face in his hands. Through his fingers he said, "Sergeant Evers didn't want me to see the crime scene photos, but I did. They were on his desk. I saw the kid hanging upside down in a tree. Her eyes were open."

He took his face from his hands. "Every time I close my eyes I see those pictures. And the whole scene at the schoolyard replays in my mind. I can only sleep for a couple of hours at a time before I wake up. I don't even want to sleep anymore; I dread it."

"That's why I involved you."

Kearns snapped his face around to stare at Farrell.

"What?"

"That's why I brought you along. Sure, I wanted to be certain it was Slocum, so I had you look at the photograph from his medical file. Except I wasn't even sure I'd be able to get his medical file, or that it contained a photograph."

"I don't understand."

"Jesus, you're dense." Farrell paused a moment. "I brought you with me today because I thought you'd want to join me. I'm going after Slocum. Not with the FBI, or the sheriff's department, or anybody else. I'm going to get him so this time he'll stay got." Farrell's eyes met Kearns' dead on. "I thought you'd want in."

Kearns was dumbfounded. "If the FBI can't do it, what makes you think we can?"

Farrell laughed out loud for several seconds. "The illustrious FBI wants to catch Slocum alright, but they've got to play by the rules. They've got to get search warrants, and court orders, and be careful not to violate anybody's civil rights, or do anything that might tarnish the Bureau's sterling image."

Farrell stopped chuckling and his expression hardened. "And while they're getting legal writs, and organizing task forces, and holding press conferences, Vernon Slocum is out there. Whose son or daughter will be next?"

"It seems like a long shot."

A mischievous grin widened over Farrell's face. "The FBI doesn't even know who they're after; we do. And all we have to do is catch him. We don't have to play by the rules. We can lie, cheat, steal; do whatever is necessary to locate the bastard and punch his ticket."

"So that's why all the bullshit today," Kearns said. He pointed to the faded photo of Slocum lying on the dashboard. "You're covering your tracks. Nobody will ever know where the file went."

Farrell smiled. "You learn fast, Deputy."

Kearns hesitated. "I've got to think about this for a minute. You're asking me to break the law."

"You've already broken the law. What're a few broken laws, more or less, if we nail Slocum?"

"Don't rush me. It's not like I'm deciding what brand of beer to order."

Farrell stuck another cigarette in his mouth and lit it.

"I'm hunting Vernon Slocum," he said around the Camel in his lips, "whether you're with me or not. I'm offering you a chance to accompany me for several reasons, not the least of which is because he is extremely dangerous. You're young, strong, and tough, and I'm not proud: I need the help. But if you're not interested, say so. I'll take you back to the sheriff's department and you can take your chances with the FBI."

"You're offering me a chance to redeem myself, aren't you?"

Farrell exhaled smoke through his nostrils. "Maybe you're not as dumb as you look."

"You wouldn't be letting me tag along out of pity?"

Farrell shook his head. "Twenty years ago I let the most vicious criminal I've ever known slip through my fingers because I didn't want to rock the boat. I figured the system would take care of him. And after thirty years of Special Agent Scanlons, and Tiffany Meades, and Vernon Slocums, I've learned differently. The system is fucked."

Farrell took a deep drag on his cigarette. His eyes became distant.

"You're not the only one who has nightmares, Deputy."

"We're talking vigilante stuff, aren't we?"

"Call it what you want," Farrell said. "I'm on Slocum's trail, with or without you. You in or out?" He extended his flask to the deputy, waiting for an answer.

"What have I got to lose?" Kearns accepted the flask. He took a long gulp of bourbon, wincing as it burned down his throat.

"I'm in."

CHAPTER 22

Buddy Cuszack was huddled on the passenger's seat of the truck. He hadn't moved since he and Slocum left Zeke Fornier's place in flames several hours earlier. Both men smelled heavily of sweat, stale cigarette smoke, and hard liquor. Cuszack also smelled of vomit.

It had taken over four hours to drive the thirty miles to the interstate from Coon Rapids, and they wouldn't have made it without the truck's four-wheel drive. Darkness had fallen by the time the duo reached I-80.

The storm subsided somewhat, but traffic on the highway was scarce. Slocum hoped by the time they reached the Missouri River the storm would subside completely. Council Bluffs, only twenty miles away, would take an hour to reach at the pace they were traveling. Slocum was anxious to be west of Iowa.

Cuszack sat wearily up, rubbing his red-rimmed eyes. He ran his filthy hands through his thick hair and beard. When his eyes finally focused, he saw Slocum behind the steering wheel driving them through the storm.

"Hey Buddy," Slocum said, in his deep, gravelly voice. "How you feelin'?"

"I feel like ten pounds of shit in a five pound sack."

"Here you go." Slocum handed Cuszack several items extracted from the pocket of his fatigue jacket. "This'll make you feel better. Go ahead, eat something."

Cuszack accepted a can of sliced peaches. The thought of eating made Cuszack feel like vomiting again, but he didn't want to offend Slocum. Slocum handed him a multi-bladed pocketknife.

"It's got a can opener, and a fork and spoon. Drink all the juice. You need some fluids in you."

Cuszack stared incredulously at the big former Marine. How could anyone be so utterly savage one minute and nurturing the next? It made him nervous. Not nervous enough, however, to disobey.

"Thanks, Vern," he mumbled. "I could use something in me besides Jack Daniel's." Cuszack had the can opened in no time and was surprised to find the peaches delicious. He was apparently hungrier than he'd initially thought.

In better spirits, and with peach juice soaking his beard, Cuszack asked, "Where we going?"

In response, Slocum offered his pack of Pall Malls and Zippo. Cuszack first lit Slocum's cigarette, and then his own.

"We're going west."

"Oh."

"Don't you want to go?"

"I got a trailer back in Coon Rapids and dogs to feed."

"Forget that shit," Slocum said. "It's behind you."

Buddy didn't answer. He slurped down the last of the peaches and tossed the can onto the floor of the truck.

"We're soldiers, you and me. Our whole lives, that's what we been the best at. Everything else we've done, we've been complete fuck-ups."

"Ah, it ain't as bad as all that."

"It's the truth, and you know it. Look at you. You was a gopher for a scumbag dope dealer who treated you like a dog. It's all you been since the war, somebody's dog. You was a fuckpunk in the VA hospital, remember? And you're a fuckpunk now."

Tears started down Cuszack's face. "Vern, that ain't true."

But he knew it was.

"It don't have to be that way, Buddy. You don't have to be a sniveling fuck all your life. You was a soldier once. You was a crew chief on a chopper in the Air-Cav, remember?"

Cuszack wiped snot from his nose and smoked his cigarette. He wouldn't look Slocum in the eye.

"I took care of you in the VA hospital, didn't I? I looked out for you."

"Yeah, Vern, but–"

"But nothing. I put you on your feet; gave you some fucking pride and dignity back. I done the same for you last night. Only you're too fucking stupid to know it."

"That ain't true," Buddy slobbered. "Zeke and Wolf were my friends, man."

"They wasn't your friends. They treated you like a slave. You were so fucked up all the time, you couldn't see it. Just like you can't see what I done for you last night. I freed you. Like in the VA. You owe me, Buddy."

Hearing Slocum say those words again sent chills down Cuszack's spine. He'd heard them before; in the VA hospital, and last night before entering Zeke's house and unleashing a bloodbath.

Suddenly flashing lights lit up the truck. Slocum glanced into the rearview mirror, and Cuszack craned his neck to look through the back window. The pulsating red and blue lights of a police car were rapidly approaching.

The snow-covered countryside added an eerie quality to the lights. The glistening white panorama turned a blinking red. Slocum put the truck into a lower gear and headed over to the side of the road.

Cuszack panicked.

"They know what you did at Zeke's! They know we're holding dope! They know about the guns! We gotta run for it! We gotta–"

Slocum silenced him with a backhand. He grabbed Cuszack by his collar and slammed him against the back of the seat.

"Shut the fuck up. He probably pulled us over because the truck's got no license plates. Let me handle it."

He braked the truck to a stop. The police car halted a car length behind. Slocum closed one eye to preserve half of his night vision. An instant later, as anticipated, a blinding spotlight was directed into the truck's cabin, illuminating the interior.

Cuszack sat petrified. With one eye closed, Slocum reached under the seat. He then switched off the ignition of the truck. With the engine quiet, the crunching sound of footsteps trudging through snow were audible. Leaving the keys in the ignition, he rolled down the window and unlatched the driver's door. He slipped his right hand into his jacket pocket.

The darting beams of two flashlights invaded the cabin. Their angle gave Slocum a general idea of both the distance and location of the two police officers directing them. One was on the truck's passenger's side, wading through the snowbank on the shoulder of the road. The other, most likely the driver of the patrol car, was approaching from the driver's side.

Slocum realized the car was not a sheriff's patrol, but belonged instead to the Iowa Highway Patrol. He could see the silhouette of their campaign hats in the halo of the spotlights.

"No matter what happens, Buddy," he whispered, "don't move. You got that? Don't fucking move."

Cuszack nodded meekly, frozen in fear. A state trooper appeared at the driver's side window.

"Evening, officer," Slocum said calmly. "What seems to be the problem?"

The trooper peered into the truck, shining his flashlight. His partner stood outside Cuszack's window. He saw the half-empty bottle of Jack Daniel's on the seat between the two occupants. When he looked at the driver, he saw a huge man with one eye closed staring back at him. Next he noticed the driver's hands out of view. By then it was too late.

Slocum slammed his shoulder into the truck's driver's door, flinging it open. The impact knocked the trooper to the snow-covered ground. In the same motion he drew the .45 from his pocket and fired three rounds at the trooper standing outside Cuszack's window. The gunshots were deafening in the confined space of the cabin, and were aimed across Cuszack's chest. Buddy stayed locked in place, temporarily blinded by the muzzle flashes.

Three holes materialized in the passenger's window, and then the flashlight was no longer shining its beam into the cabin. Slocum darted out of the truck, pulling the sawed-off shotgun from beneath his seat.

The trooper who'd been knocked senseless clawed at his holster, trying to regain his feet. Slocum kneed him in the face and he fell again. Slocum opened his closed eye, and closed the open one. He brought the sawed-off scattergun to bear on the downed trooper. The weapon roared, and the top of the trooper's head disappeared in a crimson spray.

Cuszack screamed unintelligibly. Slocum ignored his howls and crouched down, searching for the other trooper.

The remaining trooper was crouched on the opposite side of the truck. Like Slocum, he was using the engine block as cover. Slocum heard a voice over Cuszack's shrieking, and surmised the state cop was calling for help via his portable radio. He saw spots of blood staining the snow beneath the trooper's boots, and knew at least one of his .45 slugs struck its target.

Slocum found himself in a stalemate. He had one barrel left in the sawed-off, and five rounds in his pistol. He was certain the trooper had his own weapon ready, and was waiting for him to expose himself. He'd spent the element of surprise on his companion, and couldn't expect to catch the remaining trooper off guard.

He couldn't afford to wait for the trooper to make a mistake or succumb to his wounds. His radio call would soon bring every cop in the county, and the snowstorm could only delay their arrival a few moments at best.

Slocum looked under the truck, thankful he had the foresight to preserve his night vision as he'd been taught in the Corps. He could see one of the trooper's legs from the knee down.

It was enough.

Taking careful aim with the shotgun, he fired at the cop's leg. The trooper bellowed in agony and fell to the ground. Most of his foot, and the boot which once covered it, dissolved into a bloody pulp. Slocum took a hasty shot with his .45, but saw it go wide. The trooper rolled away from the truck and into the snow-filled ditch.

Slocum started to rush the trooper, but retreated when several bullets struck the fender of the truck, narrowly missing his head. He returned fire, angry with himself for wasting a precious bullet on a reflex shot.

It was a stalemate again. The trooper, though wounded at least twice, had taken cover in the ditch. Slocum's pistol was only three shots from empty, and the shotgun was now useless. The trooper had an unobstructed view of the truck, and he doubted the cop would miss again if given another shot. All the state cop had to do was wait for the cavalry to arrive.

Slocum bit his lip. He contemplated making a dash for the dead trooper's gun. That would mean breaking cover, and in all likelihood he'd be cut down. He thought about reaching into the cab of the truck and grabbing the AR-15 stashed under the seat. That would expose his legs, and leave him to the same fate as his now crippled adversary.

To do nothing, however, was certain death. Any moment more cops would swarm in. He had to act.

Slocum was preparing to rush the trooper, infantry-style, when he heard the truck's passenger door open. It was then he noticed Buddy had stopped screaming, although he couldn't remember when Cuszack had grown silent.

Shots rang out, a lot of them. Slocum could hear screams again, both Buddy's and the trooper's. He peeked over the hood of the truck, startled at what he saw.

Buddy Cuszack leaped from the truck with the AR-15 rifle. He charged the prone trooper, firing from the hip. The cop, who'd been focusing his aim at Slocum, hadn't seen Buddy emerge from the truck until too late. He was cut to pieces in a hail of fire from the semi-automatic weapon. He crumpled face down in the snow, steam rising from the countless holes in his body.

Cuszack continued to fire until the weapon's magazine was empty. Only when the bolt locked back, and the last brass casing spun off into the snow, did he cease firing. He dropped the rifle and sank to his knees, sobbing.

Slocum wasted no time. He ran to the trooper in the ditch and grabbed his revolver and spare ammo.

Pocketing the cop's weapon, he grabbed Cuszack and hoisted him into the truck. He tossed the AR-15 rifle in after him. He went to the other trooper's body next and took his revolver and spare ammo as well. He jumped into the truck, started the engine, and sped off.

Cuszack was in a catatonic state. Slocum patted him on the shoulder.

"You did real good back there, Buddy," he said. "I owe you."

A smile slowly spread across Buddy Cuszack's face.

CHAPTER 23

Deputy Kevin Kearns lay prone on the motel room floor grunting through a set of push-ups. He'd been alone for several hours since Farrell left to go grocery shopping. The retired San Francisco cop checked them into a Holiday Inn under the names Richard and Donald Henderson; father and son.

Kearns had the TV turned on, though was only half-heartedly paying attention. *Star Trek* was playing, but not the old reruns with Captain Kirk and Mister Spock. Commanding the *Enterprise* in this new show was a bald guy with a British accent. Kearns was about to switch the channel to something else when a member of the crew named Counselor Troi appeared on the screen in a uniform that showcased her cleavage. Kearns decided he liked the new *Star Trek*.

He was also thinking about what transpired within the last twenty-four hours. He was certain Sergeant Evers and the sheriff were wondering what happened to him, and guessed Special Agent Scanlon had already issued a warrant for his arrest.

He finished the push-ups and reversed his position to begin sit-ups. Exercise cleared his head. He needed a clear head now.

A few scant hours ago a stranger posing as his attorney lured him away from what was left of his ruined career.

That same stranger, now claiming to be an ex-San Francisco cop, convinced him to join forces and hunt a serial murderer named Vernon Slocum. A killer whose identity was known only to them.

Sweat glistened on his body. His brain felt as if it was also sweating.

Too much was happening too fast. He wondered if a more experienced cop would have avoided the series of events which led to his predicament. Frustrated at having no better instincts to rely on, he took out his anger on his muscles.

He pondered bracing Farrell when he returned, and telling the older cop he wanted out. Returning to the sheriff's department and facing the music. Informing Agent Scanlon and Sergeant Evers about Slocum and about the file Farrell swiped from the VA hospital. Maybe they would understand.

Not likely.

Kearns switched back to push-ups. He chuckled to himself over the irony of it all. The task force had no idea of Slocum's identity. An alcoholic ex-cop from California produced more by himself, in one afternoon, than the combined efforts of the Federal Bureau of Investigation, the Iowa State Police, and the Story County Sheriff's Department.

For all his seedy methods, the chain-smoking Californian got results.

Kearns got up to answer a loud and insistent pounding on the motel room door. He squinted through the peephole.

Farrell stood in the doorway laden with packages. He was knocking on the door with his foot. Kearns opened the door, and Farrell staggered into the room under the weight of his burden. He dropped his cargo on the bed and plopped down, out of breath.

"Getting your Christmas shopping done early?" Kearns said.

Farrell shrugged out of his trench coat and loosened his tie. "Give me a minute to catch my wind," he said, lighting a cigarette.

Farrell went to the bathroom and poured himself a large glass of water. Kearns had been exercising in his undershorts and now donned his trousers.

"Hell," remarked Farrell, noting Kearns' muscular torso. "If I'd known you were Charles Atlas I'd have brought you along to carry the groceries."

"You told me to wait here. I waited here."

"It was sound advice; by now most of the cops in Iowa will be looking for you."

"Thanks to you."

Farrell motioned for Kearns to sit down. He made an extravagant gesture of unpacking his purchases, which consisted of two large bags and an oblong-shaped box.

From the first bag Farrell produced a carton of Camel cigarettes and a bottle of Jim Beam bourbon whiskey. Kearns grunted. Next, his bony fingers brought out several pairs of thermal underwear and two packages of socks.

"We're not going to have time to do laundry," he said. "And it's cold as hell in this godforsaken state of yours."

Next came food, none of which seemed particularly healthy to Kearns. Instant coffee, doughnuts, pretzels, cough drops, breath mints, and a box of Oreo cookies.

"This is what you ventured out into a blizzard to get? These are the essentials?"

"One man's pill is another man's poison," Farrell said. "Be patient, young deputy, the best is yet to come."

He tossed the empty grocery bag aside and delved into the other. Its contents proved more interesting.

Farrell held up a Radio Shack box and handed it to Kearns. It was a police scanner.

"The guy at the mall sold me all the crystals for the police frequencies. Cost over a hundred dollars, but worth it. Here, this goes with it." He tossed Kearns a parcel. "It's an adapter that plugs into the car's cigarette lighter."

Digging further into the bag, Farrell withdrew two other items and set them on the table in front of Kearns.

"You carry a Smith & Wesson Model 19, two and a half inch, don't you?"

"How'd you know that?"

"You've been a cop as long as I have, you learn to check people for guns. Your coat pocket's a lousy place to carry your roscoe; you'll get a shitty draw. Try this."

He handed Kearns a holster. It was a Bianchi right-handed model for the S&W Model 19, two and a half inch barrel. With the holster was a box of cartridges in .38 Special +P caliber.

"You carry magnums in that six-gun?"

Kearns nodded.

"Lose them. You'll get more control with .38s out of a short barrel, and better recovery time between shots."

Kearns took his revolver from his coat pocket. The gun fit snugly in the new holster. Thumbing open the weapon's cylinder release, he ejected the six .357 magnum cartridges. He replaced them with the new .38 +Ps.

"I don't have any money to pay you for this."

"Don't mention it."

Next Farrell unpacked two flashlights and batteries. "I'm afraid of the dark," he said.

"What's in there?" Kearns asked, motioning to the oblong box. "Flowers?"

"Nah," Farrell said. "We're not at that stage of our relationship; maybe on the second date." He opened the box to reveal a shotgun. Kearns' eyes widened. Farrell hefted the weapon and held it lovingly at arm's length.

"Remington 870, twelve-gauge pump. Best goddamned law enforcement public-relations tool ever invented." Farrell placed the shotgun gingerly on the bed. He filled a plastic cup with ice and topped it with Jim Beam.

"What's the shotgun for?" Kearns asked.

"Butterfly hunting," Farrell said dryly.

"Fuck you."

Farrell ground out his cigarette.

"What do you think this is, boy: an Easter egg hunt?" The word "boy" was not lost on Kearns.

The Californian cocked his head to one side, appraising the Iowa deputy. "You think I'm a washed-up has-been who's deluded himself into thinking he's going to catch big bad Vernon Slocum, don't you?"

Kearns' silence was his answer.

"Yep, that's me," Farrell said. "A classic burnout." He took another swig. "But let's get something straight. I may be a has-been, but you're a never-been. You wouldn't know Slocum's name if it wasn't for me. You'd still be back at your hick town sheriff's department getting the third degree from a federal bureaucrat. Answering 'yes, sir,' and 'no, sir,' and wringing your hands. All because you fucked up bagging Slocum when you had the chance."

Kearns' eyes flashed, but he held his tongue.

"That's right. You fucked up. If you'd stopped Slocum in the schoolyard we wouldn't be here now. I wouldn't be freezing my gonads off in the middle of Iowa, and half the cops in the state wouldn't be missing dinner with their families. You'd be a hero, that kid wouldn't be dead, and your career wouldn't be in the sewer. Those are the facts."

"That's enough," Kearns said under his breath.

"No," Farrell said, gulping down the last of his bourbon. "It ain't enough. You've got some truth to face. We're the same, you and me. Vernon Slocum made us that way. I'm you, a few years from now. The blood of Tiffany Meade is as much on my hands as yours. I fucked up my chance to take Slocum out in Vietnam." He refilled his glass with bourbon. "It won't happen again."

"That was twenty years ago."

"Makes no difference. Just like you, I let him slip through my fingers. And another child paid for my fuck-up."

"You can't blame yourself. It was out of your hands."

Farrell grinned at Kearns. "You've been telling yourself that for a couple of days now. Sleeping any better?"

Kearns looked at the carpet.

"Well, kid," Farrell said, raising his glass in a mock toast, "if it's any consolation, I ain't been sleeping so good either." He emptied his glass for a second time.

Farrell's voice softened. "Kevin, the shotgun is because we'll need it. Do you think finding Slocum is going to be the hard part? Assuming we locate him, he's going to go out like a wolverine. If we aren't ready he'll leave us both hanging in a tree." Farrell ran his hands through his thinning hair. "Maybe I was wrong to drag you into this. I thought you understood what we're up against. I figured because of what happened in that schoolyard you'd want in. Maybe you'd better rethink this whole thing. You won't hurt my feelings if you want out."

"I don't want to quit. I know what I'm getting into."

"I'm not sure you do. I can't have you along if you're going to question everything I do. Like I said, this ain't a butterfly hunt."

"Cut me some slack. Six hours ago I didn't know who Vernon Slocum was. I don't want out."

"You sure?"

"I'm sure. Just start treating me like a partner instead of a subordinate. If I knew what you were up to, I wouldn't have to question you all the time."

"Fair enough."

The men shook hands awkwardly.

"Jesus," Farrell said. "You don't want a hug, do you?"

"Not likely. I'm going to hit the shower."

"About time; you smell like a goat. Soon as you're done we'll get a bite to eat. I'm starving."

"I forgot," Kearns called out from the bathroom. "You told Scanlon you were taking me out to lunch."

"So I lied. It was dinner."

While Kearns showered, Farrell field-stripped the shotgun and cleaned off the Cosmoline. He switched the channel from *Star Trek* to a local news broadcast.

"…our top story tonight: In the wake of a fiery explosion outside Coon Rapids today, investigators have ruled out the possibility of an accidental cause in the blaze. State arson inspectors would not comment on the incident, but this station has learned that foul play is definitely suspected. Ron Rawlings is live in Coon Rapids."

Farrell finished wiping off the packing grease and began to oil the shotgun's components.

"As you can see behind me, firefighters still haven't completely subdued the tenacious fire, which they've been battling all afternoon. It appears hazardous chemicals inside the barn are responsible for the firefighters' inability to put out the inferno. Though there has been no official confirmation, several bodies have been pulled from the farmhouse. We were also able to confirm with an anonymous member of the Carroll

County Sheriff's Department that the farmhouse was the location of a narcotics search warrant last May. We're still trying to get further on that. This is Ron Rawlings, on the scene at Coon Rapids. Back to you, Dave."

On screen, the anchorman looked down at a sheet of paper.

"This just in. Rural Pottawattamie County, east of the Nebraska State line, was the scene of a double homicide today. Two Iowa state troopers were found murdered near their patrol car, victims of an apparent ambush. The names of the troopers have been withheld pending notification of their families. There are no suspects in custody at this time, though authorities assure us every effort is being made to identify the suspect in this crime."

Farrell reassembled the shotgun. He worked the pump action, satisfied the weapon was functional. He then loaded four rounds of buckshot into the magazine but left the chamber empty.

"In other news, a candlelight vigil was held in Nevada tonight, outside Franklin D Roosevelt Elementary school. Less than one week ago, seven year-old Tiffany Meade was kidnapped here, and her beloved teacher was gunned down trying to prevent it. Meade was murdered later that day, her body discovered at a highway rest stop. Representatives from several area churches were on hand, and despite the inclement weather, a large crowd of mourners have gathered. The mood here is somber."

Farrell watched hundreds of people standing in the frigid weather. Their candles glowed eerily in the twilight, and a priest led the assembly in the Lord's Prayer. Many were crying. The image changed to a reporter interviewing Tiffany Meade's mother at home, surrounded by her family.

Farrell didn't hear the shower stop in the background. He listened to the mother of a dead child talk about a Christmas which would never be merry again. She spoke of her daughter and displayed a set of coloring books the little girl had purchased with her allowance as a Christmas present for her younger brother.

Riveted to the TV, Farrell didn't notice Kearns enter the room.

"…an unusual footnote to the Meade tragedy. FBI Special Agent Steve Scanlon, supervising the task force assigned to catch the killer, reported today that Deputy Kevin Kearns, the off-duty officer who allegedly battled the girl's assailant in an effort to thwart the kidnapping, is now missing. Scanlon said Deputy Kearns was last seen in the company of an unidentified man who claimed to be his attorney. Scanlon would not speculate what this strange new development means. We'll take a break, and when we come back, we'll have all the basketball highlights from the Cyclones' battle with the Hawkeyes. Stay with us."

Farrell reached over and switched off the television. Kearns stared at the lifeless screen. His face was ashen.

"Scanlon's implying I'm involved. It's happening just like you said."

"Don't let it bother you," Farrell said.

"Could you?"

"You got me there," Farrell acknowledged.

CHAPTER 24

Deputy Kevin Kearns woke to the sounds of a loud and off-key rendition of "Anything Goes." He sat up in bed and rubbed his eyes. The hotel room was a haze of second-hand cigarette smoke. Farrell sat at the table in his newly purchased thermal underwear, singing around the Camel in his lips. He was shaved and showered and his thinning hair was not yet dry.

Kearns glanced at the luminous hands of his watch. It was just after 6am. He'd spent a fitful night tossing and turning and hadn't actually fallen asleep until well after midnight. The last thing he saw before drifting off was Farrell, seated at the table with his bottle of bourbon and cigarettes. The retired cop was reading the thick file on Vernon Slocum they'd taken from the veterans' hospital.

"Morning, Deputy," Farrell quipped. "It's time to get up. We've got a boon to doggle, and you're burning daylight."

If the older detective showed any signs of getting no sleep, Kearns couldn't see them. He rolled out of bed and headed for the shower, his head in a fog.

When he emerged from the bathroom, Farrell was fully dressed. Their things were packed, and the contents of Slocum's file were no longer scattered on the table.

While Kearns dressed, Farrell gulped a cup of instant coffee and wrapped the shotgun in his coat. Kearns finished by belting on his revolver and donning his coat.

Soon the men were outside in the bitter cold of the hotel parking lot and loading the Oldsmobile. The snow had stopped, and the sky seemed devoid of clouds. The sun had yet to show its face over the horizon.

"Blizzard seems to have passed," Kearns commented. "Hopefully the roads will be clear."

"You drive," Farrell said, tossing Kearns the keys.

Kearns caught them in mid-air and unlocked the door. Once inside, he fired up the engine and put on the heater. Farrell withdrew the shotgun from under his coat and tucked it lengthwise under the front seat.

"We're heading for Boone, Iowa, or thereabouts; a place called Ogden. It's east of Ames, on Highway 30, according to the map."

"I know where it is," said Kearns, putting the Oldsmobile into gear and heading out of the motel lot. "What's in Ogden?"

"The medical file says Slocum grew up on a farm there. Says he has a father still living there, and a couple of brothers and a sister. Maybe one of them has a line on where he is."

"That's a good place to start," said Kearns. "But what if his family doesn't want to talk to us?"

"Let me worry about that. We'll make an investigator out of you yet."

Kearns grunted and scanned the streets for the entrance ramp to I-35 North. Farrell busied himself with removing the police/fire scanner from its box, and plugged it into the car's dashboard cigarette lighter. Soon the familiar crackle of police radio traffic filled the car.

Sitting back with a satisfied look, he gave Kearns a grin and lit a cigarette.

Kearns rolled down the window, letting in a blast of icy air.

"Are you trying to freeze me out?"

"Are you trying to smoke me out?"

"Hell, kid, a little cigarette smoke won't kill you. But pneumonia will. Close that window."

"Actually, a little cigarette smoke will kill you," Kearns said. He reluctantly rolled the window back up.

"I've been smoking longer than you've been alive, and I'm still here."

"That's because you've embalmed yourself in bourbon. You're already dead and don't know it."

"Shut up and drive, will you?" But he rolled down his window and tossed his freshly lit cigarette out the window. "I didn't want it anyway."

Kearns grinned at his victory. Farrell wrapped the collar of his coat more tightly around himself. "Let me know when we get there," he said.

Kearns listened to the chatter from the police scanner as the older cop snoozed beside him. On good roads, Ogden was about an hour away. Today, it would be after 9am before Kearns finally passed Boone on Highway 30. He gave Farrell a nudge.

"We'll be in Ogden in about ten minutes," Kearns said. "You know how to get to Slocum's farm?"

Farrell sat up from where he was slumped in the seat and ran his fingers through his thin hair. Lighting a cigarette, he pulled a stack of AAA maps from the glove box and began to shuffle through them.

Kearns followed Farrell's directions to a county road marker and turned off the highway. The road appeared to have been scooped sometime during the night, and progress, though slow, was deliberate. They'd traveled less than two miles on the flat road when Farrell said, "Should be the next farmhouse on the right."

Sure enough, a dilapidated farmstead gradually came into view. It was a large two-story home with a sagging roof and a barn in the back. The barn had long since lost its paint, and in many spots they could see light through its walls. Like the house, the barn's roof was bent under the weight of the snow covering it.

The yard in front of the house was full of junk: gutted automobiles and rusted farm implements. Kearns pulled the Oldsmobile carefully to the end of the long driveway, wary of objects that might lay hidden under the thick blanket of snow. He switched off the engine and both men stepped out of the car.

A thin trail of smoke drifted lazily from the chimney of the farmhouse, and the faint scent of burning wood filled the crisp air. Kearns looked uneasily over at Farrell, who was studying the lettering stenciled on a battered black mailbox at the end of the drive. It read, *Emil J Slocum*.

"This is the place," Kearns said.

"This place is out of *The Grapes of Wrath*," Farrell observed. "I expect the Clampetts to drive up in a Model-T Ford. Do any of you Iowans know it's the twentieth century?"

"Want to know what Iowans think of the typical San Francisco dweller?"

"I can guess. C'mon, let's knock on the door. Looks like somebody's inside."

The two men were wading through shin-deep snow towards the house. A feral growl stopped them dead in their tracks. They slowly turned to look behind them.

Less than twenty feet away stood a very large pit bull. The dog had obviously come from within one of the dilapidated hulks in the yard, aroused by the approach of the Oldsmobile. The dog had gray around its jowls, and the plume of its breath puffed from flared nostrils. Its eyes were bright and its teeth were bared. It stared directly at Farrell and Kearns, growling in a low, steady tone.

Neither man moved. The dog appeared ready to spring, and could cover the distance between the two intruders in no more than a second.

"What are we going to do?" said Kearns under his breath.

"Shut up," snapped Farrell. "Don't move; don't even step back."

Kearns noticed Farrell slowly reaching his hand into his coat. The dog growled louder, and saliva dripped from its mouth. He noticed that the pit bull, though large, was very thin, with protruding ribs and eyes sunken in their sockets. It was not a reassuring observation.

Kearns' hand crept towards the revolver under his coat. He angrily realized that unlike Farrell, his coat was buttoned, and his gun inaccessible. He realized the older cop never had his coat buttoned. Until this moment, he'd chalked it up to Farrell's slovenly style. He understood now it was a professional habit by a veteran cop. Farrell could always reach his gun. Once again Kearns mentally kicked himself for his inexperience.

Kearns was still fumbling to unbutton his coat when Farrell's worn .38 came out. The dog began to bark; loud, chirping howls intermixed with growls. Kearns knew the dog was preparing to charge. He frantically tried to work the overcoat buttons. His numbed fingers only made progress slower, and he swore at himself for his stupidity in buttoning up over his gun.

Farrell apparently also knew the huge dog was preparing to attack. He said, "Shit!" under his breath, and brought up his revolver in a two-handed aim. Kearns finally got his overcoat open, and was drawing his own weapon, when both men heard the unmistakable sound of a pump-action shotgun being racked.

"You shoot that dog and it'll be the last shootin' you ever do," came a harsh voice.

Both men slowly turned back to the farmhouse to find an old man standing on the porch. The man had an 1897 Winchester pump-action shotgun directed at them, and seemed well-versed in its operation. The pit bull was still growling.

"Beauty," snapped the man to the dog. "Get! You heard me; get on outta' here!"

The dog instantly quieted, and trotted back to its home within a junked sedan. Kearns and Farrell still didn't breathe a sigh of relief. They stared at the man on the porch.

"Out of the frying pan..." said Farrell.

Kearns recognized the man on the porch as the father of the man he'd fought in the schoolyard. The resemblance was stark, and it sent chills through the young deputy's gut.

The man stood well over six feet tall, though had to be in his late sixties or early seventies. He had a raw-boned, powerful build; the build of a man who'd made his living with his hands. He was nearly bald; stray strands of wispy gray hair fell behind his ears. He was clad in a pair of overalls and grease-stained work boots. It was his face, however, that was the most compelling.

The man's right eye was obviously sightless, a murky gray orb that gave Kearns the impression of infection. The skin on his face had the color and consistency of worn leather, and he had the same broad Nordic jaw as his son. His good eye was squinting down the barrel of the shotgun, which was still steadily pointed at Kearns and Farrell.

"Take it easy with that scattergun, Mister Slocum. Don't do anything one of us is going to regret." Farrell spoke in a clear, calm voice. Kearns was impressed with the San Francisco cop's cool demeanor. He could feel the adrenaline coursing through his own body and was mentally preparing to shoot, all too aware that the old man already had the drop on them.

"Relax, Kevin, let me handle this," Farrell said, as if reading Kearns' mind.

"Mister Slocum, would you mind pointing that shotgun somewhere else?"

"When I know who you are and what you're up to, maybe I'll consider it," said the elder Slocum, "but not until. You're government men, ain't you?"

Farrell slowly put his revolver back into its holster and brought out his empty hand, at the same time nodding for Kearns to do the same. Reluctantly, Kearns complied.

"That's right," Farrell said. "We're government men. We came to talk to you. We didn't mean to frighten your dog, but we didn't see him when we drove up. We've put our guns away. Would you please not point that gun at us anymore? It's making my partner real nervous."

Wordlessly, the old man relaxed his grip on the shotgun. "I got nothing to say to no damned government men."

Kearns had no idea what the old man was babbling about. Farrell winked at him, and turned back to Slocum.

"Mister Slocum, that's what we're here about. The government realizes you've been slighted in the past, and we've been sent to make amends. We need your full story, so we can make a report and conclude the entire incident. Perhaps make reparation. May we come in and talk to you? It's awfully cold out here, and I think you'll want to hear what we have to say."

Kearns felt the same sense of dread he felt in the VA hospital when he'd unwittingly followed Farrell on his illegal scavenger hunt. This old man, with the blood of his son burning in his veins, was no docile hospital administrator. Emil Jensen Slocum was senile, half-blind, possibly deranged, and in possession of an ancient but undoubtedly functional and loaded shotgun, which he appeared prepared to use. He was no candidate for Farrell's deceitful schemes. But just like at the veterans' hospital, Kearns found himself already mired in the impossible drama. He felt he was again in a situation that an experienced cop would have avoided with ease. He was angry with Farrell for again putting him in jeopardy, and angrier with himself for letting it happen.

"We'll only take a few minutes of your time and be on our way. You can set the record straight."

The elder Slocum stared at the two men for long minutes while Kearns and Farrell squinted back at him in the bright sunlight. Finally Slocum lowered the shotgun to his side and walked back into the house. He left the door open, and Farrell wasted no time covering the distance to the porch. Kearns scrambled to keep up.

Kearns noticed when Slocum walked into the house he shuffled along with a distinct limp. He followed Farrell inside.

Kearns' eyes struggled to adjust. The shades and shutters in the farmhouse were drawn, and going inside from the bright sunlight of the outside left him momentarily blinded. Slocum closed the door, and it became as black as night.

Kearns smelled a variety of odors, none of them pleasant: dirty laundry, urine, and feces, the rank odor of spoiled food and exhaled cigarette smoke. As his eyesight gradually returned, he saw sights no more pleasant than the smells which emanated from them.

The interior of the house was almost uninhabitable. Piles of everything from tools, to clothing, to food, were scattered everywhere. The walls were water-stained, and Kearns was glad it was cold outside. In the heat of an Iowa summer the house would be ideal for insect breeding.

There was nowhere to sit down. There was no furniture not covered in piles of one form of junk or another. Slocum shuffled in his hobbling-gait to the only available seat, a dilapidated easy chair.

On a shelf above the fireplace, Kearns was surprised to see what appeared to be a picture of the man he'd fought in the schoolyard. He was wearing a Marine Corps dress-blue uniform. Closer inspection revealed it to be a black-and-white photo, and faded with age. It was the elder Slocum, circa World War II.

"Were you in the Corps?" asked Kearns, unable to look away from the photo.

"Goddamned right, boy. Left my leg on Okinawa. You a Marine?"

"No sir. Army infantry."

"See any combat?" demanded the old man gruffly.

"No."

"All my boys served in the Corps, 'cept one. Combat, too, in Vietnam. Vern came back with more medals than me. Wade came back in a rubber bag."

Farrell spoke next. "Mister Slocum, may I use your bathroom? It seems your dog frightened me more than I thought; my stomach is upset."

"Hell, a little ole dog growls at you, and you government men shit your pants. Go ahead, it's at the end of the hall. There ain't no toilet paper, though."

Farrell gave Kearns a, 'stall him' signal and disappeared down the hallway in the direction of the worst of the smells.

Kearns struggled to make conversation, his mind suddenly blank. "Uh, you said one of your sons didn't go into the Marines. Where is he?"

"I don't know, and I don't care. He was a coward. He ran away. It was shameful. I ain't seen nor heard from him since, and if he showed his face now I'd shoot him faster than I'd have plugged you."

Kearns gulped. He didn't doubt that a bit. "Did you have any daughters?"

The old man rose to his feet and towered over Kearns, his good eye glaring.

"What about her? She send you? I don't give a goddamned who you are, G-man! You ever speak of her again, I'll kill you! You understand me, boy?"

Kearns took a step back and wished to hell Farrell would hurry up in the bathroom. He could see the burning hatred in the old man's one good eye, and the mottled orb that was his other eye didn't dilute the emotion. He was convinced the elder Slocum was insane.

"Take it easy, sir... I didn't mean to offend you. I was only making conversation. If I said something that angered you, I'm sorry."

The pointing finger of Slocum's right hand darted out and struck Kearns' chest like a rod of iron. He loomed over the deputy.

"My daughter is a slut. She's the Whore of Babylon. I don't allow her name to be spoken in my presence. You knew that, didn't you? You knew that all along. That's why you came, to remind me of Elizabeth? Ain't that so? You government men will never leave me in peace, will you? Always prodding. Well I won't allow it! Do you hear? I won't stand for it!"

Kearns had no idea what the old man was rambling about, but it was obvious Slocum was becoming highly agitated. Where was Farrell?

In answer, Farrell appeared behind Slocum. He grabbed the large old man by his hair and pulled him down into the chair. He moved to face Slocum, his .38 in his fist. Pointing it at the old Marine's face he kicked the shotgun, which had been leaning against the chair, across the room.

"Calm your ass down, old man. You've done enough ranting for one day."

Kearns breathed a sigh of relief. The elder Slocum, perhaps because of his resemblance to his son, had rattled him.

"Tell me about your wife and daughter, Mister Slocum?"

At this, Slocum seemed ready to leap from the chair and strike as his dog in the yard had nearly done.

"Go ahead, asshole," Kearns was shocked to hear Farrell say. "Go for it. You feel froggy, you leap. I'll put a bullet in your head for trying."

"You can't come in here and talk to me like that," Slocum spat vehemently. "I know my rights! Couple of government bullies, come to abuse an old man in his home. I'm a veteran! I shouldn't be treated like this! I'm gonna call–"

"Who're you going to call, baby-raper?"

Slocum recoiled at this. Kearns stood behind Farrell, aghast. What mad ploy was the renegade cop up to now?

"Go on," Farrell continued, "answer the question. Who're you going to call? Who's going to listen to a man convicted of molesting his own daughter?"

Slocum leaped at Farrell with a speed surprising for one of his age and condition. Farrell expected this, and he sidestepped the old man, chopping his neck with his revolver butt. Slocum sprawled on his face in the rubbish of his floor.

Kearns couldn't believe what he was witnessing. This time, the Californian had gone too far. It was one thing to pilfer a few faded documents from a hospital basement; quite another to enter a man's home under false pretenses and physically abuse him.

Farrell holstered his revolver. He reached down and retrieved the shotgun from the floor and ejected the shells from its chamber and magazine. Scattering the rounds, he threw the shotgun into the hall. Slocum lay on the ground trying to catch his breath, which was shallow and hoarse. Kearns feared the old man might have a heart attack.

"If I was twenty years younger," the elder Slocum sputtered, "I'd kill you with my bare hands."

Farrell stood over him and laughed. "Be glad you aren't. If you were, I'd dispose of you right now."

Farrell nodded to Kearns and then to the door. Kearns was more than ready to leave. He opened the door, flooding the interior of the house with light. As the two men left Farrell turned back to Slocum, who was struggling to get up.

"Old man," Farrell said evenly. "I'm going to catch Vernon. And when I do, I'm going to kill him."

Farrell left the house. Kearns followed with a look of amazement and horror on his young face. As Farrell waded to the car, he drew his snub-nosed .38 and aimed it at the gutted car where the pit bull resided. This time, however, no dog appeared. Both men reached the car unscathed. Getting in, Kearns started the engine immediately.

"What in the hell was that all about?" Kearns asked angrily. "How does catching this guy Slocum involve beating his elderly father up? And where do you get off telling him you're going to kill his son?"

Farrell ignored the barrage of questions and calmly lit one of his unfiltered cigarettes. After inhaling deeply, he turned to Kearns. "Kevin, I suggest you drive us away from this place. It isn't going to take Old Man Slocum long to get up, load his shotgun, and make it to the porch. I don't relish the idea of getting shot by that old coot. Do you?"

Kearns wanted to hit him. But as usual, the Californian's logic was irrefutable. He angrily drove out of the yard.

Once on the road Farrell spoke.

"Don't be pissed off, Kevin. I didn't have time to explain myself back there. I'll answer your questions before you ask them. Last night, while you slept, I read the file from the veterans' hospital. It contains the records of his therapy sessions, his psychological profiles, and medical records."

"Some bedtime story."

"In those records is evidence that Vernon Slocum, as well as his two brothers and sister, were sexually abused by their father from the time they were very small."

Kearns began to feel uneasy again. Farrell continued.

"The records of Slocum's therapy sessions indicate he was sexually abused as a child, right up until the time he left for the Marines. Vernon was the second oldest of three boys, and had a younger sister. Elizabeth was her name. Apparently their mother died under suspicious circumstances."

"What kind of suspicious circumstances?" Kearns' curiosity had overtaken his anger, and he was calmer since they had put distance between the Slocum farm and themselves.

"According to the records she had a miscarriage, and died from the resulting hemorrhaging. It was suspected, but never proven, that Slocum's wife was beaten, probably causing the miscarriage in the first place."

"How could he get away with that?"

"Child protection laws, spousal abuse laws, and mandatory reporting laws hadn't been enacted yet. Besides, this is a remote rural area now. Think about what it must have been like just after World War II."

Kearns nodded. "Even if somebody suspected Emil was abusing his wife and kids nobody would have acted on it. A man was left alone to raise his family."

"Old man Slocum didn't get away with it forever. In the early Sixties he was arrested for sexually abusing his daughter, Elizabeth. She was thirteen years old. It had probably been going on for a long time, but it came out in school when she told a teacher. Elizabeth was put into foster care and apparently old Slocum hasn't seen her since."

"I doubt she's going to show up on Father's Day with a necktie," Kearns said.

Farrell exhaled smoke. "I guess the state didn't believe a man would fuck his own boys, because after he was convicted on the charges he abused his daughter he did a couple of years in Fort Dodge and returned to his farm and custody of his three sons. Shortly after, Vernon left for Vietnam. Vernon's older brother Wade died there. The youngest son, Cole, ran away."

"No wonder the old guy came unglued when I asked him about his daughter. He must despise her for blowing the whistle on him."

"I'm sure the feeling is mutual."

"So tell me something," asked Kearns. "If you knew all this from the file we snatched at the veterans' hospital, why did we need to visit the old man?"

"Did you think I was really going to the bathroom?

While you were engaged in banter with the charming Emil Slocum, I was tossing his house."

"You ransacked his house?"

"Twenty years of working property crimes, a guy picks up a few burglary techniques. Take a look."

Farrell pulled a thick sheaf of papers from the inside pocket of his coat. Many were torn and yellowed with age. There were quite a few newspaper clippings in the pile.

"Did you find anything we can use to track Vernon?"

"I won't know until I look the stuff over. Thanks for buying me the time to find it. It wasn't easy in all that mess. Most of these papers were in a box under his bed."

"Next time clue me in before you put my head into the lion's mouth."

CHAPTER 25

"We're going to Omaha to track down Slocum's sister, Elizabeth," Farrell said, in answer to Kearns' request for a destination.

They were westbound on Highway 30 again, heading for the Missouri River and the Nebraska/Iowa border. Farrell dug under the seat for his briefcase, from which he withdrew the thick file he'd taken from the veterans' hospital.

"While you were snoozing last night," Farrell said, "I was doing homework."

"Learn anything else from Slocum's file we can use?"

"Apparently the headshrinkers found him somewhat disturbed."

"There's an earth-shattering diagnosis for you."

"Yeah," Farrell said chuckling. "Only took the doctors twenty years to come up with that one. Anyway, I was focusing on details which might lead us to his current whereabouts."

"That's where you got the address of Slocum's father."

"Right. And the information about his father's criminal history."

"It would appear your late night reading paid off," Kearns said, biting his lip. "Let's hope what we got today does as well."

Farrell shook his head. "What I found at the Slocum's farm is valuable, but for a different reason. I'll get to that in a minute."

"So you weren't bluffing back there? About the old man molesting his own kids?"

"I wasn't making anything up. And what I've read so far is beginning to form a definite pathology."

"Pathology?"

"That's medical lingo for how he became a monster." Farrell sifted through more of the papers in the file. "Slocum was the second oldest child; Elizabeth the youngest. When he was seven years-old, his sister almost two, Slocum's father beat his mother after finding out she was pregnant again. I guess beatings around the Slocum household were pretty common, but this one was particularly savage."

"You told me about this already. Slocum's wife died as a result."

"What I didn't tell you was that Vernon witnessed the incident, including seeing his father kick his pregnant mother repeatedly in the stomach. This came out in some of his therapy sessions."

"Jesus," Kearns said under his breath. "No wonder he turned out all screwed up."

"It gets worse. After the death of his wife, Emil Slocum began drinking more heavily, beating the children more severely, and on or about Vernon's tenth birthday, began molesting Vernon."

"How could a man do that to his own son?"

"I wish I knew. Or maybe I don't."

"What kind of abuse are we talking about?" Kearns asked tentatively.

"You name it, old man Slocum did it. Sodomy, oral copulation, beatings, starvation, cold water dousing, isolation, electric shocks; the whole nine yards. Most of this was revealed during narcotic-assisted hypnosis sessions. Apparently a lot of this stuff Vernon buried somewhere deep in his mind."

"Sure," chided Kevin. "He blocked it out. It's called repression. I learned about it in the academy. Lots of victims do it."

"That's right."

"Sounds like a horror movie." Kearns said.

"I'm sure for the Slocum children, it was."

"How did it end?"

"Old Emil Slocum signed Vernon into the Marines as soon as the kid turned seventeen: the minimum age of enlistment. This was a year after he'd signed Wade, Vernon's older brother, into the Corps, also on his seventeenth birthday. Soon Vernon was in Vietnam earning medals."

"What happened to Wade?"

"He was killed in action within a month of getting in-country."

"Vernon must have taken it pretty hard."

Farrell rubbed his chin. "Report doesn't really say. That time in Slocum's life was dominated by another crisis."

"His sister."

"Excellent," Farrell smiled. "You're becoming a detective. While Vernon was deep in the jungle he received word that his sister Elizabeth, who'd just turned thirteen, was taken into foster care. Vernon's younger brother, Cole, ran away."

"So while Vernon is off fighting in the jungle, one brother is killed, the other runs away, his little sister is taken into protective custody, and…"

"…and his father is sent to prison," Farrell finished. "A shining chapter in the Slocum family saga." Farrell extracted another paper from the thick file. "Vernon was in the VA hospital from the late Sixties, after I met him in Saigon, until the fall of 1986."

"Why so long?"

"He was probably doped up. It's common practice to keep mental patients under constant sedation with heavy-duty narcotics; makes for a docile patient. The side-effects of these drugs are often confused with the symptoms of whatever mental disorder the patient is supposedly being treated for. Kind of a Catch-22."

"So why was he released? Did the doctors think he was cured?"

Farrell laughed out loud. "Not likely. I can guess the answer, though it's not in the records. President Reagan cut the funding for all the mental hospitals when he took office."

"I remember reading about that," Kearns said. "Everybody was worried about what was going to happen when all these crazies hit the streets. It was all over the news. Veterans' advocacy groups and mental health professionals were up in arms about it."

"Sure. When the money ran out, thousands of psychologically ill people, including vets, supposedly too dangerous to be out walking the streets, were simply kicked loose. They were suddenly declared cured simply because the VA's budget had to be tightened."

"It boggles the mind. Twenty years in a psych-ward, and one day when it's penny-pinching time he gets turned loose." Kearns shook his head. "Didn't they know what they were unleashing?"

"I doubt it. His crimes in Vietnam were never put on record. The docs probably thought Slocum was just another combat burnout. No different than any other docile, doped-up patient."

"Hell of a way to run a railroad," Kearns said.

"Nobody ever said the Federal Government was perfect."

"Even if we find Elizabeth in Omaha, will she know where to find Vernon?"

"Have a little faith. Apparently Elizabeth corresponded with Vernon while he was in the VA hospital, and on one occasion, in 1984, came to visit. She was in her thirties then, and according to notes of one of Vernon's therapy sessions, working for the Catholic Diocese in Omaha somewhere. She'd started a career in counseling and was affiliated with Boys Town. That's where we're going now; to see if we can get a line on her that might lead us to Vernon."

"First we go to Vernon's father's place. Now we go after his sister?"

"Take a look at this." Farrell withdrew a stack of handwritten letters from inside his coat pocket. "I found these on the nightstand in old man Slocum's bedroom."

"When you were supposed to be taking a shit, and Emil and I were getting chummy?"

"Yep," Farrell said smugly. "Thanks again for the diversion. These are letters from Elizabeth to her father, some dated as recently as four months ago."

"Is there a return address?" Kearns asked.

"Yeah. Elizabeth still lives in Omaha, on Leawood West, near 132nd Street.

"I don't get it." said Kearns. "Why would Elizabeth reach out to the man who molested her as a child?"

"I haven't had much of a chance to do more than skim the letters, but it seems Elizabeth works as a counselor. In her earlier letters she mentions having a master's degree and working with abused children."

"That fits."

"I agree. A lot of people who've been abused end up as counselors; the same reason a lot of recovering alcoholics and drug addicts end up working with people who are similarly afflicted. Anyway, it seems Elizabeth has been writing to her father for a couple of years, trying to convince him to get help. At least the letters appear to be written in that tone."

"Wow," said Kearns. "This Elizabeth Slocum must be a saint. If something like that happened to me, helping the person who did it would be at the bottom of my 'to do' list."

"I gather Elizabeth got no response from old Emil. She ends all the letters with a plea for him to at least write her back."

Kearns grunted. "He called her the Whore of Babylon. I'm not sure she wants to hear what he'd have to say."

"I wouldn't," Farrell said.

"So that's our plan?" Kearns said. "Find Elizabeth and see if she can lead us to Vernon?"

"You got it."

"What if she won't help us?"

"Her father didn't want to help, but look at all he gave us. I've got a hunch Elizabeth will put us in the right direction. Sometimes when you're tracking someone you fly by the seat of your pants. It isn't always logical, but hunches can be as fruitful as anything else."

"I wouldn't know," Kearns replied sarcastically. "I'm too green to have any investigative hunches."

"Then look at the bright side, kid. You're getting a wealth of experience. Think of it as on-the-job training."

Kearns stared at the road ahead. "Omaha it is. We'll be there by late afternoon if the weather holds out." He paused and looked at the older cop hesitantly.

"Thanks for keeping me out of the dark."

Farrell stowed the letters into his coat pocket. "I promised no more fast ones Kevin, and I meant it. You do the driving and leave the worrying to me. The trail's getting warmer. When we catch up to Vernon Slocum I'm going to need you in my corner. I won't jeopardize that. I'll be dealing from the top of the deck from here on out."

"How will I know if you don't?"

CHAPTER 26

Buddy Cuszack had purpose.

He sat behind the wheel of the truck with the engine idling. His hands were steady and he wasn't trembling, even though the falling night brought the temperature down with it. The AR-15 rifle lay concealed, yet within easy reach, under the seat.

He was keeping watch.

The pick-up truck was parked at the intersection of 24th and Lake, not far from Creighton University, though far from the pleasantries of college life. This was one of Omaha's worst districts, and OPD cruisers motored past regularly. The neighborhood was mostly African-American and Hispanic, and in the low-to-illegal income bracket. Run-down houses were interspersed between tenements, bars, hotels, and mission-churches. Even in inclement weather, hookers, hustlers, and drug addicts wandered the streets, dodging the cops and searching for victims.

Cuszack was a changed man ever since he and Vernon Slocum left two Iowa state troopers in a blood-spattered snowdrift. The time before that seemed only a hazy memory. Buddy had returned to the war.

Slocum had come back. He had again pulled Cuszack from the mire of his own subservice. Thanks to him,

Buddy was no longer a man who whored himself and did the bidding of men like Zeke and Wolf. Slocum had given him his dignity back.

Buddy was a soldier again. He'd proven that in Iowa, in combat. In a firefight against two armed men. No matter that they were cops; they'd tried to kill Vernon, and therefore were the enemy. Slocum needed him, and he'd done his part. He knew he owed the big former Marine his life, but for the first time felt he was on his way to paying that debt. It felt good to be needed.

Both men hadn't slept in over two days. They'd taken back roads through western Iowa, across the Missouri River into Omaha. They stayed hidden during the day and moved at night. Buddy split the watches with Vernon, eager to stand guard and be useful. They split the crank, too. Until now, Buddy used meth when he could get it, but usually he couldn't. Now he and Vernon had a seemingly endless supply, courtesy of Zeke. He'd consumed more speed in the last two days than in the entire year previously.

The methamphetamine kept both men alert, and Buddy never felt so alive. It was good to be on a mission. He knew the meth blurred the lines between delusion and reality, but didn't care. For Buddy Cuszack, reality had always been worse.

After Buddy saved Slocum's life in Iowa, Vernon treated him differently, with respect. The two men seldom spoke, and Slocum hardly ever gave orders to Buddy any more. He didn't have to.

Buddy sat in the truck and waited, standing his watch. Vernon had left an hour ago, taking only his .45 pistol and a bindle of methamphetamine. Buddy didn't have to be told to wait; he knew. He circled the block occasionally, sometimes parking on different corners of the intersection, sometimes pulling into the parking lot of a nearby restaurant, sometimes getting out and stretching his legs. He didn't want to attract the attention of any cops.

Slocum had gone into the Lakeside Hotel, a seedy-looking, by-the-hour flophouse situated over a tattoo parlor. Buddy had kept the truck inconspicuously away from the hotel, but near enough to get there in a hurry. He was thinking tactically for the first time in years.

In the hour that had passed since Slocum had left, the traffic on 24th had gone from moderate to light. Most of the hookers had given up approaching the cars as they stopped for the changing lights and resigned themselves to soliciting the pedestrians stumbling in and out of the saloons lining both sides of the street. Buddy kept his eyes roving, scanning the perimeter for the enemy.

Slocum came out of the hotel, moving fast. Something wasn't right though; Buddy could tell. The normally-confident Marine walked too rapidly and looked to his left and right too much to not attract attention. A moment later Cuszack saw why.

Emerging from the hotel on Slocum's tail was a large, solid-looking African-American man. He was no taller than Vernon, but much broader than Slocum's sizable girth. He caught up to Slocum a few steps from the hotel and grabbed Vernon by the shoulder.

Buddy knew his cue. He put the Dodge into gear and pulled up to the sidewalk adjacent to where Slocum was standing. Ignoring the AR-15 as too cumbersome, he reached his bony hand under the blanket on the passenger seat and came up with the sawed-off shotgun. Breaking open the action, he ensured it had been reloaded since the shootout with the Iowa troopers. Under a nicotine-yellowed thumb Cuszack felt the rims of two 00 twelve-gauge rounds. He snapped the action back into place and thumbed off the safety.

The black man spun Slocum around to face him. The noise of passing traffic prevented Cuszack from hearing the words he said to the big Marine. Slocum said nothing in reply and instead looked around until his eyes met Cuszack's. Slocum smiled when he saw Buddy, and nodded.

The big African-American did not seem pleased at Slocum's silence. He put both his huge hands on Slocum's chest and pushed.

He shouldn't have. Slocum clasped both of his own hands over the hands on his chest, and instead of returning the push, stepped back. This pulled the African-American off-balance. Slocum bent his body forward at the waist, trapping the black man's hands. Cuszack heard the crack as his wrists broke from a distance of twenty feet.

Slocum separated the man's hands from his chest, holding them apart. The man was momentarily unable to resist, paralyzed by pain and shock. With his arms apart and his belly exposed, Slocum kicked the bigger man in the groin. When Slocum let go he saw the man collapse to the sidewalk.

The African-American gurgled, and two men came running from the hotel to his aid. One was a black man almost as large as him, the other a short Hispanic fellow. Cuszack's eyes narrowed. The Hispanic wasn't wearing a coat, and the butt of a revolver was clearly visible in his waistband. Cuszack stepped from the driver's seat, the cut-down scattergun boot-legged along his thigh. A small crowd of onlookers stood watching. They were focused on the downed man on the sidewalk, and paid Buddy no heed.

Slocum put his right hand inside the pocket of his field jacket and turned facing the two newcomers. The black man had a huge belly, and was holding a cut-down pool cue in one clenched fist. The Hispanic man kept both hands near his belt line where the six-gun was tucked.

Buddy sized up the newcomers and knew instinctively their plan of attack. The larger one with the club would spring at Vernon, diverting his attention. The Hispanic would then draw his weapon and fire. Slocum could get one, but not both, and they were closing fast. A siren wailed in the distance.

From behind Slocum came the deafening roar of a shotgun blast. Both barrels of Cuszack's shotgun took the Hispanic in the center of his thin chest. He staggered backwards, his abdomen obliterated in a torrent of shredded meat and bone. He fell to the ground, steam rising from his middle.

Slocum didn't even look behind him to see where the shot came from. The heavyweight African-American dropped his pool-stick and began to back up, a look of terror on his face. Cuszack saw Slocum smoothly draw the .45 from his pocket. While Buddy and the onlookers watched Slocum fired four times, hitting his large target in the upper torso. The final shot tore out the black man's throat; he stumbled on the sprawled body of his dead partner and fell heavily to the sidewalk. His wounds also created rising tendrils of steam in the cold of the Nebraska December.

Slocum went to the truck and got in. Cuszack was already in the driver's seat. A moment later the Dodge pick-up was gone. The sirens grew louder.

A marked police sedan skidded to a halt in front of the hotel, parting the crowd which had materialized there.

Officer Don Twining got out with his Smith & Wesson
revolver in hand. He and his partner, Officer Barry
DeBoer, had responded to the "shots fired" call from
seven blocks away. Both veteran cops, they were no
strangers to the violence of the streets, and on more than
a few occasions witnessed its ugliness firsthand. DeBoer
also had his revolver in hand, and Twining intentionally
left the car's rotating emergency lights on as a beacon to
other responding units.

The people in the crowd were talking and yelling at
once. Twining first checked the hands of the men lying
on the sidewalk, out of professional habit. Better to
secure the scene first, and make sure nobody can hurt
you. Questions could be asked later. DeBoer cautiously
approached the African-American man puking in the
street. Twining checked the other two men lying sprawled
on the pavement.

He checked the Hispanic man first and found lifeless
eyes staring up at nothing. In the bloody mess of the
man's torso Twining found a Charter Arms .38 revolver.
He tucked it into the waistband of his Sam Browne belt.
Normally a beat cop would leave all items at a crime
scene untouched, but the people in this neighborhood
wouldn't miss a chance to snatch the weapon for their
own purposes, and Twining was too experienced a cop to
leave a gun lying around that wasn't in a fellow officer's
hands.

DeBoer was alternately talking to the puking black man
and talking into his portable radio. Twining recognized
the man as the doorman of the Lakeside Hotel. He knew
the hotel as a flophouse for vagrants, a shooting gallery
for junkies, and an office for any number of the local
working girls. DeBoer wasn't having much luck with the
doorman, who was barely able to speak.

Twining looked over to the body of the other black man and winced. The puddle of blood from the man's throat extended from the door of the hotel to the curb. He'd seen enough torn arteries to know one when he saw it. The coppery smell of blood, the smell of gun smoke, and the pungent odor of vomit filled the night. Twining was grateful for the biting wind, which carried the scents away. At the dead African-American's feet was a cut-down – and probably lead-filled – pool cue.

Two local knee-breakers; both armed, both dead. Another badly beaten. All at the doorstep of the Lakeside Hotel. It appeared to Twining this was nothing more than a gang reprisal, or maybe a protection beef, turf dispute, or drug deal gone sour. It was a cinch the city wouldn't mourn the loss of the two dead men, and the survivor could be counted on to be uncooperative with the police. A lot of paperwork for nothing.

Twining shook his head. DeBoer seemed to be making some progress, and was getting hesitant answers from the still-puking bouncer. Two more police units pulled up along with an ambulance. The crowd edged back, and soon the scene was littered with people in uniform.

DeBoer approached his partner, his gun still in hand. He pointed to the African-American doorman, who was known to him from previous incidents at the hotel.

"Fat Eddie says it was a trick who nutted up inside the hotel. Says there were two of them; both white guys; one real big. They fled in a white pick-up truck. Nobody got a license plate. I broadcast a description, for what good it'll do."

"What does he mean the trick 'nutted up'? A no-pay?"

DeBoer shook his head. "He says the guy went up with one of the regular girls, hooker named Chrystal. Eddie figures she was doing him for dope, cause when a girl has a money customer they're supposed to leave a dollar-a-minute deposit on the room; usually a twenty. If not, the girls have to split the dope with the guy at the desk when they come down. Chrystal didn't leave a deposit."

"Then what?" asked Twining.

DeBoer holstered his sidearm. "Chrystal and the guy go into room twenty-two, and a half-hour later, only the guy comes out. Fat Eddie gets pissed, because Chrystal hasn't come down to split any dope with him. It's house rules."

"Nice to know Fat Eddie is a stickler for policy."

"Yeah," DeBoer agreed. "A real company man. So when Eddie accosts the guy outside, the fireworks start. He gets kicked in the nuts. The two stiffs, who also work at the Lakeside, come out to rescue Fat Eddie and get gunned down."

"Sounds like we should talk to Chrystal," Twining said.

"My thoughts exactly. Room twenty-two."

Twining looked over at Fat Eddie, who was being attended by paramedics. He was still retching.

"I'm impressed," he said. "You got a lot of info out of that puking piece of shit."

"Of course," replied DeBoer indignantly. "I speak fluent scumbag."

"My ass. Let's check Chrystal's room."

Officer Twining and his partner of over three years climbed the urine-soaked steps of the luxurious Lakeside Hotel. Doors held partially open snapped shut when the eyes behind them saw badges.

"Charming place," DeBoer remarked, checking the numbers stamped on the doors. "Here's twenty-two."

Twining rapped on the door with his baton. "Chrystal, it's the police department. Open up. We want to talk to you." There was no response.

Twining checked the doorknob; it was unlocked. He opened the door to room twenty-two. Greeting them was a sight that made the crime scene outside look like a Currier and Ives holiday postcard.

Hanging upside down from the ankles, which were tied to the ceiling light fixture by an electrical cord, was the body of an approximately eighteen year-old girl. She was naked, and in the low-roofed hotel room her outstretched hands came to within a few feet of the floor. Her lifeless eyes stared at the two patrolmen. She wore two smiles. One was the odd smile gravity lent her mouth as she hung upside down. The other was the ghastly red smile of her cleanly slit throat. There was a lake of blood on the floor.

Officer Barry DeBoer said nothing, his face ashen. He pointed to the chalk-white abdomen of the suspended girl. His partner only nodded. His face too was the color of the snow outside.

Scrawled on the girl's stomach in her own blood, like finger-paint from hell, were two words: Semper Fi.

CHAPTER 27

Deputy Kevin Kearns' stomach roiled. He'd been sitting in the cramped Oldsmobile sedan for the better part of two days breathing Bob Farrell's cigarette smoke. His body ached and he was irritable from lack of exercise and sleep. What he needed was a couple of hours in the gym, a steaming shower, a hot meal, and a full night's uninterrupted sleep. He'd have settled for a shave.

The road-dirtied Oldsmobile was parked in Omaha's Leawood West district, near 130th Street, not far from Boys Town. They'd arrived the night before last. They'd found Elizabeth Slocum's house easily enough.

Kearns assumed Farrell had a scam already planned, and they would simply knock on the door and elicit the whereabouts of Vernon Slocum from his unsuspecting sister. He was wrong.

Farrell told Kearns to drive around the block and look the neighborhood and house over. What they saw was a typical Midwestern suburban neighborhood in the grip of an early winter. Elizabeth Slocum's house was the same single-story tract house as a hundred others nearby, and in no way distinct. It was the most peaceful place they'd been thus far.

So Kearns was surprised when Farrell announced they would sit on the house for an indeterminate amount of time. "Reconnoitering" was all Farrell would say. That was two days ago.

Kearns had his coat wrapped tightly around him, though unbuttoned. He'd learned that lesson back at the Slocum farm. He sighed. It seemed he was doomed to be dragged around by an alcoholic ex-cop with nothing better to do than pass the time in a parked car, in suburban Omaha, breathing secondhand cigarette smoke and waiting.

He rubbed his eyes. He couldn't remember being so bone-tired. Each time he nodded off, images of Slocum, like a hell-sent demon, dominated his dreams. Sleep was no reprieve at all.

Farrell was getting on his nerves, too. They'd agreed to start working as a team, but Kearns knew that his inexperience put him at a disadvantage. He had little choice but to trust the shifty Californian and take him at his word.

The only consolation Kearns derived was from the knowledge that Vernon Slocum was near. Farrell said he could almost feel it, and Kearns had to admit the retired San Francisco cop seemed to know what he was doing. He knew Sergeant Evers and Detective Parish, along with that rat FBI Special Agent Scanlon, were no closer to identifying the killer than they were a week ago. And here he was, shivering in a smoke-filled rental car in Omaha, Nebraska, knowing not only the identity of the child killer, but actually laying in wait for him.

Maybe Farrell was beginning to rub off; he too could almost feel Slocum's nearness. Or maybe it was wishful thinking.

The police scanner alerted them to a murder scene the night before last, at a downtown Omaha hotel. Farrell and Kearns drove there. Farrell hoodwinked his way past the beat cops guarding the scene, posing as a coroner's deputy.

Kearns watched in amazement as Farrell took one corner of a stretcher and made small talk with the ambulance crew as if he'd known them intimately. He entered the hotel past throngs of onlookers, cops, reporters, and street people like he was supposed to be there.

Ten minutes later Farrell emerged from the hotel. He told Kearns to drive directly to Elizabeth Slocum's address, and there they'd been ever since.

The quiet residential neighborhood where Elizabeth Slocum lived would have been difficult to stake out had it not been for a large public park within sight of her house. Farrell explained that to sit on the street in a parked car and watch the house would have undoubtedly attracted the attention of neighbors and the police. Subsequently the Oldsmobile was nestled out of view in a corner of the park behind several dumpsters and a snowdrift that connected them.

More than once Kearns suggested they drive around the block to break up the monotony. Farrell politely disagreed, saying such activity would draw attention. He reminded the deputy their quarry was not thinking like a criminal, but instead like a soldier. If they gave up their vantage point, even for a few minutes, it would increase the chance that Vernon Slocum could slip into the neighborhood without their seeing him. Kearns reluctantly agreed.

Farrell told Kearns at length about what he'd seen at the hotel. He listened in fascination as Farrell related the details of the dead hooker, strung upside down, blood dripping from her slit throat. Inside the hotel lobby Farrell overheard Omaha PD detectives discussing the crime, and at one point had the audacity to light their cigarettes.

There was no way it couldn't have been Slocum. The modus operandi was identical, with one big exception: this time, Slocum had an accomplice.

It was just like the schoolyard in Iowa. More like a military raid than a crime. The hotel bouncers were dealt with in counter-ambush style. The upside-down prostitute made it certain. It was Lance Corporal Vernon Slocum, alright.

It was late afternoon. Farrell crammed another smoldering Camel butt into an ashtray already so full Kearns thought the entire tray would come careening down in a cancerous avalanche. Farrell refilled his cup with lukewarm coffee and added three fingers of bourbon.

As much as Farrell drank, he never seemed to get drunk. Like many long-time drinkers, he had a perfect knowledge of his alcoholic beverage tolerance. He also had a lot of practice in maintaining the outward appearance of sobriety.

"Want a snort?" Farrell asked, holding the pint towards Kearns.

"I'll pass."

"You don't approve of drinking?"

"If I gave it any thought, I suppose I would."

Farrell shook his head, grinning. "You've got to learn to lighten up, Kevin. You're going to give yourself an ulcer."

"Considering the trouble I'm in, an ulcer would be a walk in the park."

Farrell took a sip and set down the cup. Turning in the seat to face Kearns he said, "It's time to stop wallowing, OK?"

Kearns sat up abruptly to face the older man. He started to speak, but Farrell cut him off with a wave of his hand.

"I never promised this was going to be a trip to Disneyland. I never said if we caught Slocum we'd live happily ever after. All I promised was a crack at bagging him."

Farrell started to light another cigarette, than changed his mind and threw the unlit smoke to the floor of the car. He pointed his finger at Kearns.

"You knew what kind of mess you were in a split second after you punched out that FBI guy. He did nothing more than say what's always going to be on everybody's mind. No matter where you go, somebody is always going to wonder what happened in that schoolyard. You can't punch out the whole world."

"You expect me to just forget about it? Win a few, lose a few?"

"I wish I had an answer for you, but I don't. You're going to have to work it out for yourself. But I can tell you what not to do, and that's to let this thing eat your insides out. It will ruin the rest of your life if you let it."

"What life?"

"That's exactly the kind of self-pity I'm talking about. Poor Deputy Kearns. Woe is he. Enough. You think you've got it rough? I'll bet Tiffany Meade would trade places with you."

"That was below the belt."

"If that's where I've got to hit to reach you that's where I'll hit."

Farrell's voice softened. "You know I'm right. You've got to get over your guilt. Punishing yourself serves no purpose. You did all you could, and it's time to put the doubt behind you. Not that I really give a shit. If you want to slobber in angst the rest of your days, fine by me.

But right now I need you focused. I need your complete concentration if we're going to come out of this in one piece. You know what Vernon Slocum is, and he isn't acting alone; he's got an accomplice. You'd better get your head out of your butt, or when we meet up with Slocum he's going to bury us."

Kearns nodded sullenly.

"And I know what else is eating you. You think that because of what happened you'll never be a cop again. Even if we escape indictment, this will prevent any police or sheriff's department from ever taking you on. Is that what's bothering you?"

"Of course it's bothering me. I've lost my profession before I even started it."

"Believe me, you should be glad. I've been a cop thirty years, and what have I got to show for it? I've been divorced twice and have a daughter that grew up without me. I live in a dive, drink too much, smoke too much, and was as desperate for a shot at Slocum as you were. Your reason for stalking him isn't much different than mine."

"How can you say that?" Kearns blurted. "You've had your career. You've been a cop; you've caught a lot of bad guys. What's one more, give or take?"

Farrell laughed, unnerving Kearns a little. "Kid, I've wasted my life doing the job. I have nothing to show for it but a pension. I was forgotten the day I retired. My only mistake was being like you; young and full of ideals, and believing I could make a difference."

He turned to stare out the windshield into the gray sky. "Kevin, it's all shit. As a cop, all you'll ever do is make apologies to victims and get eaten up inside with frustration. Frustration at a rotten system that was loused up beyond repair long before you pinned on a badge."

"If you're so disillusioned why are you here tracking Slocum? Why aren't you back in San Francisco taking it easy in retirement?"

Farrell turned back to stare at Kearns. "I already told you; because I'm taking Slocum out. Thirty lousy years of watching the system fail has made me want to do something right. Besides, I've got nothing else to do. Or lose."

Kearns fidgeted uneasily at Farrell's words.

"You and I aren't so different. I'm a reflection of you; your personal Dorian Gray. Maybe I've dumped all my frustration and regret on Vernon Slocum. Maybe it's torn me up all these years, knowing he's out there somewhere and that I'm responsible. If I'd done the right thing in Saigon, a Christmas stocking with the name Tiffany Meade embroidered on it wouldn't be sitting empty by the fireplace this year. And maybe a good cop would be at home patrolling his beat, instead of parked in the snow with a drunk, fighting off his conscience."

"I'm sorry I asked."

"Don't be. You asked, so you're going to listen. You want to know why I'm here? You think you're the only one wrestling with guilt? You think you've cornered the market on self-pity? You're wrong."

Farrell went on, his face tight. "At least you had a shot at him. At least you went toe-to-toe with the motherfucker. You got to feel his blood under your knuckles."

His voice sounded far away.

"I knew what Slocum was all those years ago in Vietnam. Pure evil. I saw it face to face. I talked with it. And I stood there, slack-jawed, and let him get away. I told myself that it was wartime and it wasn't my concern. I'd go back to the States and forget. Go on with my police career. Be a good cop. I tried."

Farrell took a deep breath. "But evil doesn't go away; it's got to be vanquished. And once you've seen it you can't forget. The blood of Tiffany Meade is on my hands as much as yours. I knew what Slocum was, and I didn't even try to take him out when I had the chance."

Long minutes passed in silence. Kearns ran his hands through his short hair.

"I could use that drink now, Bob."

Farrell grinned and uncorked his pint of bourbon. "Sorry about that," he said. "I didn't mean to climb on a soapbox. Maybe I'm drinking too much." He shrugged. "Or not enough."

Farrell was pouring whisky into Kearns' Styrofoam cup when the deputy abruptly pulled his hand away. He ignored his spilled beverage and began hastily wiping off the condensation from the windshield of the Oldsmobile.

"Jesus, Kevin, you dumped it all over—"

"Look! That truck!" Kearns exclaimed. "It's him! It's Slocum! He's driving that truck! Do you see it?"

Farrell spit his cigarette out the window and reached below the seat. He came up with the Remington. He racked a round into the chamber.

"Yeah, I see it," Farrell said. "It's him alright. Do you recognize the other guy?"

"I've never seen him before." He hoped the tremor in his voice went unnoticed. He took his revolver from its holster and checked the six cartridges in the cylinder. He glanced over at Farrell, who was calmly staring back at him, a confident look in his eyes.

"Huddle's over, Deputy. It's game time."

CHAPTER 28

Elizabeth Pauline Slocum sat up in bed and tried to fluff the pillows beneath her to a more comfortable shape. She'd been bedridden for three days with a severe bout of the flu.

Elizabeth missed work, even when away for the two or three days a year she took sick. Though a sturdy woman, Elizabeth suffered badly during the winter months as she fought off the annual respiratory infections that spelled possible pneumonia.

She was a full-time counselor and administrator at a youth shelter funded by the Catholic Diocese. The facility specialized in problem children under the age of sixteen. Elizabeth herself had been such a child, and first learned of the home as one of its guests at age thirteen.

Elizabeth was taken to the home after being removed from her own in Ogden, Iowa. She was the youngest of four children, and two of her three brothers were in Vietnam. Many of the memories from that time in her life, the time before the shelter in Omaha, she'd tried to block out. Mostly she was successful, but sometimes the dreams returned and things she thought long buried would dredge up to her consciousness.

She remembered beatings; savage, brutal beatings. She remembered always being cold, and in darkness. She vaguely remembered the outline of her mother's face, and warm feelings associated with that image. Elizabeth recalled constant screaming, and her brothers scrambling about a cluttered room, cowering in fear. Elizabeth remembered fear very well.

She remembered the sticky-sweet alcohol smell always surrounding her father. She remembered nights when he came into the tiny, dirty room where she and her three brothers slept on a mattress on the floor. Her father would take one, or all, of the boys to his room each night. Elizabeth would try to close her ears with her tiny hands, but she couldn't shut out the screams. Then one night her father started coming for her.

By the time she was in junior high school, the pale, sickly Elizabeth Slocum attracted the attention of one of her teachers; a kind woman who somehow aroused in Elizabeth the faded images of her mother. Elizabeth had pneumonia and if the teacher hadn't taken her to the doctor she wouldn't have lived through the winter.

It was at the hospital that the physicians examining Elizabeth discovered the overwhelming evidence of long-term physical and sexual abuse. The sheriff's department was called, and when deputies kicked in the door of the squalid farmhouse the only person they found was Emil Jensen Slocum. Of his three other children, two were in Vietnam, and the youngest, Cole, had run away. With two exceptions, Elizabeth had not seen any member of her family since.

Elizabeth grew to womanhood under the gentle guidance and care of the nuns at the shelter. There she regained her health and learned nights didn't have to be filled with the screams of children.

Elizabeth loved the youth shelter, and when it came time for her to leave she did not. She earned a work scholarship at Creighton University, and spent all of her free time doing volunteer work at the shelter. After graduation she continued her education, working her way through graduate studies in psychology as a full-time counselor at the home she loved. Memories of her childhood in hell gradually faded.

Elizabeth bought a modest home and lived alone. She never thought to take a husband; she was too busy helping the endless number of children who needed her.

In 1984 Elizabeth received word her brother Vernon was in the veterans' hospital in Des Moines. She knew her oldest brother Wade was killed in Vietnam, because she'd been the recipient of his military death benefits. She assumed that because she'd never heard from Vernon he'd died in the war as well.

On a hot July afternoon Elizabeth Slocum climbed into her Volkswagen van and headed for Des Moines. She wasn't sure why she'd gone, but did. The five-hour drive to Des Moines was an odd journey back into feelings she thought she'd long forgotten, and she was anxious and uncertain when she pulled into the parking lot of the VA hospital.

Elizabeth Slocum hadn't seen her brother Vernon since she was twelve. She stepped hesitantly into the hospital and was led by an orderly to a room where visitors were allowed to meet with patients. She wouldn't soon forget what transpired next.

She walked into a clean, white-walled room which smelled of ammonia. Several men were there and most didn't look up when she entered. The men were unsettling.

Elizabeth was accustomed to working with children who had been severely traumatized in one way or another. She wasn't prepared for what she saw in these men, however.

Most of the men looked drugged, and Elizabeth guessed that was indeed what caused their appearance. From her psychology studies, she knew many patients in VA hospitals were battle-crazed, violent men, who couldn't return to the civilized world from a place where violence and killing had once been a way of life. Yet these men didn't seem violent. They were blank; human voids where minds had been. She searched through the maze of doped faces for her brother, uncertain she would recognize him.

Suddenly there he was. Elizabeth recoiled in horror, stifling a scream. It was the face of her father. He was sitting at a card table staring at her.

A rush of memories choked Elizabeth's confused mind. He was big; as big as her father, with the same angular jaw and broad shoulders. He had a look of coiled power, like a snake at rest. Yet it was his eyes that were the most disturbing. Eyes so brimming with evil she took an involuntary step backwards. She wanted desperately to look away, but couldn't. Vernon's eyes drew her into them.

Elizabeth felt twelve years old again, and in the grip of an unspeakable fear. Her older brother Vernon sat leering, a grin spreading over his face. He sensed the fear in her and relished it. He looked, to Elizabeth, like a predatory animal. She began to tremble.

She wanted to scream, but no words came. She wanted to run, but was fixed to the spot like a deer caught in the headlights of an oncoming car.

Vernon's eyes bored into her. His yellow teeth gleamed large and bright, accentuating his resemblance to a ravening insect. He began to laugh; a guttural bellow that made Elizabeth put her hands over her ears; she'd heard that laugh before. Her mind was a whirlwind. She struggled to remain composed and suppress the victim inside her.

She saw the object of Vernon's mirth and was instantly repulsed. Below the card table, Vernon had the drawstring of his trousers untied. He was holding his erect penis in his hand. He leered at Elizabeth, his eyes scorching holes in her soul. Choking back sobs, she turned and fled down the hospital corridor. Vernon's malignant laughter echoed in the halls behind her. She never went back.

The years passed. Elizabeth put aside the experience at the veterans' hospital. She devoted her time and energy to the youth shelter, and when not there scoured the welfare departments of the Tri-State area looking for abused children to add to her flock.

And now, a few weeks before Christmas, she'd taken sick again. Elizabeth suspected she would. She took sick every year at the first snow. Her propensity towards respiratory illness was a remnant of her tortured childhood.

She didn't sit idle at home. It had been nothing short of a blizzard in the Iowa/Nebraska area for almost a week solid, and she was busy with planning the holidays at the Siddartha House. She was also polishing the outline for a lecture she was to give at the community college in January.

Elizabeth sat in bed, a cup of tea at her elbow and books and notes on her lap. An earlier weather report warned Omaha residents to prepare for several more days of sub-zero temperatures and snow.

She was viewing a VCR tape she'd made of the *Phil Donahue Show*. The episode dealt with child abuse, and Elizabeth was gathering popular culture resources for her lecture. She'd just finished fluffing the pillows around her when a loud and insistent knock sounded on her front door.

Elizabeth carefully set aside her tea and padded to the front door. She wasn't expecting anyone.

When Elizabeth opened the door the first thing she met was a blast of brutally cold air. It stung both her eyes and lungs. The second thing she met was no less unpleasant.

Standing on Elizabeth Pauline Slocum's porch was as scruffy-looking a man as she'd ever seen. He was of medium height, but extremely thin. The heavy work clothes he wore hung on him like a scarecrow. He had long, greasy hair and a beard. Even in the cold wind, Elizabeth could smell the aroma of unwashed body. He looked about fifty years old. His face was emaciated, and a coat of grime covered the portions of it not hidden by hair. She had never seen him before.

"Can I help you?" Elizabeth asked, stifling a cough.

"You Elizabeth Slocum?" the man asked in a rough voice.

"Yes I am. May I help you?"

Elizabeth knew if she stood much longer in the freezing doorway pneumonia was certain. She was not overly concerned the strange man knew her name, because it was listed in the telephone directory and engraved on her mailbox. She was more concerned with getting back to the warmth of her bed.

"I got a message for you. From your brother."

Elizabeth was confused. "From who–"

The man pushed her forcefully back through the doorway and into the hall. He darted in after her and closed the door. It happened within an instant. Her eyes widened when the man drew a revolver. Elizabeth couldn't know it was taken from the body of an Iowa state trooper. The man lit a cigarette and smiled, showing several missing teeth.

"What do you want?" Elizabeth asked, trying to hide the fear in her voice.

"Like I said," the man drawled, exhaling smoke. "I got a message for you. Vernon sends his regards."

Elizabeth's memory was jarred at the sound of the name. "Vernon? Is Vernon here?"

"He'll be along in a minute," the man said casually. "I'm his partner. We figured you might be looking out the window. Thought you might recognize Vernon and freak out. So I came first to make sure the coast was clear. Pretty smart, huh?"

Elizabeth slowly backed up. She knew she needed to think clearly; to find a way to get help or get out. She watched the man. He calmly pointed his revolver at her and smoked. He was smiling.

"Like I said; Vernon will be along in a minute."

CHAPTER 29

The battered Dodge truck turned around in the cul-de-sac and backed into Elizabeth Slocum's driveway. It disgorged a passenger; a dirty-looking man dressed in dirtier clothes. The man walked nonchalantly up to the house. Then, as Farrell and Kearns watched, he forced his way in.

"Here's how we'll play it," Farrell said. "We'll take Slocum when he gets out of the truck and walks towards the house."

"What about the woman? Slocum's sister? She's obviously a hostage; you saw that guy shove her into the house. We go for Slocum, that other guy is going to kill her."

"Can't be helped. We may not get another chance at Slocum. For all we know she's an accomplice. Maybe she's hiding them out."

"You know that's not true."

"True or not, Slocum's our objective; don't forget that."

Farrell bit his lip. "I've got an idea. Drive past Elizabeth's house like you're going to pull into the driveway of that tan house two doors down."

"Are you out of your mind? Slocum will see us halfway down the block."

"Do it, goddamn it!"

Cursing under his breath, Kearns complied. He eased the Oldsmobile out of the park and onto the street. Farrell was fiddling with the volume control of the police scanner.

"This will let us know when somebody calls the police after the fireworks start. You got extra ammo?"

Kearns nodded, patting the coat pocket where he'd stashed a handful of .38 rounds. Farrell inserted another shell into the shotgun's tubular magazine to replace the one he'd chambered. Kearns stopped the car in front of the neighbor's driveway and backed up. The truck was fifty feet away and Kearns could clearly see the face of Vernon Slocum.

Slocum hadn't seen them. He was craning his neck, looking out the truck's back window at the house as if waiting for a signal. Kearns waited for orders from Farrell.

"Leave the keys in the ignition, and for God's sake don't lock the door when you get out." Kearns barely heard him.

He was staring at Vernon Slocum, a mixture of repulsion, hate, and fear swirling within him. For a brief instant he was again flooded with images of the schoolyard. He heard the sound of gunfire, and saw the schoolteacher falling dead. He remembered the powerful jolts to his shoulders as he pummeled Slocum's face with his fists. He felt the crashing blow to his head as Slocum's pistol came down on him, his last conscious thought that he was a dead man.

An elbow from Farrell brought him back. "Are you with me?"

"Yeah, I heard you."

"He hasn't seen us yet. We'll creep around the house between this one and Elizabeth's. We'll come up behind him from the neighbor's driveway. If we're lucky, he won't spot us until we're on top of him. Don't slam the door when you get out."

Kearns nodded and opened the car's door. His heart was racing, and a part of him couldn't believe what was happening. He and a man he barely knew were going to sneak up behind an unsuspecting man. If luck was with them they were going to kill him.

As if Farrell could read his mind, he said, "Kevin, this is no time for second thoughts."

"I'm OK. You watch your own ass."

Ignoring the last comment, Farrell added, "Don't hesitate. As soon as you get a shot, take it. Even if his back is turned, you got that? Don't give him any chance at all. If you do, he'll shove it down your throat. Get going."

"Aren't you coming?"

"I changed my mind. It won't do any good if we're both sneaking around the garage and Slocum gets into the house. I'll stay here and cover with the shotgun in case he moves while you're around back."

Kearns only nodded. As always, the ex-cop's logic was irrefutable. He looked back at Farrell. The Californian returned a weak smile and gave a thumbs-up gesture with the hand not cradling the shotgun. Kearns moved towards the back of the house, his revolver in hand.

Farrell cracked his passenger door and nosed the muzzle of the shotgun out to hasten his exit when the time came. He hoped the young deputy wouldn't balk.

Slocum stared at the house. Then he turned his neck around and started rubbing it. He was now facing Farrell, seated in the parked Oldsmobile two driveways away.

Seconds became hours. Farrell knew Kearns couldn't have made it around behind Slocum in the short time since he'd left; not in snow this deep.

Farrell and Slocum locked eyes. It was the same face Farrell met in Saigon; the same evil eyes. The years magically faded, and for a brief moment Farrell found himself in limbo between Saigon in 1967 and Omaha, Nebraska in 1987.

Slocum's eyes narrowed and Farrell was jarred back to reality. The game was up. The driver's door of the Dodge truck flew open. Farrell scrambled to get out of the Oldsmobile.

Vernon Slocum emerged from the truck, the AR-15 going to his shoulder. Farrell also cleared his car, and was bringing up his own weapon. The distance between the two men was perhaps sixty feet.

Both men fired. As if by the same bullet, the windshields of both the Oldsmobile and the Dodge exploded in shards of flying glass. Farrell got only one round off before he ducked and took cover behind the engine block of the big sedan.

Slocum continued to fire in two and three shot strings that tore into the Oldsmobile. Farrell knew the shotgun in his hands was no match for the assault rifle in Slocum's. He racked another round.

With bullets whistling over his head Farrell feinted standing up over the hood to draw fire. He then ducked behind the engine and scooted on his knees to the front of the car. He peeked around the headlights and fired all four remaining shotgun rounds at Slocum.

Slocum went down, his rifle making no sound as it fell in the cushioning snow. Farrell wasn't sure how badly the big Marine was hurt, if at all; sixty feet was a very long shot for 00 buck. He darted behind the engine block of the Oldsmobile and hastily reloaded the shotgun. Where in the hell was Kearns?

••••

Kearns heard the shooting start while climbing the shoulder-high fence which separated Elizabeth Slocum's yard from her neighbor's. The eruption of gunfire startled him and he nearly fell. He scaled the fence and ran through the snow towards the front of the house; there was no longer any need for stealth. He recognized the report of 5.56 mm gunfire from his military service, as well as the boom of a shotgun, and hoped Farrell could hold out until he arrived.

Slocum was on his hands and knees behind the Dodge truck. The hail of shotgun pellets Farrell sent his way missed him directly, but one of the 00 buck rounds struck the pavement under the snow. The pellets in that round flattened out and slid under the driver's door Slocum was using for cover. They peppered Slocum's left leg below the knee, sending him sprawling to the ground.

Slocum fought against the pain and rolled under the truck, out of view. The AR-15 lay in the snow beyond his reach. He drew his .45 from his coat pocket and began to crawl to the front of the truck under the chassis.

Kearns found Slocum on his hands and knees when he came around the corner of the garage. The big man was lowering his head to crawl under the truck on his belly. His back was to Kearns, and his pistol was in his hand.

Kearns' breathing stopped. He drew a bead on the center of Slocum's back, the adrenaline coursing through his body. The red-ramp front-sight of the Smith & Wesson revolver showed clearly on the green background of Slocum's faded fatigue jacket. He started to squeeze the trigger.

He choked. He was about to shoot a man in the back. It was against everything he'd been trained to do in the

Iowa Law Enforcement Academy, and against all his instincts. He saw the giant hulk of a man on his knees before him, his leg leaving a trail of blood in the snow, and he hesitated, momentarily forgetting who and what Vernon Slocum was.

A voice screamed at him from afar. "Shoot! Goddamn it, boy, shoot!"

The voice was hollow and distant. Kearns looked up to see where it was coming from and saw Farrell. The shotgun was in his hands and he was running from across the street.

"Shoot!" the older cop yelled again.

Kearns' hesitation was over. He looked back to his revolver sights and saw Slocum's bloody feet disappear beneath the bed of the truck. Cursing at himself, he crouched to peer under the truck. He was now ready to shoot Slocum; all doubt was gone. He never got the chance.

The front door of the house burst open and the bearded man they'd seen enter Elizabeth Slocum's house appeared. He was holding Elizabeth by the hair; a woman whose face bore an unmistakable resemblance to Vernon's. The barrel of a stainless-steel revolver was against her neck. She wore a look of stark terror; a sentiment Kearns identified with.

The man said nothing, but his meaning was obvious. Make a move or threat towards him, and he would dispatch the woman. Kearns wheeled to face him and leveled his weapon.

Buddy Cuszack couldn't find Vernon. He was searching the area of the truck with no success. He saw blood near the truck, and recognized the two men, one old and one young, as plainclothes cops.

"Vernon?" Buddy called. "Where the fuck are you?"

With a shriek Elizabeth Slocum wrenched herself from the grasp of the bone-thin man, leaving shanks of her hair in his fist. She didn't get two steps before Cuszack fired, the .357 slug striking her in the back.

Images of the schoolyard returned, as Kearns watched another woman succumb to gunfire before him. His jaw tightened and he emptied his revolver into Buddy Cuszack.

Cuszack danced with the impact of each .38 slug, as six of them ripped through his chest. He sank slowly to the porch. He was dead before he hit the ground.

Farrell was halfway between the Oldsmobile and Elizabeth's house, running as fast as his two pack a day cigarette habit would let him. Elizabeth Slocum lay face down in the snow on her front lawn, moaning softly, blood seeping from her nose and mouth. Kearns instinctively moved towards the injured woman.

In the next instant Slocum rose from beneath the truck, aiming his .45 pistol. Kearns raised his weapon and fired, only to be rewarded by a hollow click. He threw himself to the ground and rolled as two shots rang out, both hitting the garage wall where he'd been a split-second before.

Slocum whirled to face Farrell. Farrell realized with a plummeting heart he was caught in the open, without cover. He fired a hasty shot from the hip, knowing it would go wild even before he pulled the trigger.

As expected, the shotgun round went high and blasted a bird feeder at the top of Elizabeth's porch to splintered fragments of pine and sunflower seed. A second after firing Farrell threw himself flat, and like Kearns began to roll for his life. He dropped the shotgun.

Six .45 slugs followed Farrell, and he felt the crack and whine of their impact on the asphalt under the snow. The distance between Slocum and Farrell was better than thirty feet; not optimum conditions for accurate handgun shooting, especially at a moving target. Though nicked by numerous chips of flying concrete, Farrell was unhurt.

With his pistol empty and the slide locked back, Slocum hobbled to the driver's door of the Dodge. He clambered in, and a moment later the truck was screeching down the snow-slickened road away from his sister's house.

Farrell regained his feet and drew his two-inch .38 from his hip in a smooth, practiced motion. As the dilapidated truck sped by he fired all five bullets at the driver with seemingly no effect. In another moment the Dodge was around the corner and out of sight.

Farrell scanned the vicinity for Kearns. The young deputy was kneeling over Elizabeth Slocum's inert form. He'd placed both arms around her thick waist and was pulling her to her hands and knees. Her breathing was shallow, and with each breath frothy blood spewed from her mouth.

"You've got a punctured lung," Kearns said to the woman. "But you're going to be OK. I'm not going to leave you. I'm holding you like this so the blood doesn't fill your lungs and drown you. Stay with me; it's going to be alright."

Kearns knew in the sub-zero weather shock was only seconds away. He needed an ambulance, and fast. He looked around to the houses on the block and saw several people standing on their porches, gaping at the carnage their neighborhood had become.

"Help! I need some help!" Kearns called out. "Somebody call an ambulance! I've got a hurt woman here. I'm a police officer! Somebody call an ambulance!"

Sirens sounded faintly in the distance. Farrell ran up to Kearns and grabbed his shoulder. The deputy placed Elizabeth flat on her stomach and tore open the back of her bathrobe where the bullet entered. Elizabeth lost consciousness.

"C'mon, Kevin, we've got to get the hell out of here!" Farrell barked. "She'll be OK. There's cops on the way. Let's go!"

Ignoring this, Kearns said, "Give me your cigarettes, Bob."

Farrell looked puzzled. They had no time for whatever Kearns had in mind. "Kevin, we've got to go. Do you want to get caught?"

"Give me your cigarettes, now!" He rolled Elizabeth over on her back. Sure enough, the exit wound from the revolver slug was large and gaping. Blood-red air bubbles rose from the hole.

"Give me your fucking cigarettes! Do it!"

"Shit!" Farrell said, handing over his smokes. "This is a helluva time to take up the habit." In a few minutes, Omaha PD officers would be filling the block. He urged the younger man to hurry.

"Kevin, we've got to get out of here!"

Kearns ignored him. He removed the cellophane wrapper from the pack of Camels and tore it in half. He also tore his handkerchief in half. He placed one-half of the cellophane over the exit wound, and the other over the entrance wound in her back. He put a portion of his handkerchief over each cellophane patch. Using his necktie and the cloth belt from Elizabeth's bathrobe, he tied the makeshift dressings in place. Her breathing got noticeably better. He took off his coat and began to wrap it around her.

"Alright, you've done your civic duty. Let's go!" The sirens were much louder now.

Kearns looked up and his eyes met Farrell's. "I'm not going to leave her. She'll die. You go."

"Don't be an asshole. I'm not leaving without you. Lose the heroics and let's get the fuck out of here."

"I'm not going."

"I can't just leave you here."

"Sure you can; no point in both of us getting caught. But I can't leave her here to die. Don't worry, Bob; I won't say a word about you to the cops. That's what you're worried about, isn't it?"

Farrell glared at the deputy, shaking his head in disgust.

"I won't rat you out. Now get lost, before they get both of us."

Farrell wordlessly turned and ran for the Oldsmobile. Miraculously it started, despite the many .223 holes dotting its body. The Olds screeched out of sight. Kearns watched in silence as Farrell drove away.

Deputy Kevin Kearns knelt in a snow-blanketed Omaha suburb and rocked a critically injured woman gently in his arms.

The sirens closed in.

CHAPTER 30

Kearns sat in an interrogation room in the Investigations Division of the Omaha Police Department. It was well into the night, and he'd been there since the early afternoon. He was exhausted, but couldn't sleep. The sparse, concrete-walled room he inhabited was cold, and had only a folding chair and table for furniture.

Less than a minute after Farrell sped away in his bullet-riddled Oldsmobile, police units from OPD came screeching into the quiet residential neighborhood where Elizabeth Slocum once lived in peace. They handcuffed Kearns and took his revolver, badge, and sheriff's department identification card. As he was stuffed into the back seat of a patrol car he watched Elizabeth attended by paramedics. The last he saw of the woman was her unconscious body being loaded into an ambulance.

Kearns was taken directly to the police station and put into the interrogation room in the Investigations Division. People came and looked at him, but as yet no one had spoken. Hours passed.

His head throbbed. He had dried blood on both hands and on his shirt. They'd taken all of his property, including his belt and shoelaces. He hadn't even been allowed a phone call. Not that he had anyone to call.

He was too tired to be upset, afraid, or angry. If anything, disappointment was his dominant emotion. He'd spent the past week on a bizarre odyssey to find and stop a child-killer. The effort had failed, and he was now in deeper trouble than before. His only ally in the quest, an alcoholic ex-cop, had abandoned him to tend to the wounds of Elizabeth Slocum, an innocent woman who wouldn't have been hurt if he hadn't bungled their attempt at bagging her brother.

Undoubtedly the FBI would soon know Slocum's identity. And Kearns, for all his well-intentioned efforts, would be out of the picture. A system that failed to deal with a monster once would have a chance to fail again.

Kearns knew with certainty he'd be prosecuted. He'd given Scanlon all the rope needed to hang him now. But he'd give the federal agent no satisfaction.

The door to the interrogation room opened. Standing in the doorway were Special Agents Scanlon, Lefferty and Tatters. Kearns looked at them with bored disinterest.

"Well Deputy Kearns, I see we meet again."

Kearns smiled thinly. "How's the nose?"

Scanlon's smirk faded, and he instinctively wiped his nose with the Kleenex in his hand. "My nose is damaged, Deputy. More than enough to see you go to jail. How's your social calendar for the next few years?"

Kearns shrugged.

"I'm not going to play games with you. We know a lot, but not everything. You will supply us with information in consideration for leniency in the numerous felony charges against you."

"What charges?" Kearns asked, feigning disinterest.

"Assault and battery on me, for starters," Scanlon said. "Then we have impeding a federal investigation, escape, and quite probably murder. Any questions?"

"Yeah, I've got a question. How's Elizabeth Slocum?"

Scanlon folded his hands. "She's not your concern, if you please."

"If you please," Kevin said, "you can suck shit through a soda straw. If I find out how she's doing, maybe I'll think about talking. If I don't, you can go to hell."

Scanlon took a deep breath and let it out slowly. He was working hard to suppress his temper. "Alright, Deputy. Elizabeth Slocum is currently in stable condition at the Douglas County Hospital. She has a punctured lung but is expected to recover. Her doctors credit your first aid with saving her life. She has thus far been unable to speak, and therefore cannot supply us with any useful information. Does that satisfy you?"

"Yes it does. Thank you."

"You're welcome. Now tell us about your accomplice. The older man; the one who posed as your attorney?"

"No dice."

"Now Kevin," Scanlon said, as if talking to a three year-old. "You said if I told you Elizabeth's condition, you would talk."

"I said I'd think about it. I have."

Scanlon's lips pursed. Agent Lefferty stood up. "Fuck this asshole, sir. I say we pound the information out of him."

Kearns grinned. "You gonna do it alone? You'd better bring a lunch."

"I don't need any help with you, you little fuck. I'll kick your redneck ass."

"You know," Kearns said, "when you're angry, you sound just like Efrem Zimbalist Junior. Can you do Eliot Ness, too?"

Lefferty lunged at Kearns, who was expecting it. He stood up, pushed the table at the agent, who stumbled over it, and easily ducked under the larger man's well-advertised roundhouse punch. Kearns then hit Lefferty a sharp jab to the solar plexus. As the special agent doubled over, he grabbed the Fed's feathered hair and slammed his face down on the tabletop. Lefferty crumpled to the floor.

Agent Tatters was moving towards Kearns when the door to the conference room burst open. The station sergeant and two uniformed cops rushed in. The sergeant, a burly Irishman who stood a full head taller than anyone else in the room, wore a displeased look on his face.

"I might have known. The lieutenant said to let the G-Men alone on this, since it was their prisoner. So I let them alone, and what do they pull?"

Scanlon tried to smooth things over. "Sergeant, let me explain."

"I don't want to hear it!" the sergeant bellowed, pointing his finger at Scanlon like Darth Vader pointing his lightsaber at Luke Skywalker. "This is a police station, not the wrestling arena."

"Sergeant, it's not what you think."

"I said I don't want to hear it. You've got a cop under wraps and you're treating him like a criminal. He ain't had his phone calls, he ain't been fed, and now you and your goons are using an OPD interview room to beat the shit out of him. If you're charging him with a crime, then charge him. If not, we've got to start processing him like anybody else. Maybe the FBI didn't know it, but there are such things as civil rights." The big sergeant scowled at Scanlon. "I'm calling the watch commander. He'll listen to your double-talk, but not me. Besides, his lawyer has been waiting downstairs for over an hour. You're going to have a hard time explaining to the district attorney why Kearns wasn't allowed to see his legal counsel."

The sergeant turned to one of the uniformed officers with him. "Take Deputy Kearns to see his attorney. His lawyer's downstairs in the lobby."

"Hold on a minute," Scanlon demanded. "Who is this attorney? I want to meet him. Last time we saw Deputy Kearns he was in the company of an alleged attorney who turned out to be a phony. If you don't mind, I'll accompany you to meet this so-called attorney."

"Suit yourself. But first get that guy off my floor. And wipe up that blood."

Scanlon nodded to Tatters, who tended to the prone Agent Lefferty. Kearns and Scanlon followed the sergeant to the lobby.

Scanlon scurried to keep up with the long-striding cop. "When we meet this attorney, be prepared to make an arrest, Sergeant. We have reason to believe this person is the other suspect who was involved in the shootout today, and who's been aiding and abetting Deputy Kearns all along."

The sergeant grunted in disgust, but nodded. The group reached the lobby. Scanlon rushed ahead to be the first to confront Kearns' accomplice. He pushed rudely past the sergeant and approached the only person standing in the lobby, a lone figure in a bulky winter coat and boots. The person's back was to Scanlon.

Scanlon grabbed the person's arm and whirled them forcefully around to face him. At the same time he said, "You're under arrest."

Suddenly a hand reached out and slapped Scanlon open-handed in the face. Under normal circumstances, the slap would have been a nuisance only; but to Scanlon, with his already broken nose, it was paralyzing. He grabbed his nose, gasped, and sank to his knees.

Kearns grinned, and the station sergeant howled in laughter. The attorney Scanlon had abruptly grabbed was in fact a very attractive young woman. She was clutching a briefcase in one hand and wore a confused look on her face. Something about the woman seemed familiar to Kearns, though he was certain he'd remember if he'd met her before.

"Shall I arrest her now, Agent Scanlon?" the sergeant said between gales of laughter. Scanlon was slowly rocking back and forth on his knees, waiting for the pain to subside. The woman looked up quizzically at the sergeant.

"Sergeant, who is this man? Do you allow all visitors at your police station to be assaulted this way? I want to file charges."

The sergeant's laughter got more raucous and he bent over to catch his breath. "You hear that?" he said to Scanlon. "She wants to file criminal charges."

The sergeant was consumed in laughter. Scanlon, however, found no humor in the situation. His head was ringing. He finally stood up, his nose dripping blood.

"I'm sorry. I thought you were someone else. Please forgive me."

"I should think you're sorry," she said. "You really should be more careful, grabbing strangers and arresting them for no reason. It's unprofessional and dangerous."

Tears of laughter formed in the sergeant's eyes. He finally gained control of himself and stood up, wiping his eyes dry.

"I'm sorry, ma'am," he finally said. "What can I do for you?"

"My name is Jennifer Piper. I'm from the public defender's office. I'm here to see Deputy Kevin Kearns."

All in the room stared at the young woman. She had shoulder-length red hair, a light freckled complexion, and very clear, deep-blue eyes. What Kearns could guess about her figure under the bulky coat was complimentary. She looked more like a model than an attorney. She also didn't look a day over twenty-two years old.

"Begging your pardon," Scanlon interjected. "You don't seem old enough to have graduated from law school."

"Begging your pardon," the woman retorted sarcastically. "You don't seem competent enough to be an agent with the FBI."

The station sergeant guffawed again. Kearns didn't know who this woman was, but he liked her.

Jennifer Piper went on. "I've been standing in the lobby of this police station for over an hour and haven't been allowed to see my client. Rest assured, the district attorney will hear about this. I want to know who's responsible for this obvious breach of legal procedure?"

The station sergeant showed his palms. "Don't look at Omaha PD lady; it was out of our hands. You got a beef, you take it up with the FBI. That is," he said, starting to giggle again, "if you can find an agent who hasn't been decked."

Scanlon did his best to ignore the insult. He'd wiped most of the blood from his nose with a Kleenex and resumed his composed demeanor. "Ms Piper, I'd like to see some credentials, please? In the past we've had some difficulty with individuals impersonating attorneys."

Ms Piper bit her lip nervously. "I see," she said. "So assaulting me isn't enough? You need to further insult me by checking my ID? Do I look like a teenage boy trying to buy beer?"

"Now take it easy, lady," the sergeant interrupted, "I'll handle this." Turning to Scanlon, the tall sergeant glowered. "Damn it Scanlon; she decides not to have you arrested for battery and you still want to shake her down?

Where do you FBI fucks get off? Don't you assholes have any couth? You guys dress like you're going to Sunday School, but act like fraternity boys on a Saturday night."

"I'm sorry," Scanlon said firmly. "But I'm going to have to insist."

"Oh, alright," Ms Piper said with exasperation. "I'll have to go to my car and get my ID. It's in my purse, along with cosmetics, house keys, and a host of other things I didn't think I'd need. But Kearns stays here. I don't want him out of my sight while I'm going to my car. I don't trust you."

"We'll wait right here in the lobby," Scanlon said.

The station sergeant cut in. "If you'd like, ma'am, I'll stay here with them and make sure things are handled properly."

"Oh, that'll be all right, Sergeant," she said in a sincere voice. "You've already been marvelous. I want you to know that I harbor OPD no ill will whatsoever. You've been a big help. Who knows what Agent Scanlon would have done if you weren't here. I'll be noting your assistance to the district attorney."

"Think nothing of it," the sergeant said, blushing at the pretty attorney in spite of himself. "I'll be getting back to the patrol desk."

"Thank you again, Sergeant," Ms Piper said, offering her hand. After shaking hands, the sergeant shot a scowl at Scanlon and went back into the station, leaving Kearns, Scanlon, and the young woman alone in the lobby.

"My car's out in the public lot," Ms Piper said. "Would you like to accompany me to make sure I don't have any explosives or a tommy gun?"

"I don't find your humor particularly amusing," Scanlon snarled, all pretense of cordiality gone with the sergeant. "Get your credentials and a phone number for me to verify your employment with the public defender's office. And don't take all night."

Kearns looked at Scanlon, shaking his head. "You're a real class act, Scanlon. You change tune like a jukebox."

"Fuck you, Deputy. Last week in Iowa you were a small town cop in a bit of trouble. Now you're a small town cop in a lot of trouble. What changed your tune?"

"Fucktards like you."

The young attorney was fumbling in her leather briefcase and ignoring the exchange between the two men. Finally she looked up and addressed Scanlon.

"I'm sorry, Agent Scanlon, I thought I'd left my identification in the car. It's right here in my bag. I'll just need some help to dig it out."

Kearns watched the woman trying to balance her satchel and sift through it at the same time. She started to step forward, motioning for Kearns to hold the bag while she looked in it.

"Step back, Deputy," Scanlon said, cutting in front of Kearns. "I'll do the honors. Remember you're still in custody."

Kearns rolled his eyes and stepped back. Scanlon stepped forward and took hold of the briefcase with both hands. Jennifer Piper continued to rummage in her briefcase. Scanlon sent Kearns a smug look.

Finally, she said, "Here it is. I believe this is what you need, Agent Scanlon."

The redhead's fist emerged from the briefcase and she punched Scanlon square on his bandaged nose. It was not the feminine slap of a few moments earlier, and when it landed on his broken nose he fell unconscious to the floor. Kearns stared in surprise, his mouth agape.

The young attorney wasted no time. She reached down and grabbed her briefcase from the clutches of the unconscious FBI man, then grabbed Kearns roughly by the hand.

"Let's go!" she yelped, tugging his arm.

Kearns stood like a statue, dumbfounded.

"What are you waiting for, an engraved invitation? Come on!" Dragging the reluctant deputy she headed for the door.

Kearns allowed himself to be pulled through the doors of the police station. He looked over his shoulder at Scanlon snoring on the floor.

"Move your ass," the redhead commanded. They descended the ice-covered steps.

A silver-colored sedan screeched up in front of the steps to meet them. The passenger door popped open. Kearns noticed it had no license plates. It was an Oldsmobile.

"Get in!" Jennifer Piper said, pushing Kearns. He allowed himself to be pushed into the car. Looking back, he saw the police station doors burst open and several uniformed cops, led by the big sergeant, start down the steps with revolvers drawn.

The woman shoved Kearns into the front seat and hopped in after him, yelling, "Go! Go! Go!" to the driver. The Oldsmobile spun its tires on the icy road before gaining traction and lurched away at high speed.

The car was a block away before Kearns turned to the red-haired beauty seated to his right and said, "I gather you're not from the public defender's office?"

"Are you kidding? I haven't even graduated college, much less law school."

Looking at the driver, Kearns smiled.

"Hi Kevin," Bob Farrell said. "Good to see you again. You know, you ought to wear a coat in this kind of weather. You could catch your death of cold."

"Yeah, I could at that."

"Oh my goodness, I've forgotten my manners. Kevin, meet my daughter, Jennifer."

Suddenly the sense of familiarity Kearns noticed at the police station seemed ridiculously obvious.

"I might have known," Kearns said with a sigh. "Her kind of balls had to be hereditary." He eased into a smile. "Thanks Bob. It's good to see you, too. You'll never know how good it is."

"I couldn't leave you in the clutches of the FBI," Farrell said, lighting a cigarette. "Besides, we belong together. We're a team, you and me. Like Batman and Robin, or the Lone Ranger and Tonto."

"Or Abbott and Costello," Jennifer interjected.

"One question, Bob," Kearns asked. "An Oldsmobile?"

"Haven't I taught you anything? Oldsmobiles are the chariots of the twentieth century. Modern mechanized masterpieces. What else would I steal?"

"Steal?" Kearns said, cringing.

"Did I say steal? I meant rented. That's what I meant; rented. Right, Jen?"

"Sure, Dad. Anything you say."

"Here we go again," Kearns said, to nobody in particular.

CHAPTER 31

Special-Agent-in-Charge Steven Scanlon lay propped on a bed in the emergency room of the Douglas County Hospital with a bag of ice on his face. His hand-crafted Italian suit was splattered with his own dried blood and his Japanese silk tie, a gift from an ex-girlfriend, was stained beyond repair.

He awakened to the noisy bustle of the ER approximately one hour after being decked by a petite young woman in the front lobby of the Omaha police station. It was the second time that Deputy Kevin Kearns had been snatched from his custody by a bogus lawyer. Scanlon himself had a law degree, but was beginning to hate attorneys with a passion.

Presently Agent Phil Tatters came into the room.

"Hi, Steve. How you feeling?"

"Cut the bullshit and give me a report."

Tatters frowned and took a seat on a stool near the bed. He folded his coat over his lap and withdrew a notepad from his breast pocket.

"You want the good news or the bad news?"

"Who gives a shit? Quit stalling."

"OK, here goes. The body at the Slocum lady's house has been tentatively identified as Brent A Cuszack, a drug addict with an extensive criminal history hailing from Audubon, Iowa. I've got a couple of state DCI boys running down his history right now, but so far he's very promising. I'll get to that in a minute."

"Spare me the editorials."

Tatters continued. "The gun found next to Cuszack's body, a Smith & Wesson Model 686, has a serial number registered to the Iowa Highway Patrol. It's the gun belonging to one of the state troopers killed in western Iowa last week near the drug lab explosion."

Scanlon sat up abruptly. "I'll be damned. Our young deputy bagged a cop-killer. I wonder if he knows?"

"I don't see how he could," Tatters said.

"Keep going."

"Cuszack apparently has some connection to the lab. One of the bodies inside has been identified as a Zachary Fornier, a known drug-trafficker and methamphetamine cooker. Cuszack is a suspected drug courier. He was arrested in a raid on Fornier's farm a few years back, but got off with probation."

Scanlon removed the ice from his face and mused, "So the guy who shot the Slocum woman in Omaha probably had something to do with the deaths of his former drug trafficking associates. And he was involved in the deaths of two state troopers. I'm still listening."

Tatters flipped through the pages of his notebook. "The AR-15 semi-automatic rifle found at the scene is confirmed stolen. The serial number comes back to a batch of weapons burglarized from a sporting goods store in Ottumwa, Iowa in 1985. It's too early for a complete ballistics report, but it's a safe bet it's the same gun that killed one of the highway patrolmen."

"What about suspect number two?"

"Number two is a dead ringer for our child-snatcher. And a match to the suspect in a triple homicide in downtown Omaha three nights ago. Also, the .45 casings found in the Leawood West shootings might match those downtown, at the burned out drug lab in west Iowa, at the murder scene of the troopers, and at the schoolyard where Tiffany Meade was grabbed. Similar extractor and ejector marks on all casings. Firing pin dents on the primers look like a match, too."

"I thought you said it was too early for a ballistic analysis?"

"Who needs the lab? You can look at the brass with a magnifying lens and compare the shell casings."

"What about our child-killer?"

"We're still at a loss for a correlation between him, this Cuszack guy, Elizabeth Slocum, Deputy Kearns, and his mysterious sidekick. But there's got to be a connection."

"Of course there's a connection, you idiot. All the players converged at the Slocum woman's house. The common denominator has therefore got to be her. Check her background. I want to know everything there is to know about her."

"I'll give it top priority," Tatters said, scribbling in his notebook.

"Anything on the young woman who sprung Kearns?"

"The one who knocked you on your ass?" Tatters asked innocently, glad to finally get in a shot of his own.

"Yeah, the one who knocked me on my ass. You got a problem with that, Phil?"

"Hell, no. She was obviously some kind of trained martial arts expert, knocking out a senior federal agent with one punch like she did. Chuck Norris in a skirt."

"I don't need any bruises to my reputation to match my face."

"Oh, don't worry about that, Boss," Tatters said, unable to resist another jab. "Your reputation couldn't get any more damaged than it already is."

Scanlon said nothing, glaring at his subordinate. Tatters returned a faux-bemused expression.

He turned back to his notebook. "We still have nothing on the identity of Kearns' male accomplice. We do, however, have a pretty good composite drawing of him, thanks to you. Apparently you're the only person who got a good look at him."

The thought of the fake attorney magnified Scanlon's headache. Twice, the mystery man rescued the deputy from his grasp. If only Kearns was still in custody answers to their questions could be had for the taking. Who was this man? Why did he keep rescuing Kearns? What was their relationship?

Scanlon knew his professional reputation, and possibly his rank as Special Agent in Charge of the Des Moines Office, were in serious jeopardy. He had to find Kearns again, and soon.

"When will Elizabeth Slocum be out of surgery?" he asked.

"She's already out," Tatters said. "She's in post-op, but she hasn't regained consciousness yet."

"I want somebody watching her around the clock. As soon as she's able to talk, I want to be notified. Have a cassette recorder loaded and ready to start the minute she wakes. And keep me informed."

Tatters nodded, putting his notepad in his coat pocket. He knew his boss well enough to know when he was being dismissed. As he walked out of the room a nurse came walking in.

"Hello, Mister Scanlon. How are we feeling? I see you took the ice pack off. You shouldn't have done that."

"We're feeling like shit. And I don't need any fucking ice pack."

The nurse, an attractive blonde with the demeanor of someone who's been in the emergency room most of her career, ignored Scanlon's biting manner. She looked at his chart and clicked her teeth.

"Well, Agent Scanlon, I'm afraid we have some bad news. The x-rays are back, and it looks like your nose is going to require surgery. The last injury really did some damage. I gather your nose was already broken when it was broken again today?"

"You know damned well my nose was already broken. Is everyone in this hospital incompetent?"

The nurse only smiled, and headed for the door. "The doctor will be here in a few minutes. I hope you'll be as pleasant and cordial with her as you've been with me."

"I'll put on my happy face."

"One more thing," the nurse said, her smile widening. "There's another FBI agent in one of the other examining rooms right now. He's got a concussion and a broken nose too. He also has your temperament. Mysterious, isn't it?"

"What's that?" Scanlon asked.

"Why anyone would want to clobber two such charming men? It's beyond comprehension." Without waiting for a reply the nurse walked out.

"Kiss my ass," Scanlon said, after she'd gone.

It came out, "Kizz by ads."

CHAPTER 32

Vernon Slocum cut away the remnants of his left trouser leg with the blade of his pocketknife. Beneath the blood-soaked jeans lay his riddled calf and shin.

When he peeled back the cloth from his wounds he found matted blood and tissue stuck painfully to three dime-sized holes in his lower leg. Two of the 00 buck pellets had struck meat alone, slicing neatly into the calf-muscle on either side of the tibia. These two balls exited the rear of the calf. Though they'd bled heavily, these wounds were not Slocum's primary concern.

He concerned himself mainly with the final 00 pellet, which penetrated directly into the shin below his kneecap. This pellet didn't exit, and was embedded in the bone itself. Each time Slocum stepped on that leg, or even pointed his toe, excruciating pain resulted. This wound didn't bleed much, but instead seeped a clear liquid. This had steadily increased since the firefight.

It was only a few hours since Buddy died. Slocum didn't give his former pal much thought. He'd been a casualty. He knew the risks of the mission when he signed on, and his death brought neither sorrow nor regret.

Slocum scooped a pinch of the methamphetamine on the blade of his knife and inhaled it. The pain moved to the back of his mind.

He gently scraped away the scabbed flesh surrounding the bone-wound. The tendons in his neck and forearms swelled as he poked into the ugly hole. He held a small flashlight in his mouth like a metal cigar, its pinpoint of light illuminating his grisly work.

Slocum opened another quarter-gram bindle of methamphetamine. He used his knife blade again to scoop out some of the dirty powder, but this time, instead of ingesting it, he put it inside the bullet-holes. The meth mixed with blood, creating a paste. The numbing effect was instantaneous. He spread the makeshift painkiller in and around the bullet wounds.

He found the bottle he'd liberated at Fornier's farm. He took a long pull from it, spilling bourbon down his unshaven face and onto his jacket.

Gritting his teeth, Slocum poured whiskey into the shotgun pellet-holes in his leg. Barely a sound escaped his lips, and he tensed every muscle in his formidable body. The pain seared through his leg and into his whole being. This was not an unfamiliar feeling.

Slocum knew he was dangerously close to collapse. He hadn't slept in over seventy-two hours. He'd been staying awake with methamphetamine to keep vigilant. Buddy split the duty and made it easier for a while, but Buddy was gone. And Vernon was alone again.

Slocum was disappointed that he failed to see the ambush back at his sister's place. Had he been alert, and not so zoned on crank, he would have recognized the cul-de-sac as a trap. He would have seen the enemy waiting in ambush.

How the enemy knew he was going to get his sister, Vernon didn't know. All he knew was that the young dude who'd killed Buddy was the same man he'd fought hand to hand once before. Slocum couldn't remember where he'd encountered the older man with the shotgun, but he sensed he'd met him before too. He couldn't remember if it was in the Nam, in one of his dreams, or in one of the places he'd gone and forgotten. It was the same enemy, though. He was almost sure.

Or was it?

Slocum knew they'd stolen his mind in the VA hospital. They'd stolen his past, his memories, and his life. They'd blurred the lines between reality and dreams. He knew he had to reclaim himself. But he also knew he couldn't trust his mind; it had been poisoned by the doctors. The doctors taught his mind to play tricks on him.

After he left the hospital he hoped his mind would clear. There were still many blank spots, and he often had difficulty distinguishing the past from the present. But as time passed, his mind didn't clear; it became more clouded. It became even more difficult to discern nightmares from reality.

Only one thing was crystal-clear to him; one irrevocable truth. The key to reclaiming his life and his past.

He was a Marine.

He realized that to accomplish his mission he would need help from somebody who could be trusted; a veteran. He'd sought out Buddy.

Now he was alone again. But even alone, he had to go on.

The mission.

He'd been wounded many times before. His concern for the condition of his leg was not due to the agony it caused him, but instead for how it would affect his mobility. Slocum knew his injury was a liability and could jeopardize his mission. He needed rest and medical attention.

Slocum sat in his truck, parked on a side road at 120th and Pacific near the Westroads Shopping Plaza. The area was largely residential, and in the bitter cold of the

December night looked sleepy and peaceful. Christmas lights cast a serene glow over the neighborhood.

He took inventory. He still had a sizable quantity of cash, over eight thousand dollars, courtesy of the now-dead Zeke Fornier. He still had plenty of methamphetamine. The AR-15 was gone; the spare magazines for it under the Dodge's seat were now useless. He still had the sawed-off shotgun and his .45. He also had a magnum revolver taken from a dead state trooper. Buddy had lost the other trooper's gun, along with his life, back at Elizabeth's.

He got stiffly out of the truck. He packed his wares into the green army duffel bag, all but his .45, the Ka-Bar USMC knife, and revolver. These he stuck in the pockets of his jacket.

In a hobbling gait Slocum left the truck parked at the side of the road and headed for a group of houses nearby. Each step was agony, and shooting pains traveled through his knee into his hip.

He stopped at the first house he saw without a porch light on. He stumbled up to the porch and rang the doorbell several times. He took out his flashlight, and put it into his mouth again. He switched the duffel bag to his left hand, and drew the Ka-Bar knife with his right, holding it along his hip.

After several long minutes the porch light came on. He heard locks unbolt, and the door opened a crack. "Who is it?" came a meek voice from inside.

Slocum slammed his shoulder into the door, forcing it open. He felt the weight of a small body behind the door as it swung inward, and as soon as he was inside closed the door.

The house was in darkness, and he switched on the light clenched in his teeth. He heard a scraping sound and looked down to see a very old woman on the floor. She was extremely thin, and wore a bathrobe. Her eyes were wide with fear, and she had a toothless mouth opened in a scream that made no sound. Slocum ignored her and walked into the house, grimacing in pain with each step.

Within thirty seconds he'd made a sweep of the one-story residence and determined the old woman lived alone. The home was furnished with the knick-knacks common to elderly women, and he found nothing to indicate another resident.

He returned to the woman. He walked heavily to where she lay by the door, unable to get up. The sparse glow of the penlight in his mouth was all the light he needed to cut her throat. She thrashed briefly and was still. He turned off the porch light.

He dropped his duffel bag and went into the bedroom. The walls and dresser tops were plastered with faded photographs of what was once the woman out in the hall. There were black and white pictures of a tall, handsome man in Thirties garb. There were pictures of children and grandchildren as well.

Slocum went to the closet. He found both men's and women's clothing. The men's clothing looked big enough to fit him, even though it was outdated and smelled of mothballs.

He found a linen closet in the hall. He felt dizzy as he gazed at the stack of clean white sheets, neatly piled on top of each other. He was near the point of exhaustion, and the linen reminded him of the VA hospital.

He returned to the bedroom and lay face down on the bed. Within seconds he was asleep.

Vernon Slocum slept soundly for the next twenty hours, with only occasional nightmares to interrupt his slumber. He dreamed, as always, of children screaming in pain and carnage in the jungle. When he finally awoke it was to his own screams.

He took a hot shower and shaved with an old-fashioned safety razor he found in the medicine cabinet. He soaked his injured leg in the tub long after the shower was done. Using peroxide found under the sink, he cleaned the jagged bullet holes as best he could. He bandaged the wounds in strips of torn linen.

He hobbled back into the bedroom and ransacked the closet. Though snug around the chest and shoulders, one of the suits fit him. It took several minutes of rummaging to find a pair of shoes. The black loafers he selected were dusty and stiff with age, but fit.

In the back of the closet was a leather suitcase of a style not common for many years. He opened it to find musty towels and linen. He emptied the valise and filled it with the items from his duffel bag. He also packed the peroxide, sheets for bandages, and one of the other suits that fit.

He hobbled to the hallway and stepped over the body of the woman he'd carved the night before. Coagulated blood lay in a thick puddle around her. Her face was ashen, and her gray eyes stared sightlessly. Slocum took her by the feet and dragged her body out of view behind a sofa. He put a rug from the kitchen over the pool of caked blood.

Vernon opened the front door and looked out. Night had fallen again, and gentle flakes of snow drifted steadily down in a straight line. He guessed the temperature at a little above zero. He glanced at the address number stenciled on the top of the front door.

He went back in and closed the door. He limped into the kitchen and opened the refrigerator. A large pitcher of orange juice was the first thing he saw. Grabbing that and a carton of eggs, he closed the refrigerator. He opened cabinets until he found glassware. He broke four eggs into a glass and filled the remainder with orange juice. He drank this concoction and picked up the phone.

Dialing information, he requested the number of a local cab company. He gave the address over the front door, telling the dispatcher his destination was the bus terminal downtown. She told him it would be forty-five minutes. Thanking her, he hung up.

He went back to the bedroom and opened the suitcase. He transferred two tablespoons of methamphetamine into a flowery pillbox he'd found in the medicine cabinet. He put this, along with a roll of cash and his cigarettes and lighter, into his pockets.

Vernon then field-stripped his .45 pistol. He pushed some linen patches through the barrel with a pencil and wiped off the carbon build-up as best he could. He lightly oiled the slide rails with some corn oil he took from the kitchen. He preferred to use machine oil, but could find none in the house. Reassembling the large pistol, he filled three magazines with seven rounds each. He then put a single round in the chamber and racked the slide forward, inserting a loaded magazine into the grip. Tucking the .45 in his waistband he pocketed the two spare magazines and closed up the suitcase.

A film of sweat broke out on Slocum's forehead through this effort. His left leg throbbed badly, and walking on it was becoming more difficult. He found a cane in the hallway and tested his weight on it. Then he sat down and lit a cigarette. Before it was finished the doorbell rang.

Slocum limped to the door. When he opened it he found a short, heavy man in a parka and a baseball cap which read PARTY ANIMAL. The man was smoking a fat cigar.

"You wanna go to the bus station?"

Slocum only nodded.

"Let's go. Time's money, right?"

Slocum nodded again and walked with his cane over to where he'd set down his suitcase. Noticing the pronounced limp, the cabbie took the suitcase.

"Let me get that; looks like you got a bum wheel. What happened?"

"Hunting accident," Slocum said.

"I'll be damned," the cabbie droned on, making small talk. "Guns can be dangerous things."

Slocum again didn't reply. He followed the cabbie down the porch to the sidewalk. A yellow taxi was parked at the curb with its engine running.

"Christ," the cabbie exclaimed. "Whatcha got in this thing? Bricks?"

Slocum didn't answer. He watched the driver struggle with the heavy valise and put it into the trunk. The cabbie opened the door for him and then got in himself. On the radio, George Strait crooned, "All My Ex's Live in Texas."

"OK," the cabbie said breathlessly. "The bus station it is. You taking some kind of trip? I see you ain't got no coat on, and it's about five above friggin' zero. Where you going, Florida?"

Slocum lit a Pall Mall. He exhaled smoke through his nostrils.

"California. I'm going to California to visit a relative. Shut up and drive."

The cabbie glanced at the huge man with the tight haircut seated next to him and put the car into gear.

"You don't want to make conversation, that's OK by me. I can take a hint. It being the Christmas season and all, most folks want to spread a little holiday cheer, you know? Befriend their fellow man? Peace on Earth, and all that jazz?"

Slocum smoked in silence.

"Bah, humbug," the cabbie said, turning up the volume on the radio.

CHAPTER 33

Deputy Kevin Kearns walked out of the elevator with a pretty redhead on his arm. He was dressed in a gray suit and shiny new black shoes. The red-haired young woman wore her hair up and was wearing a conservative dress and high-heels which accented her nicely shaped legs. Both had overcoats draped over their free arms, and Kearns carried a bouquet of white roses.

The elevator stopped on the fourth floor of the Douglas County Hospital. This floor housed the Critical Care Unit. When they disembarked from the elevator, Kevin Kearns and Jennifer Farrell found themselves facing a nursing station which blocked further access to the unit. The desk attendant looked up from a series of video monitors and put down her copy of Stephen King's *Misery*, but not before marking her place with a finger.

Kearns could see patient's rooms displayed on the monitors. He nudged Jennifer and whispered, "Stall her."

"May I help you?" asked the nurse at the desk.

"I hope so," Jennifer said sweetly. "My name is Ellen Gleason, and this is my husband, Edward. We're looking for one of the patients registered here. Perhaps you could help us?"

The nurse glanced at her wristwatch. "It's after eight, and that's when visiting hours cease. You'll have to come back tomorrow."

"Please, ma'am. We drove all the way from Davenport in this weather, and the only reason we're late is because many of the roads are so bad. I know it's an inconvenience, but it's very important we see our aunt today. We understand her condition is quite serious. We're her only relatives. I know it would mean so much to her recovery if she could chat with us for a while. Couldn't you let us in? Please?"

While Jennifer kept the nurse occupied, Kearns checked the monitors. Listed by room number were patients in varying conditions of medical distress. Under the monitor labeled ICU #3, he saw Elizabeth Slocum. She lay propped up in bed with an oxygen tube in her nose and a drain tube extending from one side of her chest. She appeared asleep.

Kearns left Jennifer to argue with the nurse and scanned the corridor. Room #1 was to his immediate front. Two doors down, he saw a tall man in his late thirties. The man had a military haircut and was wearing a blue suit and tasseled loafers. His right hip bulged only slightly under the fabric of his coat.

Kearns recognized the man immediately as a federal agent. He saw no others, but wondered if the agent's partner lurked nearby, out of sight. Though not perfect, it was better than he'd hoped.

Turning back to the nurse's station, Kearns looked at the video monitors again. In the room adjacent to Elizabeth Slocum's was an extremely old woman. She looked at least ninety. Her mouth was slightly parted and her eyes were closed. Like Elizabeth Slocum, she had an oxygen tube in her nose and appeared to be asleep.

He turned his gaze quickly to the wall behind the nurse's station. Jennifer was still pleading with the nurse. On the wall was a series of clipboards. These were arranged in order by room number. At the top of the chart labeled Room #2 was the name Hapworth, Margaret A.

He interrupted Jennifer. "Ma'am, we'd sure like to see Aunt Hapworth. We don't want to be a bother, but it would mean so much to the both of us."

Jennifer's eyes widened and she kicked him under the desk. Turning to Kearns, she said, "Edward, can I have a word?"

Kearns smiled at the nurse and said, "Excuse us a moment."

Taking him aside, Jennifer asked, "What's the matter with you? We're not here to see anybody named Hapworth. We're here to see Elizabeth Slocum. Dad was very specific about that. What's gotten into you?"

"Take a look," he said, pointing down the corridor. "You see that sharp-dresser at the end of the hall, in front of room three? He's not there to deliver flowers. He's FBI, and he's obviously been posted to guard Slocum's room. We're not going to get past him with any sob story about visiting our elderly aunt. I've got an idea. Trust me, OK?"

"The hell I will. Dad calls up and begs for a favor. I haven't seen him in over a year. So I drive from Lincoln to Omaha in the middle of final exams, to see my dad, and what does he want? What's the favor? He wants me to break you out of jail. Then he wants me to break into a hospital. And now I'm apparently about to get arrested by the FBI. I won't do it. I'm not going along with any more of these crazy schemes. Now I know why Mom divorced him."

"Honey, it's OK," Kearns cooed, trying to keep her voice down. "If we can't see Aunt Maggie, then we can't see Aunt Maggie. That's all there is to it. This nice nurse has done all she can. There's nothing more we can do.

Let's not get upset, OK? C'mon, let's go get a hotel room and come back in the morning."

He led Jennifer by the arm towards the elevator. They'd taken only a few steps when the nurse called out to them.

"Hold on, folks. I can let you see your aunt, but only for a few minutes. I could get in big trouble for this."

"Thank you," Kearns said sincerely. "You don't know how much this means to us. We'll only be a minute or two."

"She's in room number two," the nurse said. "Down the hall to your right. Only a few minutes, OK?"

"Thank you very much," Kearns repeated. "C'mon honey; aren't you anxious to see your aunt?"

Jennifer smiled pleasantly until out of the nurse's view. Then she scowled at the deputy and snarled, "Don't honey me, you jerk. I hope you know what you're doing."

"Of course I know what I'm doing. Your old man taught me."

"That's what I'm afraid of."

They walked into Critical Care Unit room number two and approached the bed of Margaret Hapworth. Kearns whispered into Jennifer's ear.

"Listen carefully, because I haven't got time to say this more than once. I want you to act like you're crying, and then go down to the elevator and get in. I want you to go to the first floor. Wait exactly five minutes, and then pull the fire alarm. Then go outside, get the car, and be ready to scram when I come out."

Jennifer stared at him in horror. "You want me to pull the fire alarm in a hospital? In December? Are you mad? They throw you in jail for that! It would endanger the patients! I won't do it."

Margaret Hapworth snoozed on her bed, oblivious to the argument raging in her room. Kearns grabbed Jennifer by the arms and forced her to look into his eyes.

"Listen to me. I appreciate you getting me out of jail, but you'd better grow up. I don't like pulling these stunts any more than you, but somebody has to. Vernon Slocum has got to be found and stopped. He kills little kids and hangs them in trees. That woman next door might know where he's going to strike next. I'm going to do everything within my power to stop him. I'm not going to let Slocum get another kid. Are you with me, or not?"

Jennifer Farrell said nothing. After a few seconds she nodded weakly, still looking into Kearns' blazing eyes. He relaxed his grip on her shoulders.

"Get going. Give me five minutes, then pull the fire alarm. I expect to see you when I come out."

She wordlessly turned and left.

Kearns tossed his overcoat over the video camera mounted in one corner of the room. He then focused his attention on the intricate medical apparatus consuming one entire wall. Tubes and hoses from several of the machinery's outlets were attached to various parts of Margaret Hapworth's body.

Reaching down and grabbing a handful of these cords, Kearns said, "I'm sorry, Ms Hapworth, but I have to do this. You'll be OK; you're in the Critical Care Center, and they'll take care of you. But I need a diversion, and you're all I've got."

If Margaret Hapworth heard him, she didn't show it. He shrugged, and pulled several cords from the life-support machine.

A cacophony of alarms, buzzers, and bells filled the room. Kearns ran into the hall and began yelling frantically.

"Help! My aunt's dying! Help! Emergency! Help!"

Several nurses came running from different directions. The FBI agent came running too. They checked the apparatus, as well as Margaret Hapworth, who looked the same as she did before the crisis. The room filled with people.

Kearns took a second to ensure the FBI man was watching the event in room number two. Satisfied, he sneaked from Hapworth's room into the adjacent one.

Elizabeth Slocum was propped in a sitting position to drain her punctured lung. Kearns ran over and shook her gently by the shoulder.

"Ms Slocum," he said softly. "Wake up. Please, wake up. It's very important."

Gradually Elizabeth's eyes opened and she looked at Kearns, recognition coming an instant later. Her eyes widened.

"You," she said faintly. Kearns put his ear close to Slocum's mouth to hear her. Her breathing was extremely shallow.

"Yes," Kearns said. "I was at your house yesterday. I'm a cop. I was there looking for your brother, Vernon."

"...ank you for not leaving me," she whispered.

"Save your strength. I need to know where your brother Cole is. We think Vernon is going after Cole next, like he went after you. Where is he? You must tell me where we can find him."

She nodded, swallowing hard. He knew it was hard for her to speak, but he didn't have much time. He pressed his ear closer to her mouth.

"Address book," she said, barely audible.

"What address book? Where is it?"

Elizabeth's face contorted in pain and she struggled to get the words out. "Kitchen," she said at last.

"Where is Cole? Do you know?"

Elizabeth nodded again. Her hand reached out and took Kearns' hand. Her grip was surprisingly strong. She squeezed tightly as she spoke.

"...alifornia. In California."

Elizabeth's face was beet red, and Kearns worried the strain of speaking was hurting her. He started to get up. She pulled him back.

"Name," she said, pulling him nearer. "His name..."

She had to stop. Her breath came in wheezing gasps. Kearns wasn't sure what she was trying to communicate, but it was obviously important.

"What do you mean, 'name'? Did Cole change his name? Is that what you're trying to tell me?"

Once again, Elizabeth Slocum nodded. She was almost at the point of complete exhaustion.

Kearns squeezed her hand, hard. "Come on, Elizabeth, stay with me. Tell me Cole's name. I've got to know his name."

"...alentine," she gasped, coughing.

"Valentine? Did you say Valentine?" He was running out of time.

Slocum shook her head, choking back a cough. "...alentine," was all he could make out.

"Come on, Elizabeth, I need more. Give it to me. Is it Valentine?"

Slocum took a deep and raspy inhale. Straining with all her dwindling might, she forced out her words.

"B-Ballantine."

Kearns grinned from ear to ear. "Gotcha," he said. He kissed her on the forehead. He was standing up to leave when he saw her expression change to astonishment. He spun around to see the tall FBI man walk into the room.

Both men made eye contact. The Fed acted.

The federal agent swept aside his coat with a practiced movement of his right hand and began to draw a blue steel revolver from a holster on his hip.

Kearns threw the bouquet of roses in the Fed's face and leaped, catching him around the waist in a flying low-tackle. He pinned the man's arms to his sides. Both men went crashing to the floor, white rose petals filling the air. Kearns rolled off the larger man as the agent tucked both knees and kicked, and narrowly avoided having his teeth caved in. Both men struggled to their feet.

Kearns reached out a left and grabbed the agent's right hand, as the Fed was clearing his revolver from its holster. He twisted the gun hand inward, and punched the FBI man a quick jab to the face. The revolver clattered to the floor.

The FBI man staggered back and shook his head, then squared off. Kearns was in a relaxed stance, his right fist cocked and his left open in a blade. The Fed was bouncing lightly on the balls of his feet, and Kearns was alert to the possibility of his opponent's skill in martial arts. Sure enough, the Fed faked a punch, and when Kearns reacted his right leg darted out and kicked Kearns directly in the ribs. The kick missed the solar plexus. Had it not, the fight would have been over.

Kearns ignored the stabbing pain in his side. That his opponent was more than a match for him in unarmed combat was certain. Kearns remembered a lesson he'd learned during hand-to-hand combat training at Fort Benning.

As a recruit in Advanced Infantry Training he'd been taught if the fight lasted more than a few seconds, you were dead. Your adversary would spread an alarm. Therefore you must ignore pain, attack, and overcome your opponent's greater strength or skill with aggression and savagery. Be relentless. Attack or die.

Kearns let out a guttural howl and charged the FBI agent. The Fed struck out another kick, but Kearns barely felt it. He threw a hard right and took the larger man square on the jaw. Both men went to the floor again with the deputy on top.

The federal agent simultaneously covered his throat and groin. Kearns continued to scream in a primordial manner, and head-butted the agent repeatedly in the face.

The stitches on the left side of Kearns' head ripped open, and his own blood flowed down his face. The agent threw him off and regained his feet, but he could tell by the stiff manner in which he rose that he was stunned. It was no time to relent, and Kearns charged again.

The Fed threw another karate kick, but this one was slow, and Kearns caught the leg. He trapped the man's foot in his left elbow and stepped back, pulling the agent off balance. He hit the man as hard a right as he'd ever thrown, directly in the groin. Still screaming, he hit him two more times, the last shot to the jaw. The FBI man crumpled to the floor and was still.

Kearns wiped the blood out of his left eye and looked up. Three nurses were standing in the doorway, aghast. Kearns stumbled over to where the agent's gun had fallen and retrieved it. It was a standard FBI-issue Smith & Wesson Model 13 with a three-inch barrel, and wore Pachmayr grips. He tucked the gun in his waistband.

His side was an explosion of pain. It was a sure bet the federal agent bruised or cracked at least one of his ribs. More people began filling the doorway, blocking his exit. He was trapped.

Suddenly the deafening sound of a klaxon filled the halls. The fire alarm! Jennifer did it! The group blocking the doorway was momentarily distracted by the blaring horn.

Seizing his chance, Kearns ducked his head and charged through the group of people blocking the doorway.

Several hands tried to grab him, but he rammed his body through. He sprinted to the exit by the nurses' station. A large male nurse tried to block his path, but Kearns brushed his hands aside and brought him down with an uppercut to the gut. The impact from the punch sent shivers of pain through Kearns' ribs. He grimaced and continued his flight.

Kearns knew with the fire alarm activated the elevator would be inoperative. He ran to the stairs and found the stairway crowded with people. He shoved them aside and made his descent.

He finally reached the ground floor. Bursting from the stairwell with shouted obscenities in his ears, he pushed past the throngs and ran into the parking lot. The lot was filled with hospital employees and patients who'd left the building in response to the alarm.

Kearns wiped more blood from his left eye and searched for Jennifer. Her car wasn't in sight. People were beginning to take notice of him; a disheveled man with a torn coat and blood on his face.

Faintly, over the deafening roar of the fire klaxon, came the tiny sound of a car horn. He looked in the direction of the sound and saw Jennifer's Volkswagen Jetta on the street outside the lot. He sprinted towards the car.

He found the passenger door unlocked and piled into the car. Jennifer drove rapidly away from the hospital, the Jetta's tires skidding on the icy road.

When several blocks away, she looked over at Kearns. He was clutching his side and wincing. Blood ran down his face.

"What happened? You look like hell. Do you need a doctor?"

"I'm OK," Kearns rasped. "Besides, we just left a hospital. Get us to the hotel; I'll be fine."

"You don't look fine. Did you get what you were after?"

"I'm not sure. I think so, but I won't know until I talk with your dad. It'll depend on what he got."

"Hopefully whatever he gets won't have him looking like you do. You sure you're alright?"

"Yeah, I'm alright," he said, unconvincingly. "It was a piece of cake."

"Piece of cake, my ass," Jennifer said.

CHAPTER 34

Farrell strolled leisurely down the street, the puppy tugging mightily on its leash. He'd visited this neighborhood before; yesterday, in fact.

Farrell acquired the dog at the Omaha Animal Shelter earlier in the morning. It was a black Labrador, and no more than a few months old. He selected it because it was the only dog in the shelter that didn't bark constantly. The lady at the facility gave him a certification for the dog's shots and a nylon cord woven into a leash.

Farrell walked up to Elizabeth Slocum's house. The last time he'd been there Elizabeth lay bleeding on her front lawn, and he and Kevin were locked in combat with Vernon Slocum.

He looked around, whistling. There were no other pedestrians about, and no one seemed to be peering from any of the windows nearby.

Farrell walked past the front door and down the driveway to the rear of the house. He acted as if he were the owner and did this on a daily basis. He went directly to the back door and let go of the leash, saying, "Stay," in a loud whisper. The dog complied.

Farrell was wearing thick winter gloves and he punched his fist through the glass pane of the back door. Reaching his hand through, he unlocked the knob from the inside. A moment later he and the Labrador were safely inside Elizabeth Slocum's house.

He went directly to the kitchen. Most people kept telephones there, and subsequently address books. He located the phone, and sure enough, a small vinyl address book was beneath it. He checked the bedroom next, using a flashlight he'd brought for the occasion. There was nothing near the phone but a stack of magazines. He figured he'd better not press his luck and headed for the back door.

He found the puppy sitting as he'd left it. He'd gotten the puppy as a prop in case a cop or federal agent was watching the house. He would claim to be out walking his dog, and in fact walked back and forth in front of the house several times before approaching.

Farrell pocketed the address book and stowed his flashlight. Taking hold of the leash, he started to walk the dog out through the front door and back to his car. He'd parked the Oldsmobile on the other side of the park. He didn't want to get caught in the cul-de-sac if there was someone staking out the house.

But the dog wouldn't budge. The Labrador instead exhibited a low, steady growl. Farrell was instantly alert. He'd had the dog almost the entire day, and it hadn't made a sound. Now his ears were back, and pointing a wet nose at the rear door.

Listening carefully, Farrell could hear the crunch of footsteps in the snow outside the house. Feds. He knew it was optimistic to think they wouldn't be staking out Slocum's house, especially after the bloodbath yesterday. The footsteps made steady progress along the side of the garage, the same way he had come.

He was trapped. If indeed FBI agents, they'd now have men at both the front and rear of the house. He went to the window and peeked through the blinds. A four-door Chevy Impala had pulled up. Behind it squatted a man in a suit with a shotgun in his hands.

He looked at the dog, who was happily returning his gaze. He reached down and unhooked the leash from the dog's collar. He then walked quietly through the kitchen to the back door. He could tell by the scraping sounds outside that the person making them was almost at the back door. He gently opened it, and said to the dog in a low whisper, "OK boy, bark."

He acted like he was about to run at the dog, enough to set it on edge. The Labrador started to yelp. The dog looked back at Farrell, and Farrell feinted again, continuing with the game. The dog carried on yelping. Farrell drew his revolver and ducked behind the open kitchen door.

Soon a man edged tentatively around the corner of the door. He pointed a revolver at the dog, and then said, "Shit," under his breath. The Labrador sat by the door and made no effort to move. The man kicked the dog aside and stepped into the kitchen. The dog skittered across the smooth kitchen floor, coming to a stop against the oven.

The FBI agent stepped further into the kitchen, his revolver leading the way. As soon as he cleared the door Farrell stepped out from behind it and stuck the barrel of his own revolver against the man's neck, thumbing back the hammer.

"Don't move. Don't make a sound. If you do, I'll kill you."

The fed froze, his eyes flashing. Farrell reached out with his free hand and took the six-gun from the agent's outstretched grip. He pocketed it, and said, "If you're thinking about trying any of the moves they taught you at Quantico, forget it. Follow my instructions and you'll live through the night."

The FBI man nodded. Farrell took a set of handcuffs and a portable radio from beneath the agent's coat. Ordering him to put his hands behind his back, Farrell cuffed him. The agent complied with these instructions hesitantly, and Farrell was careful to keep his gun trained on him.

The portable radio crackled. "Hey Jerry, you OK back there? Code four?"

Farrell held the portable radio up to the man's face. "You're going to say 'Code four.' Nothing else. If you do, I'll kill you. Understand?"

The agent nodded. Beads of sweat formed on his forehead. Farrell keyed the mike on the radio. "Code four," the FBI man said.

Farrell hefted the transceiver, which weighed about three pounds. He clubbed the FBI agent on the side of the head over the temple. The Fed went down, and out.

"That's for kicking my dog, you asshole."

Farrell scooped up the puppy, which began to lick his face. He went out through the back door and made a wide arc through the backyards adjacent to Slocum's house. He used the same route Kearns used when sneaking up on Vernon Slocum. He was unaccustomed to strenuous exercise and struggled his way through the heavy snow. The warm tongue of the Labrador puppy lapped his neck as he ran.

In what seemed like hours he reached the park. Looking back, he saw the Fed still squatting behind the parked sedan in front of Elizabeth Slocum's house. He wondered how long the FBI agent would wait before going in to check on his partner.

He started the Oldsmobile, out of breath. The dog frolicked on the front seat. A minute later he was heading back to the hotel, a cigarette between his lips. It had been a close one.

He leaned over and patted the Labrador's head. "You did alright, partner," he said. The dog beamed. "But what am I going to do with you now?"

Less than twenty minutes later he was at the hotel. He tucked the puppy under his coat and smuggled it past the registration clerk in the lobby. He fumbled with his room key and opened the door.

He was greeted by an unusual sight. Seated on one of the large double beds in the room was a shirtless Deputy Kearns. Jennifer was placing a heavy-duty bandage on his head. Both looked up as Farrell entered.

"Christ," Farrell said around his cigarette. "This looks like a scene from that Indiana Jones movie. What gives?"

Jennifer ignored her father. Kearns said, "I'll have you know I went three rounds with the Bruce Lee of FBI agents today. I was almost caught."

"Again?" Farrell smirked. "We should book you a permanent room in jail. You all right?"

"No, he's not alright!" Jennifer said, standing up and putting her hands on her hips. "I don't know what you fools are up to, but it's got to stop. You run around like madmen doing all sorts of illegal things and getting yourselves hurt. This has got to end."

Kearns looked sheepish. Farrell grinned. "You know, you sound more like your mother every day."

Jennifer was not amused. "You keep her out of this. At least she was there for me. It seems the only time I hear from you is when you need something. Did you know I'm in the middle of finals? I'm trying to graduate this spring. I really didn't need to get dragged out of my dorm in the middle of a blizzard to help you and your brain-dead sidekick break the law."

"Brain-dead?" Kearns asked indignantly.

"Shut up," Farrell answered him. "Jennifer, I'm sorry," he said in his most sincere voice. "That's why I brought your Christmas present early, to show my appreciation."

With that, Farrell opened his coat and brought out the puppy. He handed it to his daughter, who took it reflexively. Kearns looked on in amazement.

"While I was out getting my ass kicked, you were Christmas shopping?"

Farrell motioned for Kearns to be silent. Jennifer didn't see this. She was too busy being assaulted by the puppy's tongue.

"Dad, I can't have a dog. I live in the dorms."

"Go on and take it," Farrell said. "You know you love it, and you'll find a place to keep him until you graduate."

Kearns could tell Jennifer wanted to be angry with her father, but her fury evaporated under the onslaught of the puppy's tongue. Farrell couldn't have timed it better.

"Listen," Farrell said. "You've got to get going. I don't know how long the weather is going to hold, and the roads are as good as they're going to get. Besides, I don't want to have you seen with us any more than you have to." Opening his wallet, Farrell handed his daughter several hundred dollars.

"Take this. It's for gas, and to buy yourself something nice for Christmas. I'm sorry I dragged you into this Jen, but I was in a bind. You really came through. I'm grateful."

"So am I," Kearns said.

Jennifer was no longer angry. "OK Dad, I can tell you're trying to get rid of me, so I'll get going. You'd better keep an eye on Kevin though; he may have broken a couple of ribs. If he starts spitting up blood you take him to a doctor, even if he doesn't want to go, OK?"

"Anything you say," Farrell said. He gave Jennifer a hug around the squirming puppy. "Now scoot."

"OK, I'm going. Can I say goodbye to Kevin?"

Farrell's eyes narrowed. "Alone? Jesus, what is this, *The Dating Game*? You've known each other, what, a couple of days?"

Kevin looked at the floor. Jennifer said, "Dad, please."

"Alright, alright, I'm going. I need to get a pack of smokes anyway. So long honey. Merry Christmas. Don't give my love to your mother."

Farrell left the hotel room, grumbling to himself. Jennifer turned to Kearns, who was still seated on the bed.

"I wanted a minute to talk to you. You're a couple of years older than me, so I shouldn't be giving advice. But I'm going to, because I don't know if I'll ever see you again."

Kearns stood up with some effort. His ribs hurt.

"Kevin," she said, stepping closer. "If you're not careful you're going to end up like Dad. Alone, and with nothing and nobody in your life. Get out of this while you can."

"Thanks for your concern, but you don't need to worry about me. The events of the past couple of weeks have made my future pretty certain. When this is all over, I'll be lucky to avoid prison."

"Quit now. Tell Dad you've had a change of heart and want to go home. It might be rough at first, but people forget."

Kearns stopped listening. He watched the sprinkling of freckles on Jennifer's face and the cascade of red hair surrounding her. His throat got thick, and words seemed hard to find. He realized he was staring, but couldn't stop.

"I've got no home. And what I've seen, I'll never forget." His smile faded and his face got tight. "I'm in the hunt; I've got to see it through. I'm going to get Vernon Slocum. Maybe some of the things I've done with your dad aren't the smartest things a guy could do, but at least he's got a plan, and the guts to carry it out. I need him a helluva lot more than he needs me. I'm sorry you got sucked into this, but I'm not sorry I met you. I feel pretty lucky for it."

She looked into his eyes. He knew he was staring again, but couldn't pull his eyes away.

Juggling the puppy under her arm, Jennifer reached down and wrote a few lines on hotel stationery. She stood up and handed the paper to Kearns.

"This is my address and phone number. When this is all over, you could visit me. We could have dinner."

A wide grin broke out on his face. "I'd like that very much. After today, I owe you at least a dinner."

Jennifer returned the smile. "Take care of yourself Deputy Kevin Kearns," she said. "And take care of Dad. You're wrong about one thing; he needs you more than you think."

She kissed him on the cheek. The Labrador puppy licked his neck. "Merry Christmas, Kevin," she said, and was gone.

Kearns stood in the doorway for several long minutes. Farrell walked in with a fresh pack of Camels in his hand.

"Close your mouth, soldier, before a bug flies into it. You look like you've never seen a girl before."

"Not like that one, I haven't. You sure she's your daughter?"

"Very funny. Now get packing. We've got a redeye flight to catch in less than an hour."

"What?"

"You heard me. I made reservations from the lobby payphone. And I snagged Elizabeth Slocum's address

book while you were out romancing my daughter. Cole
Slocum lives in Alameda, California."

"Where the hell is Alameda? I've never heard of the
place."

"It's an island between Oakland and San Francisco; my
stomping grounds. Take a look at this."

Farrell produced the address book he'd taken from
Slocum's house and thumbed through several pages until
he came to rest on a piece of paper that was randomly
placed in the book. All it read was: Cole, Bay Farm Island,
Alameda, CA.

"That's it? No phone number or address?"

"That's all I could find."

"Try under the name Ballantine."

"Where did you get that name?" Farrell asked.

"Elizabeth. She told me Cole changed his name to
Ballantine."

"She tell you anything else?"

"No. She's in pretty bad shape. Also, our conversation
was interrupted by an FBI leg-breaker."

"So that's how you ended up looking like one of Mike
Tyson's sparring partners. Christ, Kevin, you take my
daughter out for the evening and end up street brawling.
Where you going on the second date? A demolition derby?"

Kearns said nothing, merely hoping for a second date.
Farrell turned pages until he found the "B" section of the
address book. "Yep," he said, "here it is. A phone number
and address listed under 'Ballantine, C.' Good job."

"Thank your daughter. Getting the information was
the easy part. Getting out with a whole skin wasn't. If
she hadn't pulled the fire alarm when she did, I'd be back
in the hoosegow."

"My daughter pulled the fire alarm at a hospital?
Whose idea was that?"

Kearns looked at the floor again.

"I'll be damned," Farrell whistled. "There's hope for you yet. By the way, I got you a gun."

Farrell pulled out the Smith & Wesson Model 13 .357 magnum he'd taken from the federal agent at Elizabeth's house. Kearns started to laugh.

"What's so funny?"

"This," Kearns said, and produced the gun he'd taken from the FBI man at the Douglas County Hospital, an identical match to the one Farrell had.

Farrell joined the laughter. "We keep this up, and we're going to be on the FBI's Most Wanted list by dawn. I'll bet that asshole Scanlon is fuming right now."

"There's probably not an FBI guy in three counties with a gun or without a black eye."

"Let's get packed. We haven't got much time."

"By the way, Bob," Kearns said. "Thanks."

"What are you thanking me for?"

"For giving us a moment alone."

"Just because it's the Christmas season, it doesn't mean you and me are gonna be standing under the mistletoe. Start packing. And you're welcome."

CHAPTER 35

Scanlon ignored the stares of the people in the hospital lobby and headed straight for the elevator. He punched the "up" button with an angry gesture and willed the machine to hurry its descent and pick him up. Several onlookers were openly gawking.

His eyes were swollen almost shut and tinted a bruised purple. His nose was running freely, and he carried a wad of tissues in his overcoat pocket. The Ray-Ban Aviator sunglasses he wore did little to conceal his battered appearance. To the people staring at him in the hospital lobby, Scanlon looked like a man who needed to be admitted to the emergency room, not visiting the Critical Care Unit

The doctor told Scanlon his septum would require surgery soon. His broken nose had been badly re-injured by the second blow to the face. A blow he'd received at the hands of an unidentified woman posing as an attorney.

The blow to his ego caused far more damage than the injury to his nose. He and his task force were the laughing-stock of the Omaha PD.

Special Agent Lefferty's face was in much the same condition as Scanlon's, and Deputy Kearns was again responsible. After Scanlon suffered the humiliation of

Kearns' escape from his custody for the second time, the deputy apparently went to the hospital and met with Elizabeth Slocum. The special agent guarding her was now on the disabled list as a result of his encounter with the rookie deputy. It seemed Scanlon was destined to suffer setback after setback on this case.

And while Scanlon was receiving the bitter news about Kearns' escapades at the Douglas County Hospital, another alarming report came in. A man meeting the description of Kearns' elder accomplice forced entry into Elizabeth Slocum's house. Like Kearns, he'd overpowered and disarmed an FBI agent and made good his escape, despite the fact that Scanlon had left two agents to stake the house out.

The elevator finally arrived and Scanlon stormed in. Fortunately it was unoccupied. He wiped his dripping nose and punched in the button to the Critical Care Unit.

Who was Elizabeth Slocum? It was obvious she was a significant piece of the puzzle. Kearns risked capture again by going to see her at the hospital only hours after he'd escaped FBI custody for the second time.

Scanlon had to find out what role in the bizarre events surrounding this investigation Elizabeth Slocum played. What was her connection to Deputy Kearns? Was she connected to the Meade kidnapping back in Iowa, and the killing spree at the drug lab? The dead state troopers? The murdered hooker, and bouncers, at the hotel in downtown Omaha? How did Kearns end up in a shootout at her house? And who were Kearns' two accomplices? Were they somehow connected to Elizabeth Slocum?

The elevator stopped with a clank, and the doors opened. Scanlon walked out and headed for the Critical Care Unit, lost in thought. So far, loose ends were all his task force had come up with. He had nothing to tie them together. Hopefully Elizabeth Slocum could provide the knot he needed.

Tiffany Meade's death was random, for all the task force could tell. She and her family were squeaky-clean, and had no apparent links to the murdered methamphetamine dealer in Coon Rapids. The modus operandi of both murders wasn't congruent, and didn't match any known past offenses in the files. The dead hooker in downtown Omaha and the shooting of the bouncers also didn't figure. Yet these events were nonetheless connected by virtue of the fact they were committed by the same perpetrator.

The killing in downtown Omaha could have been a random sex slaying, but if so, how did Kearns and the suspect both end up in Omaha? Kearns must know something; some clue or key which had thus far eluded Scanlon. But what?

How could Kearns have discovered the identity of the spree killer? Was he in cahoots with the murderer somehow? Who was the older man acting as Kearns' accomplice? And who was the girl? What was their relationship to Kearns?

A background check on Kearns shed little light on the subject. He was born to an unwed mother in Burlington, Iowa, and spent his youth there an only child. He grew up doing farm work and going to regional schools until he graduated high school. From there he enlisted in the army as an infantryman, and when honorably discharged returned to Iowa. He settled in Ames, where he used his GI benefits to attend college at Iowa State University. He was attending college when he was hired by the Story County Sheriff's Department. There was nothing in his past to indicate any connection to a killer.

Members of Scanlon's task force also ran a check on the background of Elizabeth Slocum, but hit a brick wall. A trace of her past stopped dead at an orphanage in Omaha, where she'd been raised since age thirteen. The staff there apparently regarded Elizabeth Slocum very highly, because they refused to divulge any information about her. The nuns refused to cooperate in any investigation unless they were informed of how that information was to be used.

Scanlon had of course refused to disclose any details of the investigation, and the nuns stonewalled. He told them he would get a warrant and take their records anyway. The elder nun only smiled at him and said with so many records, for so many children, often documents became lost permanently, never to be recovered. She pointed at the shredding machine as she said this.

The meaning of the nun's statement was loud and clear. She was not going to turn over any records to the FBI. If he did get a warrant, the nuns would simply destroy the records before he could serve it and claim poor recordkeeping as the culprit. And there wasn't a damned thing Special Agent Steven Scanlon could do about it.

Some parts of the puzzle were beginning to piece themselves together, but not fast enough for Scanlon. He was riding a lot of heat from the assistant director in Washington, and the press was more relentless than ever. So far, he'd been able to explain away some of the setbacks his task force suffered by implying Kearns was somehow implicated in the slayings himself, a speculation that the deputy's behavior and the physical evidence increasingly seemed to support.

Yet Scanlon didn't really believe Kearns was associated with the killings. Even his shooting of Brent Cuszack,

an apparent cop-killer, on Elizabeth Slocum's porch was
clearly justified. But he wouldn't publicly admit that
until Kearns, his accomplices, and the suspect were in
custody and the investigation concluded.

There was another lead in an incident at the VA
hospital in Des Moines, but Scanlon and his team
couldn't correlate its significance. It was reported Kearns
and his elder sidekick gained unlawful entry into the
records division of the facility. But what they learned
there, and what, if anything, they'd taken, remained a
mystery. The records archive of the government hospital
was in such disarray that agents couldn't even determine
which portion of the vast storage area Kearns and his
partner breached.

And so it seemed Scanlon's only tangible and available
lead was the Slocum woman. Her doctor told Scanlon's
men she was not to be disturbed. The doctor ignored
Scanlon's insistence that he was on the trail of a killer
and a renegade cop who was possibly aiding that killer,
and needed immediate access to the injured woman. The
physician was adamant, and refused to let Scanlon talk
to Elizabeth Slocum. Especially after the donnybrook
between Kearns and the Omaha FBI agent staking out
her room.

Scanlon was furious over the incident. Kearns and a
female accomplice entered the Critical Care Unit under
false pretenses. They not only incapacitated and disarmed
the special agent guarding Elizabeth Slocum, but pulled
the hospital's fire alarm to cover their escape, another
felony charge to add to Kearns' burgeoning list.

Whatever it was Kearns learned from Elizabeth, he
risked a great deal to obtain it. And the older man with
Kearns risked no less, burglarizing Elizabeth's house
while it was under FBI surveillance.

No matter how much the doctors protested, Scanlon was determined to interrogate Elizabeth Slocum. She was critical to the investigation, and he desperately needed to find out what Kearns and his accomplice risked so much to know.

Scanlon walked to the nurses' station. A special agent from the Omaha FBI office was sitting in a folding chair in front of Elizabeth Slocum's room perusing a copy of *People* magazine with Sean Penn and Madonna featured on the cover and a headline announcing their impending divorce. When Scanlon entered he dropped the magazine and stood up.

"I'm here to see Elizabeth Slocum," Scanlon said in his nasal twang. "And I want to see her now." When he said this, he flashed his gold badge and ID at the nurse sitting at the station.

"I'm afraid that's impossible," the nurse said. "I'm to let no one see her. Her doctor was very insistent."

"I'm countermanding those orders."

Scanlon walked past the nurse, ignoring her commands to stop. She picked up a phone and began dialing. Scanlon strode over to the agent who'd been guarding Slocum's room.

"I don't care if you have to shoot somebody, I want at least five minutes alone with the broad. You read me?"

"Loud and clear," the agent said.

Scanlon walked into the room and found Elizabeth Slocum sitting in bed, looking pale and drained. A translucent tube protruded from her nostrils, but her eyes were alert and focused. They widened at Scanlon's entrance.

"I'm Special Agent Steve Scanlon of the Des Moines Office of the FBI. I'm heading a task force which is investigating the sex slaying of a child in Iowa, and a number of other homicides, including the murder of two Iowa state troopers. The investigation has led me to you."

Elizabeth said nothing, her breathing shallow. She furrowed her eyebrows. Scanlon paused a moment to wipe his nose.

"A man came here last night to see you. He is a rogue deputy sheriff and a fugitive. He had a reason for coming here, and I want to know what that reason was. You're going to tell me, and you're going to tell me now."

"He saved my life," she whispered with effort.

Scanlon moved closer to Elizabeth. She noticed his black eyes under the dark glasses, and the plaster cast on his nose.

"I understand you feel indebted to him, but we need information on his whereabouts, and on the whereabouts of a murderer who at this moment could be killing again."

Elizabeth struggled to speak. "I don't think I like you," she said.

Scanlon leaned his face to within inches of Elizabeth's. "I don't care what you like. I want some answers. What did Kearns want from you?"

Elizabeth fought back tears. Memories of her brutal childhood crept to the forefront of her consciousness and overwhelmed her. She thought she'd escaped that nightmare, and over the years learned to live, and love, and find purpose. But then Vernon returned; an emissary from hell. It was too much.

Elizabeth blinked her eyes. She didn't have the strength to lift her arms and brush away the flowing tears.

"Leave me alone," she said. "Go away." It took virtually all her energy to speak these words.

A tide of anger, frustration, and impatience flooded over Scanlon. He leaned over and took her by the shoulders, sending shooting pains throughout her damaged body. Elizabeth gasped for air.

Scanlon's face scrunched into a scowl. His black-rimmed eyes and dripping nose gave him the appearance of a troll from a children's story. His grip on her shoulders tightened.

"Listen to me, you fucking bitch. You're going to spill your guts, or I'll see you in prison alongside that punk deputy you think is such a hero. You talked to him. You told him something. And as far as I'm concerned, you're aiding and abetting him. You're part of the whole goddamned conspiracy. So you'd better rethink your position on the matter. What did Kearns want to know?"

There was a loud pounding on the door to Elizabeth's room. Through the window in the door, Scanlon could see the FBI guard trying to keep back a doctor and several nurses. The doctor wore an infuriated expression and the guard looked frantic. Scanlon was running out of time.

He squeezed even harder. Elizabeth's breath came in rasps, and shivers of agony coursed through her chest and back. She tried to speak.

"Talk, goddamnit! What did Kearns want to know?"

Elizabeth thought she was going to retch. The only thing keeping her from drifting into blackness was the excruciating pain Scanlon's hands were sending through her. She shook her head, gagging on the words as they came out.

"Brother... bro... th... er..."

Scanlon shook her again. "I can't hear you! Tell me!"

"Vern... on. My bro... ther."

"Who's your brother? What are you saying? Who's your brother?"

It was no use. Elizabeth slumped, and no amount of shaking would bring her back to consciousness. What had she said? Brother? Vernon? What did it mean?

The door to the hospital room crashed open and a deluge of people burst in. The FBI agent assigned to guard Elizabeth's room had his revolver out and was waving it. Several nurses pushed him into the room, daring him to shoot, knowing he wouldn't. The physician dashed past the agent and pulled Scanlon brusquely away from Elizabeth's bedside. He looked at her briefly and began barking orders. The nurses then ignored the federal agents and began attending to Elizabeth.

As one nurse administered an injection into Elizabeth's IV, the doctor, a broad-shouldered redhead with the name Hilger on his nametag, got in Scanlon's face.

"Listen to me, whoever the fuck you are. I gave orders this woman was not to be disturbed. You may have seriously impeded her recovery with your stormtrooper tactics. You enjoy shaking the shit out of injured women?"

Scanlon didn't answer. The doctor, though no taller than Scanlon, was twice as broad, and by the look of his arms under the surgical garb a regular weightlifter. The doctor also exhibited the rabid gleam in his eyes Scanlon had seen before in homicidally dangerous criminals. The special agent was suddenly very aware how fragile his nose was. This physician looked as if he could punch hard enough to push his nose to the other side of his face.

"You have to understand, Doctor," Scanlon stammered, the fear evident in his eyes, even behind the sunglasses. "We're in the midst of a major criminal investigation, and..."

"I don't give a shit if you're chasing Bonnie and Clyde. You ever come into this hospital again you'd better plan on a lengthy stay. Get the fuck out of here, and take junior G-man there with you."

Scanlon was more than happy to oblige. Motioning for the other agent to follow, he fled Elizabeth's room, ignoring the hateful stares from the nurses as he left. He headed for the elevator, the other agent on his heels.

"Call Tatters at Omaha PD," Scanlon told him. "Have him contact the Veterans' Administration in Washington. He's to scan for a Slocum, Vernon. I want any and all files on him to be forwarded to me, top priority."

"Why can't you check with the VA in Des Moines?"

Scanlon punched the elevator button. "Because that's what Kearns and his buddy were doing at the VA in Des Moines. I'll bet you a paycheck the file on Vernon Slocum won't be in Des Moines; it's been pilfered. It's with Kearns, and has been all along."

"OK, I'll call Tatters. Then what? You want me to stay here? I'm sure as hell not going to be allowed back in the Critical Care Unit."

The elevator doors opened and Scanlon stepped in. "Stay in the lobby and watch over Elizabeth Slocum. It is unlikely Kearns will return, but I don't want to take chances. And who gives a shit if you're unpopular with these assholes? You're a Bureau man; you aren't getting paid to make friends."

The elevator doors closed. The Omaha fed let out a sigh and wished he was home with his family. He watched the elevator's indicator lights trace Scanlon's progress down to the lobby.

"Yeah, I'm a Bureau man alright," he said aloud. "I get paid to watch senior Bureau men beat the shit out of crippled women."

He grunted in disgust and went to find a phone.

CHAPTER 36

Vernon Emil Slocum did not smell good.

The three-day bus ride west to Northern California was a haze of nightmarish fever dreams. His wounded leg was going septic, and the odor it gave off was beginning to alarm his fellow passengers.

The crowded Greyhound bus was filled with holiday pilgrims. Vernon sat in the back, in the smoking section, consuming an endless stream of Pall Malls and fading in and out of troubled sleep. His skin was pale and fine sweat covered his face. He knew he was running a high fever, and when the bus stopped for a one-hour layover in Cheyenne he used the time to hobble on his cane to a drugstore near the bus station. He purchased some aspirin, rubbing-alcohol, and the most potent non-prescription antibiotic ointment he could find.

Vernon also bought two pints of gin and several large rolls of surgical gauze. He returned to the bus station feeling faint and dizzy. The pain in his leg was steadily increasing, and he tried to remember the first-aid training he received decades ago in the Marine Corps. He needed to know how to treat gangrene, but his mind wouldn't let him recall anything but fragments.

Once back at the bus terminal he staggered to the men's restroom and into an enclosed toilet stall. Several of the restroom's patrons eyed him suspiciously, but were afraid to say anything to the huge, sick-looking man in the badly fitting suit. There was something about him which made even the curious avert their eyes.

Slocum removed the heavy .45 from the back of his waistband and placed it on top of the toilet tank. He took off his damp jacket. His shirt was soaked in a rancid sweat. He'd been making frequent trips to the bus's tiny bathroom during the ride and inhaling increasingly larger amounts of methamphetamine. He also sprinkled the dirty-brown stimulant into the ugly holes in his leg, to anesthetize it.

The shotgun pellet embedded in the bone of his shin taxed his tolerance for punishment to the limit. But his leg was getting worse, and the meth no longer stemmed the rising tide of pain.

Slocum leaned his cane against the toilet tank and sat heavily on the seat. He uncapped one of the pints and took a long drink from the bottle. The gin was like fire, and settled in his stomach like molten soup, but he felt the sharp edge of searing pain in his leg fade to a dull throb. He turned to his damaged limb.

Rolling up his left trouser leg, Vernon examined his shin. It was no mystery why his fellow passengers noticed an odor about him. The torn strips of bed sheet around his wounds were soaked in pus. Blood, mixed with this excretion, dried to a tacky scab around the pellet holes. He took another swig of gin, then clenched his teeth and unwrapped the bandages.

Once removed, he wished he'd left the bandages untouched. The skin between his knee and ankle was tinted an angry purple. The bullet holes were raised and full of a seeping, greenish matter. He plucked the strips of sheet from the craters in his flesh, tearing the scabs from their foundations. This renewed the flow of infected blood. He bit his lip savagely. Wave after wave of agony pummeled his body. He nearly lost consciousness and was forced to wait many minutes before continuing.

Vernon took another long drink from his pint of gin, emptying it. He uncapped the rubbing alcohol container, poured the fluid into the pellet holes, biting down on the leather-wrapped handle of his Ka-Bar knife to keep from crying out. Then he blacked out.

He regained consciousness a minute later, his leg on fire. He spit the knife out, and wiped away as much crust from his wounds as possible using a handful of toilet paper from the dispenser in the stall. Sweat dripped from his body.

Vernon opened a tube of topical antiseptic and applied it to his leg. He rewrapped the leg tightly; it had already swelled measurably since he'd removed the original bandages. He feared it might swell too much for the trousers he was wearing, which were a snug fit anyway.

Once he completely encircled his shin with fresh gauze he unlaced his shoe. He didn't remove it, afraid the swelling would prevent him from getting it back on. He didn't want to limit his mobility any more than necessary. Vernon poured aspirin into his mouth, washing the tablets down with a slug of gin from the other bottle.

He waited in the stall for his strength to return. The redressing of his leg sapped his dwindling reserves of energy. Eventually he put his jacket on and replaced the pistol in the back of his waistband. He scooped up the rancid dressings and tossed them in the toilet. He tucked the remaining gauze and medical supplies into the pockets of his coat. Before pocketing the remaining gin bottle he took another long drink.

Vernon limped stiffly over to one of the sinks and splashed cold water on his face. Looking up, he saw a mirror.

The reflection he met was a frightening one. Beneath his crew-cut was a pair of hollow, dark-rimmed, and emotionless eyes. His swollen and crooked nose sat atop a square jaw. The mouth between the nose and jaw was a thin, horizontal slash, wholly unfamiliar with the mechanics of smiling.

Vernon wiped his face with a paper towel and hobbled on his cane out of the restroom to the bus, which was boarding. He went straight to his seat at the rear of the Greyhound. By the time he eased himself painfully into the chair, his face and body were again drenched in sweat.

He lit a cigarette and inhaled deeply. The pint of gin he'd consumed was taking effect, and he felt the pain in his leg fade to numbness. He let himself drift towards sleep.

But sleep, for Vernon Slocum, did not come easily. He twitched in his seat, mumbling and dozing. He dreamed.

He was a child, in darkness, feeling the bitter cold of an Iowa winter. He was afraid; the uncompromising terror only a child can know. His father's stern and slurred voice yelled at him. He saw his brothers, and little sister. He watched them scamper and dodge blows.

He was in the closet. He was small, and smelled the waste from his own body. His bottom hurt, and his back was bloody from Daddy's belt. He could hear screams, and couldn't tell if it was Wade or Cole who was screaming. It was probably Wade, because he was the oldest. He always got punished first.

Vernon was unable to control the images drifting back and forth in his mind. He wasn't sure if he was sleeping or awake. He couldn't tell if he was seeing things which had happened, or were happening.

He lay slumped in his seat, his cigarette a burning coal in his hand. He occasionally nodded his head, as if obeying hidden commands. People sitting near him on the bus conspicuously ignored him.

Other images began to take shape, but Vernon couldn't distinguish between memory and dream. He remembered Daddy always came at night, and would take Wade, or Cole, or Elizabeth to his room. There he punished them. He knew he'd been punished in Daddy's room, too. But for some reason Vernon couldn't remember what the punishment was, or even what the inside of Daddy's room looked like.

The clearest images were always of the Corps; the clickity-clack of spit-shined boots on the parade ground, and the smell of gun oil. There was discipline in the Corps, and pride, and a sense of belonging. Daddy was proud he was a Marine. Whenever Vernon's mind faltered, he could always count on one thing: he was a Marine. Even after the doctors at the VA hospital had stolen his mind, he didn't forget that.

He was a Marine.

With that knowledge came different images and recollections. Again, he couldn't be sure if they were memories or dreams. These dreams came with sounds.

Sometimes he still heard the earth-shattering whump of the incoming mortar rounds as they slammed into the ground. He also heard screams. The screams bothered the other Marines, but not Vernon. Screams didn't bother him at all. They were his friends.

Screams reminded him of home.

Vernon watched with his eyes closed as welcome scenes unfolded before him. He saw scenes of carnage from when he was a warrior. He saw the lush, humid green of the Chu Lai peninsula. He could feel the M-60 bucking in his hands as it spewed its deadly stream of death into the foliage.

He liked the war. He belonged in it. He believed the pains and horrors of war were there to lend him a sense of the familiar. His dreams of the war always melted into an endless blur of ambushes, and firefights, and twilight patrols. He sought the crescendo of contact with the enemy; meetings which produced sexual satisfaction

Other parts of the war Vernon couldn't remember so well. These parts were like Daddy's room; dark, and out of focus. Things that couldn't be remembered no matter how hard he tried. Vernon believed the blank memories were the things taken from him by the doctors at the VA hospital.

The hospital.

Visions of the veterans' hospital, like home, were hazy and indistinct. He remembered drugs. The constant flow of pills, and shots, and liquids. He suspected the drugs at the VA hospital were the reason he couldn't penetrate the blocked memories of home and the war.

The time after he left the VA hospital was blurred beyond recollection. Vernon recalled odd jobs, and drifting aimlessly through the Midwest, sometimes living in cheap hotels, sometimes living on the street.

Then one day he was in a park in Sioux City, Iowa. He saw a man walking a child. The child was holding an orange balloon. And Vernon suddenly remembered his father, and pieces of his childhood. Why the man and his child triggered his brain to dredge up the long-dead memories, he didn't know. But he didn't question.

It was not a Marine's place to question.

And so Lance Corporal Vernon Emil Slocum was returned to duty. He'd trimmed his shaggy hair and beard to boot camp specifications. He went to an army and navy surplus store and obtained some used fatigues, and a genuine USMC Ka-Bar knife. He burglarized the home of a retired army major and acquired a 1911 Colt .45 government model semi-automatic pistol. He was again ready for action.

Ready to complete his mission.

"Mission," Vernon mumbled, over and over again. The other passengers sneaked nervous glances at the strange-looking man. They watched him toss and turn, and tried not to imagine what demons he fought in his sleep.

Fortunately for them they couldn't know.

CHAPTER 37

Cole Ballantine, formerly Cole Rodney Slocum, sat in his kitchen and enjoyed a few moments alone with his coffee. The view of San Francisco was good today; there was only a light fog over the Bay to spoil it.

The kitchen was in disarray. Piles of dishes and laundry lay scattered on the normally spotless counter tops. Cole had difficulty getting the coffee maker to work correctly, and wished for the two hundredth time his wife was home.

The Ballantine family owned a spacious waterfront home on Bay Farm Island, in Alameda. From Cole's front door he had an unobstructed view of the San Francisco's magnificent skyline, as well as the Bay Bridge.

He checked the time; 8.07am. He was supposed to have his daughter at school by 8.20.

"Kirsten," he yelled up the stairs. "We're late. Let's get moving, OK?"

"OK, Daddy. I'm coming."

Cole shook his head and returned to the kitchen. If her mother were home, seven year-old Kirsten would have been downstairs, breakfasted, and ready to go to school. He shrugged. At age seven, his daughter was already mastering the art of managing men. At sixteen, she'd be lethal.

Christmas was less than a week away, and the house was filled with the scent of pine from the Christmas tree in the living room. It was also the hectic season, with far too many things to do at work and at home. Which was why Cole objected so strongly when Marcia, his wife of more than ten years, decided to spend a few days in Sacramento with her mother.

Marcia was pregnant and due in March. For this reason he wanted her at home. But her father passed away only the year before, and she wanted to be near her mother for a portion of her first Christmas as a widow. Cole had no choice but to relent.

He tried all the excuses: it was the holidays; he couldn't cook; Kirsten would be traumatized because she missed her mother. Of course Kirsten foiled that excuse by announcing she was an adult and capable of taking care of herself. This included getting ready for school, which was why they were running late today. He returned to the base of the stairs.

"Kirsten, it's time to go! Come on!"

Cole Ballantine was a big man, like his father and brothers. He stood well over six feet in height, but was soft around the middle, a product of his sedentary job as a financial analyst. His hair was longish and unkempt, and this morning he was clad in one of his tailored business suits. He was a far cry from the scared boy who ran away from his Iowa home at sixteen.

Cole grew up in squalor on the family farm in rural Iowa. Unlike his younger sister Elizabeth, he had vivid memories of his mother, though he was only a few years old when she died. He remembered her kindness and warmth, and a soft, gentle voice. Hers was the only soft voice in the household.

Cole's father was a brutal, alcoholic tyrant. He guessed he hadn't always been that way, or Mother wouldn't have married him. At least that's what he imagined.

When his mother died, all hell broke loose. It was as if the woman was the only restraining element in the deranged man's life. With her gone, old man Slocum tortured the children savagely, beating them by day and sexually abusing them by night. Cole could still hear screams in his sleep sometimes, and would wake up in a sweat to find Marcia soothing him and telling him things were alright.

He watched his father enlist his older brother Wade in the Marines on his seventeenth birthday. He remembered Wade as a haunted soul, tortured by his role as the oldest and his inability to protect his younger siblings. Wade left wordlessly, his enlistment papers in hand, reluctant to leave his little brothers and sister, but relieved to be finally gone. Cole never saw him again. He was certain the horrors Wade faced before his death in Vietnam were daydreams compared to the nightmare he lived in Iowa.

Less than a year later, Cole's second-oldest brother, Vernon, was signed into the Marine Corps, also on his seventeenth birthday. Vernon's face beamed with pride, happy to be pleasing his father. Vernon always listened with eagerness as their father told his tales of fighting the Japs in the Big War.

By the dim light of the only kitchen bulb, their father recounted gory details of what he did to the Japanese during the Pacific campaign. He called the Japanese "slant-eyed-fucks," and laughed at his self-proclaimed atrocities. These tales terrified Cole, but Vernon loved the stories. Cole remembered his father calling Vernon "daddy's little soldier," for the stoic way he endured his beatings, and what came after them, in Daddy's bedroom.

With his two brothers gone, the beatings became more frequent and the nightly trips to the bedroom more prolonged. Cole and his sister Elizabeth, a sickly child, now bore the brunt of their father's savagery alone. When news of Wade's death came, Daddy beat Cole so badly he couldn't go to the bathroom for two days. When he was finally able to urinate it came out bright red.

The only reprieve was the days when Daddy received a letter from Vernon. The letters would be on pretty blue stationery with the USMC logo on the top. Daddy would ask Cole or Elizabeth to read the letters, which were crudely written. The letters often contained money orders, and were filled with details of military life. Daddy drank less on the days Vernon's letters came, and his moods were calmer.

But soon Vernon sent a letter announcing he was being shipped to Vietnam. Shortly after, the letters stopped altogether. Daddy's moods got darker, and he beat Cole and Elizabeth with even greater relish than before. Cole remembered that time as the worst. Elizabeth, though nearing twelve years old, had the appearance of an eight year-old. She twitched chronically, as if always about to dodge a blow. Yet when the blows came she didn't flinch at all.

Cole had only one refuge. He lingered in the library after school each day, even though it would result in a more potent beating from Daddy. There he read voraciously and dreamed of a world without fear and neglect.

He particularly liked geography books. He loved the pictures of the ocean, and tropical places where it was never cold. He dreamed of California, and read and reread books about the sunny state until his vision blurred. The school librarian would often have to evict him from the library to ensure he caught the bus home.

Cole was truant a lot, but it was no cause for concern. In rural Iowa, in those days, children were needed on the farms. Poor attendance by able-bodied farm boys was something school administrators dealt with lightly, particularly at planting and harvest time. Neither Wade nor Vernon graduated high school before joining the service. None of his teachers expected Cole to graduate either.

One day Cole Slocum could take it no more. Autumn was turning again into Iowa's fierce winter, and Elizabeth was coughing again, a sure sign the snows were coming soon. The winter promised to be a little more tolerable, since Cole and Elizabeth now had their older brother's hand-me-downs to wear. Nonetheless, it was a winter he didn't want to face.

Without saying a word to either his father or little sister, Cole left. He knew Interstate 80 was a straight route west to California, and was only two or three days walk south on Highway 169. He packed his few ragged clothes and was gone.

Cole, like his brothers, was tall and big-boned. Though barely sixteen, he easily passed for eighteen. He carried a map he'd torn from one of his beloved geography books, and told the truckers who stopped for his outstretched thumb he was heading to California to enlist in the Marines. He scrounged for meals at the truck stops along the way, and begged money from strangers. He'd never been out of Iowa before, and marveled at the world before him.

He gaped in awe at the splendor of the mountain ranges, forests, and deserts while en route to California. He ended up in Berkeley.

Berkeley was good to Cole Slocum. He lived on the street, and subsisted through the many soup kitchens and bread lines that were common in Berkeley during the hippie era. To anyone who asked, his name was

Cole Ballantine, a name taken from the author of his favorite geography book. He feared arrest by the juvenile authorities and return to his father in Iowa.

Cole was befriended by a group of hippies living on Telegraph Avenue. Under their guidance he learned to scam people out of money, scrounge for food, and thrive on the streets. He devoured college textbooks, absorbing as much knowledge as his starved mind could take. It was a time of few cares and much promise for Cole Ballantine. Cole Slocum faded into his nightmares.

The war was raging, and so were student protests. With the help of friends versed in forgery, he registered for a social security card, and got a driver's license under his new name, thereby closing forever the door to his past. With forged high school transcripts, he enrolled at Laney Community College, in Oakland.

Soon he applied and was accepted at the University of California, in Berkeley. The academic record he established at Laney allowed him to pass the more rigid registration process at the university. By then, thanks to his streetwise friends, he was an expert at manipulating the system.

Cole took part time jobs at the university. He worked by day in the library, and by night as a janitor. With his college deferment he avoided military service and the fate of his brothers in Vietnam.

In time, the horrors of his childhood and the memories of his past in Iowa were replaced by the daily routine of his new, busy, and wonderful life. When he did think of home, his thoughts were of his little sister Elizabeth. He sometimes fantasized about rescuing her; going back and exposing his father as a monster and stealing her away. But the thought of returning to that horrible place, for any reason, was a frightening one, and the shame

Cole felt at leaving his sister behind gradually waned. Occasional nightmares remained, but these were the only reminder of his former life.

He graduated college. Graduate studies followed. A master's degree in business administration resulted in a lucrative job offer in the budding Silicon Valley city of San Jose. Cole moved there and prospered.

Years passed, and he embraced the trappings of his new world. He bought a new car, explored California, and met Marcia.

Marcia was in graduate school at San Jose State, studying psychology. Cole met her one evening at the library in the geography section. She was researching a term paper, and took the initiative by introducing herself. Marcia had a gregarious, outgoing nature; so different from the quiet way he carried himself. He was enchanted immediately. They began to date, and soon they shared his apartment. Cole Ballantine was happier than he ever dreamed he could be. A year later he and Marcia were married.

Several years after the marriage, Cole was offered a promotion. He was to be managing director of a financial research team at the Harbor Bay Business Park, in Alameda. By then Marcia's career was also on solid ground. She'd established herself as a clinical psychologist with a practice in Oakland. Both were satisfied with their careers and resided comfortably in the quiet island city.

Shortly after the move to Alameda something occurred which both shocked and elated Cole. He and Marcia were lounging in bed and she was reading one of the trade publications of her profession. In the magazine was an article explaining innovative new counseling techniques for treating sexually abused children. The article was written by a child-counseling specialist from Omaha, Nebraska, named Elizabeth Slocum.

Cole was glancing over his wife's shoulder, and the name sent an electric charge through his body. He grabbed the magazine roughly from his wife's grasp. At the conclusion of the article was a picture of the author, which showed a big-boned woman with a short haircut.

It was Elizabeth. Though hardly the same thin, sickly child he'd last seen over twenty years ago, it was unquestionably Elizabeth. Before he knew it tears were streaming down his face and he was sobbing her name.

He'd always been tight-lipped about his childhood. His wife knew her trade, and her husband, and to leave well enough alone. She knew only that Cole came to California from the Midwest as a runaway from an abusive home. He never spoke of his past, or his family, and Marcia respected his privacy.

Cole cried. He clutched the picture from the magazine to his chest. She held him, and during the course of the night he told her everything.

She listened first in revulsion, then in pride. Her husband had come from a terrible place; the kind of place most children never escape from. And he'd escaped intact. He was a survivor. He'd become a stable, loving, and functional human being.

Cole wanted to contact his sister immediately, and it was Marcia who insisted he seek counseling first. She knew from her work that such a meeting could trigger problems unless he prepared for it. Marcia hadn't forgotten the nightmares her husband experienced. Now she knew their origin.

At Marcia's suggestion, Cole spent the next several months undergoing therapy. In the meantime, Marcia became pregnant. They decided Cole should fly out and visit his sister, who he'd traced by writing to the magazine.

The meeting was a joyful one. Cole and Elizabeth hugged and cried and forgave each other. She was overjoyed at seeing him, and understood the need to change his name. She was proud he had survived, and absolved him of his guilt at leaving her behind.

Cole stayed for three days, and Elizabeth gave him a tour of her life's work. He was overjoyed at what she had become. He saw her strength and goodness in the faces of the children. He came to believe the hardships of their childhood had a purpose.

They discussed Vernon, and Elizabeth recounted for Cole the incident at the veterans' hospital when she'd gone to visit him. He shuddered when he heard the story. He thought inwardly that Vernon was certainly his father's child.

Cole left after his reunion with Elizabeth filled with gratitude. He was happy to know that like him, she'd escaped and survived.

Cole wrote to her over the next several years, and she wrote diligently back. But somehow she was never able to break away from the demands of her many children and return his visit. Cole understood. She'd crafted for herself a world in which she was truly happy. He always planned to return to Omaha, but the trip was postponed indefinitely once Kirsten was born. Between their careers, marriage, and a new baby he and Marcia could never find the time.

There was never enough time. It seemed like only yesterday he was bathing Kirsten in a pan. And now she was a mature and independent woman of seven, insisting on dressing for school by herself.

"Kirsten, let's go!"

On cue, Kirsten came slowly down the stairs. This amazed Cole, who was accustomed to seeing the auburn-haired terror bound down the stairs three at a time. Today she walked regally, wearing a red dress. She also wore black tights and shiny-black patent-leather shoes. Her hair was neatly brushed to her shoulders and she wore a bright red bow.

"Your Highness," Cole said, bowing down. "I didn't know the royal ball was tonight. You look lovely. Shall I prepare the carriage?"

"Oh Daddy, you're such a dweeb! Today is the Christmas pageant."

"What's a dweeb?"

"Everybody knows what a dweeb is."

"I don't. What's a dweeb?"

"That's why you're such a dweeb, Dad," Kirsten said, speaking the way an adult does when explaining something simple to a small child. "A dweeb is a nerd who thinks he's a stud. But he's really just a nerd who's trying to be cool, and everyone can tell. That's a dweeb."

"I see. Dweebs, nerds, and studs; where do you learn this stuff?"

"MTV."

"I should have guessed."

Cole glanced at his watch again. "C'mon, honey, we've got to go. I'm late already."

"I'm ready. Are you coming to the Christmas pageant?"

"Shit," Cole said aloud. He'd forgotten all about the pageant, which Marcia had told him repeatedly to remember. Before she'd left to visit her mother in Sacramento, she'd given him a number of instructions, the most important of which was to remember to take the afternoon off to attend Kirsten's pageant. Kirsten was singing a duet of Christmas carols in the pageant with a boy from her class. Naturally, he'd forgotten to schedule the time off. He'd also forgotten to charge the battery to the video camera.

"It starts at 2 o'clock, right?" He ushered his daughter out the front door towards the car.

"Yep."

"I'll be there honey." He dug into his pants pocket for the car keys with one hand and shrugged into his jacket with the other. He did this odd dance all the way to his car, a Jeep Cherokee. Marcia had taken the BMW to Sacramento. He fumbled the car door open and tucked Kirsten into her seatbelt. She was singing "O Little Town of Bethlehem."

Cole started the car and sped from the driveway, late for Kirsten's school.

In his haste he didn't notice the car parked across the street.

Or the man inside, watching.

CHAPTER 38

Kearns marveled at San Francisco. It was a helluva lot warmer than Iowa in December.

They'd taken a cab from the airport to Farrell's apartment on Lombard Street. To Kearns, whose only experience in California was a field training exercise at Fort Ord several years previously, the City by the Bay was truly a sight to behold. The steep streets, majestic buildings, and Bay Bridge were things he'd only seen in pictures.

Once at the apartment, Farrell gave Kearns a spare key and the address of a health club within walking distance. He said he only knew of the gym because it was near a bar he frequented. He told Kearns to "knock yourself out," and settled into a hot bath with a tall glass of bourbon and his cigarettes. He also gave Kearns some money.

Kearns felt sheepish about having Farrell pay for everything, and said so. He insisted when he returned to Iowa he'd repay Farrell for his share of the expenses. But the retired San Francisco cop only shrugged and said, "Forget it. The people I took it from will never miss it." Kearns wasn't sure how much of that statement was true.

He took the money and stopped at a strip mall on the walk to the gym. He bought some shorts, socks, and a couple of T-shirts. He already had a pair of almost new running shoes, but hadn't worn them since that fateful day in November; the day he'd met Vernon Slocum.

He noticed the Christmas ornaments on the street lamps and the shops. It was odd to see such things without snow, and to see people dressed in only light clothing in December. Farrell told him it could get pretty frigid at night on the Bay, but that right now it was unseasonably warm. Kearns didn't care if the weather was seasonable or not. He liked it, and welcomed the change from the blizzard they'd left in the Midwest.

Kearns found the gym with little difficulty. He paid eight dollars to work out as a non-member, and was given a key to a locker.

It felt good to exercise. Over two weeks of intense stress, sitting cramped in cars, living in hotel rooms, eating fast food, and getting his ass kicked by federal agents made him stiff and cranky. He normally lifted weights every other day and ran on the opposite days; a routine he'd been following since leaving the army. He rarely missed his workouts, and subsequently he was in very good shape. But the events of the past few weeks had unavoidably disrupted his routine.

Kearns spent forty-five minutes running on a treadmill, and then lifted free weights for another hour. He did his best to ignore the pain in his ribs, which were still sore. He was relieved to learn they were only bruised, and not broken, as Jennifer had thought. He also knew he'd be sorry tomorrow for overdoing it in the gym today, but didn't care. He had a lot to sweat out. He finished his routine soaked in perspiration and headed for the locker room.

It wasn't until he got to the shower he realized he was in trouble. He'd been so focused on his workout he didn't notice the conspicuous lack of women in the club, or the disproportionately large number of ultra-muscular bodybuilder types using the facility. But once in the shower he felt the eyes of the other club members scrutinizing him.

This made Kearns a little uncomfortable, though not excessively so. He wasn't homophobic, and had known several covertly gay soldiers in his platoon in the army. Kearns didn't care if a soldier was straight; only if he could shoot straight. Thus he was a little peeved for not noticing the club's orientation when he walked in. The other patrons of the club assumed he must be gay, or else he wouldn't be there. The sexual vibes he was getting were fairly overt.

He finished his shower quickly. And he cursed Bob Farrell.

He could only guess at the laugh Farrell was having, sitting in his tub, knocking down bourbons and thinking of the naive Midwestern deputy working out in a gay gym in downtown San Francisco. The old bastard must be having quite a chuckle.

When Kearns finished shaving and returned to his locker, he found a huge man standing not very nonchalantly near it. The man stood at least a full head taller than Kearns' five foot ten, and outweighed him by at least sixty pounds. He'd obviously done some successful experimenting with growth hormones, and his neck was roughly the size of Kearns' waist. His eyes, jaundiced by steroid use, were fixed on the Iowa deputy. The towel wrapped around his hips looked like a handkerchief on his gigantic torso.

Kearns gulped, and headed to his locker. He would have to pass by the giant blocking his path. The man was not inconspicuous. Kearns nodded, muttered the obligatory "excuse me," and squeezed past.

"You're not from around here, are you?" It was a demand.

"Uh, no, I'm not," Kearns stammered nervously. He wanted to get his locker opened, get dressed, and be on his way. "I'm only visiting."

"Well, it's a wild city. It can get pretty frisky around here. Are you feeling frisky?" Another demand.

Kearns finally got his locker opened and reached into his gym bag. Inside, under his shorts, was the .357 he'd taken from the FBI man in Omaha. He was glad it was there. The man speaking to him could undoubtedly bend him into a pretzel without breaking a sweat. He didn't want to show the gun, but he suffered no delusions about his ability to fend off the giant in a physical confrontation. He began to dress, ignoring the mammoth homosexual standing near him.

"Hey," said the muscleman, stepping closer, "I asked you a question. Are you feeling frisky?"

"Look," said Kearns uneasily, "I'd better tell you up front; I'm not gay. I didn't know this was a gay club when I came in. I told you I was new to San Francisco, and I am. It's nothing personal. You can save your breath."

The man's face got red. Kearns slipped his hand into his gym bag on the reassuring grip of the revolver. It was a tense moment.

The moment passed. The man tossed his head and looked down at Kearns, puffing out his chest even more.

"So you say," the giant said disdainfully. "I've seen your type before. Straight guys who like to tease; stroke their egos. You're an ego-fucker. Well, fuck you." With that, the muscleman was gone.

Kearns let out a sigh of relief and finished dressing. In less than five minutes he was out the door and walking back to Farrell's, cursing the older cop.

He passed a small novelty shop on one of the street corners. Getting an idea, he went in.

Sure enough, amidst the joy buzzers, whoopee cushions, and plastic turds was a package of cigarette loads. These tiny firecrackers could be inserted into a cigarette. When the smoker lit up they got a noisy surprise and a carbon-blackened face.

Kearns paid the sales clerk and went back to Farrell's apartment. When he arrived he found Farrell still in the tub and speaking on the telephone. There was a notepad and pen on the edge of the tub, along with an empty glass and an ashtray.

"...gotta go, Tom. Thanks. I owe you one." He hung up the phone. Kearns stared at him, a scowl on his face.

"How was the workout, Rocky?" Farrell asked, bursting into a raucous laughter.

"Very funny," he said. "You're a regular Rodney Dangerfield. I almost had a date with a guy that made Arnold Schwarzenegger look like a munchkin."

"I'll bet you did," Farrell said, wiping tears of laughter from his eyes. "Did you get pumped up?" Another bout of laughter resulted.

Kearns waited for Farrell's laughter to pass. "I thought you weren't supposed to play with electrical appliances in the bathtub. I guess if the phone fell in the tub you'd be OK, on account of your electrifying personality."

"Weak, but not bad. I see you're finally developing a sense of humor."

Farrell stood up and dried himself off with a towel. When he turned to put on his robe, Kearns discreetly swiped his pack of Camels from the edge of the tub.

"While you were out worshiping the temple of your body, I was on the hunt. I phoned a buddy who owes me one at the Potrero Station. He hooked me up with

Ballantine's physical description, his driving record, and the make, model, and license numbers of the vehicles registered to him. His wife's information too."

"His wife? How do you know he's married?"

"Why wouldn't he be married?"

"I don't know. I assumed he'd be screwed up. Having met his father and his brother Vernon, I figured he'd probably be a creep, too."

"What about Elizabeth?" Farrell asked. "She's no creep. She got it together."

"Yeah, she's a remarkable woman. But she doesn't live what I'd call a normal life. She's devoted to her orphanage and her kids. She didn't opt for the typical family scene."

"I see your point," Farrell said. "But the cars registered to Cole Ballantine are jointly registered to a woman named Marcia Marie Ballantine. Her date of birth puts her six years younger than him, and at the same address."

"That means wife," Kearns agreed. "Do you mind if I use the bathroom?"

Farrell grinned, walking out of the bathroom. "Help yourself. What's the matter, didn't you want to piss at the gym? Afraid to whip it out? Think somebody was going to grab it and start jumping rope?"

Kearns said, "Hilarious," and closed the bathroom door. Once alone, he opened the package of cigarette loads and inserted several into the ends of Farrell's cigarettes. He flushed the toilet and walked out of the bathroom, returning the cigarettes to the edge of the tub.

Farrell was in the bedroom getting dressed. Kearns sat on the edge of a dog-eared sofa and looked around the retired cop's apartment.

Farrell's home was musty and needed a good cleaning. It smelled of stale cigarette smoke. A lot of the furniture looked second-hand. On the walls were various diplomas and citations from the San Francisco Police Department. The only photograph drew Kearns' attention immediately. It was of Jennifer.

He was staring at the picture when Farrell emerged from the bedroom. He knotted his tie, an unlit cigarette stuck between his lips.

"You like, gringo? I sell you cheap."

Kearns' face flushed, embarrassed to have been caught gaping at Jennifer's picture. Farrell grinned broadly around his cigarette.

"You've got the hubba-hubbas for Jen pretty bad, huh?"

"I don't know what you're talking about," he said. "I was just noticing the picture."

"If you notice it any closer, you'll drool on it. You Iowa farm boys ought to give up lying. You're no good at it."

"I'm grateful to her, that's all. She pulled my ass out of the grease. She's a damned nice lady. She has a lot of guts."

"She has a pretty good set of hooters, too," Farrell said. Kearns' face reddened even more.

"Holy hot-flashes, Batman; the deputy's blushing! He must be in love."

"Cut it out. Haven't you had enough fun at my expense today?"

Farrell headed toward the kitchenette. He withdrew a bottle of Jim Beam from under the sink and refilled his flask.

"OK, let's talk business. Cole lives in Alameda, on Bay Farm Island. His neighborhood is exclusive. It even has its own private security force. It's not going to be easy staking the place out."

"What do you suggest?"

"I'd prefer to use two cars and have each of us take a shift watching Cole's house. But in that area two cars stand about the same chance of being spotted as one, and I don't want us split up when Slocum arrives. We'll stick together. I don't think Vernon will get caught unaware again. When he comes, he'll be ready. We've got to be prepared for that."

"Christ, Bob, he may never come. After what happened in Omaha, we can't be sure he's even going to show. And we know he's injured. I don't know how badly you hurt him, but he left a lot of blood in the snow. Maybe he's somewhere licking his wounds, or hiding out. Hell, maybe he's already dead."

Farrell shook his head. "No chance. Don't ask me how I know, but I know. Slocum ain't out of action. He's a Marine. He's going to accomplish his mission, however fucked-up that mission may be. The only way we're going to stop him is to bury him."

"I know. I was only playing devil's advocate. Maybe I needed some assurance we're doing the right thing."

Farrell pulled two glasses from a cupboard and added ice to each. He poured bourbon into the glasses and handed one to Kearns, who accepted it hesitantly.

"Of course we're doing the right thing."

"If you're so sure, how come we're the ones being hunted? Why are we the bad guys, even though all we're doing is trying to end this Slocum guy's reign of terror?"

"Doing the right thing is always hard. Doesn't make it less right."

"You make it sound so simple." Kearns looked into his glass.

"It is simple. I've come to believe that most of the really important things in life are. Vernon Slocum is evil. He needs to be stopped. He's killing children, cops, hookers, and God knows who else. But the system says we can only stop him if we play by the rules. Read him his

Miranda rights, and provide him an attorney. And in the meantime, the Tiffany Meades of the world get chopped up for bait. It's simple as hell," Farrell said. "Slocum is a bad guy. We're good guys. He's the dragon, and we're Saint George."

Kearns looked up from his glass. He wished he shared Farrell's conviction.

"Sometimes I wonder why it's you and me who have to slay the dragon. Why not somebody else? I look at the picture of your daughter, and all I want is to settle down and come home every night to a girl like her. Forget this whole shitty mess. But now I'm in so deep I'll never get out. It's getting me down, that's all. I guess I'm feeling sorry for myself again. I don't see why it has to be me."

"That's easy: because you can. Because you have what others don't: the guts to get the job done. That's just how it is."

"I think there might be another reason."

"And that would be?"

Kearns looked up at his partner. "Because it's ours to do. We own it. Slocum, I mean. We both failed to take him down when we had the chance; you in Vietnam, me in Iowa, and both of us together in Omaha. We failed. Now there's blood on our hands, and we've got to make it right. Maybe this is our penance."

"Don't even go there, kid," Farrell said, not unkindly. "Sure, if things had turned out differently when we each first met Slocum, we wouldn't be here today. But we are, and the past is over and done. We've got to stay focused if we're going to take Slocum down. Dwelling on what's already happened does no good; it only distracts us. And you should know by now, maybe more than anyone, that distraction when you're stalking a guy like Vernon Slocum can be fatal."

Farrell put his hand on Kearns' shoulder. "You ask me how I know we're doing the right thing? I just know. And I know it with more certainty than I've known anything in my entire life. We're doing the right thing; count on it."

"I hope you're right."

"I don't have to hope; I know."

"Thanks, Bob. I needed that."

"Don't mention it," Farrell said. He raised his glass, inviting Kearns to follow suit. "Here's to Saint George the dragon slayer."

"To Saint George."

CHAPTER 39

Vernon Slocum waited.

He wasn't going to walk into the same ambush twice. Buddy was killed in action because he had made tactical errors. He didn't reconnoiter, or pay attention to his flanks and rear. He failed to prepare. But that wouldn't happen twice.

This time he was ready.

Vernon examined Cole's house with the trained eye of an infantry scout. The house sat on a corner with a view overlooking an expanse of lawn called Shoreline Park. Beyond that was the San Francisco Bay. The house's front door faced the street and had a nicely landscaped rear yard, complete with a redwood deck and barbecue pit. He saw no indication of security lighting or an alarm. There were no dogs in the backyard, or in the yards adjoining Cole's house.

There was very little vehicle or pedestrian traffic in the area. There was also no sign of the men who hunted him, and who almost got him in Omaha. So far things looked good. This time, Vernon was careful. And patient.

He waited.

He'd arrived yesterday, and spent the better part of a day and a half driving past the house at irregular intervals, watching. This morning he saw Cole get into a Jeep with a little girl. She had long, auburn hair tied in a bow. Vernon wondered if Cole was a good father. A father like theirs was; one who knew how to discipline children.

Vernon acquired a red Camaro. It was a newer model, with a plush interior and fancy stereo cassette player. He found it near the bus terminal in Oakland, in a convenience store parking lot. He shattered the driver's window with his elbow and was getting in when a thin African-American man ran from the convenience store, yelling at him. Vernon only smiled and pointed the sawed-off shotgun at him. The man backed away.

When Vernon went to punch the Camaro's ignition, he found it punched. The red Camaro was already stolen.

He drove directly to another convenience store several blocks away and bought a map of the Oakland/Alameda area. The clerk at the convenience store frowned when he walked in but said nothing. Vernon knew his leg was rank, but ignored the odor and concentrated on walking. Even with the cane, walking was difficult, and the swelling was beginning to burst the seams of his trousers. Spots of clear, infected fluid soaked through the fabric.

The pain in his leg was fierce but under control. He used a line or two of methamphetamine every few hours. This made his head hurt, and he ground his teeth, but kept the throb in his leg to a distant roar. He knew the drug couldn't sustain him indefinitely, but the mission was approaching a critical phase. He needed to be alert and ready to act.

Vernon scanned for the enemy. Thus far there was no sign of them. He watched when Cole left with the little girl in the morning, presumably to school. Now he watched from inside Cole's house.

Vernon waited for an hour after Cole left before he entered. He'd legally parked the Camaro then hobbled with his cane to the front door. He rang the doorbell several times with his hand on the leather-wrapped hilt of his Ka-Bar knife.

No one answered the doorbell, and Vernon limped around to the rear of the house. He jimmied the patio door open with his knife. He went in with his .45 drawn and made a thorough interior search. He saw the large Christmas tree and a picture on the coffee table of Cole, a pretty woman, and the auburn-haired little girl he'd seen earlier. He found a note in a feminine script taped to the door of the refrigerator; instructions on preparing meals. The bottom of the note proclaimed love, and stated the author wouldn't be home for two more days. The note was signed, "Marcia".

Vernon smirked. When Marcia came home she would find things she hadn't dreamed of in her worst nightmares.

He drew all the shades in the house and sat down on a thick couch. Though he'd contained the pain, the swelling in his leg was severe, and he could only stand for brief periods of time. He knew he had to conserve his strength. Soon Cole would return, and he needed to be ready to greet his brother.

He had his .45, and several loaded magazines for it. He had the sawed-off twelve gauge and more than ten shells. He had his Ka-Bar knife, sharpened as always to a razor's edge. He lit a cigarette and tried to relax.

Vernon felt in control of his faculties, but the visions and dreams which began on the bus from Omaha hadn't stopped. He knew he was in suburban California, yet he could see the dense jungle all around him. Night was falling. Soon the patrols would go out. With nightfall the enemy came. The weak and frightened would whimper; calling for their mothers, saying prayers, and babbling of home.

But not Vernon. He would make Daddy proud. He wasn't afraid. He could take it. He was a Marine.

Daddy's little soldier. Not like Cole, and Wade, who always cried in their sleep. It didn't matter about Elizabeth, because she was a girl. Daddy said she was a bitch, and a whore like Mommy, and would never measure up. But Vernon would make Daddy proud. Vernon was a good little soldier.

He dozed, unsure how long he slept. He chain-smoked Pall Mall cigarettes, waking only when the glowing red tips burned down to his knuckles. He kept his weapons handy.

Before long a car's headlights illuminated the driveway. Vernon ground out his cigarette and stood up to restore circulation to his damaged leg. He willed the pain to a recess of his mind and focused on his mission.

Keys turned in the lock of the front door. Just inside, Vernon Emil Slocum waited in the dark for his brother.

Reunion.

CHAPTER 40

"It's a wonder you Californians get anywhere at all."

The rented Oldsmobile sat stalled on Highway 580 between San Francisco and Alameda. They'd been in the car almost an hour, during what Farrell said would be a twenty minute drive.

"Hey, don't blame me," Farrell said, putting a cigarette into his mouth. "At least we Californians have somewhere to go. I just spent a week in Iowa, and it felt like twelve years. The fucking state is a cross between *Deliverance* and the North Pole."

"At least in Iowa, none of the major cities are considered the homosexual capital of America."

"Oh yeah?" Farrell retorted, lighting his cigarette. "That's because in Iowa, the people haven't evolved enough to fuck each other. They're still dating the four-legged critters."

Farrell took a deep inhale of smoke, and Kearns winced. Farrell wondered why the deputy was wincing each time he lit a cigarette lately. He was still wondering when his world exploded.

When the smoke in the car cleared, and Farrell's ears began to function again, he found Kearns laughing so hard the car was weaving in the lane. It took another few seconds for Farrell to come to his senses and realize what happened. When he did, he spat the shredded and blackened cigarette from his mouth. He wiped the carbon off his face with a handkerchief. Kearns was howling.

"Very funny, Kevin. That was the kind of prank I'd expect from a third-grader."

Kearns held his laughter in check long enough to respond.

"Not a sophisticated gag, like sending me to a gay bathhouse to work out." He burst out laughing again.

Farrell grinned, shaking his head. Eventually he too was laughing. He tossed his opened pack of smokes out the window and reached into his pocket for an unopened one.

Traffic cleared, and soon the Olds was on the Nimitz Freeway. Farrell told Kearns to get off at the High Street exit. He sat back, lighting another cigarette. This time Farrell winced. He needn't have.

"Kevin, we've got to get a few things straight before we arrive. This isn't Iowa. We need a contingency plan."

"A contingency plan?"

"Here."

He produced an envelope and handed it to Kearns. The deputy opened the envelope. Inside was a thick stack of twenty and one-hundred dollar bills.

"Bob, I'm not going to take your money again."

"It's not a handout. If we get separated like in Omaha, you're going to need a stake. We've got to be prepared for anything, and that includes successfully finding Slocum and doing him in. When that happens, we're going to be hotter than ever, and the FBI isn't making things cool right now. We'll have to split up. So don't argue; take it."

The San Franciscan's logic was again irrefutable. Kearns accepted the envelope and tucked it into his pocket.

Farrell exhaled smoke and continued. "Inside the envelope is Jennifer's address and phone number. Should something go wrong, we'll contact each other through her. That shouldn't upset you."

Kearns ignored the quip. He didn't want to tell the older man he already had Jennifer's address and phone number. They crossed the High Street Bridge, separating East Oakland and Alameda. The humor was gone now, replaced by the seriousness of what lay ahead.

"You're packing, right?"

"Both guns," Kearns said. "I brought spare ammo, too." He sensed the weight of the two FBI-issue Smith & Wesson six-guns in his coat pockets. He had a fistful of .38 rounds in each hip pocket as well.

"Remember; if you get a shot, take it."

"I haven't forgotten Omaha," Kearns said softly.

Farrell smoked in silence. He had his five-shot Smith & Wesson .38, and the Remington twelve-gauge pump-shotgun under the seat. In the back was a cooler filled with sandwiches, some bottled water, and a thermos filled with coffee. There was also a fresh fifth of bourbon in a paper sack.

The plan was to watch Cole's house for as long as it took for Slocum to arrive. Neither discussed the possibility Slocum wouldn't appear, though both harbored unspoken doubts. The provisions in the back seat were to sustain them in their vigil and to present the appearance of having a picnic at Shoreline Park should they arouse the suspicion of a neighbor, security guard, or the police.

Farrell directed them over the Bay Farm Island Bridge. Once across, they found themselves driving plush, tree-lined streets. Bay Farm Island looked like new money. Night was falling, and the streets were largely devoid of traffic.

Farrell tossed his cigarette out the window. "Drive by the house first," he said, "and we'll look it over. Don't slow down too much."

Kearns nodded, and began to scan the numbers on the houses. At the intersection of Aughinbaugh and Seaview Parkway they found Cole's house.

It was a large home, with a small yard by Iowa standards. It was new, and decorated with Christmas lights around the roof. A Jeep four-wheel drive was parked in the driveway and a red Camaro was parked in front. The shades were drawn.

Farrell checked his notebook against the license plate numbers registered to Cole Ballantine. The Jeep matched. The Camaro did not. Kearns remarked that perhaps the Ballantines had company, since it was nearing Christmas.

Farrell started to put another cigarette into his mouth, then stopped and rubbed his chin. He turned to Kearns.

"Drive over to the phone booth down at Shoreline Park. I'm going to telephone the house." Farrell tore off a page of his notebook and pocketed it. Kearns looked puzzled.

"Why are you calling Cole's house?"

"We need to be sure his family is alright, or even at home. What if Slocum's already been here, and Cole and his family are dead? Or what if they went to Grandma's in Connecticut for Christmas? Hell, maybe we got the wrong house? Or the wrong phone number?"

"I thought we were going to play it cool tonight? Stay in the car and scope the house out? I don't like this."

"If Slocum beat us here, waiting outside is pointless."

Once again, Kearns couldn't refute the San Franciscan's logic. "What do you want me to do?"

"All I want you to do is walk past the house. The front door is pretty close to the sidewalk. You should be able to hear the phone ringing if there's nobody home. Just walk past, and don't look at the house. You're a pedestrian out for an evening stroll. When you're done, come back down to the park."

"The park's a hundred yards away."

"You afraid of a little exercise?"

Kearns slowed the car to turn around. "I'll do it, but I don't like it. If Cole sees me now, he'll recognize me if he spots me again over the next couple of days. It's risky. Besides, what if a neighbor sees me?"

"You sound like my ex-wives. Have a little faith, will you?"

Kearns pulled the Oldsmobile over to the curb at Shoreline Park. Between the distance, and the rapidly approaching darkness, Cole Ballantine's house was barely visible from the payphone.

"So what are you going to say if somebody answers? May I speak to the murderer of the house?"

"Do I have to explain everything? I'll act like I'm doing a phone survey or something; ask what kind of toilet bowl cleaner the family buys. Sorry, wrong number. Whatever." Farrell opened the car door as Kearns switched off the ignition.

"Got it all figured out, don't you?"

"Trust me," Farrell smiled.

Kearns grunted and shook his head. "I'll meet you at the park in a few minutes."

Farrell straightened his tie and stepped out of the car. "Break a leg, kid."

Kearns gave a half-hearted thumbs-up and got out of the car. It took a couple of minutes to reach the Ballantine house. He slowed his pace and tried to walk casually, hands in his pockets, knowing instinctively that whenever you try to look casual you don't. The houses were close to each other, and very near the sidewalk and street; much different from the spaciously separated homes back in the Midwest.

Kearns' eyes were drawn to the large picture window in the front of the house. Disregarding Farrell's admonition not to look, he glanced around to see if any nosy neighbors were watching. Then he peered into the window. The shades were drawn, and it was impossible to see through them. To his amazement, he heard the telephone ringing faintly inside. Chalk up another one to Farrell's experience. It rang ten times and stopped.

That's when Kearns noticed the door. It wasn't ajar, but there was a set of keys still dangling from the lock. He and Farrell couldn't have seen them from the street while driving past in the darkness. Kearns looked over his shoulder to the park, but couldn't tell in the darkness if Farrell could see him. He stepped onto the small porch for a better look.

Kearns was tempted to wave at Farrell, but quickly discarded that idea. What if someone else saw him? It could draw unwanted attention. And how would he even know if Farrell saw the signal?

It would take Kearns at least several minutes to walk back to Shoreline Park, and another few minutes to either walk or drive back to the house. He bit his lip, his mind scrabbling for a plan. This was something he and Farrell hadn't discussed. Were the keys merely left inadvertently in the door when Cole came home from work? Or had Slocum already come and gone?

Kearns had to know more. He gently depressed the thumb latch on the door handle and found it unlocked. He nudged the door open. It was dark inside; the only light was coming from the Christmas tree. What he saw next sent the blood rushing through his veins.

Inside, on the floor, a man lay sprawled on his side. The man was bound hand and foot, and his feet were tied to a cord which encircled his neck. His face was blue, and blood crept from where the cord bit into his throat. On his forehead was an ugly gash over a thick bruise.

Kearns had learned of this method of binding in the police academy. The cord connecting the ankles and neck of the victim was cut to a specific length to prolong the act of suffocation. To prevent strangulation, the victim had to contort his body in a painfully strenuous manner which was impossible to maintain. To relax would tighten the noose around the neck. Death was inevitable, and only the strength of the victim determined how soon it would arrive.

Kearns drew his revolver and stepped into the house. The man's eyes widened and he tried to speak, but his only words were blood and spittle. Kearns looked carefully around the room for signs of Slocum.

He withdrew his penknife and opened the blade with his teeth, keeping his gun-hand free. He leaned down and sliced through the strangulation cord on the prone man's neck. The man instantly unfolded, gasping for air.

"You're Cole Slocum, aren't you?" he whispered.

Cole nodded, unable to speak. He was choking and gagging, but at least now he could breathe. He tried to say something and couldn't form the words.

"Where is he? Where's Vernon?"

Cole struggled with his bonds and fought to get words out. His eyes were dilated in anguish and fear. Kearns wished Farrell wasn't a block away, but couldn't risk leaving the house; not with Slocum inside. It might be their only chance to get him.

Kearns cut the bindings on Cole's wrists.

"Where is he? Is he still here?"

"...aughter," Cole gasped. "He's got my daughter!" The effort caused Cole to retch.

Kearns remembered Ballantine had a family. Cole's fear was not for himself, but for them. Apparently he had a daughter somewhere in the house. He grabbed Cole roughly by the shoulders.

"Where is she?"

Ballantine couldn't speak. He motioned with his head towards the stairs.

"Upstairs? Did he take her upstairs?"

Cole nodded. Kearns finished cutting the bonds on Cole's wrists and handed him the knife. "Cut your feet loose. Then run down the street and get my partner. He's in the park by the phone. Skinny guy in a raincoat. You got that? In the park."

Kearns stood up and headed for the stairs, his revolver in front of him. He didn't look back to see if Cole had obeyed his command.

He moved carefully up each step, conscious of the increasing darkness and the hammering of his heartbeat in his chest. He reached the top and poked his gun first around one corner, then the other. He peered cautiously into the first room at the top of the stairs.

Inside the room, which was illuminated only by a Minnie Mouse night-light, lay a small girl. She was face down and didn't move. She was not bound. Kearns couldn't tell in the dim light if her chest was rising and falling in respiration, or if she was dead. He stepped instinctively towards the child.

Suddenly, from the darkness, came a looming shape. Too late, Kearns realized he'd been suckered. His ambusher knew his attention would be diverted to the prone child. He tried to bring his revolver up but it was futile.

Vernon Slocum sidestepped the door he was hiding behind and plunged the full seven inches of his Ka-Bar knife into Kevin Kearns' chest. Kearns was already moving quickly towards the girl, and this momentum impaled him further on the blade of his attacker's knife. He weakly tried to bring his gun up, but Slocum batted it down effortlessly.

Kearns' arms went limply to his sides, and he stared into the savagely grinning face of Vernon Slocum. Slocum smelled foul, and his eyes receded into dark sockets like a skeleton. Kearns' chest exploded in pain. He saw his blood flowing down his stomach, and for an instant thought the injury was occurring to someone else. A gasp escaped his lips, and he convulsively pulled the trigger of his revolver.

The bullet went into the floor and Vernon gave the knife another brutal twist. Kearns felt the tearing of his insides, and doubled over in pain. He fell to his knees. Mercifully, he blacked out.

CHAPTER 41

Farrell heard the shot, faintly, from across the street. He sprinted from the phone booth to the parked Oldsmobile.

There was no answer when he phoned, and he'd waited at the park's public restrooms for Kearns to return. He couldn't see the Ballantine house at all; the glare of the phone booth's fluorescent light prevented him from seeing much of anything outside. Long minutes passed, and he anxiously wondered what his partner was up to. It shouldn't take this long to walk back from the house. Then came the dim but distinct sound of a gunshot.

The Oldsmobile fired up and roared down the street, screeching to a halt in front of Ballantine's house. Several neighbors were on their porches, the lights on. Apparently they'd heard the same sound as Farrell. He ignored them and bailed out of the sedan, his Smith & Wesson in his right hand.

He reached the front door of the Ballantine house and found it open. His stomach lurched with the realization that Kearns must have gone in. He gripped his revolver and called into the house, "Kevin?"

In reply, Farrell heard a low moan followed by several sharp gasps. He went inside, bringing his weapon up in the same motion.

He was startled to find a man at his feet and almost shot him unintentionally. The man was crawling towards the door. Even in the poor light he recognized the Slocum family resemblance. Cole's feet were loosely bound, and one side of his face was caked in blood from a gash on his head. A blood-red circle surrounded his neck. He tried to speak.

Farrell knelt beside him and put his left hand on Cole's shoulder. He was careful to keep his right hand directing the revolver at the darkness of the house's interior. Cole struggled for words.

"My daughter... He's got Kirsten... my daughter," Cole said in a hoarse whisper. The injury to his neck was impeding his speech.

"Vernon's got your daughter?"

Farrell knew the answer to the question before he asked it. Cole nodded vigorously in reply.

At his own mention of the name, Farrell felt his body chill. He pressed Cole for more information.

"Is Kevin here? Did Kevin come in?" Then he realized Cole couldn't know who "Kevin" was. He rephrased the query.

"Good looking kid about twenty-five? Military cut hair? Did he come in here?"

Cole's eyes widened to an anguished gaze, and tears streamed down his face from his effort to speak. All Farrell heard was "...over there," as Cole motioned with his head into the darkness of the house. Farrell's eyes were only just beginning to adjust from the brighter streetlamps outside. He peered into the void.

"Stay here," Farrell said in a voice which didn't contain his tension. He stood and began to move slowly into Cole Ballantine's house. His revolver was held at the ready, the adrenaline coursing through his body.

"Kevin?" he called softly into the blackness. "Kevin, can you hear me?"

As if in answer to his challenge, a dim shape began to form itself in the dark. As he moved towards it, he realized it was a staircase. Another shape loomed on the ground in front of the staircase. This one was formless and vague. Farrell focused his aim at the shape and drew closer.

"Kevin, is that you?"

Suddenly the amorphous shape took form, and Farrell uttered an involuntary gasp. Lying at the base of the stairs, face up, was Kevin Kearns. His eyes were closed and a revolver was in his hand. The reason Farrell was initially unable to discern his outline in the dark was because of the pool of blood emanating from his torso. The blood trail led up the stairs into even greater darkness.

He knelt next to Kearns and checked his wrist, hoping for a pulse. The hand was warm. Farrell lifted Kearns' coat and found the wound. He pressed his handkerchief against the puncture, and leaned his cheek against Kearns' nose and mouth, trying to feel respiration. All he could feel was the thumping of his own heart. He couldn't tell if Kearns was breathing, or if he was just too amped to feel it on his own sweating face.

Farrell wiped his nose and shook his head. He reached down and took Kearns' revolver from his fingers. Next he patted the coat pockets. He located Kearns' wallet, the envelope of cash he'd given the deputy, and the other FBI revolver. Tucking these into his own pockets, he looked down at his partner and friend. He had to find the phone and summon medical help. Looking around, he began to stand up.

Farrell sensed motion at the top of the stairs. From his squatting position he leaped backwards with an explosive push of his legs.

Just in time.

As Farrell propelled himself blindly backwards, he saw muzzle flashes at the top of the stairs and heard thunder. Bullets rained down on where he'd knelt only an instant before. In the lightning flashes he saw Vernon Slocum, an apparition of evil, leering at him over the sights of his pistol.

Farrell landed on his back and rolled. He couldn't tell where the shots were striking, but could feel the vibration from their impact on the floor. There were seven, maybe eight shots. He brought up his weapon to where the muzzle flashes originated, and fired until his revolver clicked empty.

Farrell jumped to his feet and ran in the darkness until he struck a wall. Putting his back against it, he slid until he found a doorway. He crashed into furniture, lamps, and a small table. Ignoring these distractions, he put his empty revolver into his waistband and drew the other .357 from his coat pocket.

He ducked into the room and waited in silence, listening. The house was noiseless except for the staccato thumping of his racing heart. Farrell mentally kicked himself for failing to bring the shotgun.

He tucked Kearns' revolver into his waistband and withdrew his empty one. He reloaded it with five fresh .38 cartridges from his pocket.

"Gonna get you," came the voice of evil from somewhere in the darkness. "I'm coming. Gonna do you like I did your friend." Farrell heard the sound of a magazine being inserted into the well of a pistol, and the unmistakable snick of the slide racking forward.

Rage welled in him; an anger deep and powerful. He took a breath and forced himself to calm down. Slocum wanted him seeing red, and thinking with his gut instead of his head. He had to stay cool or Slocum would get him, too.

"Fuck you!" he retorted, throwing himself to the floor.

Farrell realized Slocum was baiting him to give away his position. He'd complied, risking Slocum's fire for the same reason.

As expected, another volley of shots rang out; four of them. At least two hit near enough to where Farrell had been to sprinkle him with plaster chips as they tore through the walls.

But Farrell had already moved. And by firing, Slocum gave away his own position.

Farrell had him.

He peered around the edge of the door and could clearly see Vernon standing halfway down the stairs. He wore an ill-fitting suit and was leaning heavily on the handrail of the stairs, his knife in his teeth. Farrell took careful aim and started to squeeze the trigger.

Suddenly a hand grabbed his revolver and pushed it down. At the same time a hoarse voice yelled, "No! My daughter! She's upstairs! You'll hit her!"

Cole crashed into Farrell, and both fell to the floor. Farrell was focusing so intently on Slocum he had tunnel vision, and didn't notice Cole crawling towards him from the darkness of the front room.

He struggled frantically with Cole, his gun hand gripped by both of Cole's. Farrell knew Slocum would be moving forward to shoot them both point-blank as they lay writhing on the ground.

"Let go you fucking idiot!" Farrell hissed. He struggled to free his gun from Cole's grasp.

"No! You'll hit Kirsten!"

Farrell hammered Cole's face with his left fist, then his elbow. He felt the grip on his gun loosen, and he wrenched it free. He slammed the revolver down hard on Cole's head until Cole went limp.

Farrell wriggled from under the larger man and stood up. He was gasping for air from the struggle, his legs trembling from exertion, and for a moment thought he might pass out. More light entered the house, and he heard the sound of scuffling feet. The sound and light were coming from the front door.

Acutely aware of the possibility this was another ruse by Slocum to draw him into the open, Farrell nonetheless ran towards the door. He couldn't risk losing Slocum again.

No shots came. Instead, as he reached the front door, he saw something he didn't expect.

Vernon Slocum was hobbling along the sidewalk with his back towards Farrell. Even as Farrell raised his gun to shoot, he knew he couldn't.

Over Slocum's shoulder, covering his broad back, hung a little girl. Her long auburn hair flowed down past his waist. There was little chance Farrell could fire and not hit the child. His hands were shaking so badly he knew a precision shot was impossible. Especially with a .38 sporting a two-inch barrel, in the dark, at a moving target with a hostage. Yet if he didn't fire, Slocum would escape. The big former Marine was almost at the door of the red Camaro.

"Stop!" Farrell yelled. "Stop right there, you son of a bitch!"

Slocum ignored the command and opened the driver's door of the sports car. He tossed the little girl inside. Farrell staggered after him, trying in vain to regain his breath. He then realized in horror he was caught in the open. Instead of following the girl into the car, Slocum whirled and fired.

Farrell saw Slocum pivot and reacted, throwing himself clumsily to the sidewalk. The first two rounds went wild; the third landed dangerously close. It struck the pavement inches from Farrell's sprawled body. Fortunately there were no more. The slide of Slocum's .45 locked back, his pistol empty. Farrell remembered the big man expended at least four rounds in the house during his second volley.

Farrell lumbered to his feet and brought his revolver up. Slocum had ducked into the Chevrolet. Farrell lurched towards the Camaro. His only hope was to somehow get a shot at Slocum through the windshield without hitting the girl.

But by the time Farrell reached the Camaro it was in gear and screeching away down Seaview Parkway.

Farrell didn't hesitate. He ran to the Oldsmobile on legs of rubber. He got the Olds into gear as the taillights of the Camaro rounded the corner ahead.

Farrell pressed the accelerator to the floor, the Oldsmobile racing after Slocum. He cursed himself for not risking a shot at the murderer. He knew if Slocum got away, Cole Ballantine's little girl would end up hanging from a tree.

Slocum was driving his vehicle at breakneck speed, and Farrell floored his accelerator keeping up. His heart was pounding so loudly in his chest he thought it was going to pop out, and the roar in his ears was not entirely from the Oldsmobile's shrieking engine.

Slocum veered onto Bridgeway, a two-lane road that was luckily devoid of traffic. As the Camaro ran through the red lights at the intersection at Island Drive, two Alameda police cars, no doubt en route to the many calls being received from Cole Ballantine's terrified neighbors, passed the racing cars. Correctly surmising the two

fleeing cars were possibly involved in the reported
gunfight on Seaview Parkway, both police officers made
hasty U-turns to follow.

Farrell heard the sirens as he passed the cops, heading
east on Island Drive after Slocum. Slocum fishtailed and
turned onto Maitland Drive, nearly losing control. Farrell
didn't brake, but instead took his foot off the gas and
eased into the turn. When the Oldsmobile straightened
out, Farrell took a moment to ensure his revolvers were
still in his coat. In a collision, which he thought likely,
the guns could be tossed about in the car and lost. He
needed them close at hand.

Maitland Drive was a narrow residential street, and as
Farrell pursued the red car ahead of him, he was conscious
of how deadly it would be for a vehicle to emerge from
one of the many driveways. Not only would it probably
kill him and the other car's hapless driver, it would result
in the eventual death of the young hostage in Slocum's
car.

Farrell gritted his teeth. He felt a burst of adrenaline,
or anger, or hate, or all three, and noticed with some
satisfaction that his breathing was evening out and his
hands steadying. If he got close enough, he would ram
the Camaro. The child in the car might have a chance of
surviving the collision, even at high speed. If Slocum got
away however, her chances were nil.

The police cars fell behind in the distance. Farrell
ignored his rearview mirror and focused on following
the car ahead.

Slocum's car made a two-wheeled left onto eastbound
Harbor Bay Parkway. The Parkway was four-lane, and
Farrell closed the distance by smoothing his own turn and
avoiding the fishtail. He pulled adjacent to the sports car.
He saw Slocum reach down below the seat with one hand.

Farrell guessed what the big man was reaching for. In the next instant, a sawed-off shotgun was held across Slocum's chest. The dual eyes of its twin-barrels pointed directly at Farrell.

Farrell had two options.

He could slam on the brakes. Even if he didn't crash, he would lose Slocum, unable to regain the distance the Camaro would cover in the meantime. Oakland was less than two miles ahead. Once Slocum reached metropolitan traffic, Farrell would undoubtedly lose him.

Or he could ram the Camaro.

To Bob Farrell, there was only one choice.

With a grimace he jerked the steering wheel sharply right, just as the mouth of the sawed-off shotgun erupted flame. The windshield disappeared in a shower of flying glass and the Oldsmobile sideswiped Slocum's Camaro at better than ninety miles an hour. With a grinding crunch of metal both cars met and deflected, each careering in separate directions.

Farrell's sedan skidded sideways until it hit the median, where it threatened to roll but did not. The Olds bounced off the median and slid to a halt.

Farrell shook his head, dazed but largely unhurt. His face was cut by chips of flying windshield, and he was stunned by the impact, but he was otherwise alright. He regained his senses and left the car. He ran towards the Camaro, which lay on its roof in the ditch along Harbor Bay Parkway.

They'd almost reached Doolittle Drive when Farrell rammed Slocum. The red sports car veered into the ditch after the initial impact with the Oldsmobile. Once in the ditch, the Camaro toppled end-over-end until coming to rest on its roof. It lay enmeshed in a row of cypress trees.

Farrell drew one of the FBI revolvers with a hand no longer trembling. He ran, as best he could, to the upended car. He hoped to catch Slocum stunned in the driver's seat and finish him point blank.

Farrell was twenty yards from the overturned Camaro when Slocum stood up. He'd crawled through the driver's window and was wielding his shotgun and pistol. He was battered and bleeding, and wore an expression of savage fury. Farrell couldn't see the girl, and prayed she wasn't thrown from the car when it rolled. His eyes locked with Slocum's, and he thought he saw a glimmer of recognition in the brutal face.

Farrell slowed to a walk, making a conscious effort to calm his breathing. He raised his right hand and fired a hasty shot. He heard the bullet *tink* into the body of the Camaro, and hoped if he couldn't hit Slocum, at least he could suppress return fire. Farrell walked more resolutely with each step. He fired at regular intervals.

He couldn't tell if he was hitting the big former Marine, but if not, the shots were close. Slocum ducked behind the engine block of the overturned Camaro and out of sight.

Farrell emptied the first revolver and switched it to his left hand, hefting the loaded one in his right. With Slocum out of sight he no longer had a target, but kept the Smith & Wesson pointed at where he'd last seen the killer.

By the time he reached the edge of the ditch the sirens were growing louder. The cops had displayed more prudence in their driving than he and Slocum had. They had more to lose.

Farrell looked over the edge of the ditch with no concern for cover. He was again out of breath, and blood was trickling down his face. He wasn't sure how badly Slocum was hurt, nor did he care. The Alameda police would arrive in a few seconds, and Farrell had no time for hide-and-seek. He had to find Slocum, and fast.

But Slocum was not behind the Camaro when Farrell reached it. All he found was blood splattered on the windshield where Slocum had been, a lot of it, and the sawed-off shotgun discarded on the ground. Farrell searched for his adversary and found him.

Slocum hadn't merely ducked behind the car when Farrell fired. He crouched below Farrell's line of sight and fled in the ditch. Farrell could see Slocum running in a limping gait, fifty yards away. He took aim, but knew a shot would be futile.

He looked over his shoulder. The wailing sirens of the police cars were shrill now, and their flashing emergency lights were visible at Maitland Drive only a mile back. He ran quickly to the other side of the wrecked Chevrolet.

Inside, laying face down, was the little girl. He knew he couldn't open the twisted car door, so he kicked out the passenger window and reached in for her. He pulled her out of the car and checked her for signs of life.

The girl's eyes were closed, but she was breathing. Farrell felt a steady, strong pulse on her neck. She was wearing abrasions on her knees and elbows, but otherwise seemed unhurt. He noticed a purple bruise on her forehead, and surmised that Slocum kept the child quieted with a blow.

Thankfully, the girl was alive. He carried the child away from the demolished car in case it caught fire, and laid her gently on the soft grass. Smoothing her hair from her face, Farrell smiled. Slocum didn't get this one. Kearns would have been proud.

Two police cars screeched to a halt near the Oldsmobile. Leaving the girl, Farrell ducked down in the ditch as Slocum had done, and crawled parallel to where the police cars were parked. He knew from his own police experience that the glare from their vehicle's emergency

lights and spotlights would conceal him. A uniformed cop
emerged from each car. One held a shotgun, the other a
revolver. The police cars had their engines running and
flashing lights on, but the sirens were now quiet.

The two cops approached the Oldsmobile cautiously.
When they found no one inside, they moved towards the
overturned Camaro in the ditch with weapons pointed.
Farrell was now well behind them, and behind their
hastily dismounted police sedans.

One of the cops called to his partner when he spotted
the Ballantine girl lying on the ground. He ran to the
girl, made a quick examination, and spoke into his
portable radio. The cop with the shotgun looked inside
the crunched Camaro.

Farrell knew it was now or never. Both police officers
had their attention focused on things other than behind
them. He flanked them, crept out of the ditch, and darted
unnoticed to the first patrol car. He removed the keys
from the ignition. He duck-walked to the second police
car, below the line of sight. That vehicle still had its
shotgun in the electro-lock on the dashboard. It was the
same model of lock used by the SFPD.

Farrell depressed the release mechanism on the floor and
took the shotgun, a standard police Remington 870, from its
mount. He then shut down the ignition and took the keys.

Both cops heard the sudden quiet of the car's engine
being turned off. They turned to look behind them just as
Farrell racked a round into the chamber of the 12-gauge.

"Don't move."

The cops stopped in mid-turn. Farrell spoke from a
covered position behind an Alameda police car. He tried
to mute the tremor in his voice.

"Don't get stupid. I have you in the open, and I've got
cover. If you want to be heroes, go ahead. It's your funeral."

Farrell could feel the tension in the two cops as they debated whether to chance taking him on. He didn't want a shoot-out with cops.

"If I wanted to kill you, I'd have done it already. I'm not going to shoot unless you make me. All I want to do is leave. Drop your weapons. Do it now."

Neither cop made a move to comply, still standing with their backs halfway towards Farrell. Farrell fired a round from the shotgun into the rear window of the wrecked Camaro a few feet from the two policemen. He chambered another round.

"I know you're thinking: 'He can't get us both.' So which one of you wants to tell his partner's widow what you did to save your own skin? I ain't going to say it again: lose the hardware."

Both cops reluctantly complied. A shotgun and revolver clattered to the street. Farrell could hear more sirens in the distance.

"You with the shotgun: you've still got a sidearm. Drop it."

The officer did.

"Alright. Turn around, put your hands on top of your heads, and step back. If a hand comes down, I shoot."

The cops turned around and backed up, their hands on their heads. Farrell stepped from around the patrol car. Farrell couldn't see the cops' ashen faces.

"Relax. I said I wasn't going to shoot unless you made me. Neither of you have seen my face. If it stays that way until I leave, you both get home to your families. Don't turn around."

Both cops exchanged looks of disbelief, and Farrell scooped up the two revolvers and the discarded shotgun. Clumsily cradling the weapons, he backed away towards the Oldsmobile, still covering the lawmen with his shotgun one-handed. He tossed the guns into the Olds and climbed in the driver's seat. Wordlessly he put the sedan into gear and drove off, covering the lower portion of his face with his coat as he passed the two Alameda cops. He took Doolittle Drive towards East Oakland. The last thing he saw in his rearview mirror was the two cops speaking animatedly into their portable transceivers.

Farrell motored down Doolittle Drive and merged into moderate traffic. Slocum was long gone, but Farrell scanned to his left and right hoping to spot him. Slocum could have easily commandeered a car at gunpoint, or fled to the bustle of the nearby airport. In either event, Farrell couldn't linger in the area searching. While the police had no description of Slocum, they certainly had a general one of him, as well as his vehicle.

He turned onto Hegenberger Road and the cover of Oakland metropolitan traffic. The Oldsmobile had no windshield, and his eyes stung in the cold air. Normally a car in such battered condition would have attracted attention, but not in East Oakland. His mind reeled, and he struggled to accept the night's happenings. Too many images and emotions crowded his brain at once.

Every cop in the Bay Area would be searching for him.

It didn't matter that he saved a child. He'd lost Slocum.

More importantly, he'd lost Kevin Kearns.

He had never felt so alone.

CHAPTER 42

Vernon Slocum drove slowly through Oakland into San Leandro. A corpse was his passenger.

The pain in his left leg was excruciating, and wave after wave of dizziness rolled over him, threatening to make him black out. But he held on, like a Marine should. Even with the pain at its worst he knew he was going to make it. He had no choice.

But now there was other pain to contend with. Unbeknownst to Farrell, one of the bullets he fired in Cole's house struck meat. The hastily fired round punched through the flesh of his *latissimus dorsi*, the large triangular muscle beneath his left armpit. The bullet exited cleanly, but the wound it left bled profusely. Slocum knew within hours the arm would be useless.

Also, when Farrell rammed his car, Slocum's face slammed into the dashboard. Most of his teeth, both upper and lower, were spit out with saliva and blood. It all happened so fast. His ambush failed, and he was only able to get the younger of his enemies. Once again, it was the older one who'd proved the most formidable. But Slocum hoped with his partner gone, the old hunter might lose focus and give up.

Not likely.

Slocum drove a brand-new BMW sports coupe. It featured a rich-sounding stereo cassette system its owner

would never hear again. At the moment, the stereo was
playing "It's The End of the World As We Know It" by REM.

Slocum had hobbled to the highway, spears of agony
splintering his damaged leg with each step. He jumped in
front of the first motorist who approached, forcing the car
to stop. When the indignant driver stuck his head out the
window to rant in protest, Slocum shot him in the face.
He then climbed into the driver's seat, pushing the lump of
flesh that was once a slip-and-fall attorney to the passenger
side of the car.

Slocum drove aimlessly down Doolittle Drive towards
San Leandro. His left arm was soaked in blood and going
numb. Surprisingly, his shattered teeth produced more
pain than his perforated left side, a condition which would
undoubtedly change.

He pulled the car off the road and into the parking lot of
the Shoreline Café on Doolittle Drive. The café was closed
and the parking lot empty. He switched off the car's engine
and withdrew the ignition key. He knew within minutes his
wounded arm would fade, and he needed to use it while he
could.

He lumbered out of the car with great effort and opened
the trunk. Inside, he found two large suitcases. He took
them out and set them aside, dizzy with exertion. Slocum
then opened the BMW's passenger door and pulled out the
body of the car's one-time owner.

Normally, for a man of Slocum's size and physique, stuffing
the body into the trunk would have been quick and easy
work. But not tonight. Slocum had to drag the limp body from
the car where he would have once simply lifted it. He stopped
several times to let the waves of pain subside. At one point he
leaned against the car to prevent himself from passing out.

Eventually he got the deceased lawyer into the trunk. He
took a moment to pull a fat wallet from the pocket of the

dead man's expensive suit. Inside, explaining the suitcases, were ticket stubs from a Los Angeles flight. Apparently the BMW's driver was returning from a business trip to LA when he met his untimely demise. The wallet also contained credit cards and some cash.

Slocum threw one suitcase into the back seat of the car. He opened the other, and sure enough, found several towels with a hotel logo embroidered on them. He tucked one towel under his left armpit to quell the flow of blood, and used the other to pat his battered and toothless mouth. He closed the suitcase and tossed it into the car with its mate, then stumbled back into the automobile.

He was nearing exhaustion. His left leg was agonizingly painful, and had stopped bleeding entirely. Instead it was leaking more of the pus he noticed a couple of days ago. He risked a glance at the leg by rolling up the trouser bottom.

Even in the dim light of the streetlamps, Slocum could see the flesh was a putrid gray, and knew without looking his toes were black. The wound was fully gangrenous. The nutrient-robbing methamphetamine accelerated this process, but without it he would have collapsed long ago.

Slocum patted his pockets until he found his bindle of meth. He opened it with shaking hands and lifted the paper to his nose, inhaling deeply. He licked a filthy finger and used it to smear some of the dirty brown paste over his bloody gums and into the sockets that were once his teeth.

The rush came and again the pain drifted. He carefully refolded the bindle of crank and pocketed it. He then reloaded his .45. This took a long time because his fingers had trouble inserting the rounds into the magazine. He lit a Pall Mall and sat back in the seat.

First Elizabeth and then Cole. They'd left; run off. They'd run out on Daddy and the family. They'd left him to rot in the VA hospital. They thought they could run away and hide. But Vernon knew where they were. He knew where to find them.

Vernon exhaled smoke, his cigarette pink with blood. He knew he was badly wounded. He would have to alter his original plan and scrub the mission. All because of Cole and Elizabeth. They were traitors.

Traitors to their family.

Had they no pride? Were they content to be weak and afraid? Hadn't Daddy taught them anything? Was all he did for them meaningless? Did they remember nothing of home? Of their father?

They remembered nothing. They'd shit on their heritage. Elizabeth and Cole were sniveling, whining cowards, with no gratitude, and no pride. They'd left like thieves in the night, just like the Bible said. Wade was weak too, but at least he'd gone out with some honor. He'd been a Marine, and died in combat. Even though Wade was the oldest, Vernon knew inside he was the strongest. The truest. The family's honor was his burden to bear. It was his duty to reclaim it.

His mission.

But now the mission was over. He was a casualty; no longer mission-capable. He'd anticipated opposition, but not the relentless, unwavering determination of the two men who'd stalked him.

They followed him at every turn. They must have known all about Cole, and Elizabeth, and Wade, and Daddy. About the family. Elizabeth must have told them, or the head-shrinkers at the VA hospital. The doctors and counselors must have divulged his secrets. They'd invaded the deepest recesses of his mind at the hospital, and the two men who'd been sent to track him must have been armed with the things they found there.

They must have known his mission.

Yet Vernon knew the hunters weren't invulnerable. They'd certainly not engineered their traps well. Had they executed a better ambush at Elizabeth's, he would be dead. Vernon had stupidly allowed himself to be drawn into the cul-de-sac, and Buddy was KIA as a result.

Yes, the two men must have known his mission. But their ill-preparation for their own mission cost the young stalker his life. Oddly, Vernon didn't hold his enemy in contempt. His enemies had accomplished their mission. They'd prevented him from taking Cole and Elizabeth home. They'd critically injured him, and forced him to abort his own mission and retreat. Though the junior one lost his life, he'd done so honorably, and in combat.

Vernon knew he hadn't much time. Even a Marine has limits. He would have to alter his original plan and make his primary mission one of survival. It would require all his fortitude to get home, and home was a long way off.

Vernon's new mission was pathetically simple. He would drive straight home, stopping only for fuel. The credit cards and cash would allow him to use the full service facilities at gas stations without leaving the car and arousing suspicion because of his wounds. He would have some time before anyone reported the attorney and his car missing, and by then he would be well clear of California and could obtain another car. He only hoped he could hold out for the thirty or forty hours it would take to get home. His salvation was the methamphetamine, and fortunately it was still plentiful.

With luck, the meth combined with the pain would keep him alert. He finished his bloody cigarette and threw the butt out the window. He put the coupe into gear and started down Highway 61 towards the Interstate.

Vernon Slocum was going home.

CHAPTER 43

Farrell sat in the damp sand, staring off into the water of the San Francisco Bay. San Francisco Bay was cold at night, just like Farrell had told Kearns it would be. Yet the chill in the old cop's bones didn't originate entirely from the night air.

He'd ended up back in Alameda, but not by design. He drove into Oakland and cruised aimlessly until the trembling in his hands impeded his steering. The last thing he needed was to get pulled over by a cop for an inadvertent traffic infraction.

Farrell was reasonably sure his identity was still unknown to the cops, but he dare not risk going home to San Francisco over the Bay Bridge in so thrashed a car. The CHP would pull him over in an instant.

He'd wandered through Oakland. His meandering route eventually took him over the Miller-Sweeney Bridge and back again into residential Alameda. He followed Broadway Street to Bayview Drive, where it ended at the beach. Soon he was on Shoreline Drive, watching the San Francisco skyline reflect off the choppy waters of the Bay.

He pulled over near Grand Street. His hands were shaking so badly the car was weaving in the lane. His eyes were tearing, partly from the chilly air blasting through the shattered windshield, and partly from the trauma of the past hour.

Farrell left the Alameda police shotgun in the car, along with his own, and put on his overcoat. He pocketed the two service revolvers he'd taken from the Alameda cops, and also the bottle of bourbon from the back seat. He peered into the cooler at the sandwiches, but the thought of ingesting them made him gag. Farrell wasn't concerned about leaving the car. It was a rental, purchased under an assumed identity. His shotgun couldn't be traced to him either; it too was purchased back in Iowa with a false ID. Farrell opened the trunk and took out a red gasoline can. He unscrewed the cap, and poured the gallon of gas liberally over both the interior and exterior of the Oldsmobile. He'd already grabbed the yellowed medical file on Slocum they'd stolen from the veterans' hospital in Des Moines.

Though only a few weeks ago, Des Moines seemed a lifetime away.

Farrell tossed a road flare into the car's interior and walked away as it lit up the night.

He walked across Shoreline Drive to the beach. He strode directly to the waterline, through sand moist and deep. There on the hard-packed sand Farrell walked westward, lumbering under the burden of his many guns and papers. San Francisco's lights loomed large across the Bay. He heard sirens. He walked until he could walk no more. He plopped down at the water's edge cross-legged and put his face in his hands. They were still shaking. He could see the lights of the police and fire vehicles in the distance, attending to the pyre that was once his car.

Things had gone terribly wrong. Kearns was dead. His body lay on the floor of a home belonging to people he'd died protecting; strangers he'd never even met. Farrell fumbled in his pockets for the bottle of bourbon.

He knew it was over. Kearns was dead and Slocum had escaped. He'd never be able to track the deranged killer again, even if he knew where to look. His chances of finding the murderer again were zero. He'd failed. Game over.

What consolation he took in rescuing the Ballantine girl faded quickly. Slocum would find another Kirsten Ballantine, or Tiffany Meade, or whoever. It was inevitable. It's what Slocum did.

Farrell uncapped the Jim Beam and took a long pull from the bottle. The scorching rush of the bourbon took the shakes from his hands. He took another swig and stared out at the water. The bourbon lent some warmth to his body, and after another swig he felt his hands begin to steady even more.

Farrell lit a cigarette, sucking in the smoke. He thought about turning himself in. Give Scanlon and the FBI what information he possessed about Slocum and hope they could track him down, even if only for prosecution and not death. Farrell had his chance, and he'd fucked it up. Not only did he fail to bag Slocum, he cost a young deputy, a kid really, his life. A kid who Farrell tricked into becoming part of his scheme to hunt down Vernon Slocum.

Farrell drank some more bourbon. Normally, his tolerance to alcohol was quite high. But the day's stark events had whittled him to near exhaustion, and the booze was sinking in.

It wasn't supposed to go this way.

Despite the setback in Omaha, Farrell never felt he was not in control. He'd always believed he could handle the situation, whatever came up. But when he first saw Deputy Kevin Kearns, tortured by his guilt in the death of Tiffany Meade and under the grill by Scanlon and the FBI, he should have heeded the warning. He should have recognized the shadow of himself in Kearns' face. And he should have realized he was projecting his own shroud of guilt on the young deputy.

Farrell told himself he was doing the right thing, going after Slocum alone, and in convincing Kearns to accompany him, affirmed that belief. He'd told Kearns it was a simple thing, really; a matter of good versus evil. And he implied that they were on an epic quest. Doing what nobody else could do.

Saint George versus the dragon.

But the dragon won.

Farrell pulled Kearns' wallet out of his pocket. Other than a bit of cash and his Iowa driver's license, it contained nothing but a folded scrap of paper. He stared at Kearns' photo, and at the face of the young cop. A kid he had used, betrayed, and left dead on the floor of a stranger's house far from his home, for reasons which now seemed inconsequential.

With half the bottle gone, the biting cold of the San Francisco Bay seemed to diminish a bit. Farrell helped himself to another large swig, and lit another cigarette. He unfolded the piece of paper. He instantly recognized the feminine script. It was his daughter's phone number, written in her own hand. She'd obviously given it to Kevin herself.

Farrell felt hollow and drained. He spat out his cigarette and ran his fingers through what was left of his hair. He'd have to tell Jennifer, and soon. He couldn't let her find out any other way. It wouldn't take the Alameda cops long to identify the John Doe in Ballantine's house as Story County Sheriff's Deputy Kevin Andrew Kearns.

Why had Kearns gone into the house alone? Why hadn't he come back to the park? Did he hear something inside? Did Cole or Slocum draw him in?

It didn't matter. It wasn't Kearns' fault. It was Farrell's fault. It was Farrell who indirectly let Kevin die on Cole Ballantine's floor. Because it was Farrell who brought him into the mix in the first place. It was Farrell who exploited the young deputy's pain, and guilt, and coaxed him into partaking in the lethal hunt for a murderous madman, knowing full well the deputy wasn't up to the task. And it was Farrell who introduced Kearns to Jennifer. Using his own daughter like he used everybody else. He drained the bottle in a series of continuous gulps.

Farrell stood shakily up. The energy vacuum he experienced in the aftermath of the earlier adrenaline rush was intensified by the bourbon. He felt he could close his eyes and sleep on the beach forever. He had to find a place to sort things out. His mind was reeling. He would deal with this in the morning.

He staggered from the beach to the sidewalk and began to walk towards the distant lights of the South Shore Shopping Center. The stores were still open in the run up to Christmas.

Farrell hadn't gone a block when a taxicab pulled up. Its driver was apparently trolling the beach in search of patrons. Farrell raised a wobbly arm and mumbled, "Taxi!" in a slurred belch.

The cab pulled over, and a middle-aged African-American got out.

"Take it easy dude," the cabbie said. "You got to be cool. This here's a navy town. Alameda cops cruisin' the beach day and night for fucked-up motherfuckers like you. Where you goin'?"

"Need to find a hotel," Kearns slurred.

"You want fancy or economy?"

Farrell patted the thick wad of bills in the envelope in his pocket.

"I want fancy. Not in Alameda. You know a place?"

"I'll take you to the Hyatt, near the Oakland Airport. That cool?"

"Sounds cool as hell," Farrell slurred. The cabbie opened the door and he climbed in. Farrell closed his eyes.

An instant later the cabbie was shaking his shoulder. "We here. Wake up now, we here."

Farrell sat heavily up. He allowed the cabbie to lead him to the lobby, where he leaned heavily on the registration desk. He fumbled in his pocket for some bills and gave the cabbie three twenties. The cabbie grinned and walked off, muttering something about "drunk-assed fools."

The registration clerk frowned first at Farrell's breath, his bloody face, and then at his lack of luggage, but relaxed when he saw the cash. The clerk gave him a key to a room on the second floor after relieving him of several bills. Farrell staggered off to the elevator.

By the time Farrell got out of the elevator on the second floor and put his key in the lock, the walls of the hotel were spinning wildly. He entered the room, closed the door, and locked the chain. He turned on the lights to find a tastefully decorated room with a king-sized bed.

He shrugged out of his coat and jacket. The fact that his pockets contained five revolvers made this task all the more difficult. He withdrew the thick medical file from his waistband and tossed it on a table. He struggled to remove his trousers and kicked off his shoes. Then he collapsed on the bed.

Farrell fell asleep immediately, and slept fitfully for the next fifteen hours. He dreamed of a dragon which slaughtered a medieval village.

When a solitary knight ventured forth to slay the dragon, the dragon ate him.

CHAPTER 44

Special Agent Steve Scanlon wiped his dripping nose for the thousandth time and tried to relax. His flight had been delayed twice due to the inclement weather, and he was beginning to wonder if he'd ever get back to Des Moines. Not that he was in a hurry.

There was a tremendous break in the investigation within the last twenty-four hours. News of the shootout in Northern California, and the attempted kidnapping of another child, coincided with his task force's acquisition of a military 201 file. The file belonged to Lance Corporal Vernon Emil Slocum, USMC; the brother of Elizabeth Slocum.

Despite the Slocum woman's reluctance to cooperate in the investigation, his agents gained access to the master file in the Armed Services Personnel Command in St Louis. If the Bureau was good for nothing else, it was good for its vast information network.

A copy of that file was faxed to Scanlon, and it broke the investigation wide open. Scanlon spent the better part of the night perusing the documents, though a team of military and medical analysts were currently doing a more thorough job.

Most certainly Slocum was their man. A faded photograph of him in his USMC dress blues even matched the Identi-Kit composite drawings made after the Meade murder. And though Kearns and his accomplice stole Slocum's medical file from the veteran's hospital in Des Moines, they'd failed to swipe the file of Buddy Cuszack, the accomplice Kearns shot and killed at Elizabeth Slocum's home in Omaha. It appears Cuszack's stay at the VA hospital in Des Moines after his service in Vietnam coincided with Slocum's.

It was all coming together; all but the whereabouts of Deputy Kevin Kearns' elusive partner and Vernon Slocum. Scanlon wasn't sure which suspect he wanted more.

A nationally broadcast press conference was to be held at 8 o'clock that morning. Scanlon himself would have normally been given the honor of delivering the press their anxiously awaited news, since he was Special Agent in Charge. But several factors prevented his appearance on national television.

Not the least of which was his injury. Though several weeks had passed since Kearns clobbered him, both of Scanlon's eyes were still dark, with purple rings surrounding them. His nose was an endless faucet of snot and blood, and Kleenex had become a permanent part of his attire. But Scanlon knew the real reason he was kept from the conference, and it wasn't his looks.

Word had traveled far and wide throughout the Midwestern law enforcement community of his inability to keep the rookie deputy in custody. Scanlon committed the equivalent of a mortal sin; he'd embarrassed the Bureau. The final blow was allowing Kearns to escape for the second time after being knocked out by a girl posing as an attorney, the very same ruse which facilitated Kearns' first escape. Scanlon wasn't allowed at the press conference because the FBI didn't want any uncomfortable questions regarding the status of the renegade deputy or the origin of the condition of Scanlon's face.

Scanlon was therefore given orders over the phone this morning to report forthwith to his home station in Des Moines. Little else was said, but the underlying implication of reprimand was quite clear, even over the telephone.

He knew his status as Special Agent in Charge of the Des Moines Office was in jeopardy, and took his order to report immediately to Des Moines, while the investigation was still under way, as tantamount to being relieved of command.

The press conference was a success. Slocum's identity and picture were broadcast with an admonition for private citizens to notify the authorities if he was spotted. The press was generally polite, and didn't cause the FBI much grief. Except for one reporter who worked for the *Nevada Journal*, a paper published in the home county of Tiffany Meade.

This reporter repeatedly asked questions about Deputy Kearns, and wanted to know if criminal charges were being filed against him. He kept asking where Special Agent Scanlon was, and didn't seem satisfied that Scanlon had fully recovered from his injury and was busy elsewhere with more pressing cases. He fired question after question at the Bureau spokesperson, who eventually said, "That's all we have at this time," and left the podium.

Of course the Bureau didn't release all the pertinent details of the case. For example, they didn't release to the press that a man was found stabbed and clinging to life in California at Cole Ballantine's home. Or that the man was Iowa Sheriff's Deputy Kevin Kearns.

Scanlon glanced at his wristwatch, and again at the monitors which displayed the arrival/departure times for all flights. It was at least two hours before his flight would take off, assuming it wasn't delayed again. Whitney Houston was musically asking "Didn't We Almost Have

It All?" via the airport loudspeakers, adding to Scanlon's annoyance. He'd always hated the perpetually perky singer.

He opened his briefcase and pulled out the file. He sifted through the photocopies until he found the document that recorded Slocum's arrest in Saigon. At the bottom of the arrest sheet, clearly legible in the INVESTIGATING OFFICER box, was scrawled the name *SSgt Robert Farrell*. It meant nothing to Scanlon. A faded name scrawled on a faded document by a soldier in a war long over.

How Kevin Kearns, a green rookie deputy from a rural Iowa county, had tracked Vernon Slocum across the country, staying only one step behind him, was still an unanswered question. The military file was only a part of it.

The file was how Kearns knew. That's why he and his partner were in Omaha, at Elizabeth's house, lying in wait for Slocum. And that's why they ended up in Alameda, California. They'd traced the suspect's relatives using the file, somehow knowing Slocum would be doing the same.

But how did Kearns know about the file to begin with? About its significance? It meant that Kearns had to know Slocum's identity almost from the beginning.

Or his partner did.

It all boiled down to the mystery man. The fake lawyer. That son of a bitch.

It boggled the mind. A killer's trail, twenty years cold, becomes fresh again. A hayseed Iowa deputy and a phantom hunter stalk that killer, leaving the resources of the Federal Bureau of Investigation in the dust.

It would soon be over. Witnesses were being interviewed. Ballantine's Alameda neighbors, bystanders from the red-light district of downtown Omaha, the surviving teacher in the schoolyard, and anyone else who'd seen the suspect

were being shown photographic line-ups containing
Slocum's picture.

Ballistic evidence was being compared, and matched.
Slugs found in the bodies at the burned-out meth lab in
Coon Rapids, Iowa were confirmed as matching the ones
in the bodies of the Iowa state troopers, the bouncers
at 24th and Lake in Omaha, and in the walls of the
Ballantine house in Alameda. Bodily secretion evidence
from the sexual assault victims was consistent with
Slocum's medical records, and the blood left at the scene
of his crash in Alameda. Piece by piece, the puzzle was
being assembled.

All that remained was the apprehension of Vernon
Slocum. By late today his face would be known to millions
of television viewers nationwide. It was 1987, after all,
and modern technology could broadcast in minutes what
once took days or weeks to get out to the public. Hopefully
the Bureau would net the fugitive murderer soon.

Special agents contacted Slocum's former doctors at
the VA hospital, most of whom were long retired. Agents
interviewed Elizabeth Slocum to the point of exhaustion.
Incidentally, they also conducted an in-depth background
check into the history and activities of Kevin Kearns. None
of this produced any leads in discovering the identity of
Kearns' mystery partner.

This mystery man was still at large, though not as
vehemently pursued by the FBI as Slocum. Scanlon
learned the man, whoever he was, had prevented a child
belonging to Cole Ballantine from being kidnapped. But
he'd disarmed and threatened to shoot two Alameda
police officers in the process. Yet his burned out car left
no trace of forensic evidence, like fingerprints, to assist
in identifying him. Scanlon couldn't help but think this
elusive man hunter had to be a cop, or someone with

military or security experience similar to law enforcement training. He was too good to be otherwise. And he covered his tracks well.

Apprehending Kearns' partner could wait. Deputy Kevin Kearns was under guard in the intensive care unit of Highland Hospital in Oakland. He wasn't going anywhere, this time. He'd undergone surgery which saved his life. When Kearns awoke he would be induced to give up the identity of his partner in crime in lieu of reduction in the charges and the length of sentence he was inevitably facing. Unfortunately, the doctors attending to Kearns' recovery couldn't say exactly when that would be.

In any case, all Bureau focus was on locating and apprehending Vernon Slocum. And the Bureau now knew a lot about him.

Some of the most insightful information about Vernon Slocum's history came from Cole. He was cooperating fully, and told the FBI investigators interviewing him the horrific account of his childhood in Iowa; an account corroborated by special agents conversing with Elizabeth. Special agents had been dispatched to the Slocum farm near Ogden, Iowa, to interview their father, Emil J Slocum. The results of contact with the elder Slocum would be reported to Scanlon as they came in. He was still the Special Agent in Charge, at least for now.

It was a productive twenty-four hours. That's how it often went. Sometimes weeks of tenacious investigative work produced nothing. Then out of the blue a break would come, a break that would unravel the entire fabric of the crime. Scanlon only hoped he'd be around to see the eventual conclusion of the case.

"Mister Steve Scanlon. Passenger Steve Scanlon, please pick up the white courtesy phone. Steve Scanlon, please pick up the white phone."

His own name interrupting Whitney's singing ended his examination of the file. He put it into his briefcase and walked over to a white telephone on the wall.

"This is Steve Scanlon," he said in his nasal voice.

"Mister Scanlon," said a pleasant-sounding female voice. "I have an urgent call for you. Please hold and I'll transfer it."

Scanlon held the receiver to his ear and wiped his dripping nose. A moment later he recognized the familiar voice of Special Agent Tatters.

"You there, Steve?"

"I'm here. Go ahead."

"What are you still doing in Omaha?" Tatters asked.

"Trying to leave," Scanlon snapped angrily. "The flights are all delayed because of the weather. It's snowing like hell. Do you think I'd be here if I didn't have to?"

"It ain't much better here in tropical Des Moines."

"So what couldn't wait?"

"Two things," Tatters said. "First, I thought you'd want to know this morning I met the honorable Emil Jensen Slocum. One of the Story County deputies, Detective Rod Parish, drove me out there. Hell, it took us an hour by four-wheel drive just to—"

"Spare me the epic saga. What did you learn?"

"That's the point; nothing. The old guy is mad as a hatter. Met us at the door with a shotgun. Babbled a lot about Okinawa, and his days fighting the Japs. He's gonesville, Steve. Wouldn't let us on his property, and I saw no point in pressing the issue. All the things he did to his kids are past the statute of limitations, so we can't arrest or even charge him with anything. He's not a material witness, and doesn't have to talk to us if he doesn't want to. Not that he'd have any useful information. He's a dead end, Steve."

Scanlon pondered this a moment. "I still want surveillance on his house, in the event his son returns. It's a long shot, but I don't want to exclude the possibility. Have the Story County deputies help you set it up, and be sure to—"

"Sorry Steve," Tatters cut in. "No can do. That's the second thing I was going to tell you. You've been relieved. Hoersten is on the way from Chicago to take over. The task force's already been given specific orders to disregard your orders. I'm sorry to have to be the one to break it to you, but if your flight was on time you'd already know. Everybody else does."

Scanlon gripped the phone tightly, unable to find words. If he was being relieved so quickly, it could only mean one thing: the Bureau was going to front him; make him the scapegoat in the blundered investigation. It would protect the Bureau's image with the public. Scanlon had seen it many times before. When it came to the reputation of the Bureau, no single agent was safe.

"Thanks for the warning."

"So long, Steve. I'm sorry."

Scanlon hung up the phone. In all likelihood he was not only being relieved of his command, but would also face a suspension, perhaps even dismissal. Dismissal was unlikely though; the Bureau rarely fired an errant agent. The FBI preferred to keep a reprimanded agent around as a lesson to others.

Special Agent Steve Scanlon sat down heavily on a bench crowded with holiday travelers and stared through a window at the falling snow. He couldn't remember so bleak a winter. He wiped a tissue across his nose and put his chin in his hands.

"Merry fucking Christmas," he said to nobody.

CHAPTER 45

Bob Farrell lay soaking in the tub, a cigarette dangling from the corner of his mouth. He'd awakened just before noon, feeling as if he'd been run over by a train. The nausea in his stomach and the dryness in his throat were relieved somewhat by the hot bath, but the driving headache he experienced was resisting all efforts to conquer it. The cuts and scratches on his face stung.

He awoke soaked in sweat. Room service brought up a Bloody Mary and aspirin, and after gulping down several pills with the cocktail he undressed and slid into the tub.

Farrell added more hot water and ran his hands through his straggly hair. It was in need of a trim. His activities over the last few weeks left little time for a haircut. He lay in the tub and pondered.

Slocum was in the wind. Farrell was alone, without a plan, and the object of a nationwide police search. Though he was confident the FBI could not identify or apprehend him, he felt useless and lost.

Farrell spat out the remnant of his smoke and washed more hot water over his face. His mind was racing, still dazed by the events of last night. The Iowa deputy had delivered everything he'd promised, and Farrell couldn't have asked for anything more in a partner. And for his troubles, Farrell got him killed.

He got out of the bath and put a towel around his waist. His clothes were given to the room service clerk for laundering and would be clean shortly. He felt a little better, and he walked out of the bathroom on relatively steady feet.

He sat at a small desk and glanced at the objects on top of it. There was Kearns' wallet, the envelope of cash, Farrell's own wallet, his badge and pocketknife, and the piece of paper with Jennifer's address on it. He stared at the phone number for a long time. He knew he had to tell Jennifer of Kevin's death, but dreaded it.

He picked up the phone and dialed long distance. He noticed his hands were shaking again.

"Hello," came a feminine voice.

"May I speak to Jennifer?"

"She can't come to the phone right now. You'll have to call back."

"Please don't hang up. I'm her father, and I'm calling long distance. Could you tell her? I know she'll take the call."

There was a long silence at the other end. Finally, "OK. Wait a minute."

Farrell waited for what seemed like hours, clenching and unclenching his fist. Eventually he heard the receiver pick up.

"Hello, this is Jennifer. Who's this?" Her voice was thick and distant.

"Jennifer, it's Dad."

"Dad? Where are you?"

"I can't say. There's something I have to tell you."

"I already know about Kevin."

Farrell's face sagged and he sought words. None came.

"It's been on the news all morning. The FBI's been broadcasting pictures of the guy you and Kevin were stalking. They reported a big shootout in California."

Farrell suddenly realized the thickness in Jennifer's voice was from crying.

"Jennifer, I'm sorry."

"I'll bet you are," she cut in. "Playing your stupid games. I hope you're happy."

Farrell paused a long time before speaking, tears forming in his own eyes.

"I was with him when he died. I called to tell you, because I didn't want you to find out from anyone else. But I guess I fucked that up. I'm sorry. Goodbye."

Farrell started to hang up the phone. "Wait!" he heard from the receiver. He put it back to his ear.

"Wait, Dad. What do you mean, died?"

"Jennifer, Kevin was my friend. I'm sorry he's dead. I'm sorry I dragged him into this crazy scheme. I'm sorry I dragged you into this crazy scheme. I'm sorry I was never there for you, or that I wasn't a better father. I don't know what else to say. I'm sorry."

His voice was shaky, and he neared the point of crying openly. He lit a cigarette to quell the rising tide of emotion.

"Dad, what are you talking about? Kevin's not dead; at least not if what the TV says is true."

Farrell's mouth gaped and the cigarette dropped to the carpet. "Kevin's alive?"

"Where have you been? The news is on almost every station. The FBI reported a shootout in Northern California, and that two men prevented a child from being kidnapped and murdered like the little girl in Iowa. They said one of the men, in his early twenties, was found badly wounded at the scene. He was taken to the hospital where he's listed in critical condition, but expected to recover. The other guy got away. The FBI is looking for him." Jennifer paused. "He meets your description I might add. This 'other guy' supposedly took some cops hostage. Once they broadcasted the picture of that creep you two were hunting in Nebraska, I figured it had to be Kevin who was in the hospital."

Waves of relief swept over Farrell. "Did they say which hospital he was in?" he finally asked, his voice weak. He stamped out the smoldering cigarette with his bare feet.

"I can't remember."

Farrell scurried over and switched on the TV. He fumbled with the dials until he got a local news broadcast.

"Dad, you still there?"

"I'm here, Jen."

"You left Kevin there, didn't you? You ran out on him?"

"It wasn't like that. I thought he was dead... I mean... at the time... I..."

"Jesus fucking Christ, Dad! You really didn't know Kevin was alive?"

"We were in combat, Jennifer," Farrell said. "Heavy-duty shit was going down. We were trying to save a little girl. There's a lot you don't know."

"And what I do know, I had to learn from the TV. Dad, I thought you might be dead."

That thought hadn't occurred to Farrell, and it shut him up. He rubbed his eyes.

"What are you going to do? You're not going on with this ridiculous manhunt?"

"I'm not sure."

"I know what you should do," Jennifer retorted. "You should get to the hospital and see Kevin. Make sure he is OK. See if he needs anything. You're the one who put him there."

"I can't," Farrell said. "If I show up at the hospital, the FBI will grab me. I could be charged with a number of crimes, many of them felonies. No way can I go visit Kevin."

"Then maybe I'll go," Jennifer said. "The FBI doesn't know who I am. I could use an alias."

"Don't be stupid," Farrell snapped. "They'd grab you the instant they laid eyes on you. You forget Omaha?"

"The only reason you don't want me to go is because you're afraid if the FBI catches me they'll figure out who you are and arrest you."

"That's not true," Farrell said indignantly.

"Hell if it isn't," Jennifer shot back across the phone. "All you ever do is use people. You used Mom. You used me to help get you and Kevin out of a jam in Omaha. And you used Kevin to the point of nearly killing him. So don't tell me it's not true."

Farrell tried to ignore his daughter's biting words. It wasn't working.

"You go to California and you could end up in jail. Think about that."

"I'm thinking of Kevin. He's got no family. No one. He doesn't even have a home. He's going to need somebody to help him, and it damn sure isn't going to be you. You've made that quite clear. You just keep hiding wherever you are, and keep playing cops and robbers, and keep on looking out for your own skin. Don't worry about picking up the pieces."

"Listen," Farrell soothed, trying to soften his voice. "When Kevin wakes up, he's going to be covered in cops. He's very likely going to jail, if not prison. You don't want to be a part of that."

"Don't worry about me. One of the girls on my dormitory floor is dating a lawyer. He works for the Lancaster County District Attorney's Office. I asked him about Kevin. He said Kevin could build a pretty good defense for all the stuff he's done by saying he was traumatized by witnessing the kidnapping of that little girl. He had a concussion, too. He could say the injury affected his judgment, and that you suckered him into the whole thing. He said to throw you under the bus; blame you. Claim you led him along on this ridiculous safari."

"Kevin was traumatized; I agree with that. But he did what he did because it was the right thing to do. I won't let you take that away from him."

"You're only saying that because it's over, and Kevin nearly got killed. You're trying to justify it. What you did was idiotic and reckless."

"You don't know what you're talking about."

Farrell felt angry, but held it in check. He didn't expect Jennifer to understand, but he did expect her to at least acknowledge Kevin got hurt doing what he believed was right. Farrell took a long breath and chose his next words carefully. He was still reeling from learning Kearns was alive.

"I don't disagree with you, Jennifer. And for your information, I'm not going to leave Kevin dangling on the hook. I didn't know he was still alive until I spoke with you, and that changes things."

"How?" she asked.

"I'll turn myself in, pay my dues, and take what's coming to me. I'll absolve Kevin. But I won't admit what we did was wrong. It wasn't. Kevin is a good man. He has guts and conviction. He was doing what he believed had to be done. I'm lucky to have worked alongside him. It was the most right thing I've ever done."

Farrell went on, before Jennifer could interrupt. "You're right about me being selfish. Too selfish to know how much hurt I've caused my little girl. For what it's worth, I was only trying to help Kevin. I know what it's like to see little dead kids in your sleep."

Farrell held the receiver away from his face a moment and took a deep breath, wiping his eyes.

"Jennifer? Jennifer, are you still there?"

"I'm still here," she said, her voice almost inaudible. "Dad, give up this crazy idea about catching the killer. Go home. You've got to go home. You can't run forever; nobody can. You're in some trouble, but it's nothing that can't be fixed. Go home. Forget this nonsense and go home."

"I've got to go," Farrell mumbled into the phone. He set the receiver gently back on its cradle. He rubbed his eyes for long minutes, and eventually the tears abated.

Farrell watched the TV intently for the next twenty minutes, and confirmed all Jennifer had told him. Kevin was alive, and being treated at the Alameda County Hospital in Oakland. He momentarily considered Jennifer's idea of going to see him, and then quickly discarded the thought. Getting himself caught by the FBI would do neither of them any good.

He sifted aimlessly through Slocum's medical file on the desk. He stared long and hard at the grim face in the photograph. He read the names of Slocum's family, and remembered how brave Elizabeth was. He thought of Cole, who'd changed his identity to escape his past. He wondered if they ever thought of home.

Maybe they couldn't forget.

Farrell opened his own wallet and took out a recent picture of Jennifer. It was professionally done, and was undoubtedly a photo made in preparation for her graduation. Jennifer's hair flowed around her head in a wreath and she was tastefully dressed in a flattering dress. He guessed the picture would accompany her resume when she began job hunting after graduation.

He was interrupted by a knock at the door. He rose and opened it to find room service delivering his cleaned and pressed suit. He paid the clerk, tipped him, and began to dress.

Something nagged at the back of his mind; something his daughter said: *You've got to go home. You can't run forever; nobody can.*

Farrell belted his trousers and put on his socks and shoes. In a way, Jennifer was right. Everybody had a home somewhere. Even the nightmare the Slocum children endured was home. Home, for better or worse, was familiar. It was a place to let down your guard. It was the place you went when you had no place else to go. It was instinct to return home.

Could Slocum be going home? Farrell donned his shirt and began knotting his tie. Vernon was hurt. He was a long way from Iowa, where he'd spent his entire life, except for Vietnam. Perhaps he would instinctively head for that place which felt familiar and safe.

Maybe Vernon was going home?

Farrell finished knotting his tie and went over to the bed. Under the mattress he'd stashed the small arsenal of handguns he'd checked in with. There were the two FBI-issue Smith & Wesson revolvers, the two Alameda police revolvers, a Colt Trooper and a Ruger Security-Six, and Farrell's five-shot .38. He checked the loads of the two FBI .357s, ensuring both were fully charged with six rounds each. Farrell's .38 Smith & Wesson Bodyguard had only four rounds in it; one was a spent casing. He extracted the expended shell from the cylinder and inserted a fresh cartridge.

Farrell put on his coat and his overcoat. He put Kearns' wallet, his wallet and badge, and the other items into his jacket pockets. He placed one of the FBI .357s in each coat pocket, and the five-shot .38 in his waistband. Scooping up Slocum's VA file, he left the room and locked the door. The room key, and the two Alameda police handguns, remained inside.

He rode the elevator to the lobby and strolled out of the hotel. His step was lively, and he had a genuine smile on his face. Kevin was alive. That was something. An unexpected gift. With the thick file under his arm and his suit on, he looked like any other white-collar employee on a business trip.

He went directly to one of several cabbies loitering in front of the hotel.

"Airport," he barked, getting into the back of the nearest taxi.

In fifteen minutes he was at the Oakland airport. He paid the cabbie and went into the main terminal.

It wasn't crazy at all, in fact, it was quite logical in a way. It was a long shot, but Farrell had nothing better to do, and could turn himself in to the authorities in one place as well as another.

He stopped at a payphone. Inserting coins while lighting a cigarette, he asked directory assistance for the phone number of the Alameda police department.

"Emergency or non-emergency line, sir?"

"The non-emergency line please."

The operator connected him.

"Alameda police, how may I direct your call?"

"Nowhere," Farrell said, exhaling smoke through his nostrils. "It's a tip. The guns belonging to the two Alameda cops I met last night are in room two-twenty at the Oakland Hyatt. Thought I'd return them. Have a nice day."

"Sir, what's your name? Sir, wait, don't hang up. Sir…"

Farrell hung up. He walked across the terminal to the car rental booths.

"May I help you?"

"I'd like to rent a car for approximately one week. I want to pay cash for it."

"Even though you're paying cash, we'll still need a major credit card as a deposit."

"No problem," said Farrell, flashing his San Francisco star with his thumb strategically covering the word "Retired" engraved on the face. "It's departmental business. Do you want my personal credit card, or the PD's?"

"Oh, I didn't realize you were a police officer. You can skip the credit card. Give me your badge number and one of your business cards."

"I don't want to be a bother."

"No bother at all, Officer. It's not like you're going to steal the car, and we won't be able to find you."

He suppressed a grin. "You'll be able to find me alright; I'm known to every cop in the area."

For the first time in weeks, Farrell gave out one of his own business cards. Taking it, the clerk asked, "Do you have a preference for the make or model?"

"Oldsmobile. Newest you've got."

"And your destination?"

"Home. I'm going home."

CHAPTER 46

Odgen, Iowa. Christmas Eve, 1987.

Retired San Francisco Police Inspector Bob Farrell stood shivering on the outskirts of the Slocum property in the still of the dawn. There was no wind, but the temperature was well below the zero mark. The snow was knee-deep, and he was thankful he'd obtained heavier clothing.

He'd stopped at a department store in Grand Island, Nebraska, and purchased thermal underwear, heavy socks, insulated boots, and a thick wool sweater. His bones began to throb as he progressed eastward into colder climates and his California attire became inadequate.

Farrell spent the last thirty hours on Interstate 80, stopping only for fuel and to eat. He stopped in Reno long enough to place Vernon Slocum's medical and military files in a locker at the Greyhound bus station there. Then he mailed the key to the law offices of Carruthers and Lyons in San Francisco, with a list of instructions. Vinnie Carruthers would know what to do.

The road became a blur as he pushed the Oldsmobile towards the home state of Kevin Kearns. He drank a lot of minimart coffee and Jim Beam, chain-smoked unfiltered Camels, and fumbled endlessly with the car's radio dial. Mostly he got Christian stations, Country & Western, and Top Forty. Whenever he found a station he liked, he'd soon pass out of range of the station's transmitter.

By the time Farrell got the Oldsmobile into western Iowa, the blizzard had run its course. The roads were freshly plowed, and relatively clear of ice and snow. But the thermometer had dropped, and though clear skies prevailed, the temperature was a frigid minus six degrees Fahrenheit.

He knew Slocum's farm would probably be staked out. At a little after 4am he parked the Olds along the county road less than a mile from Slocum's place and laced on his insulated boots. Sure enough, as he trudged through a pasture adjacent to the farm, he saw a sheriff's department four-wheel drive cruise by and disappear out of sight. He ducked behind a hedgerow, confident they hadn't seen him.

Staking out a farm in rural Iowa was quite unlike staking out a residence in a town or city, especially in the dead of winter. There wasn't another farmhouse or building near Slocum's farm for a mile in any direction, and the soybean fields circling the property were without so much as a tree. The best the sheriff's deputies could hope to do was increase patrols around the house and look for anything out of the ordinary.

Like an Oldsmobile with California license plates.

Farrell didn't care if the sheriff's deputies found the car. He'd reached the end of the line. He knew the hunt was over, regardless of what was about to transpire. His plan was a long shot at best, and only delayed his inevitable surrender to the authorities. He wasn't going to let Kevin take the fall alone.

But the long drive eastward was therapeutic. He'd done a lot of thinking as the radio played its static-ridden renditions of Christmas favorites. He thought of

Kevin Kearns, fighting for his life and in the hands of the FBI. He thought of Jennifer, with regret. He thought of Elizabeth, and Cole, and little Kirsten. He thought of Scanlon, too, with more contempt than hate. Mostly he thought about Tiffany Meade, and the still too-clear memory of a prostitute's child hanging from a lamp in downtown Saigon.

He climbed over a barbed wire fence bordering the farm, snagging his coat. His pockets were heavy with the weight of two revolvers, and it took his numb fingers a moment to untangle himself.

Once over the fence, Farrell stopped to catch his breath and look at the farm. Walking through deep snow was more work than he'd thought, and eroded his strength and breath. But when he inhaled too deeply trying to reclaim his breath, the biting cold felt like shards of glass in his lungs. The bourbon helped.

Though still not light, the snow, under a partial moon, brought the scene to crystal clarity. He remembered the last time he'd visited old Emil Slocum, alongside Kevin Kearns.

Even under the blanket of snow the farm looked run-down and litter-strewn. Junked cars and dilapidated farm machinery still cluttered the yard, and he quickly drew one of the .357s from his pocket in anticipation of the dog. He remembered the pit bull which inhabited a rusted car, and scanned the vicinity for signs of the dangerous animal.

He could smell the dog before seeing it, and crunched quietly through the snow towards a gutted automobile where the foul stench was strongest. Pointing his revolver ahead of him, he looked inside.

On a filthy stack of old blankets the dog huddled, sleeping. Next to it, in clumps, were pieces of rancid meat.

Kearns could see hair on it, and couldn't escape the foul odor it produced. He hesitated to imagine how the meat would smell had it been July instead of December.

He left the dog undisturbed and headed towards the house. As he got closer the smell of spoiled meat got stronger, and he stifled a gag.

He reached the porch, where the smell was almost unbearable. Looking around, Kearns found the source of the putrid odor. Dumped along the side of the house, wrapped in plastic, was a large lump of meat. It had once been covered in plastic, but the dog had obviously found the pungent package and elected to feast. Remnants of the meat were what the pit bull had taken back to its lair.

Farrell turned away and backed off the porch. The smell was overpowering, and he needed a moment to catch his breath again. He walked along the opposite side of the house to see if there was another entrance besides the front door.

What he found there startled him. A large object sat under a white tarpaulin, which was constructed of several white sheets tied together. He noticed immediately that the large object had no snow on top of it, unlike every other object outside in the yard. Farrell lifted one corner of the tarp.

What he found made his blood colder than any Iowa winter. Under the sheets was a car; a burgundy-colored Ford Bronco. It wore Colorado license plates and was covered with a layer of road grit that matched the grime on Farrell's Oldsmobile in depth. He had been right: Vernon Slocum had come home.

He dropped the sheet, biting his lip. Vernon must have obtained the car in Colorado, and beaten him here by at least a day. Slocum could have easily arrived between the sheriff's patrols, which would only pass by every few hours at best. He'd then cleverly covered the car in white sheets, knowing from the road the sheriff's deputies would think the car was one of the many snow-covered clunkers dotting the yard.

Farrell's heart pounded. He ducked behind the car, out of view of the windows on the farmhouse. Vernon and his father would be sleeping inside, if inside at all, and must not have spotted him. He had no doubt that if Vernon or his father had seen him arrive they would have already killed him.

He took a moment to think. It wouldn't take long for the sheriff's patrol to spot his car, and even less time for them to put two and two together and surmise he was in the area of Slocum's farm. There weren't many places to hide the Oldsmobile, and fewer places for the driver to go on foot. And he'd left footprints in the snow leading from the Oldsmobile directly to Slocum's farm. If Farrell hesitated, his chance to nail his quarry would vanish.

Farrell was done hesitating.

He made up his mind. He'd stalked Slocum this far, and would see the hunt to its conclusion. It was ironic the trail ended where it began, decades ago, in the place that spawned a monster.

Farrell pocketed his revolver, extracted his flask, and took a long swig of bourbon with hands that might have been trembling from only the cold. He wiped his mouth on his sleeve and replaced the flask. Farrell crept again to the porch, a revolver now in each hand. He would go in and find Vernon Slocum, hopefully asleep.

Then he'd kill him.

He crossed the porch. He put his ear up to the cold wood of the door and heard nothing but the beating of his own heart and the roaring of blood in his head. Placing his shoulder tightly against the panel, he pushed.

The wooden door, brittle with age and the Iowa cold, creaked mightily and gave inward. Farrell stepped inside, closed the door, and put his back against it.

Darkness enveloped him, and he waited forever while his eyes adjusted from the relative brightness of the outside. Both his six-guns were in front of him. He listened with all his concentration for sound within the farmhouse.

There was no sound. Instead, his nose was bombarded with a smell so foul as to make the odor he'd experienced outside inconsequential in comparison. It was the aroma of blood, infection, and feces. It was overpowering, and threatened to make the retired cop vomit. He shook his head and stared into the room.

Gradually his eyes adjusted to the dim light. He recognized the same interior he'd visited once before. Indistinct shapes became furniture, and shadows faded into clarity. He felt a presence in the room. He sensed someone very near. He gripped his revolvers tightly, fingers on the triggers.

"Daddy, is that you?"

The eerie sound of the voice chilled Farrell to the bone. It was close; coming from the center of the room. He moved towards it, ready to shoot.

"Daddy, is that you? Please let me go to the bathroom, Daddy. I can't hold it any more. Daddy?"

The voice, meek and child-like, was coming from a couch with someone lying on it. Farrell got closer, and made out the silhouette of a person lying face up. He was only a few steps away, and trained the barrels of both revolvers directly at the middle of the body on the sofa.

"Daddy, is that you?"

Farrell's eyes came to rest on the form of Vernon Slocum. The sight shocked him.

Vernon's eyes were glassy, distant, and unfocused. His face was a ghostly-white, and covered in sweat. His mouth was a toothless slit of shredded flesh, the lips cracked and swollen. But it was the rest of him that Farrell found the most disconcerting.

Vernon lay on the couch, swaddled in filthy, blood-soaked blankets. His chest was a maze of makeshift bandages, and Farrell guessed at least one of the bullets he'd sent Slocum's way back in California had found its mark. What lay below Vernon's waist made Farrell's stomach again lurch and his eyes widen.

Slocum's left leg was gone. In its place was a blackened, infectious stump, ending above the knee. The couch below what was left of the leg was caked in pus-crusted ooze, mixed with dried blood. It was from there the suffocating odor of decay emanated.

Farrell's head swam, and his stomach threatened to spew. He fought back waves of nausea and tried not to think about what the dog was feeding on outside in the snow.

Vernon had come home badly wounded, his damaged leg thick with gangrene. His father had done what was necessary to prevent his son's death. The wrapped meat Farrell found carelessly dumped in the yard outside the house was undoubtedly Vernon Slocum's amputated leg.

Nightmare visions of the home surgery danced in Farrell's mind. He struggled against the need to purge, and kept his revolvers pointed at Vernon Slocum.

"Daddy, please," Slocum mumbled. His eyes stared at Farrell without recognition. "Please don't let it hurt anymore. It hurts real bad. Please make it go away."

Farrell's breath came in rasps. Vernon's body burned with fever and the trauma of his amputation. He was delirious, and babbled in the voice of a small child.

"Please, Daddy. I have to go to the bathroom. Please."

Farrell lowered the revolvers, his arms at his side. He felt sick, and weak, and all determination to kill Slocum vanished. His only emotion was pity for the barely human creature before him.

He hardly recognized the thing which lay in writhing agony on the sofa. This was not the Vernon Slocum he'd relentlessly pursued. This wasn't the killer he'd hunted since Vietnam. The Vernon Slocum he stalked had killed, and maimed, and tortured his fellow human beings with a brutality beyond description. Now, as he finally faced his quarry, Farrell felt nothing but drained. The terrible life Elizabeth, and Cole, and even Wade escaped, had kept Vernon in its grip. It had reduced him to the inhuman wretch decaying on the blood-soaked couch.

Vernon was dying, of that Farrell was certain. Even the invincible former Marine had reached his end, and death hung over him in the squalid farmhouse like a vulture. There was no longer any need to slay the dragon. Farrell stood over the dying monster in silence, his head hanging. He needed a drink.

Suddenly, from the dark recesses of the farmhouse, came movement and sound. They came from behind Farrell, and he wheeled around, fear electrifying his body.

"You leave my boy alone!"

Farrell turned in time to see Emil Slocum descending upon him. He pivoted fast, off-balance, desperately trying to bring his revolvers to bear on the lunging madman.

Emil Slocum was almost on him, a hatchet raised above his head. Farrell's eyes focused first on the weapon, then on Slocum himself. The old man was wearing a faded bathrobe, and his good leg was bare. His prosthetic leg dragged behind him as he pounced on the horrified former cop.

If it hadn't been for the artificial leg, Farrell would have been killed instantly, his head cleaved by the hatchet. In the split second it took to recognize the threat and react, the hatchet was halfway to his skull.

He threw himself backwards and instinctively raised his left arm to ward off the blow. He saw the maniacal expression on the old man's face and the glaze of his blind eye. He also saw the glistening blade of the axe.

Farrell's left forearm intercepted Emil Slocum's right wrist, where his hand held the axe. The force of the old man's plummeting arm sent the blade down Farrell's arm and deep into his left shoulder. The revolver in his left hand fell from his grasp and onto the floor.

An explosion of pain ripped into Farrell's shoulder, and he stuck the barrel of the remaining Smith & Wesson against Emil Slocum's chest. He pulled the trigger as fast as he could. The force of the elder Slocum's lunge sent them both to the ground, the gunshots deafening in the close quarters of the room.

Farrell landed hard, with the greater weight of Slocum on top of him. The impact sent agony through his body to rival the anguish in his left shoulder, tearing his breath away. His right hand pulled the trigger convulsively, though the hammer of the revolver clicked on expended casings.

With great effort Farrell pushed the old man off and crawled out from under his weight. All six of the bullets tore cleanly through the elder Slocum's chest, leaving gaping exit wounds. Emil Jensen Slocum was dead. His good eye stared vacantly at nothing.

Farrell rose shakily to his feet, gasping for air. He dropped the empty revolver and reached over to find his left arm soaked in blood. He could still raise his arm and make a fist, but this caused darts of anguish in his shoulder. The wound was bleeding profusely, and he knew it wouldn't be long before he passed out from shock and loss of blood.

His ribs were still on fire, and he worried one of them might have broken inward and perforated his lung. But a moment later most of his breath returned, and he was able to stand fully erect, despite the wobbliness of his legs. Farrell withdrew the flask from his pocket, flipped open the cap expertly with the thumb on his good arm, and took a very long pull. Though still in agony, he felt marginally better when the flask was drained. He dropped the empty flask and used his right arm to put pressure on the wound to his left shoulder.

He sensed he was being watched. He looked up, and found Vernon propped up on his elbows, staring at him. His face was caked in oily sweat, but his eyes no longer had the delirious tint to them. They were focused and alert, and staring directly at him. He realized too late that in Vernon's right hand was the gray metal of a .45 pistol.

Farrell's right hand went from his bloody shoulder to his waistband, to his .38 revolver, with all the speed he could muster. His eyes remained locked with Vernon's, as Vernon brought his own gun up and leveled it.

Both men fired; Farrell from the hip. He continued to squeeze the trigger, even as he felt the .45 slug slam into his chest. The distance between the two men was less than ten feet. Farrell tumbled backwards and down as his revolver clicked empty, all five rounds expended.

The room spun around him, and his chest seemed ready to burst. Searing pain consumed his entire being. His limbs were numb, and he fought to remain conscious as he faded in and out of blackness.

Slocum had discharged one round which found its target. Of his return fire, Farrell didn't know if he'd succeeded in hitting Slocum. He only knew he was flat on his back, shot, and unable to move. He guessed he'd hit Slocum, since his opponent only fired once.

Farrell rolled his head from side to side. His vision cleared a little, and he felt less like he was going to black out. He knew he'd taken a torso hit, and without medical help would expire where he lay. For some reason this didn't bother him as much as it should have, and he assumed the apathy was a side-effect of the shock.

He was unsure how much time passed when he heard the thud. It was a dull, muffled sound, as if something heavy was dropped, and he felt the vibration from the impact through the floor. That sound was followed by a scraping sound, which he could also feel through the floor. He struggled to sit up and determine the origin of the noise.

It took him several attempts to prop himself up on his elbows. The effort caused the sensation of near-blackout to return. He looked down and saw the right side of his chest covered in blood. He raised his head and looked around the room.

What he saw jolted him instantly to awareness. Vernon Slocum had rolled himself from the couch to the floor; this had produced the thudding sound Farrell had heard. The huge man was crawling towards the retired cop on his stomach, leaving a trail of milky, infected blood behind his stump of a leg. What Farrell could see of his chest and back was covered in fresh blood, and he realized at least some of his bullets found their mark. The scraping sound was the noise he made as he dragged himself towards the supine ex-cop.

Farrell fought to sit up. In Vernon's right hand was a Ka-Bar knife. His eyes were bright with bloodlust, and he was edging closer with every pull of his arms. He was only a few feet away.

Farrell convulsed in paralyzing agony each time he tried to get up. He felt the void of unconsciousness draw closer, and knew death was certain if he didn't move. He pushed with all his might, his eyes unable to break the spell of Slocum's hypnotic stare.

He heaved mightily and sat further upright, shaking his head to clear the dizziness this effort produced. When he returned his gaze to Slocum, not only was the big man nearer, but Farrell could see him smiling through the torn lips surrounding his mouth.

Farrell knew it was over. If Vernon had the strength to crawl across the floor after all he'd suffered, he'd make quick work of Farrell, who was finding it nearly impossible to move at all. Though death was also around the corner for Slocum, he retained more of his faculties than Farrell and would easily overpower him. It was almost humorous; in Farrell's condition, Slocum wouldn't even need the knife.

Farrell's mind scrambled for a way out. It was clear he would never get to his feet, or even move, before Slocum reached him. He remembered the revolver he'd dropped when the old man attacked, but saw it across the room, even farther than Vernon. It might as well have been in California for his chances of reaching it. He tried again to push himself up, to no avail.

This effort almost made Farrell fall back to his original position, flat on his back. He stretched his arms out to prevent this, and to brace himself. Slocum was at his feet. He resigned himself to his death, hoping it would be quick. He took little consolation in knowing his murderer would soon follow.

The outstretched hand of Vernon Slocum touched his right foot. The dizziness returned, and Farrell welcomed it, hoping the merciful blackness would spare him the defeat he was about to endure. He spread his arms out a little wider, lowering himself to the floor, letting the darkness overtake him. The last thing he saw, as he closed his eyes, was the knife in Slocum's hand and the demonic smile on his lips.

Suddenly his right hand felt something; an object. He explored it with his fingers.

An axe.

It was the weapon Emil Slocum nearly halved his head with. Farrell's brain jolted to alertness. His fingers locked around the handle of the axe like a drowning man's hand on a lifeline. He stared at Slocum's face and felt an iron grip circle his right ankle.

Slocum had reached him. He needed only to pull on Farrell's right ankle once to close the distance between the blade of his knife and his chest.

Farrell stared directly into Slocum's face and realized Slocum's journey from the couch was not without its toll. The veins stood out like snakes on his neck and the strain on his face belied the murderous rage in his eyes. Slocum pulled himself closer and raised the knife. Something like recognition passed across his features.

"Told you I'd see you around someday, Sergeant," Slocum said. His voice was a gravelly hiss.

"Hey Vernon," Farrell said, his own voice a trembling whisper.

Slocum's eyes widened at the sound of his name, and he hesitated for an instant.

"Merry Christmas, you fucker," said Farrell. He buried the hatchet in the left side of Vernon Slocum's head.

Then he collapsed.

CHAPTER 47

Ames, Iowa. January, 1988.

Bob Farrell sat in a wheelchair in his room in the Mary Greeley Hospital and from his window watched a group of small children build a snowman across the street. The children worked intently to bring shape to a sculpture familiar to winter everywhere.

It had been more than two weeks since the deputies found him, more dead than alive, in the home of Emil Slocum. As he'd suspected, a roving sheriff's patrol spotted the Oldsmobile with its California plates. It didn't take long for the sheriff's department to arrive at the Slocum farm in force.

Farrell was rushed to the emergency room of the county hospital in Nevada by life-flight helicopter, and from there to Ames for surgery. The .45 slug he'd absorbed penetrated his lung and exited cleanly. The wound in his left shoulder was more life-threatening. The laceration was quite deep, and had the deputies arrived any later he wouldn't be among the living. Farrell was told by the surgeon that if not for his high blood alcohol level and the extreme cold slowing his metabolism, he would have bled out before the paramedics reached him.

After successful operations dealing with both injuries, Farrell made a steady recovery. He was allowed no visitors other than the Story County Sheriff's deputies and FBI agents who guarded his hospital room. Apparently they were taking no more chances with him.

That was about to change.

The door to Farrell's room opened, and four men walked in past the guards. He only recognized two of them; Detective Rod Parish, from the Story County Sheriff's Department, and uniformed Sergeant Dick Evers.

Of the other two, one was obviously a Bureau man. Farrell thought the other newcomer looked like an attorney.

"Good morning, Inspector Farrell," said the Fed. "My name is Arthur Hoersten. I'm the Special Agent in Charge of the Chicago Office of the Federal Bureau of Investigation." He said it like he expected genuflection. Nodding to the other men, Hoersten said, "This is Mister Keller, with the US Attorney's Office." Keller apparently forgot the decade had changed eight years ago, and sported an ear-covering Seventies hairstyle.

Farrell nodded once. "It's 'retired' Inspector, Agent Hoersten. Shouldn't you normally ask how someone is feeling when you first enter their hospital room? Where're your manners? And where's Agent Scanlon?" Farrell thought he heard Detective Parish grunt behind Hoersten.

Hoersten didn't crack a smile. "I was told you're a smartass," he said. "Agent Scanlon is indisposed. You'll be dealing with me from now on. You're not going to like it."

"Indisposed," Farrell repeated. "That's what they said on the TV. May I see some identification please? You can never be too careful. There're all sorts of shady characters impersonating federal bureaucrats for nefarious purposes these days. And while you're at it, may I have one of your business cards?"

Parish and Evers couldn't stifle their chuckles.

"No you may not," Hoersten snapped, glaring at the two county cops. "If I were you, Mister Farrell, I'd be less smartass, and more kiss-ass. You're in a lot of trouble."

Farrell shrugged, a painful act given his stitched and slung shoulder. "You brought an entourage in here to tell me that? What do you want?"

Hoersten motioned with his head to Keller, who stepped forward and opened a file he was carrying.

"Mister Farrell, you have an impressive list of charges accumulated against you. During an approximately two-month period you've impersonated an attorney to interfere with a felony investigation; impersonated a federal officer; gained unlawful access to federal facilities; committed theft from those facilities; impeded federal investigations; effected the escape of a homicide suspect from custody; recklessly discharged firearms; obtained firearms and vehicles while using false financial instruments and identifications; assaulted federal officers; stolen their firearms; assaulted and brandished a firearm against uniformed peace officers; stolen their firearms; driven with reckless disregard for public safety; as well as engaged in a criminal conspiracy with Deputy Kevin Kearns, and your daughter, to commit some of the aforementioned crimes, including assaulting a federal agent, twice. These are just the highlights. There are also numerous other charges spanning multiple state and local jurisdictions. All of these acts are felonies. As I already said, an impressive list of charges. Any three of these could put you away for the rest of your life."

"I'm apparently a one-man crime wave."

"That's one way of putting it," Hoersten said.

"You forgot to add a couple of charges to the list," Farrell said.

"And what would those charges be?" asked Keller.

"Driving while intoxicated. I was in the bag most of the time I was crime-waving." Evers and Parish snickered again. Keller ignored them.

"Anything else?" Keller asked.

"Yeah. That I put down Vernon Slocum while the FBI sat on their asses."

Keller shook his head and stepped back. Hoersten pointed his finger directly at Farrell's face. "Crack wise while you can, dickhead. Where you're going the laughs are going to be pretty scarce. Ex-cops don't do a lot of giggling in federal prison."

It was Farrell's turn to shake his head. "I'll ask again. What do you want?"

Hoersten lowered his finger. "It's not what I want, jerk-off. It's what you're going to give me."

"What am I going to give you?"

Hoersten folded his arms across his chest. "For starters, a full statement and confession to the charges against you. Then a guilty plea to those charges."

"And why would I do that?"

"In exchange for leniency on the charges against your daughter Jennifer. I can't make any guarantees, but with your full cooperation, we'll try to convince the US Attorney's Office to reduce some of her charges to misdemeanors instead of felonies. That way she wouldn't do any prison time; only county jail time."

"What about Deputy Kearns? What does my cooperation and guilty plea buy him?"

"Nothing. He's bought and paid for. He's going to do federal time, no matter what you give us."

"And me? What have you got on the table for me if I cooperate and plead?"

Hoersten smiled. "Not a goddamned thing. You get the full package. You'll spend the rest of your miserable days in federal prison wishing you'd never fucked with the Federal Bureau of Investigation."

The room grew silent. Farrell rubbed his chin. "Let me understand the deal you're offering, Agent Hoersten. In return for my full confession and guilty plea to all charges, which would spare the federal, state, and local governments the massive time, trouble, cost and publicity of taking me to trial, my daughter gets sent to jail for up to a year, Kevin gets a long federal stretch, and I get the key thrown away? Is that the deal?"

"That's the deal," Hoersten smirked.

"When I was in Vietnam," Farrell said, "we didn't call that a 'deal.' We called it a dry-socket skull-fucking."

"I don't give a shit what you call it. Take it or leave it."

Farrell nodded to himself, deep in thought. Finally, he looked up.

"Anybody got a smoke?" Farrell asked.

"Quit fucking around. You know you can't smoke in here. What's it going to be? You going to let your daughter get fucked over, or are you going to play ball?"

"I'd like to propose a counter-offer," Farrell said dryly.

Hoersten laughed out loud. "You really are a stupid fuck. You've got to be in a position of advantage to deal, and you aren't holding any cards. You're just a burned out ex-badge with a booze habit and a long prison sentence hanging over your head. Look at the bright side though; you're probably only going to have to serve a few years before your liver or your ticker gives out and you cash in your chips. Only question is, are you going to man up for the first time in your life and do something unselfish, and think of your daughter's well-being, or are you going to be a prick and let her go down the toilet along with you?"

"You leave me little choice," Farrell said, his voice wilting.

"Actually, no choice at all. Even someone as stupid as you must see that logic. So what's it going to be? Mister Keller is prepared to take your statement right now."

"Well," said Farrell, slapping his knee with his good right arm. "Don't you even want to hear my counter-offer?" His smile returned.

"Still a smartass? Nothing you've got to say I need to hear, except your full statement and confession."

"How about this?" Farrell began. "How about I tell you and the hairdryer lawyer to rubber up and fuck each other? Then I get my Californian attorney, which you can't deny me, and you should have offered before this conversation began. Then I plead not guilty, and go gladly off to jail to await trial. Where I'll have a lot of time to fight every charge, file every appeal, and run up the cost of prosecuting me for all those complicated charges in all those different jurisdictions to astronomical levels. You're forgetting I was a cop for almost thirty years, Agent Hoersten; I know all the tricks. And I'll have nothing but time to play them."

Hoersten looked at Keller, who looked back with a blank face. "So what? We've got an airtight case."

Farrell continued as if he hadn't spoken. "And then, to really get the party started, I'll have my attorney contact the press. You remember them, don't you? Those nosy reporters? I'll make sure they get every nuance of my hunt for Vernon Slocum; especially all the juicy details regarding the FBI's ineptitude. I might even write a memoir. And I'll make certain that particular attention is devoted to the chapter on how the US Government knew what kind of a monster Vernon Slocum was in 1967 when they shipped him back to the States to be turned loose on an unsuspecting public. I'll bet the families of those two murdered Iowa state troopers would like to know all about it. And I'm certain Tiffany Meade's family would be interested as well. But do you know who'd be the most interested? Their attorneys, am I right? Hell, I might even make it on *60 Minutes*."

Hoersten's face lost some of its color. Farrell went on remorselessly.

"I know who and what you are, Special Agent in Charge Hoersten. You're the guy who is supposed to make the deal, get the quiet guilty plea, avoid the messy trial, and deliver this whole package neatly wrapped up to Washington so they can file it under 'Let's Pretend This Never Happened,' and forget it. And then you get to burnish your reputation as a 'Get things done guy,' and move up the Bureau ladder. But instead, you're going to have to report to your Bureau overlords back in DC that the whole shitty thing is about to go public and blow up in everybody's face. I'll make it my personal mission to ensure the Iran-Contra scandal looks like a tea party by comparison. Who do you think will want the story first: Mike Wallace or Dan Rather?"

"You're bluffing. Besides, you haven't got the juice. It would be your word against the Federal Government's. Who's going to believe the prison rants of a disgraced ex-cop?"

Farrell leaned back in his wheelchair, his eyebrows lifting. "Agent Hoersten, I'm surprised at you. I thought you were a more experienced law enforcement officer. Haven't you ever wondered what happened to all those files I swiped? Do you really believe I'd be in possession of Vernon Slocum's full military and medical files for almost two months, as Mister Keller already so deftly pointed out, without making copies?"

What little color left in Hoersten's face vanished completely. US Attorney Keller mirrored his complexion.

"And do you really think I wouldn't have those copied files placed with persons of trust who would ensure their delivery to the appropriate press outlets in the event of my apprehension by the authorities, or if I was to suffer an accident?" Farrell flashed his Cheshire cat grin. "Even someone as stupid as you must see that logic."

Hoersten's jaw clenched at the sound of his own words fed back to him. "I still think you're bluffing."

"Call it. This conversation is over. I want my attorney. But I suggest you call Washington and give the boys at the J Edgar Hoover building the bad news before they get it from me. Or from the evening news."

"Now just hold on a minute, Inspector Farrell," Keller said, motioning Hoersten aside and stepping towards Farrell. "No need to make threats. We are not immune to the bigger picture. We can discuss this like adults."

"Of course we can," Farrell said. "How about over a cigarette and a drink?"

"Hoersten," Keller said over his shoulder without looking back. "Get me some smokes and a bottle. Now."

"You're kidding?"

"I'm not kidding," Keller barked, "and I'm not asking. And make it fast."

"I'm a bourbon man," Farrell shouted as Hoersten stormed out of the hospital room, cursing under his breath.

"Inspector Farrell," US Attorney Keller began, pulling up a chair. "I believe we can come to an accord which would be amenable to both the United States government and to you."

"I'm listening."

Detective Parish and Sergeant Evers cast sidelong glances at each other and grinned.

CHAPTER 48

Former Story County, Iowa, Deputy Sheriff Kevin Kearns walked warily through the lobby of Highland Hospital in Oakland. Nearly three weeks had passed since he'd awakened in the intensive care unit. He'd resided there for more than a week before he was upgraded to "guarded" condition and moved to the Secure Wing of the hospital, staffed by Alameda County sheriff's deputies. It wasn't quite jail, and it wasn't quite a hospital; it was something in-between. Kearns shared a room with an African-American man who'd been shot multiple times in an apparent drug dispute.

Kearns had suffered a perforated lung, a ruptured spleen and massive blood loss at the hands of Vernon Slocum. Only the fact that the Alameda Fire Department had a station less than a mile from Cole Ballantine's home saved him. He was at death's door when the EMTs arrived. But thanks to the very experienced trauma surgeons at Highland Hospital, he was expected to make a full recovery.

The day after he was transferred to the secure wing, a harried man in a rumpled suit came in and announced he was with the Alameda County Public Defender's Office. He said that since Kearns' charges were all going to be federal, he would be arraigned by a US Attorney at a later time. Two days later a very business-like woman with a stern face and a stenographer arrived, and told him he was being charged with everything but the Lincoln assassination. Kearns said nothing, only asking for an attorney. It was all he could think to say.

Other than these visitors, Kearns had no contact with the outside world. He was offered a phone call by a deputy each day, but declined. Even if he could remember Bob or Jennifer Farrell's numbers, he wouldn't have phoned. The lines were probably recorded, and he wanted none of his troubles traced to them.

After two weeks at Highland Hospital, Kearns was almost back to his old self. His stitches had been removed, and he was allowed to exercise. He couldn't muster more than walking and push-ups, but most of his pain had subsided, and he was in better shape than he'd hoped. He desperately wanted to ask one of the deputies about any developments in the Slocum case, but dared not compromise himself by such a query.

Then one day he was given clothes - a pair of ill-fitting jeans and a hospital shirt - and told he was being released. The clothes he was brought in with were discarded on the night he was admitted, and he had no personal effects. Confused, but not dissuaded, he allowed a nurse and a sheriff's deputy to lead him to the exit. The nurse gave him instructions on how to care for his still-healing wound that were printed in Spanish, and he signed a form. Suddenly he was standing on an Oakland street on an overcast January day with a quizzical look on his face.

Kearns had no money, and it was cold. The part of Oakland hosting Highland Hospital was not in the best neighborhood in a city with few good ones, and for the first time he realized that although he had his freedom, he had nothing else. He looked around, trying to formulate a plan.

Kearns walked through the parking lot, past parked ambulances and police cars, and found himself on East 31st Street. From there, he didn't know which way to go. He was contemplating returning to the hospital to ask one of the deputies the address of a local homeless shelter when he heard a whistle.

Turning to the sound, he saw a familiar silhouette leaning against a parked Oldsmobile the color of fresh blood.

"Jesus, Kevin, you look like Oliver fucking Twist."

"I left my tuxedo at the cleaners."

Neither man spoke for a while. Kearns noted the arm sling, and Farrell the stiff manner in which Kearns walked.

"Last time I saw you I thought you were dead," Bob Farrell finally said, exhaling smoke.

"Last time I saw you, I think I was," Kearns said truthfully.

"I'm glad you're not."

The men embraced.

Finally stepping back, Kearns produced a weak smile. He looked around at the bleak Oakland landscape. His eyes met Farrell's. "You responsible for getting me sprung?"

"Something like that," Farrell smiled back, tossing his smoke to the curb.

"Where's Slocum?" Kearns asked.

"Feeding the worms, kid. His old man, too."

"You punch their tickets?"

"Yeah. Put the coins on their eyes myself."

"And the little girl? Cole's daughter?"

"Safe and sound. We did it, Kevin. We saved her."

Kearns nodded solemnly. "I guess that's something."

More silence.

"Looks like Slocum got a piece of you," Kearns finally said, thrusting his chin at Farrell's sling.

"He took a piece of both of us, Kevin."

"Yeah. I guess he did."

Kearns rubbed his head. "So what now? FBI still after us?"

"Would you be walking the streets a free man if that were true?" Farrell put his good arm around Kearns' shoulders, leading him to the car. "We're in the clear."

"How is that possible?" Kearns demanded. "After all we did you'd think we'd be public enemy number one."

"I'll tell you about it over lunch. You look like you could use a good meal."

"I could, but it's got to be mostly liquid for a few more weeks."

"My preferred diet," Farrell said. He withdrew his flask from his pocket and took a swig. He offered it to Kearns. Kearns shook his head.

"How's Jennifer?' he asked tentatively.

"Too good for a thug like you. Don't get any ideas."

"Who said I had ideas?"

"I warned you once about lying, Kevin. You prairie types aren't any good at it."

"So what now?" Kearns asked, steering the subject away from Farrell's daughter, whom he definitely had ideas about.

"Oh, yeah. I almost forgot. I've started a business."

"A business? What kind of business?"

"Private investigations." Farrell puffed out his chest. "Hanging a shingle, I am."

"A private investigator? You? Really?"

"What else would I do? Besides, you have to admit, I've got the knack for it."

"If by 'knack' you mean a propensity for drinking on the job and getting into trouble, then yeah, you've got it alright. In spades."

"So what are your plans, ex-Deputy?"

Kearns gestured to his secondhand clothes and then at the bleak Oakland landscape. "As you can see, I'm presently between jobs."

"I tried to get you reinstated at your old sheriff's department, but the feds had to draw the line somewhere. Be happy with a clean record."

"I have a clean record? How did you manage to accomplish that?"

"I'll tell you all about it another time, Kevin. So what do you say? Want to go into business with me?"

"You offering me a job?"

"Unless you have a better offer."

"I don't know the first thing about being a private investigator," Kearns said truthfully.

"What's to know? You're smart, resourceful, good with your fists and a gun, and I could use the help. Besides, we belong together. We're a team, you and me. Like the Lone Ranger and Tonto, or Holmes and Watson."

"More like Gilligan and the Skipper," Kearns said. Farrell rolled his eyes.

"So what do you say?" Farrell asked, gingerly extending his palm.

"The last time we had this conversation I ended up on the FBI's Most Wanted list."

"That was different," Farrell said smoothly. "Besides, what could happen?"

"Here we go again," Kearns said, shaking Farrell's hand.

ACKNOWLEDGMENTS

My sincerest thanks go out to my agent, Scott Miller, of Trident Media Group. His support, patience, and relentlessness are deeply appreciated. My heartfelt gratitude also goes out to my superb editor, Emlyn Rees, for his professionalism, patience, and unyielding humanity. He's forgotten more about writing than I'll ever know, and was kind enough to wield that skill to make mine better. I am humbled and honored to have Scott and Emlyn at my back.

Lastly, inexpressible thanks to Denise, Brynne, and Owen. Today, tomorrow, and forever. You know the rest.

ABOUT THE AUTHOR

Sean Lynch was born and raised in Iowa, in a Civil War-era brick farmhouse restored by his family. When not outdoors shooting his BB guns, Sean could be found reading crime and science fiction, paranormal and military non-fiction, and trying to persuade his parents to let him stay up past bedtime to watch the late-show creature feature.

After high school, Sean obtained a Bachelor of Sciences degree and served in the US Army as an enlisted Infantryman. He migrated to Northern California's San Francisco Bay Area, where he recently retired after nearly three decades as a municipal police officer. During his Law Enforcement career Sean served as a Sector Patrol Officer, Foot Patrol Officer, Motorcycle Officer, Field Training Officer, SWAT Team Officer, Firearms Instructor, SWAT Team Sniper, Defensive Tactics Instructor, Juvenile/Sexual Assault Detective, and Homicide Detective. Sean concluded his career at the rank of Lieutenant and as Commander of the Detective Division.

A lifelong fitness enthusiast, Sean exercises daily and holds a 1st Dan in Tae Kwon Do. He still watches late-night creature features. Sean is partial to Japanese cars, German pistols, and British beer.

seanlynchbooks.com
twitter.com/seanlynchbooks

When did you last google yourself?

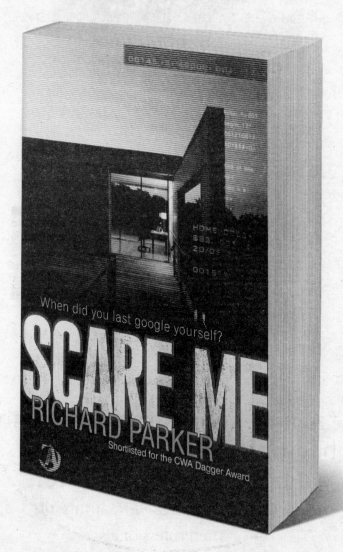

DAN O'SHEA

Introducing Detective John Lynch

PENANCE

One dark secret is about to rip a whole city apart...

"A non-stop adrenaline rush,
beginning, middle and end...
a bona fide blockbuster."

OWEN LAUKKANEN, author of

The Professionals